A Danger to the State

PHILIP TROWER

A Danger to the State

A Historical Novel

IGNATIUS PRESS SAN FRANCISCO

Cover by Riz Boncan Marsella

© 1998 Ignatius Press, San Francisco
All rights reserved
ISBN 0–89870–674–2
Library of Congress catalogue number 97–76853
Printed in the United States of America ∞

Contents

List of Principal Characters

Don Maurice de Vallecas
  judge and member of the Supreme Council of Castile

Doña Teresa de Vallecas
  his wife, a Viennese

Alfonso de Vallecas
  their eldest son, a Jesuit missionary in Paraguay

Gaspar de Vallecas
  their second son, married to . . .

Luisa de Vallecas y Pantoja
  heiress to the last Duke of Montesa

Jaime de Vallecas
  a schoolboy, later a Jesuit novice

Beatriz de Vallecas
  their second daughter

Rodrigo Logrosan
  Don Maurice's ward, betrothed to Beatriz

Doña Ana de Pantoja
  Mistress of the Robes to the Queen Mother

Henri-Lucien Charville
  man of letters and agent of the French government

Monsieur Laborde
French merchant based in Madrid

Madame Laborde
his wife

Madeleine Laborde
their daughter

Jean-Paul Houdin
clerk to Monsieur Laborde

The Marques de Torrelavega
disgraced minister seeking to return to power

Doña Ines de Torrelavega
his wife

Diego de Torrelavega
their youngest son, protégé of . . .

The Count de Pradanos
retired general

Doña Mercedes
his wife

Manso
servant of the Marques

OTHER JESUITS

Fr. Idiaquez
superior of Castilian province of the Society of Jesus (historical character)

8

Fr. Padilla

priest and astronomer, living at the Casa San Felipe in Madrid

Fr. de la Cueva

rector of the Casa San Felipe

Fr. Huber

Austrian Jesuit, priest in charge of Reduction of San Miguel, Paraguay

Fr. Mayer

Austrian Jesuit, priest in charge of Reduction of Santa Rosa, Paraguay

Fr. Joseph Pignatelli

Aragonese Jesuit (historical character — canonised by Pius XII, 1954)

OTHER HISTORICAL CHARACTERS

King Charles III of Spain

Third Bourbon king of Spain (1759–1788); previously Duke of Parma (1732–1734); King of the Two Sicilies (1734–1759); eldest son of Philip V, first Bourbon King of Spain by his second wife, Elizabeth Farnese, granddaughter of the last Farnese Duke of Parma. Widower from 1760

Elizabeth Farnese

Queen Mother, m. 1714, d. 1766

Marquis Grimaldi

Genoese favourite, Secretary of State for Foreign Affairs

Marquis Squillacci

Neapolitan favourite, Secretary of the Treasury and Secretary of State for War

Count Aranda

President of Council of Castile and chief minister 1766

Don Manuel Roda
Minister of Justice

Indians at San Miguel, Paraguay

Tarcisio
cook at priest's house, the college

Cayetano
caretaker at the college

Anselmo Cattaguru
military commander, cacique, and keeper of the arsenal

Dídaco
his eldest son, a painter

Methodius
his third son, father of . . .

Clara
engaged to . . .

Xavier Tupanchichu
grandson of chief sacristan

Crisóstomo
Xavier's friend and workmate

Jacinto Epaguini
head schoolmaster

Wenceslaus
a recent convert

Nicolás
the horse trainer

Athenagoras
the pharmacist

Agustín
an overseer

PART ONE

A Shaft of Daylight

1763–1764

ONE

"Don Maurice de Vallecas? Don Maurice de Vallecas? Have you seen Don Maurice de Vallecas?"

A page in scarlet coat and blue breeches went scurrying down the corridors of the Uzeda Palace in Madrid, seat of the Supreme Council of Castile and of the Royal Treasury of Spain. Clerks and secretaries shook their heads, and he passed on without stopping. Reaching an oblong hall filled with waiting people and with barristers at tables advising their clients, he approached an usher.

"A message for Don Maurice de Vallecas. They say it's urgent."

The usher pointed to another corridor and said, "The third door on the right. But you'd better wait. The court is sitting."

The page, who had been tipped, paid no attention but made his way quickly down the other corridor to the third door on the right, paused to look through the keyhole, then pushed the door open.

Inside the courtroom, a case was just coming to an end. Papers were being handed back by one of three judges in full-bottomed wigs and black gowns. The other two judges lounged back in their high leather-covered chairs talking together in undertones.

The page, who found himself at the rear of a railed-in platform, stepped forward and repeated his question to the judges, but this time in a tentative and respectful tone of voice.

One of the judges turned his head and took the sealed message from the page's hand. A look, half-anxious, half-puzzled, crossed his face. As soon as he had read the message, he whispered to his companions and followed the page out of the courtroom.

"Who brought this?"

"One of your illustrious lordship's servants."

"Is he still here?"

"He is outside with your lordship's coach. If your lordship pleases, I will show you the way."

The judge smiled, a little ironically, at the page's eagerness.

"Very well then", he said, taking off his gown and handing it to an

15

attendant who had followed him out of the courtroom and who handed him in return his three-cornered hat and his cloak.

The page led the way. On the steps outside, Don Maurice gave him a coin, and then one to a beggar sheltering in the doorway from the November wind.

"Drive as fast as you can", he called, as he got into his coach.

The driver flipped the reins; the mules shook their heads; the footman shouted at two boys who were clinging to the springs in the hope of a ride; and the heavy vehicle lumbered away over the cobbles.

TWO

After a journey lasting about ten minutes, the coach drew up before a three-storey house in the northwest corner of the city, at the junction of the Calle de la Madera Alta with the Calle Guzman.

"He is in the library, my lord", the majordomo said, greeting Don Maurice at the top of the steps.

Giving the man his cloak and tricorn hat, Don Maurice mounted the stairs, half-running. At the top he crossed a vestibule and pushed open a door.

The library, like most of the rest of the house, gave an impression of sparse and stiff magnificence. The furniture, sixty to a hundred years old, was heavy in design, dully glowing where gilded, ornamented with elaborate locks and embossed leather. Above the bookcases hung portraits of grave-faced men and reticent-looking women. At the far end, idly turning a globe, stood a tall figure in a cassock.

Hearing Don Maurice enter, the man looked up and then hurried toward him.

"Ah, thank God!" Don Maurice said. "You are still here. I thought I might have missed you."

"I'm afraid my message was too alarming. I wasn't sure how long they would take to deliver it."

"What has happened?"

The two men were alike, yet different. They had the same long rectangular faces, brown eyes, short straight noses. But like identical musical instruments giving out dissimilar sounds, these features expressed markedly different characters. In the father, the dominant traits were strength of character and strength of will and, what so often goes with the latter, a certain severity; the salient qualities of the son were good humour and kindness. The son, who had close-cropped coppery red hair, was an inch or two taller than the father, but they looked the same height because of Don Maurice's curling magisterial wig.

"We only heard this morning", Alfonso de Vallecas said. "We are leaving almost at once, and His Majesty wants to see all the missionaries who are going to Paraguay first. We must be at the Escorial by this evening. He will talk to us when he comes in from hunting. We shall spend the night there and start for Cadiz tomorrow morning. They are afraid we may already have missed the best ship.

"Then it is good-bye?"

"Yes, Father."

"Well, I'm glad", Don Maurice said. "It's best when it happens unexpectedly. Have you seen your mother?"

"Yes. We have said good-bye. She sent me down here to wait for you."

"Then before I ring for the others, my son, embrace me and give me your blessing."

"Who knows?" Alfonso said, when his father had knelt and he was helping him to rise. "We may see each other again after all. They may call me back to Europe."

"No. There's no point in deceiving ourselves. If you return to Europe one day, it will be after I've gone. I prefer to face that. But write as often as you can. I shall look forward to your letters. Put everything in them."

"I can say the same. You know what I want to hear. Tell me what you are thinking and what's going on in Europe, especially anything that affects our Society. And with regard to the Society, please tell me the truth, however bad it sounds."

17

Don Maurice took his son's hand.

"There's nothing to fear, believe me."

"I wish I thought so. But who would have said ten years ago that by now the Jesuits would have been driven out of France and Portugal?"

Don Maurice moved toward the brazier, which stood on a brass tray in the middle of the tapestry carpet. He held out his hands over the charcoal embers pulsating gently in the metal pan.

"My boy, the Kings of France and Portugal are libertines and weaklings. That they would make trouble for the Society was to be expected. Our own King, thank God, is a very different kind of sovereign. A more upright and honourable man than His Majesty, a more loyal Catholic, I do not know. I can say the same for the Empress. It is unthinkable that in this matter either of them would follow the policy of the French and Portuguese."

"I don't doubt His Majesty's goodness", Alfonso said. "I don't know exactly what I fear. His Majesty's death, perhaps. A new reign and a new policy. Events can change so quickly. You see, it isn't just the Society I'm anxious about. It's you and the family as well."

Don Maurice raised his eyebrows, as though now his son were passing beyond reasonable discussion into fantasy.

"Yes, Father. You. It's well known that you're a friend of the Jesuits. Remember what happened to the Távora and Aveiro families when the Society was suppressed in Portugal. Would they have been tortured and executed if they had not been suspected of being our friends? And up till then, Carvalho, who was chiefly to blame, had been thought no less humane than other statesmen."

Don Maurice's face had clouded. He refused to believe that there could be any comparison between the situation in Portugal and that in Spain.

"The case is a confused one. There must have been many Portuguese families close to the Jesuits who went unharmed."

"Will you promise, Father, should events take a bad turn, that you will make arrangements to escape abroad?"

"Son, Son, this is all nonsense."

"Then there is no harm in making me the promise."

"I suppose not", Don Maurice said reluctantly, as if he thought that to promise would be the same as to admit the danger he did not want to believe in.

"Perhaps I'm foolish", Alfonso persisted, seeing that his father was wavering, "but it would set my mind at rest."

"Then I promise with all my heart. And I never made one that cost so little", he added, just to show that he had not changed his opinion. "Now embrace me once more before I send for the others. There's no time to get Jaime and Isabel, but Gaspar and his wife are here, and Beatriz and Rodrigo."

He blessed his son and, walking briskly to the wall, took hold of a bellrope.

THREE

Before he could pull the bell, the door burst open and a four-year-old boy ran in. Over his little dress, whose stiff skirts reached halfway down his legs, he wore a miniature breastplate, and on his head a gilded helmet with two scarlet plumes. He began to circle the room shouting, "Gee-up, Beauty", and beating an imaginary horse.

"Gently, gently", called his mother, who had followed. "Gaspar," she said peevishly to her husband, who was just behind her, "please make him be quiet. He will deafen us all."

"Tonio, stop it", Gaspar de Vallecas said firmly. He was a heavy man in coat and breeches of bottle-green cloth who, although two years younger than his brother Alfonso, had the walk and assurance of a man of fifty. It was hardly surprising. In marrying his wife, Luisa, heiress to the last Duke of Montesa, the head of the powerful Pantoja family, he had himself become Duke of Montesa and one of the richest men in Spain.

The Pantojas as a clan had not taken this turn of things gracefully. That the heiress to the bulk of the family fortune and the principal family title should ally herself to a *manteista*, a member of the *noblesse de robe*, had seemed to them a disaster almost as serious as the loss of part of the Spanish Empire, and they had tried all the methods known to frantic relatives since the beginning of time—presents, flattery, tears, hysteria, hints of divine vengeance—to persuade Luisa's father not to permit the wedding. But Luisa's father was not to be moved. A hypochondriac, who had lost his wife early in their marriage and doted on his only daughter, he saw it as part of being a great aristocrat to flout convention from time to time. If there was enough money, why not marry for love?

And so had thought Gaspar, or Gaspar de Vallecas y Pantoja, as he now was, who, in spite of everything, had remained the uncomplicated, unimaginative, good-natured person he had been since infancy, taking his rise in fortune and the opposition of his wife's relations as though they were part of the natural order of things.

Luisa, on the other hand, seemed to have been designed by providence as his contradictory opposite. She was a thin, nervous-looking little woman with too much rouge, whose thickly powdered wig dwarfed her small, peaked face. A loose silk gown, the fashionable French *sacque*, half hid her enormous hooped petticoat. They had been married six and a half years.

Tonio had realised by this time that, the occasion being a special one, he could do as he pleased. To prove this, he gave a final shout, then running to his uncle Alfonso, crawled under his cassock, looking out from in front as though it were a tent. Alfonso picked him up.

"Good-bye, Tonio. Be a good boy. Try to be always obedient to your father and mother. And pray for me, and for the Indians I am going to look after, that our Lord will bless us all."

"Will you send me a spear and a hat with feathers?"

"If I can."

"Promise."

"I can't promise, Tonio, because it may not be possible."

"Will you convert many Indians?"

"That depends on God."

"As many as a million?"

"I don't know, Tonio. A million is a large number. Besides, where I'm going most of the Indians are Christians already."

During this dialogue Tonio had been playing with the sash of his uncle's cassock and had appeared more interested in trying to twist it than in hearing the answers to his questions. But suddenly he seemed to realise what it meant that his uncle was going away for good. He looked into Alfonso's face, threw his arms round his neck and began to cry.

"Don't go! Don't go! Please take me with you and let me be a martyr, too."

"But I never said I was going to be a martyr. Where I'm going, most of the priests live to be old men and die in their beds."

"Take me with you! Take me with you!"

"Let me hold him", Luisa said, putting out two hands encumbered with rings.

"No! No!" Tonio said petulantly. "Leave me alone."

"You mustn't speak to your mother like that, Tonio", Alfonso said. He smiled at his sister-in-law. "May I carry him downstairs as far as the hall?"

"Oh, certainly, if you like. I just didn't want him to be a nuisance."

"You have a splendid boy. Perhaps he will be a priest one day."

"Every boy can't be a priest", she said sharply. "My son will be Duke of Montesa."

"Of course. I was forgetting."

"You people who have given up the world may not realise what that means, but all the rest of Spain recognises the importance of the position."

She had no sooner spoken than she looked anxiously around to see if her husband had heard her.

Luisa's feelings for her husband, which she thought of as love, were a mixture of the intense possessiveness and ambiguous attitude toward authority of a spoiled and temperamental child.

What would Gaspar say? She had insulted his brother, a priest and perhaps a future martyr. Fortunately, Gaspar had joined Don Maurice at one of the windows and was looking down into the street. But God didn't move out of earshot. What would God say? Or rather, not say, but do. She had perhaps drawn down a curse on her boy instead of a blessing.

"Forgive me", she said tearfully to Alfonso. "I was carried away. You won't let any harm come to my boy? You will pray for him?"

"What's this?" Gaspar said, joining them. "Tears, Luisa?" He drew her arm through his and patted her hand. "You see how much your departure affects her. She is so sensitive. Brianchon from Paris said he had never come across a more delicately balanced constitution. It's a real affliction. Her nerves actually make her ill. I only wish", he added with a perplexed look, "that someone could find a cure."

"Perhaps the Blessed Virgin could help you", said Alfonso, who had had a serious illness three years before and was inclined to have more faith in heavenly assistance than in the efforts of doctors, even Parisian ones. "Many favours are granted at her shrine at Montserrat."

"Yes, yes", Luisa said eagerly, seizing on the idea of a pilgrimage as a method of making more certain reparation for her fault. "And we could take Tonio and little Pilar too."

Gaspar smiled. "We'll have to see. It can't be done at present. I've too much on my hands. If we're not to be ruined, your estates in Galicia will have to be attended to at once. This is no time for discussing pilgrimages."

Luisa's feelings swung back from fear to fondness. She gave a sigh accompanied by a look at Alfonso that seemed to say: "Isn't he wonderful? I have no will of my own. He does everything."

"By the way," Gaspar said, "they tell me the Jesuits in Paraguay are great stock-breeders. I was thinking it might be possible to import some of their cattle for crossing with our breeds."

"I'd have thought it would have been easier and cheaper", Alfonso said, "to get new strains from England or France."

"Nations of heretics and infidels!" interrupted a voice from the open door into the next room.

THE NEWCOMER, a sturdily built young man with unpowdered hair, wearing a black suit of old-fashioned cut not unlike Don Maurice's, was Don Maurice's ward and distant cousin, Rodrigo Logrosan. His face had the eager, energetic look of young men whose heads are teeming with schemes and ideas that they are confident will eventually be put into effect and who are burning to confront and overcome the opposition such sound ideas will assuredly meet. His parents having died when he was four, leaving him estates in Estramadura, he had lived with Don Maurice's family ever since.

In his wake came Don Maurice's daughter Beatriz, a girl of seventeen with pale blond hair like one of Velázquez' infantas.

There had been no official betrothal, but it was taken for granted in the family, and by the young couple themselves, that as soon as Rodrigo was old enough to take charge of his property, he and Beatriz would marry.

"Hullo, Rodrigo", Gaspar de Vallecas said, looking amused. "Haven't you forgiven your enemies yet? The war is over, you know."

"Why should I? The French are only interested in using us to help them fight the English, and the English want to steal our empire. The peace means nothing to them. They're continually breaking the treaty they signed in Paris only a short time ago, and if Pitt returns to power, the English merchants will force him to attack our colonies again openly. There's no need for us to trade with foreigners. We ought to trade with our empire and make more of its resources; the English would know how to. Then Spain would be great and powerful again, and we could avenge ourselves. Let the English eat their beef till they burst, and the French too. Gaspar, if you buy Alfonso's cattle and ship them to Spain, you will be a pioneer and a hero. You could strike a bargain now."

"But the herds in Paraguay belong to the Indians", Alfonso said, laughing. "What would the superior of the missions say if he heard that I'd already sold part of their property before I'd even set foot in the country?"

"I thought, Rodrigo," Duchess Luisa said, "that you were going to make Spain great again by defeating the British navy? Personally I

23

think it's a much better way than by turning my husband into a cattle importer."

"What's this?" Gaspar asked. "Has Rodrigo decided to be a naval officer now? I thought that when he and Beatriz were married they were going to live on his estate and start an agricultural revival."

"A naval officer?" Luisa exclaimed. "I expect him to be nothing less than an admiral. Yes, we've been putting our heads together. I'm going to consult a cousin of mine at the Ministry of Marine to see what he can arrange. Then, if all goes well, one day Rodrigo will be Lord High Admiral and will send the entire English and French fleets to the bottom of the sea."

Everyone laughed. Rodrigo's enthusiasms and sudden changes of mind were a family joke.

"And what do you think of all this, my dear?" Don Maurice asked Beatriz.

"She doesn't know anything about it", Rodrigo said quickly. "You're all jumping to conclusions. Doña Luisa has exaggerated. I haven't made a decision yet." He darted a fierce look at Luisa, who had promised not to mention their consultations.

Luckily for Beatriz, who felt bewildered by this discovery of an unexpected change in Rodrigo's plans, Don Maurice suddenly pulled out his watch and said it was time Alfonso was off.

The last moments had come. Tonio howled twice and fell silent, watching the others with a frightened look. Beatriz's eyes filled with tears. All in turn threw their arms round Alfonso, who hugged them lovingly.

He turned to his father. "We are ready now", he said, controlling his feelings with difficulty and reproaching himself for his weakness. Would St. Ignatius have found it so difficult to say good-bye to his family? No. For, according to his biographers, when the summons had come to leave all and follow Christ, he had obeyed unhesitatingly.

As they trooped from the room and down the stairs, his imagination presented to him in panorama the consequences of that momentous response to grace nearly 250 years earlier in the castle of Loyola.

He saw the Society of Jesus spreading over the world, transforming men's lives, founding schools and universities, training scholars and men of science, penetrating remote and unexplored countries, enriching Europe with a knowledge of hitherto misunderstood cultures and new facts of geography and natural history.

He thought of Francis Xavier, whose love of God and men had carried him across half the world to bring the gospel to the Japanese; of Matteo Ricci, whose cultivation and learning had opened the hearts of the Chinese Mandarins; of Robert de Nobili, who had exchanged the costume and customs of Europe for those of India in order to evangelise the Brahmins; of Christopher Clavius, the Euclid of the sixteenth century, who had won the admiration of Kepler and Galileo and all the most brilliant men of that age; of Peter Claver, who had spent forty years caring for the Negro slaves brought in shiploads from Africa and deposited like cattle at Cartagena; of Jacques Marquette, the apostle of North America, who had discovered the Mississippi and been the first to map its course.

These men and others like them—the perfect followers of Ignatius —had been Alfonso's heroes since boyhood. It was painful now to find himself even more unworthy of their company than he had thought he was. To comfort himself, he reflected that biographers could not know every thought of those they wrote about. Perhaps even St. Ignatius, as he trudged away from Loyola toward Montserrat, had felt a pang of sadness and wondered whether it would not have been better to continue as a soldier or to stay at home and raise a family.

FOUR

The news that Alfonso was leaving had spread to the shops and houses up and down the Calle Guzman, and a crowd had gathered outside Don Maurice's door. The people of the neighbourhood had been joined by passers-by, who had stopped out of curiosity.

"It seems only yesterday that he was in his schoolboy's cap and cape", the local cobbler said to the man who kept the secondhand clothes shop.

"I remember him when he was in petticoats."

"A vocation is a fine thing, but it's hard for the old people to lose him, seeing he's the eldest son."

"The second one hasn't done badly."

"I should think not. I wouldn't like to come up before the judge. They say he's a terror in court."

They began to discuss the recent murder of a butcher by one of his apprentices.

Standing next to them and listening to their conversation was a gentleman in a brown topcoat. He was perhaps in his early forties, thin and well-formed, so that he appeared to be taller than he really was. But it was his sharp, clever face that would have attracted the attention of anyone interested in faces and what lay behind them. He had a way of smiling that pulled up the right corner of his mouth, making attractive crescent-shaped creases in his right cheek, and his eyes, full of amusement and curiosity, moved rapidly about taking everything in as keenly as if he had some personal interest in the occasion. With him was a burly younger man, apparently a servant, wearing ill-fitting new clothes.

Just at this moment, Alfonso and his family appeared at the top of the steps. The servants crowded behind. A second later he was in the coach that stood waiting to take him back to the Jesuit house in the Calle Toledo. As it moved off, the family waved and called "Good-bye! Good-bye!" and "God bless you!" The crowd began to call and wave, too. Women who had never seen the priest or any of his relations before pulled out handkerchiefs and wiped their eyes. The street was suddenly alive with moving hands and hats.

"Who is it?" a latecomer asked, pulling the cobbler's sleeve.

By this time, the coach had turned out of sight into the next street, and Don Maurice and his family had gone back indoors.

"Another Jesuit missionary for the Indies, God bless him", the cobbler replied.

"And a good riddance!" shouted a harsh voice behind him. "We've got too many dirty Jesuits in Spain already."

People turned—at first startled, then angry—to see who had spoken. "An insult! A sacrilege! Who said that? Where is he? Which one? Arrest him! Catch him! Don't let him go!" Men shoved and pushed each other. A woman shrieked. A child was knocked over and sat crying in the gutter with a cut forehead.

The cobbler whirled around and found himself facing the servant of the gentleman in brown. He raised the hammer he had been using at his bench and was still carrying. But as he brought it down, the man dodged, and the blow missed its aim and instead hit the gentleman, who fell unconscious on the cobbles. In the excitement, the servant got away unnoticed.

"Jesus and Mary, he's dead! Holy angels and saints, I've killed him!" The cobbler dropped on his knees and began frantically feeling the body for signs of life.

The mood of the crowd changed once more. They surged forward, shouting advice, contradicting each other, and holding out handkerchiefs to bind up the gentleman's bleeding head. Some of Don Maurice's servants, who had remained on the steps, ran to see what was the matter and then raced back to the house to tell their master. Others went off to fetch a priest and the barber-surgeon who lived around the corner. A few went in pursuit of the troublemaker. But these, after looking down one or two side streets and seeing no sign of him, gave up and came back to watch the more interesting spectacle of the corpse.

At this point Don Maurice came hurrying down the steps. People fell back respectfully. Several voices spoke at once.

"We've sent for a priest, your illustrious lordship."

"He's dead, my lord."

"He's coming round, Your Honour."

Don Maurice signed to his servants. "Pablo, go and tell the maids to prepare a bed in the red room and to have plenty of hot water. Now you others, lift him gently." He turned to Rodrigo. "Get them to call the doctor."

As he was lifted, the injured man groaned. There was an excited murmur from the crowd. "God be praised! He's alive." The servants moved gingerly forward with their burden and carried it into the house. The weeping cobbler followed and sat in a corner of the hall under a bust of Cardinal Jiménez on a porphyry column. He repeated the story of the disaster, first to a footman, then to the page, and then to several serving maids.

"To think I'd live to be a murderer!"

"Oh, come now, cheer up! He's not dead yet. And you didn't mean him any harm."

"Holy St. Isidore, I've killed him!"

Don Maurice led the way upstairs. Soon after they had put the stranger to bed, the priest arrived. As there was no way of knowing how badly the man was injured, it was decided to anoint him. Don Maurice remained in the room to help and knelt beside the bed while the prayers were read. Then, after the priest had refused his invitation to stay and dine, he went to see his wife, who was recovering from a bout of what had recently become fashionable to call *une grippe*, the name being applied indiscriminately to a variety of unknown infections of varying gravity.

FIVE

Beatriz and her maid, meanwhile, were sitting together in a room on the first floor, working at opposite ends of a long piece of embroidery. For Beatriz it seemed the best way of keeping her thoughts off Alfonso's departure in the now empty hour before dinner.

"Who do you think he is, señorita? Do you think he's a foreigner?"

"A foreigner? I've no idea. I hardly saw his face."

The room was called the Maccabeus Room from the faded tapestries showing scenes from the Wars of Antiochus against the Jews, which entirely covered the walls. The designer, apparently hypnotised by the

28

stylistic idiosyncrasies of Michelangelo, had given all his figures, male and female, bull-like muscles and ferocious grimaces.

Being the room most used by the younger members of the family, it had an agreeably cluttered untidiness. Near one of the windows stood a harpsichord with piles of music and a violin case on top of it. A portfolio of engravings leaned against an unoccupied chair. Books littered the tables and window seats, and an atlas lay face downward on the floor.

"If you really want to know," said Rodrigo, coming in at this moment, "he's French."

"French? How can you tell? Is he conscious?"

"No. But he's been muttering and talking to himself."

Rodrigo crossed the room and, sitting down in front of the harpsichord, struck a few notes and then clumsily tried to pick out a tune with one finger. After three unsuccessful efforts, he got up, went to the writing table, and began drawing heads of warriors on the back of an unfinished letter. At last, tiring of this too, he got up, crossed the room, and whispered in Beatriz's ear.

Beatriz signed to the maid, who, gathering up the embroidery, retreated to the far side of the room, where she quietly continued her stitching.

Rodrigo drew a chair close to his cousin. "Look, Beatriz, I know you're cross with me, but if you'll listen I can easily explain it all."

"But I'm not cross, Rodrigo."

"There's no point in pretending. I'm not blaming you. I'm just telling you there's a very good reason for my having acted as I did."

"But why should I be cross?"

"You know what I mean. Because I didn't tell you I'd been consulting Luisa about joining the navy, of course."

"I was surprised, but, truthfully, I wasn't cross. I knew you must have a good reason."

"That's just the point. I did have a reason. It was for your sake that I didn't tell you. Supposing it all came to nothing, you would have been upset unnecessarily. That's why I made Luisa promise not to say anything until I'd had time to tell you, as I intended to."

29

"Tell me about it now."

Her gentleness disconcerted Rodrigo. He played with the fringe along the arm of his chair.

"Thanks to Luisa, there's nothing much to tell you", he said glumly. "It would mean changing our plans. We couldn't live in the country. We would have to live . . . I don't very well know where. And we should be apart for a time each year while I was at sea."

The country life she was being asked to abandon suddenly appeared to Beatriz in innumerable tempting and agreeable forms. For several seconds she struggled with her disappointment. Then, without having betrayed the effort it cost her, she said quietly, "I hate to think of being separated from you. But you know I will go anywhere in the world you want me to."

This was what Rodrigo had been hoping to hear. But now, under a perverse impulse, he felt offended that she should not be more distressed at having to give up being mistress of his family property.

"I thought you would have minded more", he said.

"Oh, of course I'm sad that we can't live at Logrosan. Everything you have told me about it has made me love it. But we must think of your future."

"My future!" he said indignantly. "It's the future of Spain that's worrying me. Oh, Beatriz, if only you could understand! What would you think of me if I ran away in a battle? Well, that's how I feel now about living in the country. Spain is in a terrible state. The empire is rotten; the people are half-starved; and the state of the army and navy makes one want to weep. If it weren't true, why would we have done so poorly in this last war?"

He waved his arms excitedly. His faced flushed at the thought of his country's plight. "It's not that there's anything the matter with us really. Properly led, we could still be masters of Europe. But we're ruled by foreigners . . . that's the trouble . . . foreigners who are always either pro-English, pro-French, or pro-Austrian. Their only interest in Spain is in lining their pockets and meddling with our institutions. In the last reign, under King Ferdinand, it was an Irishman, 'Don' Ricardo

Wall. Now it's Grimaldi and Squillacci—two Italians. The remedy is for Spaniards to take charge of their own affairs. What we need most is a strong navy, because our wealth is in our empire, which must be protected at all costs. Is it a coincidence that Ensenada, who tried to build up the fleet in the last reign, is now out of favour at Court? Of course, a man of my age can't achieve much. But one day, with luck, I may get to the top. Then I shall see that something is done."

"Oh, Rodrigo," Beatriz said enthusiastically, "if only the King would make you President of the Council of Castile some day. Think of all the good you could do. I believe there wouldn't be a single poor person left if you were ruling Spain. Or, if you were at the Ministry of War, you could help all the widows of the poor dead soldiers and sailors, and the families of those who are alive, too. They are paid so little. I wonder if . . ."

Beatriz knew little about government but a great deal about the difficulties of the poor, and she therefore regarded the Treasury as the most interesting department of state. Had she had the chance, she would have emptied it as quickly as possible into the hands of the needy.

"If you were ruling," said Rodrigo, in a better humour now, "the country would be bankrupt in a week."

"But there must be so much money in the Treasury."

"Not enough for you. And I suppose it might just as well go to the poor as be filched by foreigners. But I should keep some back to build the fleet."

"Not too much, I hope."

"What a miser you are! Don't you want to see Spain great again?"

"Yes. Oh, yes. Of course. But . . ."

Beatriz hesitated. She felt that when Spain had been unquestionably the greatest power in the world, her countrymen had been rather less noble; obsessed, in fact, with gold mines and silver mines and galleons loaded with bullion. If Spain were great again, might not her younger brother, Jaime, instead of wanting to be a priest, go off to the Indies and return one day, no longer devout and gentle, but bellowing orders, glittering with jewels, and followed by a retinue of slaves, parrots, and

31

monkeys? But perhaps it was possible for a country to be both powerful and noble.

"Oh, yes", she repeated, to make up for the lack of warmth with which she had spoken the first time. "And if you had a strong fleet, you could rescue the poor Christian slaves from the Barbary pirates. Oh, Rodrigo, what a splendid admiral you will make!"

"Not so fast. I haven't seen the sea yet. But good subordinates are as necessary as good leaders."

SIX

Doña Teresa de Vallecas was in her boudoir lying on a chaise longue while being read aloud to by a maid.

Austrian by birth, she had met and married Don Maurice in 1730 when he was in Vienna on a diplomatic mission for King Philip V.

Almost invariably cheerful and always serene, she had that natural charm which is like a substitute for goodness though not necessarily the same thing. And she also had that goodness which is acquired, not natural, and makes charm by itself seem tawdry. Even some of the Pantojas, Luisa's relations, once they had submitted to the indignity of meeting her, had felt their prejudices dissolve.

Her boudoir and bedchamber, which had been specially furnished for her by her husband in order to soften her exile, were the only rooms in the house decorated according to the taste of the times. Nearly everything in them came from Vienna or Paris. There were pastel portraits, china figures, enamel and gilt boxes. Chairs with rippling contours and curving legs stood about on the savonnerie carpet like overdressed courtiers, and the tables, cabinets, and looking-glass frames also seemed to have been designed by men ignorant of the right angle and the straight line. The china blue ceiling was decorated with small white clouds, and the walls were panelled in yellow silk.

When Don Maurice entered the boudoir, the spaniel lying curled up on her lap jumped down and ran forward barking.

The maid put down her book, curtsied, and left the room.

"My love!"

"My dear one!"

Doña Teresa put out both hands. Don Maurice took them and, still holding them, sat down at her side. They remained like this for some time in silence, each taking comfort in the other's closeness.

"He must be almost at the Escorial by now."

"A priest and a missionary!"

"We are greatly blessed."

"I wonder if he has reached the Palace yet. On a clear day you can almost see it. But there wouldn't be any point in looking, would there?"

"No, my love", Don Maurice said gently. "Just follow him with your thoughts."

"I will! I will! I know you're right", she cried. "And I'm happy and glad that he's going. It's just . . . it's just . . ." And the tears that had been gathering in her eyes ran down her cheeks.

Don Maurice got up and helped her to find her handkerchief; then he arranged the cushion behind her head.

"My love," he said firmly, when she had finished drying her tears, "I've some news about Rodrigo."

She looked at him gratefully and made herself smile.

"He's not into debt, I hope?"

"Nothing as bad as that. He's concocted a plan with Luisa to join the navy."

"Oh, goodness! When will the dear boy make up his mind what he wants to do with himself? He has a new plan every six months."

"He's too much unsettled at present to make a sensible decision. We must take steps. I know I opposed the suggestion you made some weeks ago, but now it seems to me wise and farsighted."

"A foreign tour?"

"Yes."

33

"Do you think he'll agree?"

"After a protest or two. Most young men like to travel, and Rodrigo, in spite of his prejudices against foreign countries, has a good mind and an inquiring one. Once abroad, he will soon become interested in what's going on outside Spain. Also, I'm reluctant to have him marry Beatriz in his present frame of mind. I certainly hope they will marry eventually. But it won't do them any harm to be separated for a year or so. It will give them a chance to test their feelings for each other. . . ."

He was interrupted by a knock on the door.

"Yes?" Doña Teresa called.

The maid rushed in.

"What's the matter, my child? You look as if you had run to the Retiro and back."

"Señora, there is a lady in the hall who has called to see you."

"But your mistress can't possibly see anyone, Benita," Don Maurice said. "Surely you know that?"

"Yes, señor. Antonio has told the lady that the Señora is ill. But she insists on speaking to her."

"Insists! Who is she?"

"She calls herself Doña Ana Pantoja, señor."

"What! Tell Antonio that on no account . . ."

"Benita, leave the room", Doña Teresa said quickly. "Wait next door till I call you."

"Yes, señora. But don't be long or the lady will be here. Antonio won't be able to stop her."

"How dare she!" Don Maurice broke out when they were alone again.

"Please, Maurice", Doña Teresa said soothingly.

"Of all the Pantojas, she is the worst and the most troublesome. In fact, I suspect her of having been the ringleader in their opposition to Gaspar's marriage. Do you realise they spread rumours that you were an Austrian spy?"

"I know, I know, my love."

"That there was hereditary lunacy in our family, and that one of my ancestors was sent to the galleys."

34

"One can't deny they were thorough." Doña Teresa had the beginnings of a smile. "But perhaps—"

"Then what does this woman mean by coming here? Does she think she can insult us and then force her way into our house?"

"Perhaps she wants to say she's sorry."

"Nobody who was sorry would set about showing it in such a thoughtless way. She could have said she was sorry long ago, or she could wait till you were better. On no account shall she enter this house."

"She already has, my love. So now that she is here, we had much better see her."

"I forbid it."

"Please, Maurice."

Don Maurice would never have consented if he had not suddenly realised that his wife was going to be much more upset by having Doña Ana Pantoja turned away than by anything that lady might say or do.

"Very well", he said at last. "But at the first sign of rudeness she leaves."

Doña Teresa rang a bell beside her chair.

"Quick, Benita! Fetch my brush and comb. Oh! And a small looking glass, too. And tell Antonio to bring the señora up here."

SEVEN

As she entered the room, Doña Ana Pantoja stopped and blinked, dazzled after the sunless passage by the light that fell through the high windows on all the glittering things in Doña Teresa's boudoir.

Tall and, in spite of her nearly eighty years, unbent, she was dressed completely in black and carried in one hand gloves and a small fan. Her expression was dignified, but her eyes—the chief traitors—drooped sadly at the corners, proclaiming against her will that position and lineage had not brought happiness. Pride had prevented her from marrying;

35

none of the men who had asked for her hand had seemed good enough. And loyalty had kept her from surrendering a position she had long ago begun to find irksome. For forty years she had been lady-in-waiting and finally mistress of the robes to Elizabeth Farnese, the Queen Mother, who, after the death of her husband, Philip V, and during the reign of her stepson Ferdinand VI had lived in retirement at San Ildefonso, a palace north of the Guadaramas, sixty miles from Madrid. Her ladies and attendants had led a melancholy life, and although on the accession of her son, Charles III, the Queen Mother had returned to Court, from Doña Ana's point of view the improvement had not been great. She found herself, in old age, the companion and servant of a difficult invalid and without children or grandchildren of her own to love and find relief in.

Without noticing Don Maurice, who had drawn back into a corner, Doña Ana went straight to his wife.

"Doña Teresa de Vallecas, I have done you a great wrong", she said. "I did not mean to come here to apologise, but God in his wisdom has brought me to do this without my intending to. I long ago repented of the harm I did you and your family and of all the efforts I made to prevent your son from marrying Luisa. Insofar as I have been able, I have tried to restore your good name. I do not say this expecting to be thanked. It was my duty. However, pride has kept me from acknowledging my crimes in person and from asking your forgiveness. I knew I ought to. But I put off doing it. Then suddenly Her Majesty sends me here with a message for you. You can imagine my feelings. But I consider it a blessing that I am not allowed to run away from my duty. So, Doña Teresa, here I am at last, very willing now to have been brought here against my will, and I most humbly beg your pardon for all the wrong I did you."

"My dear madam", Doña Teresa said. "I forgave you long ago. Please, please sit down."

As Doña Ana moved toward a chair, she caught sight of Don Maurice.

"Ah, Don Maurice, in my eagerness to unburden my conscience, I didn't see you. But I most sincerely ask your pardon, too."

"I forgive you with all my heart, madam", said Don Maurice, who had been impressed by the ungrudging completeness of Doña Ana's apology and was feeling ashamed of having spoken so harshly of her, even though he had had reason to. "I must confess that up to now I have found it hard to forgive you on my wife's account."

"Well, Don Maurice, I can appreciate that. In your shoes I should have found it hard to forgive, too. Your wife, I can see from her beautiful smile, is different. But you and I, Don Maurice, have, I think, much in common. Oh, it's a poor compliment, I know. But whatever feelings you may have had, I can assure you I thoroughly sympathise with them."

She signed to Don Maurice to move her chair closer to Doña Teresa's and sat down.

"I'm so very sorry, Doña Teresa, to find that you have been ill, and I'm sure Her Majesty, if she had known, would have asked me to express her sympathy. I hope it has not been too serious."

"We were very anxious about her for several weeks", Don Maurice said. "She is recovering now, but she is still weak."

"Of course. And strangers are tiring, so I promise I shall not stay long."

"Oh, no", Doña Teresa said. "My husband is overanxious about me. This is such a happy day for us, now that everything has been put right, and I hope you will stay a long time."

"We will see", Doña Ana said with a smile that showed that Doña Teresa had won her. "Your husband must be obeyed." She looked around. "What a beautiful room! I was brought up in very different surroundings. Hard chairs, stools without backs, hardly a carpet. I don't expect you know our old Spanish houses. But I must come to business. I believe you have a daughter, Don Maurice?"

"Three, madam."

"Three? I was told only of one."

"Ines, a nun; Beatriz, just grown up; and Isabel, being educated at a convent in Segovia. My youngest son, Jaime, is also still at school—with the Jesuits in Toledo."

"Well, that makes it easy. Her Majesty doesn't need nuns, not for what she has in mind, nor does she need schoolgirls. How old is she?"

"Which one?"

"Tut, tut, Don Maurice. For a famous lawyer, how slow you are! The one who is not a nun and not in the schoolroom."

"Beatriz is nineteen, madam."

"Well, Her Majesty is looking for somebody to read to her, and she would like to have your daughter. She says her ladies-in-waiting drawl when they read, and her maids don't know how to pronounce the words. As you see, Her Majesty doesn't have a very high opinion of us. However, she has heard a lot about your daughter . . . from a person whose name I am not to mention . . . how good and devout and well-educated she is, and how fluently she speaks Italian, and she is anxious to have her services as soon as possible."

Don Maurice was standing beside the brazier, close to his wife's chair. Their eyes met, each asking the same question which instantaneously received the same answer: "Just the thing to occupy Beatriz if Rodrigo goes abroad."

"Please will you thank Her Majesty," Don Maurice said, "and tell her that we shall both be honoured to have Beatriz undertake these duties. How often would Her Majesty want Beatriz to read to her?"

"That is a point I was to discuss with you. Her Majesty, as you probably know, still keeps the same hours as during King Philip's last years, when he was subject to melancholia. She rises at five in the afternoon and sometimes doesn't go to bed before seven in the morning. Of course, when she came to Spain such habits were quite contrary to her inclinations. However, she always set herself to please her husband and fell in with his wishes. Now, after so many years, she does not want to change. I was to suggest that while the Court is in residence at one of the Sitios away from Madrid, Doña Beatriz should spend one week in every four in attendance on Her Majesty, and that at Christmas and Easter when we are in Madrid she could come twice a week for the night. We can try that for a beginning. Later on we can see." This was

Doña Ana's way of saying that later on the Queen Mother might have tired of her new reader and would want a change.

"But surely," Doña Teresa said naïvely, "Her Majesty does not want Beatriz to read to her all evening."

"Her Majesty wants to be amused. She wants someone young and new to talk to and generally to help her pass the time. I hear your daughter has a gift for storytelling. If so, don't let her be shy of employing this accomplishment."

"She can dance and sing nicely, too."

"I'm afraid Her Majesty is no longer interested in dancing, and I doubt whether Doña Beatriz's voice would give her much satisfaction since she has been used to listening to the great Farinelli."

"Oh, of course not", Doña Teresa said humbly. "I was forgetting."

"However, if she can play an instrument like that one over there," said Doña Ana, pointing without enthusiasm to a clavichord, "I imagine that a tune now and then would be acceptable." She took Doña Teresa's hand affectionately and familiarly, and her manner changed. "But I am tiring you. It is time for me to go. Don Maurice, we can discuss the final arrangements when you have spoken to your daughter. Good-bye, Doña Teresa. Look after yourself, and, now that I am forgiven, I hope it will not be long before we meet again. I shall take good care of your daughter. Don't be afraid on that score."

She rose, and Don Maurice rose too in order to take her down to her coach.

At the door she turned and said, "Try hot goat's milk with two or three drops of oil of sassafras. It's excellent for almost any complaint."

EIGHT

On a Tuesday morning, a week after the departure of Alfonso de Vallecas for Paraguay, the Marquis Grimaldi stood at one of the windows of his room in the Foreign Secretary's apartment lapped in an unexpectedly warm ray of sunshine and an engrossing daydream.

A handsome, well-built man who had begun to put on weight—just enough to give his features and limbs a pleasant roundness without making him look fat—he had, in leaning against the window frame, automatically adopted a pose as though he were having his portrait painted.

Don Jeronimo had originally come to Spain during the reign of Philip V on a diplomatic mission from the Genoese Republic. With his gifts as a conversationalist and pleasing manners, he had soon found patrons in Madrid to persuade him, and to help him, enter the service of Spain. Then, as Spanish representative, he had been sent successively to Vienna, Hanover, the Hague, and Stockholm. On the accession of the present king, Charles III, in 1759, he had been moved to Paris and finally recalled to Madrid to become Foreign Secretary.

It was a career to be envied. But it had one drawback. As an Italian, Don Jeronimo was unpopular, and being sensitive and at heart timorous, he minded. The worst of it was having to share his unpopularity with the other Italian Secretary of State, the Marquis Squillacci, who, in addition to his post as Secretary of the Treasury, had recently been made War Minister as well. He regarded Squillacci as a narrow-minded busybody, devoid of political tact. It was Squillacci, he told himself, who had given the Italians a bad name. But this did not make things any better. The mob was undiscriminating in its animosities.

However, on this occasion no unpleasant thoughts disturbed him. As he sank deeper and deeper into his reverie, there passed before his imagination people he had known in his youth—relations, friends, boyhood companions, tutors, servants, rivals—and one by one they expressed wonder and admiration at finding him where he was.

He sighed deeply, like a thirsty man on a hot day after drinking a glass of clear, cold spring water. But a knock on his door abruptly broke his reverie.

He started, feeling embarrassed and irritated, as though caught admiring himself in a looking glass. A secretary entered carrying a bundle of papers, which he placed on the minister's desk.

"Has Rubeo come yet?" Don Jeronimo asked sharply.

"He is downstairs, Your Excellency. Do you wish to see him now?"

"Yes, send him up. I hope he is thoroughly frightened."

"He's been here an hour, Your Excellency, so he's had plenty of time to dwell on the consequences of Your Excellency's displeasure."

The secretary's respectful and flattering tone smoothed Don Jeronimo's momentarily ruffled sensibilities.

"Well, I shall have to be lenient with him this time. Men like Rubeo are hard to come by in Madrid."

The secretary inclined his head deferentially to show that he was not prepared to disagree.

"Your Excellency," he said, "before I have Rubeo sent up, there's a matter I ought perhaps to mention to you."

"What is it?"

"The French Ambassador was at the Prince of San Martino's last night and complained to me again about your communicating directly with Versailles through unofficial channels."

"Really?" With a look of self-satisfied amusement, Don Jeronimo left the window and flung himself in a chair. "And how was his complaint phrased?"

"He didn't complain. He only hinted."

"Why doesn't he speak to his Court about it? It's as much to blame as I am."

"Yes, Excellency. Shall I tell him that?"

"No. But you can tell him if you like that it's against your principles to trouble your minister with unfounded rumours. And now, send Rubeo to me."

"Yes, Excellency."

After a few minutes the door opened a second time, revealing, immobile on the threshold, a terrified little man, not more than five feet two inches tall, with small eyes set close together and cheeks like the top of a

41

wizened mushroom. Holding his hat with both hands over his stomach as though expecting a blow there, he looked less like a police agent than a shopkeeper. Someone standing in the passage pushed him forward, causing him to stumble over the edge of the carpet, and, in trying to recover his balance, he ran several steps forward, which brought him to within a foot of the minister, who watched coldly as he straightened himself and retreated to a respectful distance. His pinched and usually pitiless face looked forlorn and abject.

"I'm on his track at last, Excellency", Rubeo said, as soon as he had got his breath back. "I haven't found him yet, but I'm on his track."

"It's about time. Madrid is not a big city, and Monsieur Charville has been lost for over a week. There are countries where you would have been in prison for less than this."

"Your Excellency," Rubeo said unhappily, "I've been thirty years in the pay of His Majesty's government and never to this week have I had a failure."

"A boast you won't be able to repeat in future. How do you think it is going to sound when the news gets abroad that a distinguished stranger staying in Madrid has disappeared completely and can't be found? Monsieur Charville is a man of letters, well-known in many countries, and a protégé of the Duc de Choiseul, the most powerful man in France and head of the French government."

"If only Your Excellency had allowed me to inform the magistrates—"

"Monsieur Charville is travelling on private business. There are reasons why he does not want his presence here advertised. You must find him, or I've finished with you."

"Give me two more days, Excellency. I promise to find him in two days. The man I set to watch him . . ." He corrected himself. "The man whom, at Your Excellency's suggestion, I attached to him as a guide and interpreter, and who disappeared at the same time, has been found. I've brought him along, Excellency. Shall I call him in?"

"Very well."

Rubeo went to the door, opened it, and called out in a very different tone of voice from the one he had been using to the minister, "Stand up. Come here. And take your hat off."

There was a murmuring of voices, and then a big, surly looking man shuffled into the room, the same who had caused the uproar outside Don Maurice de Vallecas' house. His eyes were bloodshot, his clothes crumpled, and he had two days' growth of beard.

"Is this the best you can do?" Don Jeronimo asked disgustedly. "Do you mean to tell me you entrusted Monsieur Charville to a ruffian like this?"

"He looks bad now, Excellency, I admit. We've only just found him. That's why I brought him along as he is. He's been hiding for over a week, sleeping in his clothes." Rubeo turned to the man. "Haven't you, you scoundrel? When you were given that coat, weren't you told to keep it decent?"

He jerked the man's arms and slapped his chest several times with the back of his hand. The clothes gave off little puffs of dust. "But you wouldn't recognise him, Excellency, when he's been cleaned up a bit. A really fine man, upright as a soldier."

"He looks like an idiot."

"He's not as stupid as he seems, Excellency. I'm afraid he's been drinking. But it's most unusual in him. When he's sober, he can talk like a book and knows how to show strangers the sights of Madrid and explain its history as if he could read and write. Come now, tell His Excellency where you last saw the French gentleman."

The man stared at the ground and shuffled his feet.

"In the Calle Guzman?" Don Jeronimo asked smoothly.

The man slowly raised his eyes, and Rubeo stared.

"Then you know where he is, Excellency?"

Don Jeronimo looked at him mockingly.

"I do. And now", he said, turning on the other man, "you will answer some questions for me. You were in a fight?"

"That's right", the man muttered.

"Say, 'Yes, Excellency'", Rubeo snapped.

43

"Yes, Excellency." This time the words came out in a growl.

"Who started it?"

"I did."

"How?" said Don Jeronimo.

"There was a crowd outside the de Vallecas residence. The old Conde was at the top of the steps saying good-bye to his son, a Jesuit, who was going away to the missions. As the son was getting into the carriage, I shouted, 'Good riddance! We've got too many dirty Jesuits in Spain already.'"

"Blockhead", said Rubeo.

Don Jeronimo held up his hand.

"And then, you coward," he said, "you went and left the man you were supposed to be guarding on the ground and took to your heels."

"I'm no coward", the man said threateningly, and took two steps toward the minister as though about to strike him.

The movement was so sudden, and the change in the man's manner from half-suppressed insolence to anger so unexpected, that Don Jeronimo instinctively stepped backward and clutched the edge of the bronze-inlaid table behind him.

"You scoundrel! So that's the sore spot. You're ashamed of your cowardice, aren't you? That's what's behind your insolence. Take him away, Rubeo; get rid of him."

"Ah, but I'll still be in Madrid. You mayn't wish to see me, but I'll be watching you."

"What! You dare to threaten me? You dare to threaten one of His Majesty's Secretaries of State? You scum! I'll have you . . . I'll have you . . ." Don Jeronimo searched his mind. Flogging? The galleys? Death? So keenly did he feel the insult to his dignity that the most extreme punishment did not seem too heavy. However, his experience as a diplomat kept him from being too specific. "I'll have you . . . If you're not careful, I shall have you punished with the utmost severity. Now go."

Rubeo jerked the man's arm and pulled him toward the door. He was about to open it when the minister called out, "Stop!"

"You will answer one more question. You had orders to take particular care of this French gentleman. Instead, you deliberately started a fight by shouting insults about the Jesuits. Why?"

"I was told to. To see how the people reacted."

"Who told you?"

"That's my business."

Don Jeronimo signed angrily to Rubeo to take the man away and, picking up a handbell on his desk as they backed out of the door, rang it violently.

NINE

"My coach", Don Jeronimo said to the servant who answered the bell. "And my hat and cloak."

A different servant brought the hat and cloak, and a cane with a gold knob.

A few moments later Don Jeronimo passed into the anteroom, which was filled with waiting people. Some were officials, a few were prosperous-looking gentlemen, but by far the greater number were poor place-hunters, mostly from the provinces, whose faces, either anxious or listless, told how many anterooms they had already waited in without success. At the sight of Don Jeronimo, five or six of these men jumped to their feet, and one, whose poverty and hopelessness made him bolder than the rest, dodged past the ushers to thrust himself into the minister's path.

"If Your Excellency would be graciously pleased to read this memorial. It is a new copy. I fear the other copies cannot have reached Your Excellency. I have had no reply. If Your Excellency would condescend to give me his patronage. I have waited a year, Your Excellency. I have a family, and they must eat. If Your Excellency would please . . ."

An usher pulled the man aside. Really, Don Jeronimo said to himself, their boldness is passing all bounds. I must change things. They ought not to have direct access to me. But an empty anteroom would not have pleased him either.

He went down the wide stone staircase to the ground floor, acknowledging with an effort—for he was still agitated by his interview with the police spy—the bows of the pages and clerks he met on the way.

Before stepping into his coach, he murmured an address to the footman holding open the door.

The coach started with a lurch, and the horses, which had grown restive while waiting, dashed away over the cobbles. Don Jeronimo passed a hand over his face. Horrible pictures raced through his mind —of being attacked in the street, murdered in his bed, ambushed on a lonely road. But saner thoughts soon took their place. The interest his coach attracted reminded him of the immense distance between himself and the spy. The kind of things he had been imagining just did not happen to people of his sort.

After a short drive, the coach turned through iron gates into a courtyard and stopped at the bottom of a flight of steps leading up to the main entrance of a new house built in the French style. Usually half a dozen footmen were hanging about the door. Today, a single elderly servant was on duty.

"The gentleman you are expecting is in the Chinese room", he said, as he took Don Jeronimo's hat and cane. "I have given orders that no one is to go near that part of the house, so you will not be disturbed. This way, if Your Excellency pleases."

"Thank you, Fernando. I can find the room myself."

Don Jeronimo went quickly upstairs and along a gallery hung with French and Italian pictures, broken at intervals by niches containing Roman copies of Greek statues.

Their owner, the Prince of San Martino, whom the King, on accession to the throne of Spain, had brought with him from Italy and made second in command of the Italian company of the bodyguard, allowed Don Jeronimo to use his house when the minister wanted to meet people without attracting attention. They had been young men together in Rome.

Without a glance at the works of art, Don Jeronimo pushed open a door at the end of the gallery and entered a small room whose blue wallpaper was speckled with oriental birds and whose one window looked onto an interior court. Before the fireplace, with his back to the door, a man in a brown suit sat warming his hands.

"My dear Charville!" Don Jeronimo said eagerly. "What a relief to see you at last. A thousand, thousand apologies for the churlish welcome Madrid has given you. But your eye. It isn't seriously injured, I hope. Oh, I shall never forgive myself."

The man had risen. Don Jeronimo seized his hands, shook them both, gripped his shoulders, stood back to get a better look at him. He did, in fact, everything people do when they wish to leave no doubt they are pleased to see someone. Meanwhile an equal variety of expressions appropriate to the occasion—pleasure, concern, sympathy, distress, indignation—appeared on Don Jeronimo's face. The other took it all with a look of quiet amusement. A patch over his right eye half hid a fading yellow bruise that discoloured the temple above it.

"Please don't disturb yourself, Monsieur le marquis. The eye was not injured."

"Ah, thank God! I was afraid you had lost it. What a tragedy! To think of the immortal works the world might have lost."

Monsieur Charville smiled. "I think I could probably have written as well with one eye as with two, Your Excellency. Now if I had lost half my head . . ."

"My dear friend, not 'Excellency' to you."

But the Frenchman knew how to assess the protest at its proper value.

"You must allow me, Excellency, to bathe in your reflected glory", he said, pushing forward a chair. "With regard to the eye, I assure you I only wear this patch because the bruise is still rather dark underneath and without it I look a bit gruesome."

Don Jeronimo sat down as, after a moment, did Monsieur Charville.

"I am relieved," Don Jeronimo said, "deeply relieved, that you haven't taken greater harm, though what has already befallen you is bad enough. And to meet with the accident in such an unsuitable place! You couldn't, in a sense, have fallen into worse hands."

"On the contrary", Monsieur Charville said. "I think myself most

47

lucky. Don Maurice de Vallecas and his charming family have been all hospitality. I am enchanted and fascinated at finding myself so quickly in the heart of the real Spain, with its courtesy and generosity. I think I may say that I am already treated as a friend by all. Even a young ward who, it seems, has an aversion to foreigners has taken me into his confidence. Surely one could not have had a more fitting introduction to the Spain we have had painted for us in the pages of the Abbé Lesage's *Gil Blas* than this combination I have encountered of violence and magnanimity."

"But haven't you discovered . . . ?"

"Of course. The Jesuit son. I know. Probably a most worthy man like his father and brothers. I saw him only for an instant, as he was departing, before I sank into unconsciousness beneath the cudgel that irate citizen of Madrid aimed at my guide. By the way, what happened to him?"

"The scoundrel! They brought him to me this morning. He'd been hiding. When I saw what a ruffian they'd given you, I was furious. Oh, my dear friend," he wailed, "if you knew the way things are run here. The uncouthness! The barbarity! Sometimes I understand what it was like for Ovid on the Black Sea."

"Come, come, Excellency", Monsieur Charville said with a laugh. "It isn't that bad. Spain, after all, is a great country. Maybe superstition has made the light of civilisation wander a bit. But in your exalted position, think how much you can do to lead her into the paths of reason and philosophy. Might we not compare this country to one of the great bulls that her sons are so fond of fighting? The bull is a noble beast, full of fine qualities. It is for you to tame the Spanish bull."

Don Jeronimo, pretending to be still annoyed, sat frowning at the buckles on his shoes with the fretful look of a cross child who has to be cajoled into behaving properly.

"Take courage, Excellency", Monsieur Charville continued. "You have the confidence of His Majesty. He is all-powerful. What more can you want?"

Don Jeronimo sighed. "There are so many influences working against

48

us", he said. "In theory, a considerable number of Spaniards profess to love philosophy and believe in progress. But in practice they are so attached to their outmoded customs that they will do little to alter them —as you must have seen for yourself. You couldn't have fallen into a more typically Spanish household. I will speak to the Prince, and you can stay here for the rest of your visit."

"I would prefer to stay where I am. I am happy there."

"But in view of your work . . ."

"You forget. I am a simple antiquarian. My work lies in the libraries of Madrid, where I am expecting to find many treasures for this new book of mine."

"My friend, you know what I mean. Your other work."

"And what better place to avoid all suspicion about that." ·

There was a pause. Then Don Jeronimo's frown suddenly changed to a smile.

"Of course, of course. I see your point."

"You underestimate Don Maurice", Monsieur Charville continued. "He is an intelligent, well-informed man who has read a number of our modern French authors—books such as *Émile*, *De l'Esprit*, *Candide* and *Mahomet*, the *Lettre sur les aveugles*, and I don't know what else. We were talking about them last night. Naturally, he doesn't care for many of their views. But he understands their importance and recognises the authors' abilities. He asked whether I didn't think it true that the editors of the Encyclopaedia and their friends were only attacking the Jesuits because they ultimately want to destroy the Church . . ."

"Exactly what I should have expected from a doddering old idiot like de Vallecas. That kind of thing is said to discredit people who are trying to reform the Church intelligently and rid it of an Order that is solely intent on getting power for itself."

The warmth with which Don Jeronimo spoke warned Monsieur Charville of his blunder.

"I meant, of course," he said quickly, "that Don Maurice understood our authors in a general sense. But I was forgetting. Let me give you Monsieur le duc's letter."

Don Jeronimo took the packet, ripped it open, and quickly scanned the contents. Then he read it a second time, and his look of pleasure changed to one of fretfulness and annoyance. He went to the door, glanced outside, and returned to the fireplace.

"I don't know what to say to this", he exclaimed, impatiently striking the paper with a forefinger. "It's all very well for Choiseul to boast of having turned the Jesuits out of France, but it's child's play compared to banishing them from Spain. Doesn't he realise how religious the King is? You must forgive my saying so, Charville, but our work here would be much easier if His Majesty were a libertine like the King of France. 'When are we going to get rid of our Jesuits?' he asks. When, indeed? I thought he was going to send you here with some real damning evidence against them. Hints and insinuations will have no effect as far as His Majesty is concerned. And I strongly resent his holding up Portugal as an example. I'm not a barbarian like Carvalho. Whatever happens here, we've no intention of torturing and butchering people."

During this tirade, Monsieur Charville sat with his eyes down and his hands on his lap. When it was over, he said in a conciliatory voice, "And is the King really as attached to the Jesuits as you say? There are plenty of devout people in France who detest them. Indeed, I am often amazed by the inconsistencies into which hatred leads so many eminent Christians." He smiled. "Who would have expected to find bishops and cardinals fighting on the same side as the contributors to the Encyclopaedia?"

"If you are talking about the Jansenists," Don Jeronimo said, "they hardly exist here, more's the pity. Not that I sympathise with all their views. They are altogether too austere for me. Nevertheless, one has to admit they are concerned about the purity of the faith."

"And is there no way of persuading your King that the purity of the faith, or the good of the Church, requires the extinction of the Society of Jesus? Let's put it like this. We want the Pope to suppress the entire Society for good. No Pope, neither this one nor the next, is going to do that if he can avoid it. But he won't be able to avoid it if Spain and the Empire, as well as France and Portugal, suppress the Society. All

Europe will see they are a danger to national and international stability. However, it's no use trying to put pressure on the Empress. She will never go against her conscience, unless so many people are doing what her conscience forbids that she can persuade herself the Empire will suffer unless she follows suit. This is why Monsieur le duc asked me to tell you personally what great importance he attaches to winning over your King. If we succeed, the Society is certainly doomed. If we fail, it will survive. It seems to me we must somehow convince him that the Jesuits are a threat to his personal authority. Could you not start by suggesting that . . ."

"Impossible! Impossible!" Don Jeronimo exclaimed, his face flushing. Nothing upset him so much as the idea of having to tell the King anything that might be received unfavourably. He also felt like a man who has run up bills and is faced with having to pay them. When in Paris he had privately boasted to his friends of the speed with which he would put an end to the Jesuits were he ruling Spain.

"I assure you, it's impossible", he continued. "His Majesty is the most strong-willed man I know. If I tried to force him in one direction, he would take the opposite."

"Not force, my dear sir. Lead."

"Lead or force. It comes to the same thing. It's impossible."

Monsieur Charville saw that to press Don Jeronimo further was to risk losing his friendship altogether. He also realised, from the way the minister was fidgeting and sitting on the edge of his chair, that he was anxious to get away.

"I can appreciate your difficulties", he said. "We must move slowly. *Autres pays, autres moeurs.*"

"Yes, yes. You have grasped the situation perfectly."

"So I would be right in saying that, while the King is the chief obstacle to our success, we have sympathisers in high places?"

It now suited Don Jeronimo to paint as black a picture as possible.

"Among the secretaries of state, only myself", he said. "My colleague, Squillacci, thinks of nothing except extorting taxes from the people. Arriaga is out and out for the Jesuits. Campo-Villar is a nonentity. On the lower levels, the only man on our side is Campomanes in the Council of Castile. Of the grandees, Alba is the most hostile to the Jesuits, but the old man is getting on, and he's so anxious to return to power that I doubt whether he is interested in much else. Not a promising picture, but the only one I can truthfully paint."

"Not very promising at present. Nor was it in France a few years ago. But things will improve, Excellency. So I will tell the Duke that for the moment we must bide our time, that the cause of enlightenment advances, and that more minds are receptive to ideas of progress, but that an attack on the Society now would be abortive."

"Good! Perfect! And forgive my unmannerly outburst against the Duke. I regard him as one of my dearest friends. But there is so much misunderstanding of the position here that it sometimes exasperates me."

"By the way . . ." Monsieur Charville pulled a book out of his coat pocket as though he had only just remembered it. "The Duke thought you might be interested in this. It's called *De Statu Ecclesiae*. The author, a German, uses the pseudonym 'Febronius' but is known to be a high ecclesiastic. He puts very clearly the true relationship between Church and state and lists all the encroachments the Holy See has made on the legitimate rights of sovereigns. It might interest His Majesty, too."

"Hmm. I will have to see. I can't promise to show it to him. It will depend on finding the right opportunity. And now I won't detain you any longer, as I have a meeting of the Council of Ministers. If you need to see me again, send a message through the Prince. When do you leave us?"

"About the middle of January. My researches will keep me here at least till then. After that I go on to Naples, Rome, and Vienna."

"Well, my friend, I wish you every success in your work. You know what an admirer of your genius I am. Your latest volume has been the delight of my rare leisure hours, and I look forward impatiently to your next. I must quit you now, but greet the Duke from me when you write. Fernando will come to you as soon as I have gone and will let you out by the garden."

Don Jeronimo grasped Monsieur Charville's hand, gazing into his eyes with an appearance of affectionate admiration, then turned and left the room.

TEN

A few minutes later, Monsieur Charville followed the footman down a back staircase and across a wintry garden. The footman opened a gate with a rusty lock in the far wall and let him into the street.

Monsieur Charville looked about him. What a relief, he thought, not to have that ruffian of Grimaldi's hanging onto my coattail any longer. I was afraid His Excellency was going to offer me another one. A guide and interpreter, indeed! As if I couldn't tell a spy when I see one.

Hearing a whistle, he looked round and saw his valet, Dubois, signalling from the door of a shop farther up the street. He beckoned to show it was safe to join him. Since losing Don Jeronimo's ruffian, he had been using Dubois as a "bodyguard".

"This is the address I want to go to now, Dubois", he said. "Keep an eye out to see if we're followed."

"I thought of that, sir. They're all a poor dirty-looking lot here. But I haven't seen any that look unusually suspicious."

"Good, but keep a look out, all the same."

"Rightee-ho, sir." Dubois cocked his hat at an angle and glanced contemptuously at a sow which, with its litter, had wandered into the street and was reclining on a heap of rubbish. He was a tall, fine-looking fellow, a member of the Duc de Choiseul's household who had been lent to Monsieur Charville because he could speak some Spanish. Having spent all his life since boyhood in the service of the very rich, he had acquired an unusual capacity for measuring people's exact social status and adjusting his manner accordingly. For the moment, his attitude toward Monsieur Charville was a mixture of patronage, deference, and nursemaid-like solicitude, as though at any moment the gentleman might, through inexperience, tumble down and have to be picked up and dusted. Had he been able to look into the future and see whether Monsieur Charville was destined to rise in society or sink again to where he had come from, his manner would have crystallised into one or other of the first two attitudes. But not being able to do this, he suited his manner to his temporary master's indeterminate position.

Monsieur Charville, having been all his life in a subordinate position himself, knew that such a man could, if he took against him, do him a lot of harm. He had therefore openly consulted Dubois on questions of dress and etiquette to flatter his vanity—an aim not requiring any very special skill.

"If we run into any crowds, sir, I wouldn't stop to find out what's going on."

"Very good, Dubois. I wish I'd had you with me the other day. If I had, I might not have got this black eye."

HENRI-LUCIEN CHARVILLE, whom we now meet properly for the first time, was forty-five and for twenty-seven years—that is to say, for most of his adult life—had been first a clerk, then an agent for a tax-farmer in Languedoc. He was unmarried and, until moving to Paris three years before, had lived in a small house in Carcassonne with a spinster sister to keep house for him. They had only had his salary to live on. Their parents, who had kept a shop, had died when they were small children. Henri-Lucien had been educated by the Christian Brothers at the expense of a distant cousin. He had left school at sixteen, and the same relation had got him the place in the tax-farmer's office.

By this time he had only two ambitions: to be rich and to be a famous writer. He did not want unlimited riches, or riches for their own sake, nor did he want them for the sake of comfort or pleasure. His personal tastes and habits were almost austere. No, he wanted them as the only finally effective means of escape from dependence on others and, to a lesser degree, because he saw how much money commanded respect. Unfortunately, he did not know how people who made a lot of money began. The tax-farmer kept a close watch on his employees.

However, the desire, the longing, the passion for literary fame came first. He had not only had the normal desire of a talented young man to express and communicate his thoughts. The narrowness and obscurity of his circumstances had bred in him a kind of horror at the idea of remaining forever unknown in a small provincial town. It was something almost metaphysical, as though not to be known and famous were equivalent to falling into a state of non-being. He had a small group of friends, all members like himself of the local literary and archaeological societies. But, aware as he was of his own superior abilities, both they and the meetings of the society made him ever more conscious that he was living in an intellectual backwater.

His talents, he had discovered, were of two kinds, not usually found in combination. He could tell stories and say clever things that made people laugh. On the other hand, he had the natural scholar's excellent memory and love of amassing and marshalling large quantities of detailed information.

His sister was the only human being capable of stirring in him anything like affection. It was not demonstrative, but considerate and fiercely protective. Devout and a bit simple, she gave him in return the unfathomable, incomprehensible, utterly undeserved love of an old-fashioned family servant. Otherwise, at this period, women meant little to him, except as a means for satisfying masculine physical needs— needs he sometimes thought he would be glad to be without. Only on reaching Paris had he discovered how agreeable the company of intelligent women could be. He also discovered how to make himself agreeable to them. He practised charm like an art. But love in the sense of emotional involvement he still found unintelligible and, as far as he was concerned, something to be avoided at all costs. When in love, it seemed to him, otherwise reasonable men and women became either absurd or demanding, or both.

His attitude to religion was similarly uncommitted. He did not hate it. He had liked his teachers, the Christian Brothers, and he saw nothing superstitious or ridiculous in people saying prayers and lighting candles in front of saints, as his sister did, if it made them happy. It was even, if God existed, reasonable. But did it matter whether God existed? Faced with Pascal's wager, he would have chosen unbelief as the better bet, simply because there is only one life to be enjoyed, and if the choice proved wrong, God would not mind all that much. Although a nonbeliever, he had none of the missionary zeal of his new Parisian friends for overthrowing Christianity and turning humanity into a race of paragons by making them all philosophers. The idea seemed to him as silly and misguided as falling in love. Men would always be much the same as they had been from the beginning. Get rid of one set of ideas and rules, and there would soon be people imposing a new lot. The art of life was to know how to circumvent rules when necessary and keep one's head above water by swimming with the prevailing current. Why the current flowed in one direction at one time and another direction at another time no one could say. To try and swim against it was to risk drowning. If quixotic men like the good Jesuit Fathers wished to do so, that was their choice. He had no grudge against them. He was only siding with their opponents because it was in his interest to do so. His interest and theirs happened at this time to conflict. At another time their interests might have coincided.

Most people who met Henri-Lucien would have had difficulty in believing how much unabashed egoism lay behind the amused, intelligent face.

But how fast the years at Carcassonne had gone by, how quickly middle age had come on with his longings still unfulfilled. Sometimes he had felt something like despair, which it had taken all his powers of self-control—and they were remarkable—to contain. But he knew that bitterness and despair are signs of failure, that the world has no time for failure, and that he must therefore force himself to remain urbane and smiling.

For many years he had focused his hopes on a book he had been writing about Roman Narbonne. He had travelled widely over the region on behalf of the tax-farmer, acquiring along the way a good knowledge of its geography and monuments. The Carcassonne episcopal library had provided him with the classical authors he needed, and he had combed all the local archives he could find. The manuscript was now two thousand pages long. Then one day he had come across Voltaire's *Lettres philosophiques*, and they had revolutionised his thinking. He had put his own book aside and had quickly written another one of 160 pages, full of entertaining stories, incidents, and reflections, in which the present state of the province was compared with its condition, or supposed condition, under the Roman Empire. Then everything had been orderly and efficient; now there was nothing but incompetence and decay. He made fun of the provincial governor and his officials, mocked the state of the roads and inns, lamented the derelict condition of the farms. Much of what he described was true, but he had no intention of remaining in Languedoc to help put things right, and, since he was still working for the tax-farmer, he had said nothing about the methods by which the taxes were collected.

He had called the book *The Journeys of Quintus Querculus* and sent the manuscript to a friend in Paris. A few weeks later he had heard that a publisher had accepted it. Sure in advance of success, he had asked the tax-farmer for a month's leave of absence and had set out for Paris. There the publisher, a Monsieur Dardu, had advised him to use a pseudonym. There were powerful people, not least the governor of Languedoc, whom his book might offend. For a day, Monsieur Charville had hesitated. If he used a pseudonym, he would be much less well known. But in the end he had decided on prudence.

The Journeys of Quintus Querculus, by "Gallonius", had sold out three days after its appearance. Four more editions had followed during the course of the month, and soon it was being published abroad. "All Paris" was wondering who "Gallonius" could be. Monsieur Charville had written to the tax-farmer resigning his post; he had also written to his sister, instructing her to shut up the house in Carcassonne and join him in the capital. Dardu had introduced him to Grimm, who had introduced him to d'Alembert and Mademoiselle de Lespinasse. Diderot has asked him to write an article on Roman transport for the last volume of the Encyclopaedia. Madame du Deffand had invited him to her salon, where he had met Rousseau, whom he had instantly disliked.

If only he could have given up the wretched pseudonym that prevented the public at large from knowing who he was! But Dardu had warned him to be careful; the police had visited his office to question him about "Gallonius". They had come a second time and been more pressing. Dardu had taken Monsieur Charville to see the Duc de Choiseul and had asked the minister to give "this new glory of France" his protection. The inquiry into the identity of "Gallonius" had stopped, and his enemies had temporarily had to forego any hopes of revenge. A year later, "Gallonius" had published a second volume of *Journeys*, no less admired by his public than the first and even more provoking to the governor of Languedoc.

Then one day at the Baron d'Holbach's, he had overheard Grimm saying to the young Condorcet that it was a pity "Gallonius" in his *Journeys* had treated his subject so superficially. Monsieur Charville had thought indignantly of the enormous manuscript left locked up in a cupboard at home. There was nothing superficial about that. But what publisher would have touched it if he had sent it instead of *Quintus Querculus* to Paris. Only now that he was famous could he hope to get it printed. And printed it should be. He would get his sister to bring it with her. He would revise it, expand it, turn it, in fact, into a history of Roman Gaul, which would establish his reputation for seriousness once and for all.

On mentioning his plan a few days later to his new patron, the Duke had made a proposal of his own. He needed, he had said, an agent to make contact with sympathetic personalities at the courts of Madrid and Naples and to urge them to prosecute the attack on the Jesuits more vigorously, also to find out what, if any, steps had already been taken. All expenses would be paid, and he could also use the journey to collect material for a companion volume about Roman Spain. He would thus appear to be travelling as a scholar with private means.

To this proposal Monsieur Charville had instantly said "Yes". Grimm's criticism of his book had temporarily tarnished the charms of Paris for him, and now that he was "a name" himself, his attitude toward his new friends had altered. A sense of rivalry had replaced his earlier feelings of admiration and respect. The sting of envy had succeeded the sting of frustrated ambition.

ELEVEN

"Dubois, I think we are lost."

"Trust me, sir, and you won't come to any harm."

"I do trust you", Monsieur Charville said. "All the same, I'd rather not take any risks, so please will you go into that shop and ask the way again."

They had been walking for a quarter of an hour since leaving the Prince of San Martino's palace and now found themselves in a narrow street running downhill.

With bad grace the valet did as he was told.

"Just as I thought", he said, coming back. "But we can take a shortcut through that church opposite. The place we want is . . . well, I'll explain when we get there."

Two minutes later they stood in a crowded street before the door of a large old house that had once been a nobleman's palace but was now divided up and given over to trade. While Monsieur Charville was waiting for someone to answer his knock, a loaded wagon came out from an archway at the side of the building.

"Who's there?" a voice demanded from inside the house.

"A gentleman to see Monsieur Laborde."

The door was opened by a servant girl. She said something in Spanish and led the way upstairs. At the top she opened another door and signed to Monsieur Charville to go into the room beyond.

"Oh, I beg your pardon", he exclaimed, trying to back out when he found that he was in the presence of two women.

The older of the women, who wore an elaborate lace cap, was sitting by the fire mending a stocking, while the other, a girl who looked not yet twenty, was writing in an account book at the table. At the sight of Monsieur Charville, the older woman shrieked and put a hand to see if her cap was in order. With the other hand she thrust the stocking out of sight behind her chair.

"Oh, that girl!" she said, ignoring Monsieur Charville and addressing her daughter in French. "If I've told her once, I've told her a thousand times not to show customers up to the salon. There was never a race to equal these Spaniards for misunderstanding what you say."

"Please don't let me disturb you, madame", Monsieur Charville said in French. "There has been a mistake. I was looking for Monsieur Laborde."

"Then you are a Frenchman, monsieur?"

"Yes, madame. I have that happiness."

"Mon Dieu!" the lady said, her expression transformed, "then you can't know how delighted I am to see you. Madeleine, do you hear? The gentleman is French. Pray, sir, be seated. And you will take a glass of wine with us? Yes, yes, I won't listen to a refusal. Madeleine, here are the keys of the cupboard. Quickly now! So you want to see my husband, sir?"

"If I may."

"Yes, yes", Madame Laborde said, but she seemed to be in no hurry. "In a minute or two I will have my girl fetch him. And to think I was calling her a half-wit. This is the first sensible thing she's done. But you must excuse our appearance. We're not dressed for receiving callers. You look like a married man, so you know that women can't be waiting to make themselves agreeable to gentlemen all the time. And please forgive this wretched little salon."

"On the contrary, I was admiring it."

"You flatter me, sir. But what can you do to a room with such a dismal outlook?"

The windows looked onto a large untidy yard and a line of warehouses. However, the room itself was pretty and comfortable enough.

While she was talking, Madame Laborde bustled about trying to distract Monsieur Charville's attention from certain things that seemed to her too homely to be seen in a lady's salon, such as the account book and her sewing box. Embroidery would have been different.

"Have you been acquainted with my husband for long, monsieur?"

"I'm a stranger to him. I've come on business."

"Ah, sir, then you won't realise that we haven't always lived in this prison. Yes, that's what I call it. I suppose you know Monsieur Laborde was in the silk business at Lyons with his brothers. We had a fine house there, close to the river, and lived in quite a different style." Madame Laborde dropped a pair of curling irons inside her daughter's spinet and deftly kicked a shabby slipper out of sight under a cupboard. "Then just over a year ago they decided to open a branch in Madrid. Someone—how I'd like to wring his neck!—told them that silks were hard to get in Spain and there was a fortune to be made here. So it falls to my husband, being the youngest, to take his family into exile. We lead a most melancholy existence. Since coming to Spain, Monsieur Laborde has taken up with banking, too, and thinks of nothing but making economies. We just have this small apartment over the shop, and Madeleine and I spend nearly all our time here trying to keep each other from crying. May I ask, sir, how long it is since you came to this horrible country?"

"Mother, you oughtn't to speak like that", Madeleine said, as she came back into the room carrying a tray with a decanter and glasses. "This gentleman may be partly Spanish, and besides, you know how much kindness we have received since we have been here."

But Madame Laborde was not in the mood for trifles like gratitude and discretion. She was one of those extroverted women who tell their troubles to the first person they meet, and she had been cooped up for a month with no one to talk to except her daughter and the maid.

"I should hope they would show a little pity to two poor exiles", she said. "They are Christians, after all. But beyond that . . ." She threw up her hands. "Besides, I can see that this gentleman is French to his fingertips. From Paris, too, I feel sure. I imagine you wouldn't think much of Lyons, sir. But Madeleine and I are very homesick for it. Still, bad as things are, I could have resigned myself to them if Monsieur Laborde hadn't got it into his head a few weeks ago that Madeleine must marry a . . ."

"Oh, Mother!"

"Well, my pet, if you won't stand up for yourself, your mother must. I believe in calling people by their proper names. A most odious man here in Madrid, was what I was going to say, whom Monsieur Laborde is only interested in because he's so rich. A Frenchman, of course, but one I'm thoroughly ashamed of. He calls himself Mesnier. He might just as well call himself Monsieur l'Avare. He thinks about money even more than Monsieur Laborde does."

"Mother, I'm sure this gentleman doesn't want to hear about our private concerns."

The gentleman smiled in a fashion that could have been interpreted several ways.

"Well, my dear, I can't see the harm in sharing one's troubles."

"I'm sure this gentleman will forgive my saying so, but we have each other to confide in, Mother."

"You have me to confide in, but whom do I have?" Madame Laborde asked indignantly. "I assure you, sir," she went on, turning to Monsieur Charville and rushing ahead to prevent her daughter from interrupting again, "that this is not the whole story. Before my husband fell in with this odious Monsieur Mesnier whom I mentioned just now, he had promised to let Madeleine marry a fine young man called Berouet, a boy of good family who was working in the business here. It was all settled, and we were as happy as could be. But suddenly Monsieur Laborde changes his mind. Without a word to either of us, he sends young Berouet off to Lyons to work in the office there and tells me I'm to have Mesnier for a son-in-law. Well! I just laughed in his face. 'Mesnier!' I said. 'Do you think I'm going to let you sell our daughter to that snivelling money-lender, a man nearer my own age than Madeleine's?' Oh, yes, I didn't mince my words. 'If you carry on with this low scheme,' I said, 'you're going to be frying in Purgatory till Judgment Day—that is, if you don't go to a worse place.' Well, sir, wasn't I right? What other fate could a man expect who is prepared to barter his daughter for gold. Oh, I frightened him properly. But not enough to bring him to his senses and make him ashamed of himself. Money has eaten right into his heart."

"Can I offer you some wine, sir?" Madeleine asked.

"Of course the gentleman will take wine, my dear. And so, sir, it's war, open war. My husband is set on the marriage, and my daughter and I are equally determined not to give in to him. But it isn't pleasant. He won't let us go out. We can't receive visitors. We mayn't send letters —and since we've stopped getting any, I'm sure he's keeping the ones that do come for us. It's like living in a besieged city. But what can two defenceless women do? We're completely without resources."

My God, Monsieur Charville thought, she's going to ask me to lend her some money.

Madame Laborde misread his expression.

"Oh, you needn't worry, my good sir", she said. "I should have no hesitation in throwing myself on your generosity if that would solve our dilemma. But we can't travel back to France alone. And even if we could, the only place we could go is my son's house, and my son is completely dependent on the goodwill of his father and uncles, who are capable of turning him out of the business if he helps us. However, the shoe isn't entirely on one foot. I have ways and means of fighting back. Only a woman's weapons, but sharp enough for all that. I know how to make my husband uncomfortable, and he hates that."

Madame Laborde was interrupted by a cough, and looking around she saw the person she was speaking of standing in the doorway.

Monsieur Laborde, a portly man in breeches and shirtsleeves, stood gazing at them with indecision and embarrassment. He looked, indeed, very much like a monarch in difficulty with his parliament. His authority had been flaunted. Ought he to be firm? Or conciliatory? Having lost his nerve, either policy seemed likely to be disastrous. A pen stuck in the side curls of his wig did nothing to counteract the impression of diminished dignity. Nor did the lifeless way his arms hung down on either side, like flitches of bacon.

In the past, when it had been unnecessary, he had made a great show of ruling his family. But now that his wife and daughter were no longer willing to obey, he had discovered how weak he was. There was a limit to what he could bear. Snuff in the soup, beetles in his bed, a toad in his slippers . . . they were beyond the limit. For the last fortnight he had been eating and sleeping in his office.

"Well, Monsieur Laborde," his wife said, "this is a surprise. Providence, as you see, has sent us a visitor to help us pass the morning, which is more than you have done. How this gentleman managed to get in, I don't know, seeing that you choose to have us live in a fortress. But here he is, and we thought we would enjoy a little of his society before you monopolise him."

"Good morning, sir", Monsieur Laborde said, ignoring his wife. "How can I help you?"

"I have a bill of exchange that I should like you to negotiate for me", Monsieur Charville said. "I had no intention of disturbing Madame and Mademoiselle . . ."

"Oh, I assure you, sir," Madame Laborde said, "we were delighted to be disturbed."

"If you will step downstairs, sir," Monsieur Laborde said, "I will see if I can oblige you."

"Well, monsieur," his wife said to Monsieur Charville, rising from her chair, "I see that Monsieur Laborde is determined not to oblige us, so we must say good-bye. Madeleine and I have very much enjoyed your visit, and we hope you will call again. I suppose now that Monsieur Laborde has seen you, he won't have the door shut in your face."

"It is very kind of you", Monsieur Charville said, without committing himself. He was still not certain that Madame Laborde might not intend to borrow money from him or, worse still, ask him to give her and her daughter refuge at his apartment in Paris. "Good-bye, mademoiselle."

"Good-bye, monsieur."

"And perhaps you will be good enough", Madame Laborde continued, "to champion our poor cause with my husband. A few words from you may touch his heart and make him feel some compunction, for nothing my daughter and I have said has had any effect. God will most certainly reward you for it."

Monsieur Laborde flushed but said nothing. He held open the door for Monsieur Charville, who bowed himself out of the room, again without making any promise.

"Oh, Mother," Madeleine said, as soon as they were alone, "how could you have told him all about us like that? It was cruel." She looked as if she were about to cry.

"I'm sorry, my pet. But I did it for your good. Your mother isn't a fool. She hasn't lived in the world for forty-three years for nothing. We don't know who this stranger is. But it's quite possible that he's somebody important."

"But even if he is, why should he take any interest in our affairs?"

"Powerful people like to show they have influence", Madame Laborde said with finality, as if she spent her life at Court and were a friend of kings. "Besides, what could interest a man more than the sight of two women in distress? It appeals to their sense of gallantry. He is more than likely to say something to your father, trust my word."

TWELVE

Monsieur Laborde's office on the ground floor of the building was very dusty and full of ledgers and metal boxes.

"Well, sir," he said as they entered, quickly pulling a counterpane over an unmade bed, "is the bill endorsed?"

"Not yet. Perhaps you would kindly lend me a pen?"

Monsieur Laborde removed the pen from his wig and held it out to Monsieur Charville, who looked critically at the nib, tossed it onto the desk without using it, and sat down in Monsieur Laborde's chair.

"Thank you. And now, Laborde, I'd like a word about your wife. Of course, all women talk a lot. But isn't it a handicap in a business like yours to have a wife who is quite so indiscreet?"

"That's my affair", said Monsieur Laborde, too startled for a moment by Monsieur Charville's presumption to think of being indignant. "Give me the bill, take your money, and our business is done."

"Not until you've answered my question. Do you ever discuss your affairs with your wife? Some husbands do. Some husbands don't. If you are foolish enough to belong to the first category, everybody in Madrid must know what goes on in your office."

"See here, sir", Monsieur Laborde said angrily. "I don't know who you are, and I don't care. You can be King Louis himself, but I've stood enough of your insolence. Get out!"

As soon as Monsieur Laborde had spoken, he regretted it. Everything about Monsieur Charville—the cool way he sat in the chair trifling with a paperweight—told him that his visitor must be a person of much greater importance than his name and clothes suggested.

"Your wife's tongue is very much my concern, Laborde. I'm in Madrid on business for Monsieur le duc de Choiseul. This paper will satisfy you that I'm not lying. My name is Charville, and I want the use of your office for half an hour or so while I write a letter. But I have been wondering whether you are a fit person to have charge of the correspondence between the French Court and its agents in Spain. We need reliable, discreet men. Not men who chatter to their wives."

"Sir, I promise you my wife knows nothing. Absolutely nothing. I never even discuss my own affairs with her, let alone this other business."

"Of course, you realise that were the Duke dissatisfied with your services, it would be enough for him to inform the Marquis Grimaldi indirectly about your activities, and you would be expelled from the country, or worse."

"Sir, I am a true Frenchman, a patriot. I would be hanged, no, I would let myself be burned at the stake rather than betray Monsieur le duc's confidence. Besides, what do I know? Only that my men carry certain letters back and forth between Paris and Madrid. I never ask what's in them or the names of the gentlemen who bring them. All I ask is to see their credentials. I assure you . . ."

Monsieur Charville picked up the pen from the desk again.

"That's all right. I take your word for it. Do you have a man going into France today or tomorrow or some time early next week?"

"On Monday, sir."

"Very good. Monday will do. And now I would like to be left alone."

"Certainly, sir, certainly. You will find everything you need on this desk—paper, ink, pens, sand. Just ring that bell if you want anything else. I'll be in the next room." And like a rabbit fleeing from a weasel, Monsieur Laborde escaped through the door in the opposite wall.

Merciful heavens! he thought, as he stood in temporary safety on the other side, wiping his forehead with a handkerchief. What a mess I've got myself into! Why on earth did I get involved in this kind of dirty work? Why didn't I stick to banking and the silk trade?

Suddenly he realised that the three clerks in the room were looking at him curiously. "What are you staring at?" he said angrily. "Get on with your work. No. Take this bill to those people in the Calle Toledo, Robert, and tell them it must be paid at once. Marcel, go and give them a hand in the warehouse. Jean-Paul, run upstairs and tell Madame Laborde that if she and Mademoiselle want to go for a walk, you are free to escort them in half an hour."

LEFT TO HIMSELF, Monsieur Charville sucked the tip of his pen, then swiftly began to write a report to his master.

Your Excellency,

I reached Madrid on 3rd November and saw the Marquis Grimaldi this morning. I was unable to see him sooner on account of an accident I had.

He was going to describe the accident, but knowing that the great have little interest in hearing about the misfortunes of subordinates, he continued instead:

I will not trouble you with its details. However, in consequence, I am now the guest of a certain Don Maurice de Vallecas, a member of the Council of Castile, a man in high favour with the King and very close to the Jesuits. I am thus safeguarded from any suspicions that might be entertained about my presence here.

He read and reread the paragraph and was pleased. It sounded as though he had made friends with Don Maurice through his own ingenuity. He went on writing.

I fear I must report that my meeting with Monsieur de Grimaldi was not very satisfactory. He is no longer so eager to suppress the Society as he was when in Paris. Nothing can be done here without the King, on whose favour his position depends, and what the King thinks about the Jesuits nobody seems to know. Monsieur le marquis will not risk bringing disgrace on himself by mentioning the subject and possibly antagonising His Majesty. I pressed him to be bold, but without result. We can expect nothing from him for the future. Should some other man do the work, Monsieur de Grimaldi will, if it is safe, join him. But he will not take the initiative himself. Our meeting was plainly a disappointment to him too. He seemed to think he was going to hear himself praised for what he has not yet done.

With regard to the King, accounts differ. But from various sources I have formed the following picture. As Your Excellency knows, His Majesty is a keen defender of the rights of princes against the encroachments of the Holy See. This indicates a frame of mind that could be receptive to our ideas. But at the same time he is strict in his religious duties; he prides himself on being an upholder of the Catholic faith, and I have it on good authority that he personally detests Monsieur Voltaire. He is not opposed to reforms; indeed, I understand that he is anxious to attract foreign manufacturers and craftsmen to his country. In one sense he is on the side of progress. But the spirit of the Encyclopaedia is too far ahead of him to win his sympathy. After all, as Your Excellency will appreciate, he is a monarch. Monsieur Voltaire and Monsieur Diderot handle religion and authority too roughly to please him. He will fight the Holy See where he thinks his rights as a sovereign are in jeopardy, but at the same time he would want to preserve the appearance before the Pope of being a dutiful son. It would be difficult for him in the present circumstances to suppress the Jesuits, supposing that he were ready to, and still keep this reputation.

Monsieur Charville then repeated what Don Jeronimo had told him about the other ministers.

The Marquis praised only Monsieur de Campomanes. What I did not tell him was that I had already contrived a meeting with that gentleman and had mentioned your name to him and disclosed some of my sympathies. Campomanes spoke warmly of what we have achieved in France, and he is working to prevent our French Jesuits from being given asylum in Spain. But he confirmed Monsieur de Grimaldi's view of the impossibility of having the Society suppressed here within the foreseeable future. He also said that even if His Majesty were prepared to act against the Society, he would not do so until after the death of the Queen Mother, who has been devoted to the Jesuits all her life.

Monsieur de Campomanes is a successful lawyer, and while he is ready to do more for us than Monsieur de Grimaldi, he too is unlikely to do anything that might damage his career.

I have still to meet Monsieur de Torrelavega, who, you will remember, was prominent in the last reign. In recent years he has lived on his estates in the north but is said to be in Madrid at present. I have heard that he is hostile to the Jesuits, and his wealth and absence from the Court should give him an independence and readiness to act not enjoyed by Messieurs de Grimaldi and Campomanes. On the other hand, he is said to be a fanatical admirer of the English, which means that he is not likely to be all that well disposed toward us.

Your Excellency will see that I have not tried to disguise the poor success I have had so far. But I know Your Excellency wants to hear the truth, however discouraging . . .

Monsieur Charville paused. I wonder if that's so, he thought. Possibly not. But if I say it, he will have to agree. He can't pretend that he would rather hear an encouraging falsehood.

He began to write again.

. . . since without the truth it will be impossible to make an effective plan.

However, I am confident that we shall succeed in our design, even though its fulfilment is farther off than we anticipated. I shall work to gain sympathisers here so that we can count on a body of men who

69

can take advantage of any crisis, disaster, or public disturbance and lay it at the door of the Jesuits. His Majesty must be made to fear them, or the Society must be placed in a false position so that its survival appears to be in conflict with His Majesty's interests.

As Your Excellency will appreciate, all this will take time, so that I may have to spend longer in Spain than I had anticipated. In view of this, might I beg that Your Excellency would be pleased graciously to have placed at my disposal a further sum of money for my expenses.

For the rest, I shall continue to devote myself to the studies Your Excellency has so generously encouraged me to undertake.

Assuring Your Excellency of my devoted service, I remain Your Excellency's obedient, humble servant,

C.

Monsieur Charville sat back in his chair and bit his lower lip. He crossed out the sentence asking for money. I'll leave that to my next report, he thought. People hate being asked for money, even when it's not their own. He rewrote the last page, scattered sand over it, and read the whole letter through. Afterward he enclosed it in three envelopes, which he sealed with separate seals, and then rang the bell.

A cowed and obsequious Monsieur Laborde reappeared. Monsieur Charville gave him the letter.

"But I don't want it to go until you have a really trustworthy man making the journey", he said.

"The man going on Monday is a jewel, sir. Never asks any questions he oughtn't to. Would you care to see him?"

"Looking at him won't tell me much."

Monsieur Laborde locked the letter in a safe.

"I'm sure, sir," he said, when he had hidden the key inside his shirt, "that you are too fair a gentleman to believe everything my wife has said about me. She's an excellent woman at heart, but her feelings are too strong to make her a good judge of what is best for our daughter. I'm certain that when she sees how happy Madeleine is with Monsieur Mesnier, she will persuade herself that it was she who arranged the marriage."

"Your family is your own affair", Monsieur Charville said coolly. "As long as my letter reaches Paris, I shall be satisfied. Here is my address while I am in Madrid. If any letters come for me, please have them sent round at once."

Dubois was waiting in the flagged passage outside, and Monsieur Laborde let them into the street through the arched gate used by the carts and wagons.

THIRTEEN

They had gone only a short distance when they heard running footsteps. Looking round, Monsieur Charville saw the clerk Jean-Paul pelting down the street after him.

"Could you wait a minute, sir", he called. "Madame Laborde would like to speak with you."

The lady, who had just left her house, was walking toward them on the arm of her daughter.

I hope to God, Monsieur Charville thought, looking the young man up and down, that Laborde isn't going to send my letter by a boy like this.

Just at that moment, Madame Laborde and Madeleine approached.

"I can never thank you enough", the lady began, "for your great kindness. My daughter and I are anxious to know how we can express our gratitude."

"I don't know that I have deserved it", said Monsieur Charville, who had by now classified Madame Laborde as a talkative and possibly dangerous nuisance, and was thinking that Don Maurice was very punctual for meals and that his house was three-quarters of a mile away.

"Oh, sir, we are not to be put off with such modesty. After two weeks of imprisonment, Monsieur Laborde throws open the door, sends us for a walk, and begs to be allowed to come and dine with us. Do you think we don't know whom we are indebted to for this change."

71

"If you are attributing some alteration in your husband's behaviour to me, madame, you are mistaken. I have not spoken a word to him about your affairs. Good-day, madame. Good-day, mademoiselle."

He bowed and, ignoring Jean-Paul, walked quickly away.

"What a remarkable man!" Madame Laborde exclaimed as she looked after him.

"I think, perhaps, we were mistaken, Mother", Madeleine said. "This gentleman didn't seem in the least pleased at being thanked. He certainly wouldn't have denied speaking to Father if he really had. Something else must have happened to make Father change his mind."

"My child, when you know human nature as well as I do, you will think differently", Madame Laborde said with decision. "One occasionally meets people—they are few and far between, it's true, but they do exist —who will get in a passion rather than admit to having done a kindness, although they spend most of their lives helping others."

"It still seems rather strange for a gentleman with such good intentions to speak to two women so rudely."

"Just human nature, my pet—of a particular kind. Besides, if he wasn't talking to your father about us, what was he doing all that time? It doesn't take three-quarters of an hour to negotiate a bill of exchange."

They set out for the Atocha gate. Beyond it lay a walk called Las Delicias, the only feature of Madrid that pleased Madame Laborde. From there she could see the Manzanares, and although it was only a trickle by comparison, it reminded her of the Rhone and her home. As they went along, she continued to expound her theories about Monsieur Charville's character, position, and occupation.

Undoubtedly, she said, he was a gentleman of rank, possibly a marquis, and an intuition told her that he was visiting Madrid for the purpose of luring French talent back to France. France must be suffering from the loss of gifted men like Monsieur Laborde. Their visitor might even be a friend of King Louis and in that case could get Monsieur Laborde appointed purveyor of silks to the Court.

Here she fell silent and began to plan in her mind how best to present this new idea to Monsieur Charville the next time he called.

72

"Be careful, mademoiselle", Jean-Paul said, drawing Madeleine to one side as a coach rolled by sending up four jets of mud from its wheels.

"Oh, thank you. I wonder who the lady was inside. She looked terribly annoyed. Perhaps it was because her coachman nearly splashed us."

"That was Madame de Squillacci, the wife of the King's chief minister, mademoiselle. He is Secretary of the Treasury and Secretary of State for War. So you can imagine how powerful he is."

A few yards farther on they passed some soldiers marching toward the Retiro Palace.

"How smart they look!" Madeleine exclaimed. "Our own soldiers couldn't do better."

"Excuse me, mademoiselle," Jean-Paul said, "but that is a detachment of the Italian bodyguard."

"Why, Monsieur Jean-Paul, what a lot you know", she said with surprise. He was so small and slight—only an inch or so taller than herself—that she thought of him as a boy rather than a man.

"I keep my eyes and ears open, mademoiselle. The more you know, the more use you can be."

"You like Spain, don't you?"

"Yes, mademoiselle."

"I thought so. But don't you miss your family?"

"I have no family, mademoiselle."

"Oh, I'm so very sorry."

"There's no need to be. I lost my parents long ago. But the good God looked after me. When I was twelve, a priest—he was a canon of the Church of St. Étienne in Lyons—took me in. He ran a school in his house for the sons of gentlemen. He let me take part in their lessons, and in return I helped to wait on them. I learned many useful things that way. And you, mademoiselle, are you not fond of the Spanish, too?"

"Yes, indeed. They are more serious than French people, but I believe they are also kindhearted. Do you know, Monsieur Jean-Paul, I think that the Spanish love God more than we do. I wonder why?"

"I know what my master, the Canon, would have said."

"What would that be?"

"Jansenism, mademoiselle. He used to call it the Calvinist frost that had blighted the bloom on our Catholic life in France. He said it made ordinary people too frightened of God to love him and gave bad men an excuse for saying religion turned people into hypocrites and Pharisees."

"Fear of God is a very salutary thing, young man", Madame Laborde said suddenly.

"Yes, madame."

"Oh, Mother, you weren't listening to what Monsieur Jean-Paul was saying."

"Yes, I was. He was saying that people don't fear God enough. It's what I'm always telling Monsieur Laborde." And the older woman plunged back into her daydream again.

"According to the Jansenists," Jean-Paul continued, "our Saviour did not die for all men, only for a few. This is just one of a number of their teachings condemned by Pope Clement XI back at the beginning of the century in a document called the bull *Unigenitus*. That's why the Jansenists hate the Pope and are continually stirring up trouble against the Jesuits. The Jesuits have always been their strongest opponents. The Jansenists reply that the Jesuits win power over people by preaching a lax morality. They say the Jesuits make religion too easy. But it isn't true."

They passed through the Atocha gate. Ahead of them, they could see the river sparkling between the trees of the avenue. The centre of the walk had been trampled by the hooves of horses and was deep in mud, but along the side, close to the trees, a narrow path was still dry. Madame Laborde went in front. Jean-Paul and Madeleine followed side by side.

"I wonder, Monsieur Jean-Paul, that you didn't think of becoming a priest."

"Why, mademoiselle? Just because I can repeat what I've heard in a sermon? If I described the play I saw last night at the Teatro de la Cruz, would you say that I ought to be an actor?"

"Did you really go to the play? Oh, how I envy you! I wonder if my father would let you take my mother and me to the theatre sometimes."

"It would have to be after Christmas, mademoiselle. I'm leaving for France on Monday."

"On Monday? And I was just thinking how much I would enjoy another walk like this. You say so many interesting things, Monsieur Jean-Paul. You don't know how disappointed I feel." She fell silent. After a minute or so she said suddenly, "Will you be going to Lyons?"

"To Paris first, then Lyons, mademoiselle. I take your father's letters and bring back the replies."

"Young man," Madame Laborde said over her shoulder, "you are much too inexperienced to travel about so much. I've spoken to Monsieur Laborde about it before. Sending mere boys on a journey like that! It's not right."

"Don't worry about me, madame. I've travelled from the day I was born. My parents were acrobats, and I was born on the road."

"Oh, how fascinating", Madeleine said.

"Would you like me to do a turn for you, mademoiselle?"

He stepped onto the grass at the side of the path, rubbed his hands quickly, took a short run, turned a somersault in the air and landed on his feet. Madeleine clapped her hands.

"Bravo! Bravo!"

"Well, Monsieur Jean-Paul, we didn't expect you to be able to do a thing like that", her mother said, surprised that a young man she had thought of as rather insignificant should have such a marked personality of his own. "And what else can you do?"

"Shall I recite you some poetry, madame?"

"Good heavens! You didn't learn that from acrobats, surely?"

"No. I was taught by the actors they sold me to after my parents died."

"They sold you?" Madeleine said. "How terrible!"

"You are very good to be so sympathetic, mademoiselle. But the actors who bought me treated me kindly. I spent three years with them before they sold me to the Canon. Let me see. What do I remember best?"

He frowned and began to declaim, with the gestures appropriate for tragedy, some lines from a play called *Polyphème*, by a now-forgotten author named Delamarche. Experienced theatregoers would have been amused by his efforts to speak in a bass voice, uttering threats against Mars and Jupiter, but neither Madeleine nor her mother was critical. They both applauded.

"Oh, that was beautiful!"

"You speak like a real actor", Madame Laborde said. "Though, personally, I could never understand how Christians could waste their time listening to all that nonsense about gods and goddesses."

"Great people like that sort of thing, madame. But I prefer songs." And in a clear tenor, this time without mannerisms, he began singing a song about two lovers called Dodo and Nanette.

By now they had come to the end of the walk, where a gardener was burning a heap of leaves. The smoke from his bonfire drifted across the path in a thick curtain. Madame Laborde suddenly remembered that there were things she wanted to buy before dinner, so they started back toward the city.

When they reached home, Madeleine allowed her mother to go upstairs ahead of her.

"Monsieur," she said, turning to Jean-Paul and speaking quickly in a low voice, "you say you are going to France on Monday. If I give you a letter, do you think you could deliver it for me when you get to Lyons", she hesitated for an instant, "to Monsieur Berouet?"

"Yes, mademoiselle. Gladly. And I'll bring back an answer as well."

FOURTEEN

In the Palace of the Escorial, the pages and maids of honour to Elizabeth, the Queen Mother, stared out of the windows at the dusk falling over the countryside and yawned as they waited for their mistress, who was just waking up.

At six o'clock the Queen appeared from her bedroom, walking with a stick and leaning on Doña Ana Pantoja's arm. The ladies in the private drawing room rose and curtsied to the floor. She greeted each with a few words and passed on to one of the larger drawing rooms.

The early part of the evening was taken up with callers—the Papal Nuncio, the ambassadors of the Bourbon Courts, the Bishop of Jaen, some elderly noblewomen, and, finally, the widow of an official who could not get her pension and who had obtained an audience with the Queen through Doña Ana.

At eight the doors opened, and a chamberlain announced the King. Charles III came in quickly, went straight up to his mother, and, before she had time to make even a show of rising, gave her a respectful kiss.

He was short in body, and his face, with its strange long nose and small eyes, suggested a country landowner from one of the more remote provinces. However, he was far from a nonentity. To have acquired and kept a reputation as a strong ruler when he was fundamentally uncertain of himself, lacked imagination, and was not quick-witted showed abilities of at least some sort. An exalted idea of his authority and rights as sovereign was the mainspring of his public actions, but he had the sense to recognise his limitations and had learned how to use abler men without becoming their puppet. Except on state occasions, he always dressed simply, without orders or decorations, and tonight he was wearing a plain dark coat with brass buttons. His life was equally simple: a routine of attention to business interspersed with much hunting to keep himself fit and his courtiers occupied. Any balls and galas were held of necessity, not for pleasure. He ate the same supper every night —an omelette and salad. He had now been a widower for three years. Always faithful as a husband, he was—to the wonderment of most other courts and chancelleries—to live chastely for the rest of his life.

"How are you today, Mother?" he asked as he sat down.

"As well as I can expect at my age, I suppose, Charles. Old age is detestable."

"We all have to come to it, Mother. The great thing is to keep up one's spirits."

"I do my best, Charles. But when you are blind and nearly eighty and surrounded by other old women . . ."

The King, fearing a catalogue of complaints, began to talk about his afternoon's shooting. Afterward he spoke about the improvements he was making at Aranjuez, the royal palace about thirty miles south of Madrid.

"Grimaldi has been showing me the plans for some gardens he saw at The Hague. We are thinking of having them adapted. Aranjuez has too many long prospects and vistas. We want something more intimate."

Like most people who have been trained to take the lead in conversation so as to fill silences or to avoid hearing what they would prefer not to hear, the King discussed each subject exhaustively, and only when there was no conversational ore left in it, passed on to another.

Doña Ana, watching from her corner, thought: Two people afraid of each other. But what is he frightened of? Doesn't he realise that by never consulting her or allowing her to take a part in affairs, he has broken her spirit? She is now much more in awe of him than he ever was of her.

The Queen was longing to ask her son who he thought would be the next King of Poland. After having had a half, and often more than a half, share in running the foreign affairs of Spain for thirty years, it was hard to know only what was the common gossip of the Court. But if she asked about Poland, she might annoy him, and then he might refuse to do anything for the widow she had promised Doña Ana she would help.

With an effort she sacrificed her curiosity and asked about the señora's pension.

"But of course, Mother. Give me her name."

He beckoned to the gentleman-in-waiting, who wrote down the name in a small notebook.

Before leaving, the King kissed his mother again, this time with some feeling. He was pleased with her for not trying to wheedle information about state business out of him. Then he went to supper.

"Could anyone have a more devoted son?" the Queen remarked to Doña Ana. "I have only to ask something and he grants it."

But dutiful, rather than devoted, was what the Queen actually thought of her son. In spite of having had her request about the widow granted, she felt puzzled and hurt. Why didn't he ask her advice about politics? Could he think she didn't understand them? Impossible! Was he under the impression that affairs of state would tire her? But she had hinted again and again that she wanted to be taken into his confidence.

She stopped in her reflections, breathing heavily, and told herself with indignation that he could not love her. For the Queen, government was not so much a responsibility toward millions of subjects whose happiness depended on right decisions. She regarded it more as a game of cards, in which it was mean of her son not to let her take part, particularly since she was such a good player, and in partnership with her in the past he had done so very well out of the game.

When, just under fifty years ago and still a little known minor Italian princess, Elizabeth Farnese, as she then was, niece of the last Farnese duke of Parma, had come to Spain to marry the recently widowed Philip V, it had seemed unlikely that any child of her own by him would become King. It was against all expectation that her eldest son, Charles, after more than twenty years, had succeeded to the throne on the death of his stepbrother Ferdinand. She had, therefore, during her husband's lifetime, used Spanish money, arms, and influence to win thrones for her sons in Italy, the country of her birth. Charles she had succeeded in making King of the Two Sicilies, and Philip had been established as Duke of Parma.

The other European powers, having become accustomed to regarding Spain as an extinct volcano, had been infuriated at finding the Court of Madrid suddenly following an energetic foreign policy. It was as though an ordinary housewife, determined to provide well for her children, had forced her way into the stock exchange and, to the rage of the brokers, had upset the market by buying and selling on her own and making off with a fortune. In revenge, through their propagandists, they had started a campaign of character assassination against her. Although she had neither committed adultery with her ministers nor connived at the murder of her husband, she enjoyed a far worse reputation internationally than the Semiramis of the North, Catherine of Russia, who was reputed to have done both.

Someone, the Queen decided, as her fingers played nervously with a jewelled vinaigrette, had turned her son against her. Was it the favourite, Losada? Was it Grimaldi? Was it that scoundrel Tannucci?

When she began speculations of this kind, her suspicions generally ended with Tannucci, who was now ruling the Two Sicilies for her young grandson, Ferdinand, Charles III's third child. A meddlesome intriguer, was her opinion of the Neapolitan minister, an infidel and freemason in all probability, who, under a veil of devotion and respect for religion, was sapping the authority of the Holy See and stirring up more trouble for the Society of Jesus.

Charles could not know what Tannucci was really like. Were he to find out, he would surely get him dismissed. Her son had always been a devoted Catholic. But was he, without realising it, being influenced by Tannucci's ideas? Why, for instance, had he suddenly become interested in the canonisation of that miserable Bishop Palafox, who had been such a hater of the Jesuits a hundred years ago? And why had he chosen a Franciscan confessor instead of a Jesuit? On the other hand, he allowed Jesuits to educate his children. She did not know what to think. She had lost touch with her son. She no longer understood him.

The Queen's next visitor was her confessor, Father Bramieri, with whom she spent a certain time each day talking about spiritual subjects.

"We have been reading the life of St. Benedict, Father," she said, "and we have been scandalised by the behaviour of the monks of Subiaco."

"They won't have been the first monks to behave scandalously, Your Majesty, you can be sure", the priest replied with a smile. "I forget for a moment what they did."

"Tried to poison him. Forced him to become their abbot and then turned against him because his rule was too strict. Can you conceive of such wickedness? Why be monks at all, if you are going to go in for murder? And to poison a saint!"

"I don't know that his being a saint made any difference, Your Majesty. It would have been just as wrong to poison a sinner. What has to be remembered is that even after taking vows in religion, men remain men. God does not take away their free will because they have dedicated their lives to his service in a special way. And then, too, different temptations beset different ages and callings. In the past, men were rougher and wilder, and so their sins were most often sins of passion and violence. In modern times, sins of the mind are more common. It certainly looks as if the devil won a notable victory at Subiaco. But the monks probably repented, and one ought not to feel that one could not fall into an equally grave sin, unlikely though that may seem."

"You are quite right, Father. We can think of a number of people we would have been tempted to do away with if we had had the chance. And we treated Madame des Ursins badly, thoroughly badly. She had to go, of course. When we came here from Parma, she was running the country entirely in the interests of the French. King Philip was quite under her thumb. But we should never have sent her away in the snow the way we did. That was cruel. May she forgive us, and may God have mercy on her soul."

"She does forgive you, madam, you can be sure. Even in Purgatory there is only love."

The Queen then discussed the Foundling Hospital in Madrid, which Father Bramieri had been to visit for her. Before he left, she sent for Doña Ana and had her give him one hundred escudos for it.

At eleven the Queen dined. Two of the dishes were not to her liking, and she sent them back. She also complained that the room was dark and ordered more candles to be brought in.

"What is this, Doña Ana?" she asked crossly, peering with the aid of a magnifying glass at the menu. "They write so ill, I can't read it. Have the man who does these taught to form his letters properly. Nobody takes trouble nowadays."

"The new reader has arrived", Doña Ana said, as a distraction.

"What reader?"

"Doña Beatriz de Vallecas, ma'am."

This news made the Queen more cheerful, and she gave orders that Beatriz was to be sent for as soon as her dinner was over.

FIFTEEN

Several rooms away, Beatriz, who was being instructed in court etiquette, had just sunk to the ground in a curtsey, and now one of the Queen's ladies was stalking around her, criticising her performance.

Beatriz had reached the Escorial late in the afternoon and had been placed in the care of a Doña Dolores de la Peña. This lady was now writing letters in a corner of the room, and her companion, Doña Inmaculada Hernandez, had taken charge.

"Again, please", Doña Inmaculada said shrilly. "Now how many curtsies will there be? That's right. One at the door, and one before you kiss Her Majesty's hand. And when you leave? The same? That's right. Ready now?"

Beatriz tried again.

"Your eyes! Your eyes!" Doña Inmaculada shrieked, as Beatriz sank down for the tenth time. In her eagerness to give satisfaction, she had kept her eyes fastened on those of her instructress. "Heavens, you don't stare royalty in the face. Again, please."

"My good Doña Inmaculada," Doña Dolores said mildly, as she looked up from her writing, "you'll wear the poor child out."

"Nonsense. I never saw such a healthy young woman. Indeed, her complexion seems better suited to the countryside than the Court. However, she hasn't done too badly. I've seen worse curtsies."

"You don't know what a compliment she's paying you", Doña Dolores said with a smile. "Doña Inmaculada is very strict about these things. If you've satisfied her, you'll satisfy anybody."

Teacher and pupil sat down to rest, and Doña Inmaculada began to tell Beatriz what she must do to please the Queen.

"Above all, if Her Majesty falls asleep while you are reading to her, don't stop. Act as though you hadn't noticed. When she wakes up, she will tell you to read the passage again, pretending she wants to hear it for a second time only because she found it so interesting. Quite a common weakness in the elderly, which we shall all doubtless come to sooner or later."

She looked at Beatriz meaningfully in case she had failed to realise that she, too, like the rest of them, would one day be old and no longer pretty.

At this moment they were interrupted by the ladies who had been waiting on the Queen at dinner. They entered chattering and laughing like a flock of tropical birds just released from a cage and made straight for the fireplace. Then, after warming themselves for a few minutes, swept into a farther room with a rustle of silk and taffeta dresses.

At midnight, Beatriz was summoned to the private drawing room. Doña Ana was with the Queen. When Beatriz had made her two curtsies and had kissed the Queen's hand, so that she could at last with propriety raise her eyes, her first impression was of a baby's face balanced on top of a bundle of black brocade and of two plump hands covered with rings. Her next thought was: "She's just an old lady, like Grandmother." The idea surprised her, but she immediately felt more at ease.

"Come closer, my child, so that we can see you", the Queen said. "There, you must kneel down."

Beatriz did as she was told.

"Yes, we can see you now. There is a definite likeness. Is she not like her grandfather, Doña Ana?"

"I did not have the honour of knowing the gentleman, ma'am."

"Don't be a goose, Doña Ana. Of course you did."

Doña Ana inclined her head respectfully.

"What a delightful man! So good, so trustworthy, so tactful, so considerate." The Queen fell into a daydream that lasted about a minute. "It was long before you were born, my child, but your grandfather was very useful to us in the twenties and thirties—especially in the business of the French and Austrian marriages. Oh, those marriages! You can't imagine the time we had getting little Maria Ana's dowry and jewels out of the French when they broke off their engagement to King Louis and sent her home. Thank God, they did break if off, though. He'd certainly have made her wretched, the wastrel."

Doña Ana frowned and glanced at Beatriz. This was unsuitable talk for the ears of a girl.

"The child is still kneeling, ma'am," she said.

Doña Ana pointed to a stool close to the Queen and whispered to Beatriz to sit down on it.

"Bless us, so she is! Now tell us about your family", the Queen continued. "We expect you hear all that is going on in the great world from your father."

"Oh, no, ma'am. Papa never talks about his affairs."

This answer seemed to disappoint the Queen.

"That is a very dutiful reply, my child. But we might have expected as much from the granddaughter of our old friend."

"But, Your Majesty, I didn't say it to be dutiful. It's true."

"Don't answer back", Doña Ana said sharply.

"Let her alone", the Queen said. "She means what she says, and what she means isn't disrespectful. We have forgotten, Doña Ana, that the young speak from their hearts. If only we old people could be as candid."

That's all very well, Doña Ana said to herself, but if a young lady you didn't care for were to talk to you candidly, you'd soon put her in her place.

She thought this without bitterness. She had studied her mistress' character for years and, in spite of all she had learned, was still fond of her.

"Your father is wise, my child", the Queen continued. "Knowing about politics and affairs of state has never made anyone happier. And there is much in them to embitter the heart. They don't give one a very elevated picture of mankind. Let the young keep their illusions for as long as possible. We give very little attention to public affairs now. At our age there are more important things to consider. We will not be very much longer in this world and must prepare for the next. The King consults us from time to time—more than we could really wish. You see, we have such a long experience of ruling. But we hope that as he gets more accustomed to Spain, which he was absent from for so long, he will need our support less and less. Tell us, my child, when are you going to be married?"

The unexpectedness of the question confused Beatriz.

"What does the child say? We can't hear?"

"She says nothing, ma'am. She is blushing. But she is to marry her cousin. They were brought up together."

The Queen's eyes twinkled. She clapped her hands, and her rings glittered.

"How lovely. Tell me about him, my child."

But to spare Beatriz, Doña Ana answered instead.

"He has recently finished his studies at Salamanca, ma'am, and is going to travel abroad for a year."

"That's enough, Doña Ana", the Queen said abruptly. "We've plagued the child sufficiently for the time being."

We! Doña Ana thought.

At the end of an hour, twelve musicians appeared. On a signal from Doña Ana, Beatriz was about to retire, but the Queen commanded her to stay. The musicians performed three pieces by Porpora and two by Carlo Broschi. Then a tenor sang an aria from *Lo Frate Inammorato* by Pergolesi, and this was followed by the instruments again.

The Queen listened attentively. In the middle of a piece she stopped the players, reprimanded them, and ordered them to play the passage again. At its conclusion, the first violin came to apologise.

"Shocking, señor", the Queen said. "Worse than a village band."

The musician bowed low and begged pardon humbly—much more humbly than necessary, Beatriz thought, considering the smallness of the fault. But the musician knew how many other musicians were ready to step into his shoes.

"Well, señor," she said playfully, when the concert was over, "we will ask Doña Beatriz de Vallecas what she thinks of your playing."

"Oh, ma'am, I've never heard anything to equal it."

"Aha, señor! Do you hear that? She says that never before has she heard such dreadful playing."

"But, ma'am, that wasn't at all what I meant", Beatriz cried, fearing that she might have ruined the man. "I meant that I had never heard such heavenly music. I could detect no faults; it all sounded perfect."

The musician gave her a smile that showed a larger number than usual of his fine white teeth.

The Queen laughed. "You will have to learn to be more discriminating", she said.

After the music, Beatriz read aloud part of an Italian translation of a French romance about a pair of lovers called Amaris and Hubegonde. Doña Ana thought it insipid and unreal, but the Queen loved it, and so did Beatriz, when she had read far enough to pick up the thread of the story. Both ladies saw themselves as Hubegonde. As for Amaris, in Beatriz's imagination he looked like Rodrigo, while in the Queen's, he resembled Philip V as he had looked the first time she saw him.

Beatriz then retired to the anteroom, and for the next hour or so the Queen dictated letters to Doña Inmaculada. Afterward, toward five o'clock, she ate supper and talked with her ladies. At half past six she went to her private chapel to hear Mass.

By the time Mass was over the sky was beginning to pale. Wrapped in a fur-lined cloak with a hood, and supported by two of her ladies, she descended to the terrace outside the Palace, there to take the early morning air. She walked slowly several times up and down the gravel while the sky grew gradually lighter and country noises began to come from beyond the palace grounds—the barking of dogs, the crowing of cocks, the rumbling of cart wheels. An officer in one of the courtyards shouted a command, and a sentry stamped.

When she had been put to bed, the Queen sent for Beatriz again. Propped on a mountain of pillows and wearing an enormous ribboned cap, she looked to Beatriz more than ever like her grandmother and even less than before like her idea of a queen.

"Now, my child, you must read us to sleep", she said. "But no more of Amaris and Hubegonde. Our confessor tells us we are too fond of romances. There ought to be some serious books on that table. No? Well, where can they have been put? Doña Ana! Doña Inmaculada! Doña Dolores! Look, all of you."

The ladies began to search the room and called in the maidservants to help. The Queen, who was all the time growing more excited, directed the operation from the bed. Curtains were pulled aside, tablecloths lifted, closet doors opened. At the height of the commotion she remembered seeing the books in the drawing room.

"There," she said, with a sly look at Doña Ana, "if your memories were as good as ours there wouldn't have been all this fuss."

When the books were brought, she told Beatriz to read the titles.

"*The Life of Saint John Francis Regis*", said Beatriz, examining the first.

"We've read the most interesting parts of that."

"This one is by somebody called Febronius."

"Febronius! Febronius! I've never heard of him."

"It seems to be in Latin, ma'am. The title is *De Statu Ecclesiae*."

"The state of the Church? I hope the author doesn't find fault with it. That's all anyone seems to think about these days. Doña Ana! Doña Ana! Where does this book come from?"

"I've never seen it before, ma'am."

"But someone must know. It can't have walked into my apartments."

Doña Ana went to consult the other ladies, and one of them suggested it might be the King's, as she remembered seeing him carrying a book.

"Not the kind of book the King usually reads", the Queen said. "Still, I don't see who else it could belong to. Have it sent back to him." Then, turning to Beatriz, she continued: "We will have some more of St. Benedict's *Life*. And let us hope that in the next chapter those wicked monks who tried to poison him will have repented."

SIXTEEN

The Queen was the kind of woman who could not like, or dislike, people by halves. Her enthusiasm for her new reader was so great that she insisted on keeping Beatriz with her for the greater part of the day —or rather, of the night.

The ladies-in-waiting took this success good-naturedly. It was difficult not to like Beatriz, and she made their lives easier by putting the Queen in a better temper. Also she was young. Nearly all the members of the Queen's household were in their sixties or seventies. Shut in by themselves, and living mostly by night, they felt strongly their isolation from the busy world of their children and grandchildren, their nephews and nieces. Everything suggested that life, for them, was over. Beatriz's pretty, youthful face was like a flower blooming in a basement.

Beatriz soon realised that the Queen, like most old people, lived a large part of the time in the past, going over its mistakes and putting them right in her imagination. If her criticisms spared no one in European public life for the last fifty years, she was just as scathing about some of her own actions. And her censures fell thick on Grimaldi, some even touching the King.

When the Queen spoke this way, Beatriz, from embarrassment, sat silent with downcast eyes, an attitude that won Doña Ana's approval.

Later in the first week the Queen's uncertain temper manifested itself in a more dramatic fashion.

Carvalho, the all-powerful Portuguese minister—he had not yet been created Marques de Pombal—seeing how long it was taking the anti-Jesuit party in Spain to get the Society suppressed, had concluded that the Queen Mother was to blame. Up to this point he had taken little account of her. In his opinion she was a troublesome old harridan, who had fortunately long since had all her teeth drawn and her claws blunted. However, it now seemed as if she had a claw or two that had grown sharp again. So he had decided to try to win her over. This, with the complacence characteristic of an all-powerful statesman, he had thought to achieve by a flattering message and a present of some Chinese porcelain, which he had instructed the Portuguese Ambassador in Madrid to deliver to her.

Beatriz was sitting in the anteroom when the Ambassador of his Most Faithful Majesty arrived and was taken into the Queen's presence.

After a minute or two, she heard a strident "How dare you, sir . . ." as though a furious peasant woman had gotten into the Palace. Beatriz leaned forward to look through the open door. The Queen was hidden from her by the Ambassador, whose back she could see deferentially bowed.

"So your master wants me to sell the Spanish Jesuits to his companions in crime here. How much am I to be paid?" the Queen demanded. "Thirty pieces of silver. No, that's too much. We're only trafficking in men. A trumpery box of china will do."

"Your Majesty, I protest . . ."

"So do I, sir. I protest against the imprisonment and burning of priests, against the torture of innocent servants, against the strangling of honourable gentlemen, and against strapping them to wheels and breaking them to pieces with hammers."

"I assure your Majesty . . ."

"What? That the Aveiros, the Tavoras, and Father Malagrida are still alive?"

"Your Majesty has been misled."

"Do you deny these things, sir?" With each question the Queen's voice grew shriller. "Are you going to tell me that the dungeons of St. Julian are empty?"

The Ambassador, seeing that is was useless to defend himself, backed toward the door.

The Queen's voice followed him.

"Tell Señor Carvalho that I don't expect presents from executioners."

With a flushed, angry face, the Ambassador strode through the anteroom. An official hurried beside him. Beatriz caught the words: "Deeply regret . . . Her Majesty indisposed . . ."

THE SAME WEEK an incident occurred, this time of apparently little significance, but one that was to have consequences affecting Beatriz personally.

One of the governesses of the royal children, the Countess of Quiroga, came to the Queen Mother's apartments to visit her friend, Doña Dolores. Beatriz had seen the Countess several times already, but that lady had scarcely noticed her. On this occasion, however, the Countess went straight over to Beatriz, sat down beside her, and started to talk. Within a few minutes, Beatriz, who had hitherto thought her proud and disagreeable, had completely revised her opinion. The Countess, a still handsome woman, knew how to be amusing about life at Court without saying anything that jarred by being disrespectful.

"I was watching you at Mass the other morning", she said. "It is such a pleasure to come across a girl who thinks of something besides dresses and young men."

Beatriz looked embarrassed.

"Oh, I hope you don't mind," the Countess said, "but I wanted to ask you a favour. There is someone I would like you to pray for. Will you?"

"Of course. May I know who it is?"

"I can't tell you the person's name, or age, or sex. But I can say that this person is in great need of prayers. I believe he or she neglected their religious duties for a long time and is causing the family much anxiety."

Beatriz was immediately interested.

"Oh, poor person! How unhappy he must be!"

"I didn't say it was a man, you know."

"How unhappy he or she must be!"

"Then you will say a prayer for my friend?"

"Most certainly. But I will also write to my aunt—she's a Carmelite —and ask her to pray for him, which will be much better."

This conversation was the beginning of something that was more than an acquaintance, if not quite a friendship. Beatriz thought much about the Countess of Quiroga's friend and said many prayers for this unknown person who was in such great need. On subsequent visits to the Palace, whenever she met the Countess, she would ask if there was any news of her friend.

"Yes," the Countess would say, "there's been a definite improvement." Or, with a mournful look, "Things have taken a turn for the worse again. You will keep praying, won't you?"

And each time Beatriz felt more curious than before to know who the Countess' friend could be and what was the matter with him.

SEVENTEEN

For about a year, a group had existed in Madrid called the Society for the Dissemination of Useful Knowledge. Once a month the members met to listen to a talk on some learned subject such as gravitation, political economy, or classical inscriptions. The idea had been Don Maurice's. Familiar as he was with what was taking place in the salons and coffee houses of France and Italy, he had sensed the need for widening the intellectual horizons of his friends and acquaintances in a way that did not simultaneously lead to their becoming infidels.

In January of the new year it was the turn of Gaspar de Vallecas and his Duchess Luisa to entertain the Society at the Montesa Palace. Gaspar had been one of the first to join, and Luisa was an enthusiastic member—partly because the idea seemed daringly novel, partly because it was the kind of thing that would annoy her relations. So far no other Pantoja had joined.

On the Monday the Society was to meet, Gaspar, who had been shooting with the King near Aravaca, returned to the Montesa Palace just as it was growing dark. After handing his shotgun to his valet, he ran up the steps, went straight to his room, washed the blood and dirt from his hands, and then, without changing his clothes, hurried to his wife's apartment.

In the Duchess' bedroom, a woman in her fifties was seated in a chair facing the open door of the dressing room. At the sight of the Duke, her hitherto lustreless eyes lit up with pleasure, and she gave him her hand to kiss.

The Marquesa de Torrelavega, who had been a friend of Luisa's mother, was the kind of woman for whom worry had become the mainspring of existence. Some of her troubles were genuine enough. Her husband, a minister in the previous reign but now out of favour was brutal and unfaithful. Her children were selfish and quarrelsome. But these real causes of suffering she aggravated by unnecessary anxieties about money and rank, both of which she had in abundance.

"Good evening, Doña Ines", Gaspar said, in his open, friendly way.

"So you've come to gather some useful knowledge. That's good. Where's Luisa?"

Doña Ines nodded toward the door.

"Having her hair dressed. I gather you are expecting the French Ambassador tonight. We, being out of favour at Court, are, of course, out of favour with him, too. But one can't expect an ambassador to be anything but a weathercock, can one? And then, of course, the English Ambassador is such a particular friend of ours. I do feel that Lord Rochford is a great addition to Madrid society."

Gaspar smiled down at her and nodded, but it was plain he had not taken in what she said.

"Excuse me", he murmured, and vanished into the dressing room to embrace the Duchess.

Doña Ines felt a pang of envy at seeing the eagerness with which he hastened to his wife after being separated from her only since midday. She heard the Duchess protest that she could not be kissed because it would disarrange her hair, then Gaspar came back smiling happily.

"And what's the news, Doña Ines?" he asked, sitting down opposite her with a hand on each knee. "I hope you're not thinking of running away to the country again."

"No. We have had enough of rural life in the last two years. We shall stay on in Madrid for another month at least, thank God."

"Good, good. Though personally I hate Madrid. If it weren't for Luisa, I'd live all the time in the country. Wouldn't I, my love?"

"I can't hear what you're saying", the Duchess cried petulantly from next door. Then she spoke to the hairdresser. "There's too much pomade. No. Leave it. I haven't the patience to be fussed over any more. I'll just have to look like a gypsy. I'll dress now."

"She hears perfectly well", the Duke said with a sly look at Doña Ines. "It's only that she doesn't want to admit what a long-suffering husband I am."

He broke into a laugh in which Doña Ines joined, wondering at herself as she did so, since Gaspar's jokes were not clever like Lord Rochford's. The Englishman's jokes were the kind people repeated. If you tried repeating Gaspar's, no one understood the point. But when he made them himself, you laughed out of sympathy, infected by his good humour.

"By the way," he said, "did your husband order any sheep from that address in England I gave him?"

"Really, Don Gaspar, what a question to ask a woman!"

"Oh, come! We don't have to go through pretences of that sort. The wives of the Patriarchs knew all about sheep, you can be sure, so I don't see why they should be beneath the dignity of the noblest Spanish lady."

Doña Ines laughed. "If that's your opinion," she said, "I will confess the truth. I know more than enough about the wretched creatures. First they were landed at Cherbourg, then we heard that a storm had driven them onto the coast of Cornwall, and finally they were delivered to a nobleman in Lisbon. We couldn't have worried about them more if it had been the fate of the Fleet we had been following. But we have them at last, and their bleating has given me many sleepless nights."

"And have they lambed yet?"

"Now let me see . . ."

Doña Ines felt sorry when Luisa finally appeared, and Gaspar, forgetting about the sheep, rose and took her hand.

"I've never seen that dress before. You look beautiful, Luisa." He turned to Doña Ines. "Aren't I fortunate to have such a lovely wife?"

"Ines didn't come to hear me being flattered by my foolish husband", the Duchess said, smiling with pleasure. "You would think by this time he would have asked after our children, wouldn't you, especially since one of them is ill."

"But I was just about to . . ."

"On the contrary, you were discussing livestock", she said, teasingly. "Can you imagine it, Ines, a father who thinks more of his animals than his children!"

Doña Ines could easily imagine it, being married to just such a man, but she did not say so.

"Stop it, Luisa, and tell me how Pilar is", the Duke said.

"You had better go and find out for yourself. And can you speak to

Tonio? He kicked Francisco again today. It's the second time. He really must be punished severely. I don't see how else we can stop him."

"Again!" Gaspar exclaimed in a shocked voice. He took leave of Doña Ines and, with a worried expression, hastened off to the nursery.

Luisa smiled and led Doña Ines into her private sitting room.

"Little Pilar is not as ill as I pretended. But as we haven't much time before the members of the Society arrive, I thought I had better get rid of Gaspar. Is your boy Diego coming this evening?"

"His father is bringing him."

"Good. Beatriz and her parents will be here as usual, so it will be easy. I will introduce you to them after the speaker has finished. Then, while you are talking to the parents, Diego and Beatriz will have an opportunity to get to know each other."

"And do you think there is a chance that your father-in-law and mother-in-law and the girl herself will be interested in the match?" Doña Ines asked. "I will be frank, Luisa." She hesitated, looking for the right words. "There is much about Diego that I could wish otherwise— both in appearance and manner."

"First appearances are always deceptive", said the Duchess, who, when she had determined on a course of action, was not to be put off. "There are very few men who don't cause their parents anxiety. Once he is married to Beatriz, she will transform him."

"Yes, but meanwhile she will have to meet him in his untransformed state."

"Listen," said Luisa impatiently, "everything is playing into our hands. Her cousin Rodrigo, with whom she imagines she is in love, is to travel abroad for a year. He's not a bad young man—indeed I am fond of him—but he and Beatriz would never be happy together. He's quite unpolished, and she is such an exquisitely sensitive creature. It's really their own good I'm thinking of. Very well. While Rodrigo is away, Diego will have a clear field for over a year. That ought to be time enough to win her affections. I've also told my cousin Elvira de Quiroga, who sees Beatriz at Court—Elvira is a governess to the royal children —to try and get her interested in him."

"Luisa, how can I ever thank you."

"That's not all, though. I have work for you, too. It will be just as well if we can persuade Rodrigo to fall in love with someone else while he's abroad. You know Italy. If you could write letters of introduction to families in Naples, Rome, and other places where they have pretty daughters, I will undertake to give them to him. When he has met a few Italian beauties, he will forget he was ever in love with Beatriz."

Hearing the sound of carriage wheels, Luisa broke off and, gathering up her fan, led Doña Ines through several fine rooms into one larger than the rest, dominated by a portrait of Philip V on horseback. Under the portrait stood a solitary armchair. Beside the chair was a gilded table with a carafe of water and a glass on it. Opposite were fifty smaller chairs placed in rows.

EIGHTEEN

Luisa's motives for making trouble between Beatriz and Rodrigo were, like the causes of war in history books, both general and particular.

In general, she eased her restlessness by interfering in other people's lives; and in particular, she thought she had found a means of forcing her relations, the Pantojas, to have a higher opinion of the de Vallecases by marrying Beatriz into the Torrelavega family, which the Pantojas had to recognise as only a degree less exalted than their own.

Luisa was like a revolutionary with a secret belief in the divine right of kings. Encouraged by her father, she had married for love. But she had not had the strength of character to be indifferent to the criticisms of her uncles, aunts, and cousins. She had wanted to have her own way and, at the same time, to be approved of for having had it. Therefore, the mésalliance must be shown not to be a mésalliance.

So far she had had little success. When, therefore, she had received a letter from Doña Ines de Torrelavega saying that she was looking for a wife for her fourth son, Diego, and asking Luisa if she knew of a suitable girl, she had immediately replied that she did indeed. Her sister-in-law Beatriz would be an ideal wife for Don Diego, and, to make the match more attractive, she had promised that, if it came off, she would privately double the amount of Beatriz's dowry. Being accustomed to forcing reality to fit her fantasies, neither the apparent impracticability of the scheme nor the suffering it must cause Rodrigo and Beatriz had made her hesitate or reflect.

What Luisa did not know was that Doña Ines' letter had been inspired by her husband, whose motives were even more tortuous than Luisa's.

THE MARQUES DE TORRELAVEGA was typical of those noblemen all over Europe who as a class were not particularly interested in either learning or progress, and certainly not in liberty, equality, or fraternity, but who, foreseeing neither the social nor political consequences of the Enlightenment, instinctively allied themselves with it insofar as it was a movement dedicated to removing or relaxing the restrictions of religion.

In the previous reign, the Marques had been successively Ambassador in London and Secretary of State for the Marine and, while in London, had become an ardent admirer of the English, not because he believed, as his Whig friends did, that England was the home of liberty, but because he saw it as a despotism run by, and in the interests of, his own kind. France he despised, because it typified the triumph of royal power and the subjection of the nobility.

However, with the death of Ferdinand VI and the accession of Charles III to the throne of Spain, he had been dismissed from his post and had withdrawn, in a malignant frame of mind, to his estates at Sala de los Infantes, near Burgos. Since then he had been watching for an opportunity to return to power.

With regard to his family, the Marques could not have been said to love any of his children. However, with one exception they satisfied his pride; his daughters were beautiful, and three of his four sons, reckless and handsome. Only Diego, the youngest, had no qualities that could please his father. It is true, he was tall and broad-shouldered, but his features were heavy, his eyes blinked stupidly, and his limbs seemed to be held together on strings like a puppet's. The Marques, who believed he had a right to generate only good-looking children well endowed with the gifts that make for success, regarded Diego as a malicious joke played on him by that providence in which he did not believe. But Diego was growing up and had to be provided for—if possible at little or no cost to the family, yet still in a fashion suited to the dignity of the Torrelavegas.

The Marques' first plan had been to force the monks at the local monastery of San Torquato to elect his son as their superior. The old abbot had just died, the Prior was a cousin of the family, and so too was the bishop of the diocese, a man whose family had purchased a mitre for him at the age of twenty-three by a combination of falsehoods and bribes, and after indignant protests from the Papal Nuncio. As for the monks, they were harmless but weak men, frightened of the Marques' power; so after the dispensations necessary on account of Diego's age had been obtained, they had compliantly elected him.

The next day the Marques had arrived at San Torquato with all four of his sons. The community assembled in the guesthouse to receive them. Diego's eldest brother was holding him affectionately by the arm, or so it was meant to appear.

"Reverend Fathers, allow me to present your new Abbot," the Marques had begun, "a young man who—I'm not afraid to say even though I'm his father—has been remarkable for piety and devotion since childhood and from the age of six has been eager to embrace the contemplative life. You will find him, I believe, a second St. Benedict."

The monks had listened with expressionless faces, wondering whether the Marques meant to deceive or insult them.

Flushed and agitated, the Prior put some formal questions to the Abbot-elect. But instead of answering, Diego had started forward, staring at the community with mad, goggling eyes.

"I won't be a monk", he had shouted. "If you accept me against my will, you'll damn yourselves. You can all go to hell if you want to, but I'm not going with you."

Then, sinking his teeth into his brother's hand, he had wrenched himself free and had dashed from the room.

"After him! After him!" the Marques had shouted, like a huntsman hallooing at his dogs, and the three older brothers had rushed in pursuit.

The terrified monks, recalled to a sense of duty by Diego's outburst had hurried off to the chapter house to decide what to do.

"We're sorry, Your Excellency," the Prior had said on their return, "but the election is invalid. The candidate is not a free agent."

"Nonsense, Father Prior," the Marques had replied, "he's been longing to join you. What you've just witnessed is stage fright."

"I'm afraid we must disagree. Besides, it's too late now. We have just elected another Abbot. Our Father Guestmaster."

The Marques had blustered and threatened, but in vain. By this time the monks were far more frightened of incurring the wrath of God than the displeasure of the Torrelavegas, so the Marques had had to content himself, on his return home, with giving Diego a more severe beating than usual and keeping him locked in his room for three weeks on a diet of bread and water.

This setback had not prevented the Marques, when, in the summer of 1763, he was staying in England with his friend Lord Buckinghamshire, from complaining to his host of the idleness, viciousness, and ignorance of monks—failings that would have been increased a hundredfold if Diego, who had had the most meagre of educations and already paid the minimum attention to the sixth commandment, had been elected abbot of San Torquato. In reply to Lady Buckinghamshire, who had asked whether it was true that the worst kind of monks were the Jesuits, he had said that undoubtedly monks of the Jesuit brand surpassed all others in worthlessness and immorality.

SOON AFTER RETURNING from his visit to England, the Marques had heard someone mention the great favour enjoyed at Court by the Duke of Montesa.

"Montesa?" the Marques had said to his wife. "Is he that upstart who married old Montesa's daughter? Didn't you used to know her?"

"It was her mother I knew", Doña Ines had said timidly. "I haven't seen Luisa since she married Gaspar de Vallecas."

"No matter. Write to her. Make friends with her again. Tell her you're coming to Madrid and would like to visit her."

In cultivating the Duke, the Marques had foreseen the possibility of recovering a place at Court and, what interested him more, a role in government. This had been his original intention in having his wife write to Luisa. But when he had read Luisa's reply, he had become almost equally interested in her proposed match between Diego and Beatriz. Marrying one of his sons to Montesa's sister would, by binding the two families together, not only help smooth the path to royal favour but be a much more advantageous method of providing for Diego than making him a Benedictine abbot.

Accompanied by his wife and six children, he had immediately started for Madrid and during the journey had decided, as a preliminary measure, to get Diego into one of the regiments of the royal bodyguard where the young man could be drilled into looking more presentable.

NINETEEN

"And when you press the lever, an electric current flows along the rod and makes a spark . . . as I was saying at the Medina Celis' . . . so you still accept Tournefort's theory? . . . No, I'm converted to Linnaeus . . . How extraordinary! Paper money? I would never trust that."

A buzz of conversation filled the great drawing room of the Montesa Palace as the disseminators of useful knowledge stood about waiting for the proceedings to begin. Several of the men were in court dress. Here and there a star of an Order caught the light or a ribbon made a band of colour across a dark coat.

At last, when all the members of the Society who counted socially were present, Luisa glided with Monsieur Charville in her wake toward the chair under the portrait of Philip V and held up her hand for silence.

By an extraordinary stroke of good fortune, she said, they were privi-

leged tonight to have a distinguished French scholar to speak to them—
a gentleman for whom her father-in-law, Don Maurice de Vallecas, and
other leading members of the Society had so high a regard that they had
just arranged for him to be made an honourary member of the Spanish
Academy of History.

"May I ask you to show your appreciation of this well-deserved
compliment to our foreign visitor", said Luisa, though she had no real
idea why it was deserved. A round of hand-clapping was accompanied
by a nodding of heads and polite smiles.

"His subject", Luisa continued, "will be medieval Provence and its
rulers. Most of us are used to thinking of Provence as part of France.
But long ago it was a separate kingdom, a centre of chivalry and poetry,
subjects both dear to Spanish hearts. Monsieur Charville . . ."

With a nod toward the speaker, she moved to a sofa at one side.

Monsieur Charville spoke in French for about three-quarters of an
hour. At the end, the applause lasted well over a minute. The ladies had
found the address on Linnaeus the month before dry and difficult to
follow, whereas this talk had been full of stories and more like a chapter
from a novel. The men had enjoyed the descriptions of battles and feuds,
and everyone had appreciated the speaker's final tribute to the part the
Catholic religion had played in softening the manners of the barbarians.

"Delightful . . . remarkable . . . fascinating." The room resounded
with exclamations of pleasure and admiration. Luisa gestured toward the
back of the audience. "I think we already have someone who wants to
put a question."

"Do you think, monsieur," asked a pretty woman, the panniers of
whose dress overflowed her chair in drifts of embroidered satin, "it
would be a good thing . . . do you think it would be possible to revive
the laws of chivalry?"

Everyone looked at Monsieur Charville. He was smiling urbanely, a
little as an adult might at the question of a small child.

"I think, madame," he said, "that I must distinguish between the two
parts of your question. Do I think it would be a good thing if the laws
of chivalry were revived? Yes. Most certainly. I approve any measure

that will make men more courteous to women. Do I think a revival of chivalry is possible? That is a more difficult question. I can only answer with the proverb, 'Where there's a will, there's a way.' "

There was a general murmur of approval.

"So you think", asked a man at the back, "that we are less courteous than our ancestors?"

"Sir, I will speak for France only, as my acquaintance with Spain is slight. I'm afraid the answer is 'Yes.' "

"Do I understand then, sir,"—this time it was a priest who spoke— "that you regard European civilisation as having in some sense declined since the days of the Counts of Provence? Are you not, on this point, in very marked disagreement with current opinion in your own country?"

"Maybe I am, Father. Maybe I am. But I hope you will not judge the state of letters in France from the writings of a small clique."

A gentleman wearing the star of the Order of the Knights of Calatrava challenged Monsieur Charville's thesis about Provence and suggested that, as it had in fact been a hotbed of pagan and Moslem influences, the ending of its independence had been a blessing.

Monsieur Charville answered good-humouredly, but the gentleman insisted on his point. The priest who had put the earlier question rescued Monsieur Charville by asking about the laws of inheritance. Was the rule of primogeniture observed, or had the rulers of Provence followed the unfortunate precedent set by Charlemagne?

Before Monsieur Charville could reply, a big, awkward-looking young man toward the back of the audience got clumsily to his feet. His clothes, though obviously new, looked as if they had been made for somebody different.

For a few seconds, Diego de Torrelavega stood blinking at the priest, with an expression that was both cowed and defiant.

"They say you're a Jesuit, Father", he said in a husky voice.

"I am."

"Then perhaps you can tell us how the rulers succeed each other in the Jesuit empire in Paraguay."

Everyone in front turned round. An angry voice said, "Sit down, sir", and a gentleman immediately behind Diego tried to pull him into his chair by tugging at the edge of his coat.

"There is no Jesuit empire in Paraguay", the priest said quietly. "Paraguay is a part of His Majesty's dominions, ruled over by a governor. The Jesuits there are missionaries."

"If that's so, how do you explain this coin?"

"May I see it?"

Diego held out the coin, which was passed from hand to hand along the row. People leaned over the shoulders of those in front of them to look at it.

The priest examined both sides of the coin.

"Very interesting", he said. "I had heard of these but never seen one. It shows the head of a man," he added for the benefit of those who had not managed to see it, "and the inscription reads 'Nicholas, Emperor of Paraguay'. They are made, I believe, in Amsterdam. Our enemies want to make people think that our aim is worldly power. All I can say is that we must be very incompetent and unworldly power seekers, seeing how easily we have been turned out of France and Portugal. No sir, I'm afraid I must disappoint you. There's no emperor and no empire in Paraguay. But thank you for letting me see this coin. I'd like to keep it, if I may, to add to my collection of curiosities."

With a friendly smile, and without waiting for further permission, he slipped the coin into his pocket.

Diego sat down heavily on his chair and scowled at the people who were staring at him. There were angry whispers. "Who is he . . . ? Scandalous . . . ? Is he a member?"

To divert attention, Luisa stood up quickly and signed to her major-domo. The doors to the picture gallery and billiard room were thrown open, and footmen came in carrying trays of iced drinks and sweet cakes.

TWENTY

The company left their chairs and broke into groups, some discussing the incident in subdued voices, others talking with exaggerated loudness as though nothing had happened. But gradually the sense of uneasiness passed, and the conversation took a political turn. In place of names like Linnaeus and Descartes, those of Frederick of Prussia and the recently murdered Tsar Peter and his wife Catherine were to be heard. Some of the men drifted into the billiard room.

In a corner away from the rest, Doña Ines de Torrelavega was sitting with her son.

"What got into you to speak like that?" she asked in an angry, plaintive whisper. "You've ruined everything. Your father will be furious."

"Why should I care?" Diego replied sulkily.

He was in his least tractable mood. He had been planning to go to a comedy at the Teatro del Principe, but suddenly he had been ordered to change his clothes and, with as little consideration as a cow or a sheep being driven to market would receive, had been told he was being taken to meet a young woman he had never heard of, whom it was intended he should marry. Accustomed as he was to being badly treated, he had still felt outraged and consequently was in a more resentful and rebellious frame of mind than usual.

"You know very well why you should care", Doña Ines said. "Where did you get that coin?"

"I found it in his room."

"Your father's?"

"Yes."

Doña Ines gasped.

"Why should I care?" Diego said again, looking sullenly at his mother. "Let him beat me. One day, when I'm strong enough, I'll thrash him till he's half-dead."

"Don't talk like that. You sound like a heathen."

"I put a spoke in his wheel tonight, though. He's pretending to love

103

the Jesuits in order to make up to this Duke of Montesa, isn't he? But he hates them like poison. Which is the girl?"

"It's much too late to trouble yourself about that now. You've put the whole thing out of the question."

"If that's her with the yellow hair, she's not bad."

"You're disgusting. You talk like a common foot soldier."

"And if I do, who's fault is that?"

The justice of the retort went straight to his mother's heart, and she had to check her tears.

The strange thing was that Diego, although so unsatisfactory, was now the only one of her children whom Doña Ines really loved. Had she been able to show the affection she felt, she might have changed his character. But she was not brave enough to stand up for him to his father, and she was so preoccupied with his shortcomings, which always put her husband into a fury, that she was continually nagging and finding fault with him. As a result, the young man had never realised that his mother cared for him.

They had both been so engrossed in their argument that they had not noticed the priest's approach. Now, when they looked up, he was already standing before them, a short figure with a round face, a small nose, protruding ears, and a large mouth. His cassock had a neat darn near the left shoulder and his far-from-new shoes turned up at the toes like miniature rowing boats.

"May I join you?" he asked.

Doña Ines, more flustered than ever by the memory of Diego's behaviour, made room for the priest beside her on the sofa.

"I don't know how to look you in the face, Father", she said. "What you must think of my boy! I feel deeply ashamed."

"Not another word, señora, please. Young men are easily influenced by what they hear. Those who deliberately spread these stories and are old enough to know better are the guilty ones. I'm delighted to have had the opportunity of putting the real facts before this young gentleman. I'm convinced that he is too honest not to see their force. But let me introduce myself. I am Father Padilla. I live at the Casa San Felipe;

halfway down the Calle Redondilla, opposite the fountain. The door of our house is next to the church. If you are stopping in Madrid," he turned to Diego, "come and pay me a visit, and I will show you my observatory."

"You are an astronomer, Father?" Doña Ines asked.

"Yes, señora. A very lowly one—though I have the honour of corresponding with the great Boscovitch."

"That is much too modest, Father", said Luisa, who came up at this moment. "Don't believe a word he says, Ines. He is famous. He has discovered stars, meteors, comets, and different things on the moon. People write to him from all over the world."

"Now what can I do", said Father Padilla, laughing, "but run away and hide my head in shame. And it is just what I shall do—taking this young gentleman with me . . . if I may have your permission and this lady's, and if the gentleman himself is agreeable—for I am anxious to present him to an old friend of mine whom I think he may find interesting."

Diego, who had been expecting the priest to lecture him, was astonished at finding anyone taking a personal interest in him and had been listening with his mouth open. Now he got up and, after his mother had smiled her permission, followed Father Padilla across the room like a half-tamed but still suspicious wolfhound.

"So that's the end of that", Doña Ines said to Luisa with a sigh.

"Nonsense. It's the end of nothing. It's the beginning."

"Be sensible, Luisa. The de Vallecases are never going to let their daughter marry him after this charming episode."

"Why not? Anybody could see that he didn't really mean it. He was obviously just repeating something he had heard."

"Not from us, I can assure you", Doña Ines said quickly.

"Of course not. These stories are all over the place. Now listen. Beatriz is an odd girl. She's always interested in people with something wrong with them—cripples, epileptics, half-wits. Not that Diego is any of these", she added, seeing the expression of pain that flitted across Doña Ines' face. "I only said that to show you that cleverness and handsome looks don't count with her as they would with another woman. I always suspected that she was attracted by her cousin Rodrigo simply because he was an orphan. A disadvantage of that kind seems to appeal to her. I won't introduce Diego to her tonight, but his arguing with Father Padilla like that is probably the best thing that could have happened. At least he will have made an impression on her."

"I don't doubt it."

"But this is an important point," said Luisa, with the resourcefulness of a barrister thinking up ever more ingenious reasons to support an ever weaker case. "An unfavourable impression is better than none. She is now certain to think about Diego a lot. People who dislike each other to start with often fall more deeply in love later, and when she realises that Father Padilla is being nice to him, she will begin to start seeing his good points."

"Well, Luisa, you know your sister-in-law Beatriz better than I", said Doña Ines in a dispirited voice. "Do as you think best."

MEANWHILE, in the picture gallery, Gaspar de Vallecas was showing Monsieur Charville his additions to the Montesa collection. They had stopped before a large picture of the risen Christ.

"I should like to know your opinion of this", he said, with an anxious note in his voice.

"A masterpiece!" Monsieur Charville said in an awed tone.

"You really think so?" Gaspar asked eagerly.

"I'm convinced. Is it a Dolci?"

"No. A Mengs."

"Of course. I should have known from the *impasto*."

"As a matter of fact, I was fortunate to get it. Losada was after it, but he haggled over the price, and Mengs was so irritated that he let me have it instead. You don't by any chance think there's anything wrong with it?"

Monsieur Charville tilted his head first to the left, then to the right, backed away, and finally studied the paint work from a distance of a few inches.

"Perfection!" he said.

"Hullo, Torrelavega", Gaspar said, as he saw the Marques approaching. "Come and tell us what you think of this picture. Charville won't hear a word against it, but I'm not sure that the Magdalen's arm isn't a bit out of proportion."

At hearing the name Torrelavega, Monsieur Charville looked quickly round.

"Ah, Montesa", the Marques said as he came up to them. "I have been wanting for the past half hour to apologise for my son, but the Bishop of Teruel has been detaining me. I'm on my way this minute to find the young scoundrel and order him to beg your pardon in person."

"Leave him, leave him. We all do foolish things at his age."

"No. Beg your pardon he shall, and the Jesuit Father's too. And he shall do it on his knees. This is a serious matter. I don't know where he has picked up these stories, but I will not tolerate them, and he must be punished."

"As a favour to myself and my wife," Gaspar pleaded, "please say no more about it."

"For your sake, then, Montesa", the Marques said, after pretending to hesitate for a moment. "But you are too lenient. Let me warn you. You don't know what boys of his age are like."

Gaspar de Vallecas smiled, having persuaded himself that under an abrupt manner the Marques hid a warm heart and was probably an indulgent father. He presented Monsieur Charville, and then, noticing a lady on the other side of the gallery by herself, he excused himself and hurried over to talk to her.

The Marques, annoyed at being left alone with Monsieur Charville, to whom he had taken a dislike on a number of grounds—for being a Frenchman, a man of letters, and "a sycophant of the clergy"—did not bother to look pleasant. The evening had been trying in more than one way, and he was feeling more than usually short-tempered.

Monsieur Charville, on the other hand, who had for several weeks been trying without success to meet the Marques, was so surprised at finding him a guest of the presumably devout Montesas that he began to wonder if he had been misinformed. Could a friend of Don Maurice de Vallecas' son possibly be an enemy of the Jesuits? He decided to take a chance.

"It will probably surprise you, sir," he said in a low voice, "but I have a message for you from Monsieur de Choiseul, which I think you will be interested to hear."

"You are most certainly mistaken, sir."

"I think not", Monsieur Charville replied quietly.

The Marques, whose face had assumed what even for him was an exceptionally haughty expression, stared hard and suspiciously at Monsieur Charville for a full half-minute. Then he suddenly beckoned to a footman.

"This gentleman is feeling ill. Where is there a window that can be opened without inconveniencing the ladies?"

"If Your Excellency will come this way." The footman led the Marques and Monsieur Charville into a deserted anteroom. After throwing back the shutters of one of the windows, he withdrew, leaving them alone together.

TWENTY MINUTES LATER, Don Maurice, who wanted to take his wife and family home, sent Rodrigo to look for their guest. After searching through the rooms, Rodrigo noticed a door leading off the picture gallery. As he pushed it open, he heard Monsieur Charville saying ". . . And when he has been thoroughly frightened, it will be easy to fasten the blame on *them*." He wondered briefly what the words meant, but almost immediately, as Monsieur Charville turned smilingly toward him, they passed out of his mind. It was only after a number of years, and in very different circumstances, that he would recall them and understand their meaning.

TWENTY-ONE

About a week later, Father Padilla was sitting in his observatory on the roof of the Casa San Felipe, the Jesuit house attached to the Church of San Felipe. It was just before five in the morning.

There were fifteen priests living at San Felipe: the rector, the four fathers in charge of the parish, and three scholars; the other seven used the house as a base from which they went out to preach missions in the towns and villages around Madrid.

As an astronomer, Father Padilla was not expected to do parish work. Nevertheless, he used to hear confessions in the church and take the last sacraments to the dying, lest, as he used to say, he should forget that the souls of men take precedence over stars.

Recently, Father Boscovitch, the famous Dalmatian Jesuit astronomer, had written to ask his opinion about certain irregularities in the movement of the planet Mercury, and it was this subject that Father Padilla was working on now.

He was always content when alone in his observatory, which, he sometimes thought, looked like a Moorish tomb that had been dropped onto the tiles by a passing magic carpet. As he gazed through the opening in the dome at the night sky packed from horizon to horizon with stars, he used to think, "If I could make a universe and fill it with creatures as infinitely small to me as we are to him, would I regard them with the feelings of a father? No. I would look on them as toys and, after a time, grow tired of them. But he, great and magnificent as he is, loves us always, thinks of us always, and never tires of us. It is amazing."

At six, after shaving and making his meditation, he went down to the church.

He had just finished Mass and returned to the sacristy, when, as he turned to put away the chalice in a cupboard, he noticed a scared-looking boy standing in the doorway.

"Good morning, Carlos. What's the matter?"

"Please, Father, come quick! It's my brother. Someone's knifed him. He's dying."

Father Padilla ripped off his chasuble and began tugging at his cincture.

"I'll come at once."

A few minutes later, preceded by an altar boy in cassock and surplice and followed by Carlos, he was making his way through the streets, carrying the pyx containing the Blessed Sacrament under a white and gold cloth. At the sound of the acolyte's bell, people knelt on the cobbles and removed their hats.

After turning down a narrow street, they crossed an almost deserted marketplace. A solitary stroller was gazing up at the sky. On coming close to the little procession, the stroller hesitated, then he too removed his hat and knelt down. Afterward he stood up and followed. Since it was customary for men meeting a priest in these circumstances to escort him to his destination as a sign of respect for the Sacrament, Father Padilla walked on without looking to see who the man was.

Beyond the marketplace they entered an alley where a dozen people were standing outside a dilapidated house with a carved stone entrance. One of them said in a low voice, "The top floor, Father." The acolyte led the way up a rickety staircase. At the top a door stood open onto a crowded garret. Near the single window a huge man in tight-fitting breeches, and with his hat still on, sat sobbing on a stool. Some women were trying to hush a wailing child. As the acolyte entered, silence fell, and everyone dropped to their knees.

While Father Padilla was wondering whom to address, a short woman in black came through a door opposite and took him into an inner room where, on a disordered bed, lay the police spy who had been appointed to keep a watch on Monsieur Charville and had later frightened Don Jeronimo Grimaldi half out of his wits. A young woman was kneeling beside him, trying to stop the blood that was oozing from his side and soaking the bedclothes.

"Who is it?" the man asked weakly.

"The priest", the girl answered.

"God and his Holy Mother be thanked!"

Father Padilla took the man's hand.

"How are you, my son?"

"I knew they'd get me, Father. I'm dying."

"Then you must accept God's will and make a good death."

As the priest prepared to hear the man's confession, the two women went back to the outer room. There they found everyone gazing at the tall awkward-looking young man who had followed the priest and acolyte up the stairs. He was now leaning uncomfortably against the doorpost, trying to seem at ease.

The older woman frowned.

"Uncle," she said sharply to the huge man in a hat, "give the gentleman your stool. Please be seated, sir."

Diego de Torrelavega thanked her shyly and sat down. There was a long pause during which nothing could be heard but the shiftings and stirrings of the waiting relations and friends and an occasional murmur from the next room. Diego stared hard at a spider hanging from the ceiling. Then the bedroom door opened, and Father Padilla said, "We are ready now."

The two women went inside again. Without waiting to be asked, Diego followed and knelt in a corner. He had never seen such a poor, bare room. But almost immediately his attention was attracted by the man on the bed. While the priest was anointing him and reading the prayers, the man's eyes kept travelling back and forth from the crucifix that stood between two lighted candles on the window ledge to a smudged picture of the Blessed Virgin on the wall. But after he had received Communion, he lay with his eyes shut, as if dead. Father Padilla leaned down and said something in his ear. Then he left the room, followed by the women. Diego lingered until last, wondering if the man had really died. He kept looking at the dried blood on the bedclothes with a disturbed mixture of feelings.

In the outer room Father Padilla was comforting the man's mother. After listening for a moment in the shadow of a large cupboard, Diego slipped out and went to wait downstairs in the street.

TWENTY-TWO

For a full week Diego had been trying to decide whether or not to accept Father Padilla's invitation to pay him a visit.

I'll go this morning, he would think. Then: No, some other time —he's sure to preach at me. And a little later: I wonder what his observatory is like. I'll call this afternoon. But by afternoon he would be saying to himself: He didn't really like me. He was just making up to *him*. ("Him" was the word he used when thinking of his father.) And this conclusion would be upset in turn by the memory of the way Father Padilla had talked to him at the Montesas' soirée. It was the first time in his life that he had been made to feel he was worth talking to for his own sake and was not just an appendage of his family. He wanted to repeat the experience and would again be on the point of setting out for San Felipe when some new thought would stop him.

Now, as he stood in the street waiting for Father Padilla to come downstairs, he was still in two minds as to how he was going to act when they met. It would depend on how Father Padilla reacted. If the priest were to show any coolness, he was ready to be truculent and off-hand. But if he were friendly, he would be pleasant.

Recently Diego's life had become a lot more agreeable. His mother, realising that if he was to make a favourable impression on the de Val-lecases it was necessary to build up his self-confidence and self-respect, had persuaded her husband to treat him more reasonably, especially in front of other people, and to give him enough money to buy clothes suitable to his position in society. At Remusat's, the fashionable French tailor in the Calle Atocha, he had been helped to make his choice by Signor Vitelli, the dancing master his parents had engaged for him. But as the new clothes were of a brightness not often seen in the streets of Madrid and as he was not sure if they were splendid or ridiculous, he had decided to try them out this morning so as to get used to them before he met too many people.

At last Father Padilla appeared, and Diego realised happily that the priest was pleased to see him.

"I thought you might have forgotten me, Father." He laughed loudly and suddenly and with a heartiness that bore no relation to his remark.

"My memory is not that bad", Father Padilla said, as he shook his hand. "In fact, I was thinking about you only this morning."

"About me?" Diego sounded even more pleased. "I don't believe it."

"Now, why should I say so if I wasn't?"

"Honestly?"

"Of course."

Diego chuckled, as though the idea of anyone thinking about him early in the morning were preposterous, but also novel and delightful.

"What were you thinking about me?"

"Among other things, that I hoped to see you again."

"Was that all?"

"No. But as we are only a few minutes from where I live, perhaps you could spare the time to come and look at my observatory."

"May I really?"

"Of course. Come along. We'll be there in five minutes."

After walking for a few yards in silence, Diego eyed Father Padilla sideways and asked, "How do you like my new clothes?"

"Very much. I see you favour the French style."

"It's what Signor Vitelli recommended, so that's what I told the tailors to make. But I don't know that I trust that jumping jack. He may have given me the wrong advice. Anyway, my father's paid for them."

"On the contrary, Signor Vitelli seems to have very good taste and an eye for colour."

"You think so, Father?" Diego spoke eagerly. "I was afraid they might be too bright. But who cares?" he went on, his voice suddenly growing defiant. "I'm used to looking a fool. If people want to waste their breath laughing at me, let them. Laughter can't harm me." He threw his cane into the air and deftly caught it again. Then he pushed his hat on one side, and his face grew more cheerful. "By the way, Father, what luck it was my meeting you like this. We might have missed each other. I hadn't got anything to do this morning, you know, so I said to myself, I'll go and see if Father Padilla is in. Of course, later in the day I'm

113

pretty busy. The ladies are beginning to ask me to their *tertulias*. Then there are the theatres, and five days a week I take fencing lessons, besides which I'm trying all the coffee houses in turn. I was to have had a dancing lesson this morning, but I'm not going. The shoes pinch my feet, and the Signor gets on my nerves. As a matter of fact, I'm used to getting up early, and Madrid's a dull place, I think, before midday. Do you know, when I was crossing that square, I was watching a flock of pigeons. I was thinking that if I'd had my gun, I'd soon have made quick work of the fat devils. I'm a first-rate shot, you see. So is Don Gaspar de Montesa, whose party we met at. They say he's not a real duke—only the sort who gets called duke because his wife is a duchess. Anyhow, I'd give anything to have his guns. He took me to see the royal shoot the other day. Oh, God, I nearly choked to keep from laughing. A great fat buck jumped out of a bush nearly on top of the King. Off went his gun. Bang! Bang!" Diego raised his stick as though taking aim. "I was watching from a hillock behind, so I could see he'd missed, but the buck fell down dead all the same. Hey, what's this, I thought, till I saw the barrel of Don Gaspar's gun smoking and realised that he'd shot it. The King was as red as a turkey cock. Then somebody said, "Good shot, sire", pretending the King had shot it instead of Don Gaspar, and everybody else said the same. Don Gaspar was as red as a turkey, too. What a joke! I thought I'd die trying not to laugh."

"If I were you, Don Diego," Father Padilla said, "I'd be careful whom you tell that story to. It might reach the wrong ears and cause offence. We're all human beings, you know. Even a King doesn't like to miss an easy shot in front of his friends. What about you? Don't you ever miss anything?"

"Look, Father, do you see the kite sitting on that roof over there? What would you say the distance was? A long shot anyway. I could bring him down from twice the distance. Why, I could do it sitting on a horse. You should see me ride, too, Father. I could teach these fops in Madrid a thing or two. I bet their horses have all been trained not to prance about or go too fast. One day I'm going to England where they hunt foxes and jump huge great fences and ditches six feet across.

My father says so. He's been there, but he won't take me because he's ashamed of me. He thinks I'm a half-wit. Maybe I am. But when I do get there I'll have the time of my life. And maybe it won't be so long, either, because they're going to marry me to a young woman with a lot of money, and I'll be able to do as I like then. Though I'm not sure I really want to get married. No girl who's anything to look at is going to marry a fellow like me unless she's forced to, and it won't be very comfortable living with a wife who wishes she'd never set eyes on me. My father can have me thrashed black and blue and carried into church by force, but he can't make me say the words, can he?"

"My son, you should speak of your father with more discretion."

Diego, who had been talking away without thinking much of what he was saying, happy to have someone to listen to him, stopped with a look of surprise.

"But my father often thrashes me", he said. "See here!" And he began to pull up the sleeve of his coat.

"Leave that alone, and listen to me", Father Padilla said quietly. "If your parents are really trying to force you into a marriage against your will, then it is something that must be discussed seriously. If not, you should be more careful about what you say."

Diego looked crestfallen. "Oh, I didn't mean you to take it like that", he said. "Besides, my father has stopped beating me for the present. After all, he wants to persuade people that I would make a good husband for their daughters. It wouldn't do to have me going about with bruises and black eyes. What's more, they're going to make me an officer in the royal bodyguard. I shall be on my own then."

He's not so dull as he looks, Father Padilla said to himself, and to turn Diego's thoughts to other things, he began to talk about the people they passed, the kind of life they probably led, how much they would earn, what their trade might be, and the part of Spain they might have come from.

"I say, Father", Diego broke in abruptly as they approached San Felipe. "What a long time you took hearing that man's confession. I thought you were never going to come out again."

Father Padilla paused at the foot of the stairs.

"When a man is dying, he thinks carefully over his past. We die only once, and the state we are in then is the state we shall remain in for all eternity—either God's friends, or at enmity with him. Do you want to make your confession, too?"

"Oh, no, Father," Diego said quickly.

"Why keep our Lord waiting, my son?"

"Waiting?"

"Isn't it, perhaps, rather a long time since your last confession?"

Diego, who had made as if to mount the steps, stood still. He could feel his cheeks flushing. As was his habit when in difficulty, he was about to lie. Then he thought again how good the priest had been to him, and for the first time in his life he found that he had to tell the truth.

"Yes," he said, "a very long time."

"What about it, then?"

Diego hesitated, then said, "You'd better hear my confession now, Father."

They went into the church.

"I'll go to the sacristy while you examine your conscience", Father Padilla said. "Take as long as you like. I'll wait for you in that confessional over there."

Diego knelt down. He saw all his sins clearly enough: anger, hatred, lies, neglect of his religious duties, fornication, theft—the money he had stolen from one his brothers and a cousin. The only sin he seemed not to have committed was murder. Oh, my God, what am I going to say? he thought, as he saw Father Padilla leaving the sacristy and going toward the confessional. If I tell him everything, he'll give me a roasting and won't want to know me any more. No. It will be all right. He's not like that. He's different.

Then a new thought struck him. If I say I'm sorry for my sins, I shall have to try and be better. Otherwise, I shall be committing a sacrilege and making things worse. His sins suddenly seemed to be clutching at him, like greedy relations clinging to a rich cousin on the point of leaving them. Think how miserable life will be without us, they seemed to say. You won't be able to stand it. Everything will seem boring and pointless. Besides, you can't get rid of us. We are too strong for you.

"Holy Mother of God, help me", he said, and got up and went into the confessional.

It took him some time to get everything sorted out and said. But, with help from Father Padilla, whose profile was dimly visible through the grille, it was done at last; he made an act of contrition and received absolution. Afterward the priest gave him some words of advice and encouragement.

"Whatever is said or done at your home, try to accept it patiently and humbly. It won't be easy at first. But if you persevere, with God's help it will become so. Remember what our Lord had to go through for us. The worse people treat you, the more you must pray for them. If you continue to do this, God will eventually give you great inner peace."

"Father, I'm afraid of committing the same sins all over again, even though I don't want to."

"That is because you rely on yourself. We must rely on God. He will always give us the grace we need when we ask for it, but he doesn't give it in advance. That is because he wants us to realise our weakness and to depend wholly on him. However, if you do fall into serious sin again, don't be discouraged. No matter how often it happens, go to confession and start again."

TWENTY-THREE

Upstairs, in Father Padilla's room, they looked at his curiosities, which, together with his books, papers, and astronomical instruments, littered the shelves along two of the walls. There were bottles and jars, stuffed birds, dried lizards, lumps of rock and ore, fossils, shells, fragments of carved stone, coins, bunches of dry seaweed.

Diego, who was in a daydream, at first said little, but on seeing an air pump, he became interested. Father Padilla showed him how it worked.

"And what's this?" he said, excitedly. "Is it a diamond?"

"No. It's crystal. Isn't it beautiful? And this is a meteorite."

"What's that?"

"A piece of a star."

"I wish I could find one. Are they lucky?"

"No, Don Diego. As Catholics, we don't believe in luck. But they are interesting because they tell us something about the composition of the stars. If you like, please keep it."

"Do you really mean that, Father?"

"Yes, yes. We will say it's in exchange for the coin you gave me at the Duke of Montesa's. Besides, I have another here. Now, what do you think of this?"

"What is it? Is it alive?"

"No, it's preserved in spirits."

"It looks like a dragon."

"A wingless dragon. It's actually a young alligator from the Amazon."

Diego, fascinated by the reptile's grotesqueness, held up the jar to the light. He was hoping the priest would give him this, too, but was ashamed to ask.

"I wish I could go to Africa", he said.

The royal bodyguard, Father Padilla thought, is not composed of scholars, but I'm sure they know that the Amazon isn't in Africa. This boy is uncommonly ignorant. If he isn't helped, he will be the laughingstock of the other officers.

He took a book from one of the shelves.

"Perhaps you would like to borrow this", he said. "It will tell you something about meteorites, but there's a lot of other interesting matter in it if you care to read on. Look, here's a section on animals. And here's another on rocks and stones—we call it geology. And this one tells you about the different continents and what they produce."

They went up to the observatory. There Diego's delight was complete. He gazed through the telescope, revolved the dome, and opened and shut the aperture. Then he went out on the roof and with a hand telescope looked at what was going on in the streets of the city.

Before he left, Father Padilla invited him to visit the Casa San Felipe again one evening the following week, so that they could look at the stars.

Diego walked home, revolving in his mind plans for reforming his life and rooting out all his bad habits in a week or two. When he reached the Torrelavega Palace, the old doorkeeper—the only person, apart from his mother, who had any feeling for him—came hurriedly down the steps.

"Don Diego! Don Diego! Where have you been? His Excellency has had us looking all over the place for you. He sent for you to go out with him more than half an hour ago."

"Oh, my God, I'd forgotten. What shall I do, Sancho? I was to have gone with him to see the Duke of Baños, the commander of the Spanish regiment of the bodyguard. They want to make me a soldier. My father will be furious."

"I know, sir, I know. He already is. Ah, if only you would be more careful."

"I mean to be, Sancho, but you know what I am. And I was feeling so happy just now." He ran up the steps, trying to collect his thoughts, which were rushing about like rats disturbed in a barn. I *must* keep my temper, he said to himself. Whatever happens, I mustn't answer back. I must show him that I'm different.

But still his heart beat violently.

As he entered the hall, his father appeared at the point where the two upper flights of stairs, starting from opposite sides of the hall on the first floor, converged at a landing halfway down, before descending to the ground floor in a single final cascade of shallow steps.

The footmen on duty glanced at each other and grinned, looking forward with relish to witnessing the tempest that was about to break over Diego's head.

"Stop where you are", the Marques shouted as soon as he saw Diego. With his eyes fixed on his son, he came slowly down the last flight.

"Where have you been, sir?"

"Talking to Father Padilla, sir."

"Who's he?"

"The priest I met at the Duke of Montesa's."

"Ah! With the Jesuits. So that's the kind of religion they teach at San Felipe. Encouraging young men to idle their time away in gossip while neglecting their duties toward their parents."

"He didn't encourage me. He knew nothing about my appointment."

"How dare you argue with me, sir."

"I didn't mean to argue—"

"Do you realise that by your negligence and lack of consideration, you have not only jeopardized your own future, you have put me—your father—in the delightful position of having been grossly impolite to an intimate friend of His Majesty . . ." What the Marques really disliked was having been put in a position of having to write a letter of apology.

By this time he was only a few steps from where Diego stood as if cemented to the marble floor.

"Father, I'm sorry, I forgot . . ."

The word "father", spoken pleadingly, seemed to act on the Marques' temper like a detonator.

"Mind your manners, sir. Address me as you are accustomed to", he shouted, then, with all his might, struck Diego twice in the face. Diego reeled over and fell backward, while the Marques turned on his heel and remounted the stairs.

The souls of servants in the great households of the past tended to bear the imprint of their masters' and mistresses' vices and virtues, and the Torrelavega servants were no exception. They were mostly a hard, callous lot. But there were limits to the enjoyment even they could derive from seeing a fellow human being humiliated. Diego seemed suddenly one of themselves.

As soon as the Marques was out of sight, two of the footmen and a page ran forward to help the young man to his feet. His father's heavy gold ring had made a gash across his forehead and another down his cheek. He could barely see for the blood streaming over his eyes, and had difficulty in keeping upright. Supporting him on each side, the footmen helped him to his mother's apartment while the page ran ahead to warn her of his arrival.

At the sight of the blood, Doña Ines gave a half-stifled shriek and signed to the servants to take him into her dressing room.

"Water and a towel", she said to the maid.

Diego had been lowered into a chair where he half lay with his head propped against the back and his legs sticking out stiffly in front like two posts. Doña Ines knelt beside him and started bathing his face. After a minute or two, realising the gashes were not as deep as she had thought, she began as usual to reproach and upbraid him. It was her way of expressing love.

"Poor Mother", Diego said. "I'm sorry I cause you so much sorrow and worry. Please forgive me. I mean to try and be different."

He endeavoured to smile, but the pain from the gash in his cheek made him wince, so he caressed her hand.

Doña Ines looked at him in astonishment. It was the first affectionate gesture he had made since he was a small boy of six.

TWENTY-FOUR

The following afternoon, Father de la Cueva, the rector of the Casa San Felipe, was crossing Madrid to call on Don Maurice de Vallecas.

As he went along, he struggled with resentful feelings toward Father Padilla, the immediate cause of the difficult interview that lay ahead. What a nuisance Padilla is, he said to himself. Always worrying over things that don't really concern him. Of course, I suppose he was trying to do his duty, but he should be careful to see that what he thinks is his duty won't result in more harm than good.

Although Father de la Cueva tried to be just, or thought he tried, Father Padilla irritated him unreasonably. His accent, his laugh, his manner of eating, everything about the older man seemed to get on the rector's nerves. He couldn't account for it. The other Fathers didn't have that effect on him.

Then there was Padilla's scientific work with its inconvenient hours, which upset the orderly running of the house. Was it really necessary for priests to be astronomers? Of course, the Church had always encouraged learning, and rightly. But when there were so many souls to save . . . And that wasn't all. Padilla was spending far too much time with influential people. Not just men of science, but people of rank, especially women. If it goes on like this, he said to himself as he picked his way over the cobbles and past the street vendors' stalls, I shall have to put a stop to it. It's the kind of thing that gets us a reputation for being greedy for power.

Was there in this thought a touch of jealousy at Father Padilla's popularity as a spiritual director? Father de la Cueva was an upright man, hard-working, conscientious, and efficient. He had done well at his studies and had been sent to Rome for further training. Afterward he had been assistant to the late Provincial of the Society. But he did not have a winning personality. He gave the impression of seeing other people as problems, items of duty to be ticked off a list, rather than as human beings to be valued each for his own sake. Moreover, while he certainly did not enjoy the company of the rich and influential—they intimidated him—he had, perhaps, more of the wrong kind of respect for their opinions and fear of offending them than was appropriate for a priest.

On reaching Don Maurice's house in the Calle Guzman, he was immediately taken up into the library and a few seconds later was joined by Don Maurice himself.

"This is a great pleasure, Father", Don Maurice said. "And what can I do for you? How can I help you?"

"Your lordship is most kind. The warmth of your feelings for our Society is well known and a great consolation to us. But this time I have come to render you a service, not to ask for one. At least, I hope your lordship will think it a service."

"You sound doubtful, Father."

"It is a delicate subject, my lord."

"Come. Let's hear it. I'm not a man to take offence easily. And besides, how can I, since, as you say, you have come to do me a good turn."

"Well, my lord, yesterday one of our priests, Father Padilla in fact, whom your lordship knows, was sent for to bring the last sacraments to a man who had been stabbed in a brawl—or so it appears. He seems to have been some kind of informer or police spy. He made his confession, and afterwards he told Father Padilla that last autumn he had been appointed to act as guide and interpreter to a foreigner whom he had every reason to believe was an agent of the French government, sent here to stir up trouble against the Jesuits, and he begged Father Padilla to pass the information on to his superiors. The Frenchman's name, he said, was Charville. You will understand my embarrassment, your lordship. I believe that is the name of the gentleman staying in your house. I deeply regret having to tell you all this, but after discussing it thoroughly, both Father Padilla and I decided we had no alternative."

Father de la Cueva looked quickly at Don Maurice. There! he thought, he is offended in spite of having said he wouldn't be. I thought all along that telling him would do more harm than good.

Don Maurice got up and paced about the room, biting the side of his finger and muttering, "Impossible! Impossible!" Eventually he stopped in front of the rector and, to the priest's discomfort, stood frowning at him in silence. He had assumed that Monsieur Charville was a Frenchman of private means travelling for his own pleasure and interest. Why should he not be? Europe at this period was full of such gentlemen voyaging in pursuit of scholarly hobbies of one kind or another; and nothing Monsieur Charville had said had led Don Maurice to think otherwise.

He came to himself abruptly.

"Forgive me, Father", he said. "Please don't think I'm angry at what you've told me. You have done right. In the circumstances, you had no other course. But you can understand my feelings. A gentleman I have given my friendship to, whom I have trusted completely, whom I still trust," he added with emphasis, "falls under the suspicion of having deceived me. I will be frank. I don't for a minute believe that Monsieur Charville is a French agent. But for the sake of his honour and my own peace of mind, I should like to clear the matter up. Is it possible to question this man further? Informers, as a class, readily jump to conclusions on insufficient evidence."

"I'm afraid he died last night."

"It's most embarrassing . . . most embarrassing."

He sat thinking for a while. Suddenly his face lit up.

"I believe I have found the answer. I have a ward—you may know him —whom we are sending on a European tour, and I have been thinking of asking Monsieur Charville if he would consent to accompany him as mentor and guide. I would like the boy to have someone older to keep an eye on him. He has taken rather a fancy to this gentleman, who was in any case already planning to visit Italy and Germany before returning to France. I will therefore put my proposal to him immediately. I think you will agree that if he accepts it, we shall know the information you have received is without foundation. An agent of the French Court is not likely to want the company of a lively, intelligent young man who is sure to notice anything unusual about his movements and who will hamper his freedom."

Father de la Cueva agreed that this would decide the question and, pleased that the interview had been so much less awkward than he had expected, took his leave.

On his way out, a gentleman standing in the hall bowed courteously. I suppose that's Charville, he said to himself. He certainly doesn't look as if he were deceiving anybody. What a mistake it is to be oversuspicious!

DON MAURICE decided to put his proposal to his guest the following morning. Meanwhile he found himself anticipating the moment with a certain anxiety.

If Monsieur Charville accepted, all would be well—not a trace of suspicion could attach to him. But if he refused? A refusal would not prove anything one way or the other. Don Maurice had only thought of this after Father de la Cueva had gone. The Frenchman could have good reasons for not wishing to accompany Rodrigo, reasons which would have nothing to do with his being a French agent. How could the mystery be cleared up then?

Having made rather a parade to his friends of his liking for this erudite Frenchman, Don Maurice was anxious, among other things, to vindicate his own judgment.

Early the next morning, he sent a servant to ask Monsieur Charville if he could spare a few moments in the library.

Why is he so nervous? Monsieur Charville wondered, as he listened to Don Maurice's proposal, which included highly advantageous financial arrangements.

"Of course, I realise that I am asking a quite exceptional favour", Don Maurice said, fearing that Monsieur Charville might think he was being asked to act as Rodrigo's tutor. "Your historical researches, of course, come first. But, my friend, I know no one from whose society Rodrigo will benefit so much, and I am anxious about his welfare. Please think it over. Now I must ask you to excuse me, as I am due at the Council. You know how prompt His Majesty always is, and how equally prompt he expects his servants to be."

TWENTY-FIVE

As soon as Don Maurice had gone, Monsieur Charville set out for a walk. It was easier for him to think things over walking than sitting. What am I going to say, he wondered, as he made his way down to the El Pardo road. His first reaction had been to refuse. He saw all the difficulties that Don Maurice had foreseen for anyone trying to combine the duties of a French agent with those of a travelling companion to a young man of wealth and position. And suppose, he said to himself, the boy runs into debt while we're abroad or gets himself killed in a duel? However, after considering how much money Don Maurice's offer would enable him to save, he finally decided to accept it. All his expenses, while he was in Rodrigo's company, would be paid by Don Maurice. This meant he would not have to spend any of the money he was receiving from the French government for his expenses. It would go into his bank account as pure profit. On top of this, Don Maurice had asked him to accept two hundred escudos as an expression of his esteem and gratitude and in compensation for the inconvenience he was going to be put to. Monsieur Charville had refused the two hundred escudos, intending to accept them if they were offered a second time.

He turned off the road and on to a path that led around the city walls to the north, between vegetable gardens and orchards of bare fruit trees.

His journey to Spain was turning out to be unexpectedly profitable in other ways. To buy his good will, Monsieur Laborde had made him an interest-free loan, which the merchant had invested for him in some mines near Bilbao.

For some time he loitered along the path, daydreaming about these improvements in his financial situation like a voluptuary lingering over the first mouthful of an exceptionally fine wine. At last he had got a foot on the ladder to financial independence. It was only the bottom rung, but his goal was at least now achievable and in sight.

Reentering the city through a postern, he made his way with some difficulty through a maze of alleyways to the Calle Guzman. At the far end, a neatly dressed man was walking toward him with a lady on either arm. As they came nearer, Monsieur Charville saw, with annoyance, that the ladies were Madame Laborde and her daughter, Madeleine. He walked more quickly so as to get to Don Maurice's house before they came up. But Madame Laborde recognised him and was gesticulating enthusiastically.

"Monsieur! Monsieur! we have letters for you."

They met in front of Don Maurice's door.

Their escort, a man in early middle age, Monsieur Charville took to be Mesnier, the future son-in-law chosen by Monsieur Laborde. His trim little body supported a shrewd little face. Madeleine looked depressed.

She had not heard from her lover for three months, and, to make things worse, she had, from weariness and for the sake of peace, agreed to allow Mesnier to pay his court to her. As a result, her mind was torn between conflicting anxieties—that her lover had forgotten her and that she had been unfaithful to him—which left her feeling alternately bereft and guilty.

"Good morning, madame", Monsieur Charville said coldly, as he took the letters.

Unabashed by his tone, Madame Laborde began to ask solicitously after his welfare, as though he had been one of her early admirers, whom she was now seeing again for the first time since her marriage. How had he been? She hoped the people he was staying with fed him properly. For her part, she couldn't stand Spanish food; it turned her stomach. She and Madeleine had been well. But their prospects? As melancholy as ever!

This last remark was accompanied by a grimace in the direction of Mesnier, supposed to be unnoticeable to all save Monsieur Charville.

"Will you all step inside for a moment, please," Monsieur Charville said, "while I see if these letters need an immediate answer."

They entered the hall, the footmen brought chairs, and the visitors sat down while Monsieur Charville took his letters to a window and stood there reading them. Madame Laborde looked about her and commented out loud on what she saw.

"Well, I must say! It's handsome enough, though it is in Spain. I would never have thought it. But the cornice could do with some paint. Now I like the young girl in that portrait over there. She's sweet. But what ugly clothes. These people must be very rich. Unless you are, you can't afford to keep so many able-bodied young men idling away their time doing nothing. I'd have them all scrubbing floors and painting the place up a bit. Look how still they stand, Madeleine. Almost as if they couldn't see us."

"Oh, do be careful, Mother. You talk so loud, and some of them may understand French."

Madame Laborde lowered her voice and continued her observations in a whisper. Monsieur Charville, meanwhile, had finished reading his letters and now thrust them into his pocket.

"Will you please tell your husband that I will call on him shortly", he said to Madame Laborde. "And thank you for your trouble."

"Oh, not at all, sir", Madame Laborde replied, still under the illusion that Monsieur Charville was able and willing to rescue her and Madeleine from their exile. "And when you get back to France, you will remember, won't you, to say to the right people what a great loss it is to French trade that Monsieur Laborde wastes his time and energies in this wretched town, where most of the people can't tell silk from calico. You won't forget, will you?"

"I shall remember all you have told me. How could I not, madame?" Monsieur Charville replied with an irony that was noticed only by Madeleine.

"There, you see", Madame Laborde said to Madeleine when they were in the street again. "He's as good as promised."

"He's done nothing of the sort, Mother. I doubt if he even knew what you were talking about."

"What's he promised?" asked Mesnier.

This was the first time he had spoken since they had met Monsieur Charville. While sitting in the hall he had gazed about him in silence, pricing everything, adding it all up and calculating what it would fetch at auction in France.

"Ah, never you mind", Madame Laborde said.

"Why? Do you want Monsieur Laborde to go back to France?"

Mon Dieu, she thought, he's so silent I forgot he was there. Now he'll go and tell Laborde and ruin everything.

At this moment a carriage drew up at the door they had just left. Involuntarily, they turned to look. A few seconds later, Doña Teresa de Vallecas, accompanied by Beatriz and Rodrigo, appeared from the house and got into it.

"What a lovely face!" Madame Laborde exclaimed as Beatriz glanced in their direction. Madeleine watched enviously as Rodrigo handed his cousin into the carriage. Nothing, I'm sure, goes wrong in her life, she thought.

THE FIRST OF THE TWO LETTERS Madame Laborde had brought was from one of the Duc de Choiseul's secretaries, asking Monsieur Charville with offensive peremptoriness why the Duke had not heard from him.

The second was a grovelling note from Monsieur Laborde, saying he had just learned that his courier who had gone to France before Christmas had been robbed at an inn near Chateauroux and that some of the letters he had been carrying were missing. It was possible that his "distinguished client's" letter was among them.

After waiting half an hour, Monsieur Charville put on his great coat again and followed Madame Laborde to her husband's house.

Thank God the courier was robbed in France, he thought. What a mess I'd have been in if my letter to Choiseul had fallen into the wrong hands on this side of the frontier. Next time I must be more circumspect. However, the cloud has a silver lining. I'll be able to frighten Laborde so much that he'll do whatever I want.

Monsieur Charville spent a half hour with Monsieur Laborde, during which he not only threatened to report the incident to the Duc de Choiseul but mentioned the words "Bastille" and "galleys". At the end, the silk merchant, who had never had such a terrifying experience, tore up Monsieur Charville's "promise to pay" for the investment in the mines and "forced" him to accept a further loan as an outright gift.

"WELL, MY FRIEND?" Don Maurice asked anxiously when he and Monsieur Charville met before supper.

"The answer is 'Yes'", Monsieur Charville said smilingly. "I shall be delighted to go with Rodrigo."

"Ah, what a weight you've taken off my mind."

TWENTY-SIX

The travellers set out in the middle of February. They were to visit Naples, Rome, Florence, Vienna, Munich, and Paris, and any lesser courts and cities they felt inclined to stop at on the way.

Rodrigo had a brand-new travelling chariot for himself and Monsieur Charville and an old one, repainted, from Don Maurice's stables, for the two valets and the luggage.

The farewells took place in the hall where the family had gathered to see Alfonso off three months before. This time Doña Teresa was present, as well as the two youngest members, Jaime and Isabel, who had been released from their schooling for the occasion. Everyone, for different reasons, felt strained, and each longed for the farewells to be over—Rodrigo and his cousins because they were going to miss each other, and Monsieur Charville because the sight of their distress and the expressions of gratitude and friendship they showered on him disturbed the order of values he had established for himself.

Eventually it was all over. The final messages were shouted through the open carriage window and the last waves exchanged as the carriage turned out of sight at the end of the street, and the family went back into the house to pass as best they could the remains of a lustreless day.

A FEW HOURS LATER, when Rodrigo and Monsieur Charville were well out of the city and on the road to Tarragona, Jean-Paul Houdin was riding in from France through the Atocha gate.

Without stopping at his lodgings to wash or change, he made his way straight to Monsieur Laborde's, where, after tethering his horse to a wall, he went in by a back entrance. There had been changes while he was away. The courtyard had been cleared of the carts and rubbish that had annoyed Madame Laborde, the ground had been paved, and groups of evergreens stood about in tubs. This was Monsieur Laborde's way of telling his wife and daughter that concessions in regard to Mesnier would be rewarded.

Jean-Paul went upstairs to Madame Laborde's salon, where he found her alone.

"Why, it's Monsieur Jean-Paul", she said. "What a pleasant surprise! We'd begun to think you were never coming back."

"Is Mademoiselle Madeleine in?"

"She's somewhere about. You don't mean to say that you've brought us news of our dear Berouet? I'll call her."

"No, please don't." He lowered his voice. "I'm glad I found you alone, madame. I've bad news I'm afraid. It's best for you to tell her. Mademoiselle gave me a letter to take to Monsieur Berouet. Madame, he's married."

Madame Laborde jumped to her feet.

"Married! It's impossible! He can't be. Oh, my poor child. It will break her heart. The wretch! The villain! He's worse than Laborde, worse than Mesnier. Are you certain, monsieur?"

"Absolutely, madame. They told me when I got to Lyons."

"Oh, the monster! To think he could do such a thing to my poor little Madeleine. I'd like to wring his neck."

At this moment Madeleine herself came in.

"Monsieur Jean-Paul!" she exclaimed. "So you're back. Oh, I'm so glad. Did you . . . ?" And then she noticed his expression. "My God, what's happened. Berouet! Is he ill? Is he dead?"

"It's all right, my pet", Madame Laborde said, drawing her daughter toward her and stroking her cheek. "I'll explain it all in a minute. Berouet is quite well." She signed to Jean-Paul that he had better go. "Come and see us in a day or two," she said, "and thank you."

"Madame. I'm leaving Monsieur Laborde's service", he said, thrusting a piece of paper into her hand. "This is the address of my lodgings. If you need me, please send for me. I will do all I can to help you."

Before Madame Laborde could answer, he was at the door. The last thing he saw was Madeleine clinging to her mother and looking after him with frightened, questioning eyes. Outside, feeling miserable and angry, he sat down on one of the worn stone steps.

The old lady is right, he said to himself. I'd like to twist that fellow

Berouet's neck, too. To think that any man who had the chance of marrying Mademoiselle Madeleine would throw her over for a middle-aged widow with some money.

He thought how much he would have liked to have been in Madame Laborde's place and have Madeleine clinging to him for comfort. But what would be the use, he said to himself. You can understand her falling in love with a man like Berouet. He comes from a respectable family. He has looks, even charm of a sort. But the thought of marrying me would never cross her mind. I've only my wages, and my parents— may they rest in peace—were as poor as the twelve apostles. Not that I wouldn't be able to make her much happier than twenty Berouets could. I'm not a coward, and I'm better educated, and . . . and . . . But you can't go around with a notice pinned to your coat telling people what you're like inside.

He got up, dusted off the skirts of his coat, and went downstairs to the office.

MONSIEUR LABORDE was writing in a ledger.

"Ah, Houdin", he said, looking up with his usual uneasy smile as Jean-Paul entered the office. "Had a good journey?" Then he remembered the theft of the letters and his expression changed.

The wrath of superiors, like lightning, tends to travel relentlessly downward until it exhausts itself in the earth. The Duc de Choiseul had been angry at not hearing from Monsieur Charville and had expressed his displeasure by an arrogant letter from his secretary; Monsieur Charville, exasperated at being criticised, had vented his bitterness on Monsieur Laborde; and Monsieur Laborde, frightened and resentful, had made up his mind to let Jean-Paul feel what it is like to be threatened by superiors with unmentionable penalties. Had he thought about the matter, he would have expected Jean-Paul to react by kicking a dog, cursing a beggar, or insulting his landlady with complaints about his dinner.

"Ah, Houdin", he repeated. "It's about time you were back."

"I came as fast as I could, sir."

"I gave you an important commission. You let yourself be robbed. What have you got to say for yourself?"

"Only that I want to leave your service, sir."

"Leave my service?" Monsieur Laborde was taken aback. He had meant to scold, not to dismiss. Efficient clerks and couriers were hard to come by. Besides, there was something hostile in Jean-Paul's manner that alarmed him. "Who said anything about leaving my service?" he asked in a more conciliatory tone.

"I did."

"Oh, come now." This time, Monsieur Laborde's manner was almost ingratiating. "Perhaps I was irritable when you first came in. After all, the theft of those letters caused me a lot of unpleasantness. But you don't want to pay too much attention to a sharp word or two."

"I'm sorry, sir, but I still want to leave. I'd be glad if I could have my wages."

"Why? Wasn't I paying you enough?"

"If you must know, sir, I don't like some of the business that goes on here."

Monsieur Laborde suddenly flushed.

"What happened to those letters?" he demanded loudly.

"I wrote and told you, sir. Some of the letters were missing. The thieves must have thought they had money in them. Others had been opened and were lying scattered around the room. These I resealed and delivered to the people they were addressed to."

"You read them first, though."

"Have I said I did?"

"Don't lie to me. I can see you read them. Well, there was nothing in them you have any right to object to. You ought to be proud to serve your country."

"That depends on how it's done. Come, sir, pay me my wages, and I'll save you the trouble of getting angry with me."

By now, Monsieur Laborde was beside himself. Jean-Paul was one of half a dozen couriers travelling for him between Paris and Madrid with letters from French agents in Spain concealed in the lining of their valises. He had never told his couriers what kind of letters they were, but he had assumed they understood. There was no need to hide business letters in secret pockets, so if Jean-Paul was suddenly pretending to be shocked by this traffic, he must have been bribed by the Spanish to betray his employer. There were objections to this idea. If it were true, the Spanish would surely have told Jean-Paul to keep his job at all costs. By now, however, Monsieur Laborde was far too excited to think logically.

"Wages?" he roared. "I'm not paying any wages to spies and traitors. If you ever tell anyone what you read in those letters, it will be the worse for you. A word from me, and as soon as you go back to France, they'll put you in the galleys for life. Now get out!"

"Well, sir, if it comes to that, a word from me here in Madrid in the right quarters, and they'll be closing down your business and sending you back to Lyons or, more likely, putting *you* in the galleys. Come on, pay me what you owe me."

"Get out! Get out! No. Wait. Take the money. Here it is, and may it choke you."

Both were red in the face, and both could feel their hearts pounding. Monsieur Laborde counted out the coins and then threw them down on the table. Half of them rolled off and fell on the floor. Jean-Paul picked them up and went out, slamming the door.

The ugly, mean-minded moneylender! he said to himself. Trying to cheat me out of my wages. I might have known he wasn't up to any good from the way he treats his daughter. To think of all the dirty work I've done for him without knowing it.

TWENTY-SEVEN

After putting his horse in Monsieur Laborde's stables, Jean-Paul made his way to his lodgings near the Hospital of San Fernando, where he had a room over a cobbler's workshop. The cobbler and his family were so pleased to see him back that he first had to drink a glass of wine with them and tell them about his journey.

When at last he reached his room, he dropped his baggage in a corner and locked the door behind him. Next, he took off his coat, opened the lining under the right arm with a pair of scissors, and drew out some folded sheets of paper. Having glanced over them to make sure they were all there, he put half of them—a copy of Monsieur Charville's letter to the Duc de Choiseul—in his pocket. The rest—the original letter—he hid in a crevice between the tiles and one of the rafters. Then he washed and changed his clothes.

A quarter of an hour later he was standing in front of the Casa San Felipe.

In reply to his repeated ringing of the bell, the door was at last opened by a middle-aged priest, whose rather forced smile failed to conceal an underlying impatience.

"Good-day, Father", Jean-Paul said. "Could I see the Superior, please?"

"I am the Superior", Father de la Cueva answered.

He led the way to a parlour, furnished with a bare table and two chairs.

Excitedly, Jean-Paul explained who he was, where he had been working, the contents of the letter he had been carrying to Paris, and how he had come to know them.

Father de la Cueva took the letter, read through it rapidly, and then a second time more slowly.

Jean-Paul watched him, anticipating with a feeling of pride his thanks and congratulations. But when Father de la Cueva had finished reading and had raised his eyes, instead of appearing pleased, he looked displeased and suspicious.

"Thank you", he said. "I will take care of it."

"You'll make sure His Majesty reads it, won't you, Father?"

"That's for others to decide."

"But Father, if the King reads this, he'll know who your enemies are, and then he can put them in prison."

"And what reason do I have for thinking your story is true?"

"Why, Father . . ."

"How do I know this letter is not a forgery?"

"But I told you, Father—"

"You may be lying."

Jean-Paul was silent.

"You say you were employed by this Monsieur Laborde. Suppose I asked him to confirm what you have told me about yourself, would he?"

"No, Father", Jean-Paul said, crestfallen. "I thought you'd trust me. I know my intentions are honest."

"And you expect me, on the strength of your word, to risk the safety of my Order by showing His Majesty a letter like this? The first thing our enemies will say is that we've fabricated this letter to discredit people we don't like and, unless I can bring unimpeachable evidence to the contrary, they'll be believed. We shall then have the whole Court against us. This letter insults almost everyone in authority—from the King downward. For all I know, that's just what's intended, and your bringing this thing here is simply a trap."

"Father, I swear—as I hope to be saved—that every word I've told you is true."

"Perhaps you are personally innocent", Father de la Cueva said, his tone softening a little. "You look and sound honest, but that doesn't mean that you may not be the dupe of men whose motives are far from it. In all probability this letter was put into your luggage and deliberately left on the floor by the thieves in the expectation that when you found it, you would act exactly as you have done, and that we should be fools enough to take it as genuine."

"But, Father, how would the thieves know what was in the letter?"

"You assume that the men who broke into your room really were thieves. Why? There's nothing so very difficult about staging a robbery. Our enemies have used more ingenious ruses than that in their efforts to destroy us. Where do you go to Mass on Sundays? At one of our churches?"

"Yes, Father."

"Do you usually go to confession to our priests?"

"Yes, Father."

"There you are, then. You were the ideal person for their purpose. You are young, enthusiastic, not overly suspicious. They knew you were favourably inclined toward us. I've little doubt that the thieves who robbed you at Chateauroux had followed you all the way from Madrid."

"Good heavens, Father, do you really think all this is true?"

"It's more than possible. I know quite a bit about this Monsieur Charville, and I have every reason to believe he had as little to do with this letter as you or I. Somebody wants to involve us in blackening Monsieur Charville's character so that we shall fall out with a gentleman in a high position—a friend of our Society—who is a close friend of Monsieur Charville."

"Don't forget, Father, that I saw Monsieur Charville at Monsieur Laborde's."

"What does that prove? You tell me Monsieur Laborde is a banker. Lots of perfectly innocent people must call on him."

"That's true enough." Jean-Paul was silent for some moments. "Well, Father, I'm thankful it was you who answered the door and not some other priest who might not have understood everything so clearly."

"Almighty God arranges these things," Father de la Cueva said with a deprecatory smile, "and if any other letters of this sort fall into your hands, be sure to let me have them."

PART TWO

Indian Baroque

1764–1765

TWENTY-EIGHT

June was nearly over. The midwinter sun of the southern hemisphere was melting the early morning clouds and dispersing the mists that had earlier blanketed the marshes and lain like drifts of snow along the rivers.

On an earth road, a party of horsemen in single file, ten Indians in white tunics and a European priest, whose cassock and black broad-brimmed hat had, from exposure to the weather, acquired the greenish sheen of a jackdaw's wing, were mounting the side of a shallow valley. At the top of the hill, the travellers stopped. Before them stretched an undulating plain, covered with grass and palmetto bushes. Here and there a hillock or copse broke the open expanse, and a quarter of a mile off herds of cattle were grazing. In the far distance the plain was bounded by a dark line where the forest began.

Alfonso de Vallecas lifted the flap of his saddle and tightened the girth. Then he took his feet out of the stirrups and stretched his legs. He had been on the road only a short while, but he was still stiff from the previous day's ride.

It was over half a year since he had left Spain. The sea voyage itself had taken three months. He and his fellow missionaries had slept six to a narrow, constricted cabin in the bows. Near Cape Verde, a storm had blown their ship several hundred miles off course; and for the last fortnight the biscuits had had weevils, the meat maggots, and the water had gone bad.

On March 15 they had dropped anchor in the River Plate. The twelve priests, their clothing hanging loose on their emaciated bodies, had been set ashore at Buenos Aires, and for the next two and a half months they had lived at the local Jesuit house attached to the church of San Francisco Borja, recovering their health and learning Guarani, the language of the Indians they were to work among.

Finally, on June 1, they had started on the last lap of their journey. A flotilla of boats and rafts had been setting sail that day up the rivers Paraguay and Paraná for Candelaria, the chief of the thirty Jesuit Reductions, or mission towns, in the area where the Paraná and Uruguay, after converging to within about fifty miles of each other, follow a parallel course for one hundred miles from northeast to southwest. Candelaria was the seat of the local Jesuit superior. The boats and rafts, which had brought cargoes of timber and hides to Buenos Aires, were now returning with smaller but equally valuable cargoes of raw materials and manufactured goods from Europe, necessaries that could not be obtained from the countryside or made by the Indians of the Reductions themselves.

The journey of over five hundred miles upriver to the subtropical land of the Guaranis had lasted nearly three weeks. From Candelaria, Alfonso had now been riding for several days northward to his ultimate destination, the Reduction of San Miguel Guazu, where he was to act as assistant priest, or *padre compañero*.

Before giving his Indian guides the sign to move on, Alfonso looked back at the place where they had spent the night, two huts half-hidden in the trees near a bridge over a stream. One was the hut of a herdsman, the other a rest house.

The Reductions were linked by a system of roads, better than the majority of roads in Europe at that time, and, where the distance between towns was more than a day's journey, there were rest houses for travellers and for the Indian couriers carrying messages from one Reduction to another.

"Reverend Father," said the leader of the party to Alfonso, "we should be at San Miguel by sunset. One of the men wishes to ride ahead and warn them of your arrival, so that they can be ready to welcome you. Does he have your permission?"

"Is it necessary to warn them?"

The Indian looked puzzled. It was as though a general had said: "Is it necessary for men to salute me?" or a king had asked: "Must they really bow?"

"Very well, then", Alfonso said. "Let him go, by all means."

The Indian took this message to the would-be herald, who set off at a gallop. The rest of the party followed at a walk. Having reached open ground, the Indians broke their file and rode line abreast behind Alfonso. They talked quietly among themselves. He listened and watched, both to improve his knowledge of their language and to learn more about their characters. So far, he had found them serious, simple, and, if a bit reserved, disarmingly trustful. This judgment, however, did not allow for individual differences that must exist; as yet, one swarthy, reticent face with high cheekbones, tilted eyes, and downcast glance looked much like another. They prayed with the ardour and confidence of the poor and of newly converted peoples everywhere. Each evening, for instance, before they lay down to sleep, they recited the Litany of Loreto in front of a portable statue of the Madonna, which they carried with them and lodged for the night in an arbour of leaves and boughs. On rising, they said their morning prayers in the same way, before removing the statue and continuing the journey. At their request, Alfonso had led them in these devotions, leaving him to wonder whether there was much need for him at San Miguel. Weren't the citizens of Madrid in greater need of missionaries?

At Candelaria, he had confided his doubts to one of the priests who had come out with him from Spain, an Irishman called Fields.

"My very own thoughts", Father Fields had replied with energy. "It looks as if the Lord wants to take us to paradise by sedan chair."

Father Fields, however, was not prepared to follow such an uncertain way to heaven without plainer signs of its being God's will. So, on reaching Candelaria, he had asked to be sent to one of the more dangerous missions among the Moxos and Chiquito Indians, near the border with Peru, rather than to one of the well-established Guarani Reductions.

After riding for an hour, Alfonso and his party reached the edge of the forest, where the road disappeared into a tunnel of shadows. Around its entrance hovered hummingbirds and butterflies, sucking nectar from the same flowers. Giant trees rose up on every side, their trunks concealed by thickets of shrubs and ferns. Moss, looking like green sheep's fleece, hung from the boughs, and farther overhead the creepers let fall showers of brilliant blossoms. Moist leaves and tendrils brushed their faces. The air was still and heavy.

Alfonso gazed about him in wonder. Here, everything in nature seemed grand, powerful, immense, and resplendent. It was as though in Europe God were expressing his thoughts on a harpsichord, in the Americas on a cathedral organ.

TWENTY-NINE

At midday they stopped to rest. The Indians quickly built a fire and prepared *yerba*, a kind of tea made from pulverized leaves of the ilex. They served it to Alfonso in a dried gourd, together with some meat and a cake of manioc flour. After they had eaten, the Indians slept, and Alfonso, opening his breviary, said the Office of the day, which was the Feast of St. John the Baptist.

An hour later they untethered their horses and rode on, still following the path through the forest. Soon they heard the splashing of a waterfall. The cacique who was leading the way came back to speak to Alfonso.

"There is a path to the right here, Reverend Father. It is not so good as the road, but it is shorter. We shall reach San Miguel an hour sooner by the path. Which would you like us to take?"

"Whichever you think best."

The cacique shifted in his saddle and looked sideways at the ground. He plainly favoured the path but just as plainly did not want to be responsible for choosing it.

"Do you know this other path?" Alfonso asked. "Is there any danger of our losing our way?"

"Oh, no, Reverend Father."

"Very good. We will take the path."

They turned off through the bushes, which, as they moved forward, whipped and tore at their faces and clothes. Alfonso, who could scarcely see, kept his horse's head close to the rump of the horse in front. Then the undergrowth cleared. The path took a zigzag course downhill between the boles of the trees. Suddenly the waterfall came into view, shining in the sunlight that fell through a gap in the forest ceiling.

As the cacique was crossing the pool at the foot of the waterfall, a horse neighed somewhere on the opposite bank. The Indians reined in their horses and sat listening. Then the cacique and the man behind him spurred their animals up the bank and disappeared. Boughs snapped and twigs crackled as they broke through the undergrowth. A few moments later the cacique gave a yell. The Indians with Alfonso shouted in reply, and three more of them forced their horses up the bank and into the trees. Alfonso wondered what to do, not knowing what kind of danger to expect. But before he had time to come to a decision, the cacique and his companions returned on foot, driving three men in front of them— a Spaniard and two mestizos.

"Go and get the horses", the cacique said to one of the Indians who had stayed with Alfonso.

The Spaniard's eyes moved back and forth as he sized up his captors. He had assumed a bold, couldn't-care-less expression, in spite of the fact that he looked half-starved and his muddy clothes were in rags. The two half-casts showed no emotion but stood with lowered eyes, seemingly ready to accept any fate, however unpleasant.

"Only Indians are allowed in the territory of the Reduction, Reverend Father", the cacique said excitedly. "These men must be taken back under guard to wherever they came from."

"Do you understand what he's saying?" Alfonso asked the Spaniard.

"That gibberish? I'll be damned first."

"He says that Europeans are not allowed in the Reductions."

"Then what are you doing here?"

"Only the Indians are allowed *and* their European priests", Alfonso said mildly. "Did you know that?"

"What I know is my own business. You Jesuits make the laws in these parts. So what you decide goes."

"They are looking for gold", the cacique interrupted. "Many Spaniards visit the Reductions secretly to find gold. They think there is gold because the King does not allow them on our land."

Alfonso signed to the cacique to keep silent, and then turned to the Spaniard again.

"Since I am a newcomer", he said, "and not certain how the regulations apply, I must ask to you accompany me to San Miguel, so that we can put your case to Father Huber, the parish priest there."

"I am forced to go with you. You and your men outnumber us."

"But if you're innocent, why should you object?"

The man frowned, bit his lip, and then laughed, shrugging his shoulders.

"Very well," he said, "I'll go with you." he said. "What does it matter? If you want to make a fool of yourself, go ahead. But only if we ride side by side. I'm not going to be seen surrounded by these barefooted devils, as if I were a criminal."

"As you wish."

After the Indians had disarmed him, the Spaniard, still closely watched by the cacique, went to his horse, mounted, and rejoined Alfonso, who then gave the order to move on. There was just room on the path for them to ride abreast.

"The cacique says you were hunting for gold", Alfonso said, looking at the Spaniard with curiosity.

"I suppose you believe everything that damn cacique tells you."

"All the same, you do think there's gold in the Reductions, don't you?"

The man laughed. "Everyone knows the Jesuits have got gold mines here."

"Everyone knows? You're quite wrong. Won't you take my word for it?"

"No, I won't." The man smiled, showing two gold front teeth—the only gold, apparently, he had so far come by. "Why should a lot of clever men like you Jesuits shut yourselves up with these cursed Indians unless you're hiding something worth having?"

Well, Alfonso thought, I suppose that's a kind of compliment. At least he doesn't pretend to have better motives than he attributes to us.

"If you've nothing to hide," the Spaniard continued, "why not let honest people look around?"

The question, which he considered unanswerable, pleased him greatly.

"It's not honest people we're afraid of", Alfonso said. "Unfortunately, some of the colonists would set the Indians a bad example. When the Indians saw them breaking the commandments, they might say to themselves: 'These Spaniards are Christians like us. If they can do these things, why shouldn't we?' Since we cannot know in advance which colonists are going to behave well and which badly, we have to exclude all Europeans."

"I'll tell you what, Father," the Spaniard said, falling suddenly into a friendly, confidential manner, "I don't altogether blame you Jesuits for keeping your mines a secret. You're on to a good thing. It's human nature to keep it to yourselves. But you can't blame us either if we try to outwit you and lay our hands on some of that gold, too. Would you like a piece of advice? Be generous. We colonists are reasonable men. We'd be content if you let us have a half-share in your mines. Tell that to your superiors. Tell them that if they'll just be sensible, they'll make a lot a friends and lose some powerful enemies."

"But there isn't any gold to share."

"All right, Father. To please you, we'll forget about the gold for the present. But what about business and trade? You're not going to tell me you Jesuits don't trade. Because I've seen your goods being unloaded at Asunción and Corrientes. Now I don't happen to be in trade myself. As a gentleman, I wouldn't dirty my hands with buying and selling. But I know a trader or two, and they complain that you always undersell them. And they say they're not going to put up with it much longer."

"But our priests don't trade. They only help the Indians to dispose of what they, the Indians, produce by their own work. That isn't wrong."

"You spoil the market for the other traders. They think that priests ought not to engage in business. What do you say to that?"

147

Alfonso was tempted to say that men with low minds could be expected to see only low motives in other people. "I can only repeat what I said before," he answered, "that we don't trade and never have traded. We act on behalf of the Indians, who, without our help, would certainly be cheated by the colonists who buy their goods."

The Spaniard condescendingly patted Alfonso's shoulder. Alfonso heard an indignant snort from the cacique, who was riding just behind him. "You're young, Father", the Spaniard said. "You imagine that all the priests in America are only thinking about heaven and saving other people's souls, the way you are. But priests are men, like the rest of us, and after a time they start thinking of the good things of life, too."

"That's true", Alfonso said. "Priests are men with men's failings. But that isn't an excuse for making rash judgments and for spreading lies about them. Can you really wonder that we keep you from mixing with the Indians?"

"They might hear some home truths, you mean. Discover that Reverend Father isn't as holy as he seems?"

"Look", Alfonso said sharply. "You ought to be thinking of your own soul, not spending so much time misjudging other people. You're going to die one day. Have you ever thought how you're going to account to God for all the calumnies you've spread?"

The man swore and pulled savagely on his reins, causing his horse to rear. Then he smiled again and patted Alfonso's shoulder for a second time, as though to say: "We both know you're obliged to talk this professional twaddle, but I don't hold it against you."

At this point the path grew so narrow that they had to ride in single file. Alfonso, glad not to have to talk any more, wondered whether he had spoken too sharply.

After another hour, the forest ended, and they came to a marsh, where the Indians argued for several minutes before deciding the best way to cross.

On the left, a lake stretched into the distance, with sleeping wild fowl floating here and there on its surface.

Beyond the marsh, the rising ground brought them to another plain with great herds of grazing cattle, like the one they had passed in the morning. Half a mile off, a cluster of trees sheltered a low group of buildings. This, the cacique explained, was one of the *estancias*, or ranches, belonging to San Miguel.

We must be getting near, Alfonso thought, with a sudden unexpected feeling of apprehension. San Miguel was to be his home for many years, possibly for life. What would his new superior be like? Suppose he bungled his work, or the Indians didn't take to him, or under his supervision the crops failed and the herds diminished? All the way across the plain thoughts like this kept tormenting him.

They entered the trees again. Here they met the road they had left earlier in the day. After another mile they could see sunlight at the far end. The cacique, who had ridden ahead, stopped and turned in his saddle.

"San Miguel", he shouted.

Alfonso spurred his horse and cantered forward to join him. The Spaniard, who had been whistling, fell silent.

THIRTY

Before them, half a mile off, Alfonso saw the roofs of the town and, rising higher, the ochre-coloured walls and towers of the church. The metal crosses on top of the towers winked in the late afternoon sun, as though someone were signalling with them. Between the edge of the forest and the nearest houses, the ground was cultivated. But although it was still an hour to sunset, there was not a man or woman in sight. The town was surrounded by a palisade, and the road ran straight through the fields toward a group of ilex trees in front of the main gate.

As Alfonso took in the scene, the confusion of the familiar and foreign stirred him in a way he could not fully understand. The town itself might have been a town in Spain, but everything else—the trees, the crops, the birds, the flowers—was foreign to him. It was like looking at a portrait of a parent or a brother and sister in an exotically new and unknown frame.

Suddenly, he heard a shot. Immediately another shot sounded from the direction of the town, and a puff of smoke showed white against the dark green of the ilex trees. The second shot was echoed by a third. Then the bells of the church began to peal, hesitantly at first, but then loudly and tumultuously. A few seconds later a cavalcade emerged from the trees, followed by a crowd of men, women, and children on foot.

Alfonso and his party advanced to meet them. His escort fell back, leaving him in the lead.

At the head of the approaching cavalcade, riding a chestnut mare, was the parish priest, the *padre cura*, in his cassock and a large straw hat. He was flanked on either side by an Indian on a white stallion. The Indians, who sat erect in their saddles, looking neither to right nor left, were dressed like European noblemen. Each, on his straight black hair cut in a short bob, wore a tricorn hat with a white ostrich feather curled inside the brim. Their blue coats had deep cuffs and wide skirts, which lay on their horses' flanks like braided saddlecloths. A lace jabot at the neck overflowed onto an embroidered yellow waistcoat, and crimson breeches completed the outfit. Lower legs and feet were bare. In their white-gloved hands they carried coloured batons. Other town officers, only a little less ornately dressed, followed immediately behind, and then a crowd of two thousand or more on foot, the men in knee-length cotton tunics and loose trousers falling a few inches below, and the women in shifts reaching to the ankles. A few had cloaks of unbleached wool that they had twined around them toga-fashion. Squeezed between the adults, the children looked like loose peas in a heap of pods.

When the two groups were about ten yards apart, they halted, and the murmur coming from the crowd as it advanced suddenly stopped.

Alfonso and the parish priest dismounted. They approached each other and embraced.

"Welcome, Father! Welcome to San Miguel!" the old priest said with emotion. "I am Father Huber. And you . . . ?"

"My name is de Vallecas. Alfonso de Vallecas, Father."

"I am glad, very glad. We have longed for your coming, all of us, for more than a year. Welcome to your new home!"

Before he had finished speaking, the Indians broke into applause. Pressing forward from behind the horsemen, they spilled into the fields so as to see the new priest better. The two "grandees" shouted and waved their batons.

"You are more than kind, Father", replied Alfonso, equally moved. "I never expected a welcome like this."

When they had mounted their horses again, the combined cavalcade turned about and moved back toward the town, led by a band of pipes, piccolos, oboes, clarinets, trumpets, cornets, and drums, playing a Haydn march. Reaching the ilex grove, they passed through the gate, and down a wide street bordered by palms and paraiso trees, to the plaza in front of the church. Everywhere Indians stood expectantly, under the trees, in the side streets, on the verandas of the houses. The plaza was full to its limits, and the boughs overhead swayed beneath the weight of small brown bodies, as though the trees had borne a crop of children.

An Indian ran forward to take their horses, and the two priests entered the church. Columns with Corinthian capitals separated the nave from the aisles; paintings in carved gilt frames hung over the altars; and the sun, shining though the west window, lit up a frescoed ceiling.

They approached the sanctuary side by side and knelt a moment before the tabernacle. Then Father Huber motioned Alfonso to a heavily carved and gilded chair, and he himself went up into the pulpit, which, equally ornate, looked from a distance like a huge and wonderful barnacle-encrusted shell from a tropical sea. A brightly painted St. Michael killing a green and silver dragon surmounted the canopy above. Meanwhile, the Indians pressing into the church behind them were ranging themselves in rows on either side of the nave—the men and boys on the left; the women, girls, and young children on the right. In the half-light of the church, the whites of their eyes shone like mother-of-pearl beads, line upon line, and every pair was fixed on Father Huber.

"Beloved children in Jesus Christ," he began, "today we must thank God with all our hearts for sending us a new *padre compañero*. We have all prayed that he would come soon. And now, after testing our patience and perseverance a little, God has, in his own good time, answered our prayers and sent us the desire of our hearts. He is here at last, the good priest who has left his home far away over the sea to come and help us all to get to heaven. He is young, he is strong; he will, please God, be a second father to you for many years. So thank God very much today, and try to make this good Father feel at home by letting him see how glad you are to welcome him. To show that we appreciate his sacrifice, let us all try each day to be better Christians than we were yesterday. Now we will sing the Te Deum."

The congregation murmured its approval.

Leaving the pulpit, Father Huber went to the centre of the sanctuary, where he was joined by Alfonso. Out of sight, cellos and violins began playing the hymn's opening bars. But the sound of the instruments was soon drowned by the hundreds of chanting voices. Just as a few moments before, the souls of the Indians had seemed to be all in their eyes, now those souls appeared to be all in their voices.

Sung vespers followed, with the organ playing, and after the last 'Amen', Father Huber and Alfonso, preceded by an acolyte carrying a processional cross, returned to the west door.

A worried-looking official was waiting for him on the steps outside.

"What shall we do with him, Reverence?" He pointed to the Spaniard who, no longer on horseback, stood with his two companions at the bottom of the steps, surrounded by their Indian captors.

"Take them to the guesthouse and set a guard outside the windows", Father Huber said. He turned to the Spaniard. "You will have to spend the night here, I'm afraid. Tomorrow you will be escorted to Villarrica."

"Don't think you can treat a Spaniard and a gentleman like this and get away with it", the man said hotly.

"If you persist in trespassing, you must put up with the consequences. I have to carry out the Governor's orders."

"The Governor's orders! You Jesuits have got the Governor in your pockets."

"You will be here only for a night, and, as you know from experience, you will be comfortable and well looked after." Father Huber smiled ironically. "If anyone is disrespectful, you have only to tell me."

"Order these men to let me go."

"I'm sorry, it is impossible." He turned to the Indian official. "Take him away, and see that his supper is a good one."

"You wait", the Spaniard shouted. "We'll get even with you yet. We'll find your gold sooner or later. Then we'll put an end to your trading and moneymaking." The threats ended in a string of oaths.

The Indians near enough to hear what the man was saying, cried out in protest. Those who could see only his furious face laughed and clapped.

"Poor fellow", Father Huber said, as the man was led away, still shouting. "I'm afraid he's learned the art of conversation in a bad school. That's how the devil talks: begins with lies, contradicts himself, then gets angry and ends with abuse."

"I'm amazed", Alfonso said. "He said nothing about having seen you before."

"He's been here five or six times. Eighty percent of the colonists are convinced that we have secret gold mines, but most of them won't go to the trouble of looking for them. Only occasionally do we get a man like this fellow, who not only believes in the existence of the mines but is really determined to find them."

While he was speaking, the Indians had been coming up to Alfonso one by one, kissing his hand and pressing it to their forehead.

"My children," Father Huber said, "you will have the chance of welcoming the *padre compañero* tomorrow. Now he needs a rest. He has come a long journey. So he will bid you good night."

THIRTY-ONE

The priests' house, or *collegio*, was attached to the north side of the church.

Father Huber opened a wicket in the wooden gates, led the way across a courtyard, under a veranda, and into an oblong room with a low ceiling. The furniture—a table, a few chairs, a dresser, a cupboard, two chests—was all heavy and made of dark wood. There were books on the top shelves of the dresser, and crockery below. Portraits of priests with yellow faces and slanting eyes hung on the whitewashed walls. Among them was a portrait in bright colours of a cacique wearing a feathered headdress.

"This is our community room", Father Huber said. "You and I are the community, Father—except when we have visitors." He smiled and pointed out of the window. "That gate in the garden wall leads to the cemetery. I like to read my breviary there. Our Indians love their dead; they keep the graves beautifully." He walked to the end of the room and threw open two doors. "This is your room. And this one is mine." He smiled again. "If either of us falls sick, we are in easy reach of a priest." He led the way back to the courtyard. In the angle closest to them, an outside staircase rose to the upper floor. "There are rooms there", he said, "for the Bishop and Governor and other visitors. And here is the kitchen."

An old Indian was bent over the hearth. As soon as he heard the priests come in, he wiped his hands on his apron and hurried to greet them. It was difficult to believe that a smile showing only a few blackened teeth like old tree stumps could be so winning.

"This is our faithful Tarcisio", Father Huber said. "He has cooked for the priests of San Miguel for fifty years. You were not in the church then, Tarcisio?"

"No, Reverend Father. What would the Lord have said to me if I had neglected the dinner and served you cinders?"

"He has one other man to help him look after the house", Father Huber said. "But they sleep out with their families. We won't interrupt you, then, Tarcisio. He is making something special in honour of your arrival, Father, and he has never had a failure yet. That door at the other end of the veranda leads to the sacristy and church. And now I expect you want to wash after your journey."

Father Huber had given Alfonso the larger of the two rooms, the one with a window on the garden, keeping for himself the smaller one, which had a high barred window looking on to the veranda.

When Alfonso had changed his shirt and put on the second of his two cassocks, he returned to the community room.

Father Huber and an Indian he had not seen before were kneeling on the floor in one of the far corners trying to light a stove of sun-dried bricks. They had not heard Alfonso come in. Without intending to overhear what they said, he stood and watched them.

"It won't light, Your Reverence", the Indian said crossly. He was younger than Tarcisio—about sixty—but his face was only a little less wrinkled and leathery.

"Come, Cayetano," Father Huber said in a coaxing voice, "let's try once more."

"I don't know what Your Reverence needs a fire for suddenly. You never have one when you're by yourself."

"The young Father isn't used to our climate. The evenings are chilly, and he may feel cold."

The Indian muttered. It sounded to Alfonso as if he were saying that old men, not young ones, needed to be kept warm. At the same time he thrust his arm into the stove and up the chimney.

"Look here!", he said, pulling out a handful of straw and sticks covered with bird droppings, "and there'll be more higher up. But what can you expect when it hasn't been lit since his lordship the Bishop was last here more than a year ago."

"Can I help?" Alfonso asked, coming forward.

Father Huber started and turned his head.

"Ah, Father! I didn't realise you were there." To hide his embarrassment, he began to fill the inside of the stove with sticks and shavings. "I'll try once more, then you can have a turn. I designed the thing, so if I

155

can't make it burn, it shows I'm not much of an inventor. The trouble is, I haven't got it right for the draught. It's always been a nuisance. There, now. Perhaps it will burn at last. You've done the work, Cayetano, and I shall get the credit. What do you say to that?"

In another minute the sticks were burning fiercely. Father Huber pushed a log on top of them, closed the door of the stove and adjusted a primitive damper. The Indian picked up the remains of the birds' nests and left the room, looking as if he thought the fire had lighted with the deliberate purpose of contradicting him.

"Cayetano will be in a better temper shortly", Father Huber said. "He is easily ruffled if I do anything he thinks is not in keeping with the dignity of the college."

And sure enough, Cayetano returned three minutes later, smiling as if nothing had happened. He was carrying a large oval dish, heaped with meat and vegetables, which he set on the table. When Father Huber introduced him to Alfonso, he expressed surprise and delight, as though they were meeting for the first time.

Father Huber said grace.

Earlier, when riding at the head of his parishioners and talking in the plaza to the Spaniard, Father Huber had looked commanding and majestic. But now, as with bowed head he invoked God's blessing on their meal, his work-worn body gave the opposite impression. His shoulders drooped, his chest was sunk in, his skin was as brown and wrinkled as Cayetano's, and he had as few teeth as Tarcisio. His shock of wiry hair was dead white.

During the meal Father Huber talked animatedly; he took little food himself but kept urging Alfonso to eat.

"You must keep up your strength, Father. A strange climate is full of dangers. The health must be protected by feeding the body well. It must have time to adapt to its surroundings before you start mortifying it. Some of the young priests who come out from Europe won't listen to advice. They all want to imitate St. Aloysius—except, of course, his obedience. Then they fall ill. It is a pity. Before you go to bed I will

156

give you some medicine. We call it 'Cure-all'. But let us be truthful: it cures some things. It also prevents them, which is better."

"May I ask, Father, which part of Germany you come from?"

"The Empire. I'm Austrian."

"Then we are compatriots. My mother is Austrian."

"It isn't possible?" Father Huber said excitedly. "Let me look at you. Yes, now I think I can see it. You haven't a Spanish face. But which part of Austria?"

"I have never lived in Austria myself. But I speak German."

"Ah, merciful God, how good and gracious you are! Only yesterday, when I was riding through the fields, I thought how much I would like to speak German with someone for an hour or so. Have you ever noticed, Father, how often when we give our lives to God, he answers not only prayers but a wish, a mere wish?"

He began to question Alfonso in German about his journey and the news from Europe. Alfonso described the successes of England and Prussia in the recent war and what he had heard of the activities of the French parlements and of the other events leading up to the suppression of the Jesuits in France.

Father Huber, who seemed already familiar with the details of the war, criticised the tactics of the Austrian commanders at the battles of Liegnitz and Torgau and praised the generalship of Frederick of Prussia. In gentler terms, for fear of hurting Alfonso's feelings, he bewailed the losses of the French and Spanish at sea and commended the naval strategy of the British.

Of the war being waged against the Society of Jesus he spoke less but listened carefully to everything Alfonso said.

"Ah," he exclaimed, when Alfonso had described the plight of the Jesuits imprisoned in Lisbon, "the devil did not think—when he started his tricks in Portugal—that he was preparing the way for so many glorious confessors of the faith."

But after a moment he sighed and grew thoughtful.

"Don't forget", Alfonso said, momentarily adopting his father, Don

157

Maurice's, tone to cheer up the older man, "that we have His Majesty and the Empress on our side. The whole world knows what good, devout Catholics they are. Bad though things are, our enemies may well by now have done their worst."

"We must hope so. We must hope so. But princes are strange people, Father. They're not like us. It's hardly surprising. From childhood on, they hear little except flattery. Only God knows how their minds work and can understand their ways. Doubtless if they were never deceived, we could depend upon them. But it is difficult for them to learn the truth."

They were nearing the end of their meal when there was a knock on the door, and a tall, middle-aged Indian came in to report that the town was quiet and the gates had been shut. He was followed by the head sacristan, who said he had locked the church.

"It's time for us to make the rounds," Father Huber said. They put on their cloaks. As they went out, Father Huber unhooked a lantern from one of the posts along the veranda.

Night had fallen and the sky was overcast. The air was full of the smoke of wood fires, which made the inside of Alfonso's nose tingle. Everywhere he looked, lights flickered between the trees, and he could hear hundreds of voices in conversation, broken from time to time by laughter or the crying of a baby. A dog barked, then another, then several together until, at a volley of shouts from their masters, they fell silent.

They tried the door of the church, then visited the gates of the town, which, Father Huber explained, were to keep out wild beasts as well as undesirable human beings. They ended their round at the hospital, the orphanage, and the refuge for the old with no family to look after them. They were all one-storey structures with thatched roofs.

At the hospital there were two sick Indians in the men's ward. One was asleep; the other, as Father Huber and Alfonso came in, watched them with glittering, feverish eyes. When they approached his cot, he took Father Huber's hand and pressed it to his forehead.

"Will I be well soon, Reverend Father?" he asked.

"Yes, my friend, soon. Very soon. How do you feel now?"

"Better. But I have bad dreams. I'm afraid. Please stay with me, Father."

"I will pray, and the dreams will go away."

Father Huber dipped a sprig of ilex into a holy water stoop near the door and sprinkled the patient and his bed. Then he knelt down. While he was praying, the Indian fell asleep. They walked away on tiptoe.

"Except when bringing the last sacraments," Father Huber said, "we never go into the Indians' houses or the women's half of the hospital and refuge."

The orphanage consisted of a single room. In the semi-darkness, half-lit by a lamp winking before a statue, they could dimly see eight small bodies wrapped in blankets, asleep on the floor. A wicker screen separated the far end of the room from the rest. The childless couple who cared for the orphans were sitting behind it, talking in low voices. Hearing the footsteps of the two priests, the man came to see who was there. He led them outside and began to tell a long tale about the state of each child. Father Huber listened, asked questions, criticised what he considered one or two faults, praised the man in general for his care of the children, prescribed a remedy for colic, and gave his blessing.

At the old people's refuge, the men were sitting outside on the veranda. They were greatly excited to see Alfonso, and one of them offered him his pipe to smoke. The two priests talked and joked with them for a while, then returned to the college, where they found Tarcisio and Cayetano waiting outside the gates.

"I have closed the shutters, Reverend Father," Tarcisio said, "and here are the keys."

After saying good night, the Indians made off across the plaza, their short figures disappearing quickly in the darkness.

Father Huber followed Alfonso into the college and locked the door behind them.

THIRTY-TWO

"Tell me, Father," Alfonso said, when they were settled before the stove in the community room, with the almond-eyed priest and the bright cacique looking down at them from their picture frames and the heavy furniture looming in the shadows beyond the lamplight, "how is it that, although so far from Europe, you know so much about the last war? Most people in Spain know less."

"I have friends who keep me informed. They know I'm interested in military science."

"You were a soldier, then?" Alfonso asked with surprise.

"You jump to conclusions", Father Huber smiled. "However, this time you happen to be right."

At first he seemed reluctant to talk about himself, but seeing that Alfonso was interested, and wishing to oblige him, he told his story.

His father had been a well-to-do merchant in Linz and had meant his son to be a merchant, too. But at fifteen, attracted by the fame of Prince Eugène, the young Franz Huber had run away to join the Imperial armies.

"In those days," Father Huber said, "we were fighting King Philip of Spain and trying to turn him off his throne. Now I am the next best thing to his son's subject. But then I wasn't interested in what wars were about. I thought only of horses, my honour, and winning the praise of the Prince. This was all that was in my mind when I arrived at Audenarde just before the battle. I must have been the most junior officer in the army, yet I was still hoping the Prince would notice me. That's how young men are. But I wasn't to see action that day. We were kept in reserve. I was so disappointed and ashamed that when we joined the troops who'd been fighting, I scarcely dared look at them. As soon as I could, I got behind a hedge, made some rents with my sword in my uniform, and smeared powder on my face and mud on my clothes." Father Huber tipped back his chair and laughed.

He had been present at Denain when the Allies had been defeated by Marshal Villars.

"But the Prince was not to blame", he said. "The Dutch and English left us in the lurch." Each time he mentioned Prince Eugène, he spoke with emotion. Fifty years of the religious life had not obliterated his love and veneration for his hero.

"I remember that battle particularly well", he went on. "After it, I was promoted. How proud I felt! I looked forward to dying as a general or a marshal. Then suddenly God changed everything. I had seen plenty of the horrors of war. Sometimes my heart smote me when I saw our soldiers plundering the peasants' corn. But, for the most part, we looked on these things as unavoidable. However, there came a time when I could no longer stifle my better impulses. We had been besieging a town for months. When it fell, the slaughter was terrible. Among other things, I saw a child's head smashed by a horse's hoof. I don't know why that particular incident stuck in my mind, but it did. A soul redeemed by Christ, I kept saying to myself; and soon after that, I left the army and entered our Society."

He was silent for a minute, gazing at the stove.

"But don't imagine", he said, suddenly speaking with emphasis, "that I'm condemning my fellow soldiers. Crimes are committed in all armies —very often great ones. But the temptations are great, too. It is easy to think you would resist them if you have not been exposed to them. I always pray a lot for soldiers. Now there", he went on in a lighter tone, pointing to one of the portraits, "is a man as great in his own way as the Prince."

"Do they ordain Indians here?"

"Some of our Fathers who were born out here had Indian blood in them. But in this case the artist, not the sitter, was the Indian. A clever boy. I had him paint the likeness from an engraving, and he gave the subject some of his own features. That is Father Montoya, one of the early Jesuit missionaries and, in a sense, the founder of this Reduction. About 150 years ago he converted great numbers of Indians near the source of the Paraná. It is a long way east of here, above the falls of Guayra, in Portuguese territory. With great difficulty he settled his converts in villages and began to teach them how to till the land.

"After a while the inhabitants of São Paulo heard about it—the Paulistas, or Mamelucos, as we still call them. I won't call them Brazilians. There must be in that town men of almost every known race, white and coloured, and I doubt if the name of God is mentioned in it—except as an oath—once in a twelvemonth. And you can imagine that they were, if anything, worse 150 years ago, when the authority of the Portuguese in those parts was weaker than it is today. Their chief business was slaving and still is. Even now they trouble us from time to time.

"Needless to say, no sooner had the Paulistas heard of Father Montoya's Indians, only a couple of hundred miles away, than they set out to capture them. They slaughtered and carried off so many that Father Montoya decided to lead the remainder far enough downstream to be out of their reach and within the power of the Spanish crown.

"The voyage down the Paraná lasted many months. At the Guayra falls they had to abandon their rafts and cut a way through the jungle. Hundreds died on the journey. Some of the survivors joined the rudimentary townships that our priests had already started in this area. The rest Montoya settled in new ones. He himself took over San Miguel, where the priest was sick and dispirited, and put new life into it. Many of our families are descendants of the Indians he brought down the Paraná. Others are descended from Indians converted since his time. About a hundred came to us seven or eight years ago. I don't know if you remember, but they were driven off their land when . . ."

The incident Father Huber was referring to had begun while Alfonso was still a schoolboy.

Around 1750, the Courts of Spain and Portugal, wishing to straighten the frontiers of their colonial empires in South America, had agreed to an exchange of territory. A treaty had been signed and commissioners appointed to implement it. However, the territory to be handed over to Portugal by Spain had included seven Reductions south and east of the river Uruguay, and the Spanish statesmen responsible for the treaty seem to have been unaware of, or uninterested in, the Portuguese government's intentions toward them.

When the Portuguese commissioners arrived, they had ordered the Indians and their pastors in these Reductions to move to Spanish territory. There had followed ten years of revolt, attempted repression, official investigations, charges, and countercharges. Some of the Indians had refused to leave; some had fled to the forests and reverted to savagery; others, led by their priests, had tried to make new homes for themselves on the Spanish side of the frontier but, since the best land was already occupied, had barely managed to survive. Others, again, had sought refuge in already established townships.

The Jesuits, torn between their duty to the civil authorities and their duties to the Indians, had done what they could to obtain justice for their flocks and, where that failed, to persuade the Indians to submit peacefully. That they only partially succeeded should have surprised no one.

At the end of ten years, Charles III, on succeeding to the Spanish throne, had annulled the treaty with Portugal. The territories in question had reverted to their original owners, and the Indians of the seven Reductions, now greatly reduced in numbers, had been allowed to return to their homes.

In Europe the incident had occasioned a torrent of pamphlets and broadsheets accusing the Jesuits of inciting the Indians to rebel against their rightful sovereigns and propagating the legend that the Reductions were an independent state ruled through a puppet emperor, Nicholas.

"Oh, yes," Alfonso said, "we've heard all about that in Europe."

A strange bird call broke the silence outside.

"Unfortunately," Father Huber went on, "the Portuguese and Paulistas aren't the only people who raise problems for us. Some of the Spanish are almost as bad. I'm not thinking of small-fry like the fellow you met this afternoon. It's the big landowners, the *encomenderos*, as we call them, with the right to employ Indian labour on their estates provided they feed them and have them instructed in the faith. They resent the Reductions because they see them as a vast pool of Indian labour they would like to get their hands on and can't. Most of the Indians see working for the *encomenderos* as a form of slavery."

He leaned forward, picked up a poker, and stirred the embers in the stove.

"You know," he said, in a lighter tone, "when I came to Paraguay thirty years ago, hardly anyone I knew back home had even heard of the Guarani Reductions. All they talked about then was the danger of having the French in the Low Countries. Now I am continually getting letters from friends and relations asking whether the Indians have billiard tables and ride in carriages and things of that sort. Our friends often seem as wide of the mark as our enemies. I would like to think that at least some of our enemies are merely ignorant and misguided . . ."

"You credit them with a better faith than I do", Alfonso said. "Anyone who isn't prejudiced in advance must surely see that a handful of priests, unarmed and without soldiers or police, couldn't rule thousands of Indians against their will, much less run a despotism."

"I suppose they persuade themselves, like our friend this afternoon, that we make the Indians obey us by telling them they will go to hell if they don't." Father Huber laughed, showing a greater extent of toothless gum than usual. "But if it were possible to rule simply by the fear of hell, kings and princes would surely try it. Think of what a lot of money they would save. No need for muskets, sabres, prisons, and gaolers, eh!"

An old clock in a battered case on the dresser caught his eye, and he broke off.

"The pleasure of speaking German has made me forget that you must be longing for bed, Father. Forgive my selfishness."

After they had recited compline together in the church, Alfonso went to his room. Father Huber stood for a moment, framed by the open door, holding a candle in one hand and with the other shading the flame from the draught. "Please remember, I'm your friend as well as your superior. If you have any troubles, I hope you will confide in me. I, too, know what it feels like to leave all one's friends and to arrive in a strange and distant country."

THIRTY-THREE

In Europe, among the leaders of the Enlightenment, the Guarani Reductions had long aroused ambiguous feelings. As the work of the Jesuits, they were suspect. On the other hand, in the Reductions the Jesuits had apparently achieved, or come close to achieving, one of *les philosophes'* most cherished goals—the construction of an ideal state according to a single master plan, where everyone would be happy and fulfilled forevermore.

How had the Jesuits succeeded in organising a state so close to their dreams? Where had they found the key? Was it in Plato's *Republic*? Or Thomas More's *Utopia*? Or Campanella's *City of the Sun*? The question had been debated back and forth across Europe for decades. However, it remained unresolved, because enlightened opinion had missed the point.

The Jesuits had not gone to Paraguay to apply a political theory, however familiar some of them may have been with the books just mentioned. They had gone there to convert the Indians from savagery to Christianity, which meant, in the first place, teaching them to live together in harmony according to the principles of the gospel, the natural virtues, and natural justice. The special features of life in the Reductions, which so fascinated the philosophers, were due simply to the difficulties of achieving this aim, given the peculiarities of the Guarani character and the conditions prevailing in Paraguay in the seventeenth and eighteenth centuries.

When the Jesuits had first made contact with the Guaranis about a century and a half earlier, they had found them not at all like the noble savages so popular in the drawing rooms of women like Madame d'Épinay and Madame Geoffrin. Had those ladies had firsthand knowledge of the Guarani's personal habits and public behaviour, they would have almost certainly called them "beastly". Though not the most bellicose Indian tribe, the Guaranis were constantly at war with each other, ate like wild animals, sometimes smeared their bodies in rancid fish oil, from time to time indulged in cannibalism, lived under the rule of witch doctors, and believed in a chief deity who lived in a mysterious dark region infested by bats. Nor, until early missionaries arrived, had it occurred to them that they could live differently and better. Their natural good qualities—their gentleness when well-treated, their skill as craftsmen, their remarkable musical gifts—began to flower only as they were civilised.

At first, the Jesuits had tried to share their wandering, unsettled life in the forests. But they soon saw that it would be impossible for their new flocks to go on living in this way as Christians; they moved about in small groups, sometimes in contact with each other, sometimes not. So with the approval of the Spanish crown and the help of their caciques, the Jesuits had persuaded them to adopt a settled way of life in scattered townships and had taught them to farm. The townships and their lands came to be called Reductions, because the Indians were gathered into them, or "reduced", from the surrounding forests. The Indians had been compliant because this new life had proved better than the old— they had been less often hungry—and because, banded together, they had found it easier to resist their Indian enemies and the Spanish and Portuguese slavers. Some communal ownership had proved necessary because the Indians had no foresight and, if dependent on their private plots alone, would have eaten in six months the food intended for a whole year.

"WE DIVIDE OUR WORK into the material and the spiritual", Father Huber said, after Mass the next morning, while he and Alfonso were eating their breakfast of *yerba* and bread. "I take the former, you take the latter. You will be responsible for everything to do with the church, religion, and schools. I shall be helping you only with confessions. But this morning you had better take a tour of the Reduction so that you will know your way about. Anselmo Cattaguru will be your guide. He is an elderly cacique, not a clever man, but very much respected."

"And do I call him cacique?"

"No. We keep the title, but it is scarcely used. The caciques are descendants of the old tribal chieftains. A lot of them get elected as military commanders and civil officials. Otherwise they are hardly distinguished from the other Indians. Those who have commanded troops in battle, like Anselmo, are called 'captain'. You will find that captain is a popular title in Paraguay. I'm surprised the fellow you brought along with you yesterday didn't call himself captain."

"Is he here still?"

Father Huber looked amused.

"He left in the night—of his own accord—with his two companions. I suspect the guards fell asleep. I'm afraid I shall have to be stern with them."

"What will you do?"

"I've sent a party off to look for them with orders to take them straight to Villarrica, but I doubt if it will find them. Still, there's little harm they can do. We enforce the law only because if the news got around that we were turning a blind eye to its infringement, we should soon be pestered by swarms of these ruffians."

While they had been talking, the sound of singing had been coming in through the window.

"The men are starting for the fields", Father Huber said. "Come. I always ride with them if I can. Anselmo will be waiting outside."

The old cacique was sitting on a stone mounting block outside the college door. Over his white tunic he wore a red cloak, the insignia of his military rank, and his leather belt was heavily worked in intricate multicoloured patterns. A mat of thick grey hair surmounted his grave, dignified face. On seeing the priests, he rose and bowed solemnly, clutching in one hand an ornamented baton. Father Huber's pony was tethered to a ring in the wall beside the mounting block.

Alfonso had hardly greeted the cacique when his attention was attracted by the crowds in the plaza.

Over on the south side, a procession had begun to form, headed by a burly Indian with a pole topped by a crucifix in his right hand. An iron mattock hung from his belt, and although, as he turned this way and that to see what was happening, it swung and knocked against his thigh, it seemed to cause him no more discomfort than if it had been a paper knife. The Indians behind him were singing a hymn to the accompaniment of a band of piccolos, flutes, and trumpets.

Meanwhile, from all around, more men were pouring into the plaza, laughing and talking as they came. They went first to the storehouse, behind the college, to collect their tools. Then they waited on the grass while the officials—distinguished by coloured sashes worn diagonally over the back and chest and by different coloured borders to their tunics—hurried to and fro, allotting the men their tasks and arranging the work parties in line so that those intended for the fields nearest the town were in the rear, those working farther off were in the middle, while those who had farthest to go were in front. The leaders of the individual work parties each carried a pole, topped by the statue of a saint.

"Now, Anselmo," Father Huber said, "see that you show the *padre compañero* everything."

"Trust me, Reverend Father", the cacique said.

Father Huber turned to Alfonso.

"Anselmo showed the Governor around when he was here. Good-bye then, Father. We will meet at midday."

A hush fell on the throng. Father Huber mounted his pony and rode to the head of the procession, raising his straw hat, as he passed, to the statue of the Blessed Virgin on its column in the centre of the square.

"In the name of God, forward!" he cried.

The band began to play again, the church bells rang, the Indians broke into another hymn, and so the procession moved off down the broad earth road lined with women and children waving good-bye.

"Today," Anselmo said, as he watched them go, "today they work in Tabambae. Today and tomorrow and the next day. The day after that and two more days, they will work in Abambae. And then it will be Sunday. On holidays the men go fishing and hunting, and on big feasts we have games and plays and tournaments."

Alfonso already knew from Father Huber that Tabambae was the community land that was worked on Monday, Tuesday, and Wednesday and that Abambae was the land divided into individual plots and allotted to heads of families, which was worked the remaining three days of the week—a system of labour that only occasionally had to be altered to take account of the weather, the ripening of crops, or the attack of pests. Artisans worked two days a week on the community land.

While Anselmo had been talking, a second procession, this one made up of youths and boys with a sprinkling of adults, had been forming. These, he explained, would be working in Tupambae, God's land. The produce of Tupambae was for the support of the sick, the old, widows, orphans. The adults in this group were men who had committed small offences. Working for a spell in Tupambae was their punishment. The punishment lay in being seen publicly as offenders, in not being able to work their own land, and in having to work alongside boys.

This procession, too, moved off to the sound of music and singing.

It was a beautiful morning. The sun was just looking over the tops of the trees, while the cloud that had formed in the night had broken up into countless pieces, now slowly becoming diaphanous, which lay against the blue of the sky like small white islands against the blue of the sea on a map. Birds sped through the air like coloured darts or hopped on the ground in search of insects. Children shouted, chased each other, and tumbled about. In the distance, the women's dresses gleamed against the shadows under the verandas. It was as though during the night the earth's face had been washed with a sponge.

"If it pleases Your Reverence," Anselmo said in correct but curiously accented Spanish, "we will take a turn through the streets first, and you can see what fine children we have. The men in the workrooms will not have settled to their tasks yet."

San Miguel was laid out in straight lines. The streets ran north to south, or east to west; the plaza was exactly in the middle, and the palisade and ditch surrounding the whole were very nearly a perfect square.

On his arrival the night before, Alfonso had entered the plaza from the south—the side occupied by the hospital and the refuge. On the east was the church, flanked by the college and orphanage, and behind it lay the cemetery, running back as far as the palisade. On the north were two school buildings. The workshops, storehouses, and farm buildings were on the western edge of the town. The rest of the area enclosed by the palisade was filled with houses.

Alfonso and the cacique left the square by the main thoroughfare on the south and turned into a tree-lined street running at right angles to it. The houses, set back a little from the trees, were built in blocks of ten to lessen the danger from fire. They were simple one-storey buildings of reddish-brown stone, with tiled roofs that projected in front to form a veranda supported on wooden posts. The houses were all alike except in the small ways that showed the different tastes and characters of the occupants. Some were better kept than others. A number had their fronts plastered and painted, like south German or Austrian farmhouses, with pictures of saints and animals or designs of fruit and flowers. Here and there wicker cages containing pet birds hung from the rafters of the verandas. Elsewhere the verandas were half-hidden by vines.

The children playing in the street were all under five, the others being in school or at work. They ran up to Alfonso as he passed and stopped to stare, thumb in mouth. One or two of the bolder ones took hold of his cassock and trotted a few steps at his side. They were called back by their mothers, who stopped their work to greet the priest in shrill voices, like the cries of startled parakeets. One would be sweeping the floor, another scouring a pot, a third feeding a baby, a fourth returning from the well with water in a jar, a fifth hanging up washing.

"And this is where my eldest son, Dídaco, lives", Anselmo said, stopping before a house no different from the rest, except perhaps in being conspicuously neater and more brightly painted than its neighbours. He looked shyly at Alfonso.

"How beautifully kept it is!" Alfonso said. "Did your son paint the pictures?"

"Yes. He is a good son, but he is not a soldier like me. We will see him at work later, if Your Reverence pleases. He is always painting pictures. There are several in the church. Your Reverence would think they had been done by a Spaniard."

By "a Spaniard", Anselmo meant a non-Indian, the Jesuits of the Reductions having come from all parts of Europe.

"Daughter!" he called.

A woman in her fifties appeared at the door of the house. She held a tiny baby. Anselmo beckoned to her.

"This is my son's wife, Your Reverence. She is looking after her grandson while her daughter is at work. Daughter, this is the *padre compañero*."

"I saw the Father yesterday in the church", she replied.

Her placid face was heavily lined. She smiled at Alfonso and asked him if he would like to hold the baby. Alfonso took it and rocked it for a moment or two.

"Now, Daughter," Anselmo said, "His Reverence has held the child long enough."

"That is not so, Grandfather. See how the little hand clings to His Reverence's finger."

"Never mind. Take her indoors."

Without ill-humour, she took the baby and carried it back into the house.

"Tell me about this picture", Alfonso said, peering at a scene painted on the wall to the right of the door. "It seems to represent a battle."

"You are right, Reverend Father."

Anselmo nodded and looked away at the far side of the street, as though suddenly fascinated by a woman shaking a blanket.

"I can see the soldiers on the right are Christians by the crosses on their tunics. But who are the others?"

"Those are the Paulistas, Reverence."

"Ah, yes. I've heard about them. And when did this battle take place?"

"Ten, twelve years ago. I forget, Reverence."

"It must have been a fierce fight." Alfonso went a step or two nearer the house. "Why, Anselmo!" he said, "The Captain looks remarkably like you. Was it really you?"

Anselmo stared at the ground, frowning so as not to show his satisfaction.

"Well, I congratulate you. It's a brave thing to defend your country-men, and I am glad your son has put this picture here so that people will remember your victory. Where did the battle take place?"

"Many miles from here, Reverence, near the Sierra de Mabaracayu.

We chased the Paulistas more than a hundred miles before we caught
them."

"And you were wounded? I notice that you limp."

"No. That was before. When I was a young man. The Paulistas
captured me and took me to their city. What a place, Reverence. If I
hadn't been there, I wouldn't have believed there was such a wicked
town in the whole world. People of all sorts—Portuguese, Spaniards,
Africans, Indians, all mixed up together—and the women just as bad as
the men. Not a priest in the place to marry them to the men. Not a
church. All day they are swearing, quarrelling, stealing, murdering each
other. I thought I must be in hell. And for the slaves it is terrible. They
are beaten for nothing. A hundred lashes for dropping a dish. Or kicked
to death. Or the tongue cut out, or a hand cut off. I've seen a man
roasted over a fire. It makes you tremble to think of it. But, thanks be
to God, I got away." And he crossed himself.

Alfonso, having never witnessed evil on such a scale, wondered how
much of Anselmo's story could be true.

The old man must have read his thoughts for, drawing aside his cloak
and lifting the hem of his tunic an inch or two above the knee, he
exposed the end of a scar.

"From here to here", he said, touching the top of his hip. The scar
was plainly many years old, but it was still a dull crimson and made a
depression in the thigh half an inch deep. Flesh and skin were knotted
together like badly darned cloth.

"Mother of God!" Alfonso exclaimed, shocked as he had never been
before. "What made that?"

"A hot iron, Reverence. They wanted to lame me to prevent me from
escaping. But I got away, all the same."

"What! Five hundred miles with a wound like that?"

"I thought of my wife and children. I wanted to get back to them. It
took many months. Some Indians hid me in the forest until my leg was
healed. Two of them asked to become Christians. I baptized them and
brought them with me."

As they made their way along the streets, Anselmo stopped outside the houses of some of the other military commanders and of leading officials, praising them as he did so in a voice loud enough to be heard by the women at work inside. This was to prevent the ill-feeling that would be caused were it noticed that the new priest was being shown only the houses of Anselmo's relations.

In civil matters, the Indians ran the towns for themselves with the guidance and help of the Jesuits. The officials responsible for their government corresponded more or less to those of any average Spanish town and were elected annually. They included the *corregidor*, or mayor, his deputy, the *teniente*, four *regidors*, or councillors, three *alcaldes*, or supervisors, a "head of police", and the *alférez real* or royal standard-bearer. Together these officials made up the *cabildo*, or town council. The Indians recognised themselves as subjects of the King, not of the Jesuits, no matter how much they depended upon the latter. Among the lesser officials, civil and ecclesiastical, were the overseers in the fields, the leader of the orchestra, and the sacristans and beadles. All of these posts were much coveted because of the privileges attached to them: authority, a wand of office of some kind; the right to wear a special cloak, a coloured sash, a tunic with an embroidered border; a place of honour at the many festivals.

New officials were elected the first of every January from a list drawn up by the retiring officials and took over from their predecessors on the feast of the Epiphany, with the Spanish colonial government giving the Jesuits the right to challenge nominations they thought unsuitable.

THIRTY-FOUR

As Alfonso and Anselmo approached the western edge of the town, with its workshops, granaries, storehouses, and farm buildings, the sound of hammering and sawing grew louder, and they could hear the roaring of the smithy fire as the smith worked the bellows.

In the first building they stopped at, fifty women were spinning cotton, chatting as they worked. Each held a distaff and balanced a shallow basket on her lap. At the end of the room a statue of St. Ann, mother of the Blessed Virgin, also holding a distaff, overlooked the scene.

Alfonso and Anselmo watched from the doorway.

"That is my granddaughter", Anselmo said, pointing to a girl of about fourteen. "She is the daughter of my third son, Methodius, and will be married next year to the grandson of one of the sacristans."

The girl was not especially pretty, but her face had an attractive freshness and innocence.

"What is her name?"

"Clara, Reverend Father."

"And her future husband's?"

"Xavier. Xavier Tupanchichu."

"And are you pleased, Anselmo?" Alfonso asked, as they moved on.

"Yes. Very pleased. It was the *padre cura*'s work. When he arranges a marriage, the couples are nearly always contented. He knows which ones will suit each other. Xavier is sixteen and a half. It is time for him to marry. If a man cannot make up his mind by the time he is seventeen, the Padre chooses for him. Xavier is good, but he is undecided. However, he will be kind to Clara. He will make her happy. The Padre used to say: 'Xavier, you are fifteen . . . whom are you going to marry?' 'Oh, Reverend Father,' he would reply, 'there is so-and-so and so-and-so, but I don't know which to choose. I will decide in three months.' Then the Padre would say: 'Xavier, you are nearly sixteen now, have you decided yet?' And Xavier's face would grow long. He didn't know which of the girls he liked best. 'Another three months, *padre cura*,' he would answer. After another three months, he thought that maybe he would like a different girl altogether, and then it was not her, but perhaps another, and then he wasn't sure if he didn't prefer the first one after all. 'Well, Xavier,' the Father said at last, 'if you haven't decided by the end of May, I shall have to find a wife for you.' And so it came about, and now Xavier smiles all day long."

Anselmo led the way to one of the long barns where the crops were stored. The air inside was full of fragrant dust. As they entered, rats scuttled across the floor and vanished under the sacks piled up to the rafters on both sides. These, Anselmo explained, were filled with the dried and prepared ilex leaves from which the Paraguayan tea was made. The *yerba* of San Miguel was famous for its high quality, and the Reduction exported large amounts.

"The Governor of Buenos Aires drinks the *yerba* of San Miguel", Anselmo said proudly.

Another barn was filled with sacks of maize, and in yet another, dried manioc, which had an unpleasant, sharp smell, was hanging on strings stretched across the ceiling.

At the carpenters' shop, ten or more Indians were busy shaping rafters and posts, smoothing planks, and nailing together door frames.

Nearby was a hut for the cabinetmakers, joiners, and instrument makers. Between them they made the church furnishings and designed and repaired the musical instruments for the orchestra and bands. A large proportion of the Indians were musical and with training could play and sing the most intricate European pieces. The products of this workshop were also exported downriver to towns like Asunción, Corrientes, and Buenos Aires.

The senior workman left his bench to greet Alfonso.

"Your Reverence would like to see what we are doing?" His ease of manner showed that he was used to showing visitors around his workroom. "This man here is carving a chair for the church at Santa Rosa—to be used by the Bishop. It is in very hard wood, so it takes him a long time, but the ants won't eat it."

The man was kneeling on the floor with his back to them. The foreman bent down and touched his shoulder.

"Hey, Agatho, the new Father is here." Then the foreman looked up at Alfonso and said: "Deaf!"

Alfonso examined the chair, which was equal to anything he had seen in Spain. He ran his hand over the back and arms.

"Beautiful!" he said.

The deaf workman watched Alfonso's lips and then expressed his thanks with toneless cries.

175

"Dumb, too", the foreman said cheerfully. He stooped to pick up the sheet of paper with the design the man was working from.

A violin with a broken peg was hanging from the wall. Alfonso asked if he could look at it, and the foreman took it down and gave it to him.

Leaning against a bench, Alfonso began to tune it, testing the strings with his thumb. The Indians gathered round him to watch.

"The Padre can play?"

"A little. But the violin was not made here."

"Yes, yes." All three Indians nodded their heads emphatically and laughed with satisfaction.

"When the Bishop came," Anselmo said, "he told us that the Pope does not have violins in his church to compare with ours."

"I'm certain the Pope would be very pleased to have a violin as good as this", Alfonso said. "Was this made from an Italian model?"

The foreman looked puzzled.

"Brother Adolphe taught us how to make them."

"Brother Adolphe? That sounds like a German name, but this looks like an Italian instrument. Does the Brother come here often? I would like to talk to him."

"Brother Adolphe is dead."

"He died before my father was born."

"We never saw him."

"But this is how he made violins."

Alfonso's questions seemed to have upset the Indians, so to dispel the strain he tucked the violin under his chin and played a tune pizzicato. Smiles immediately reappeared on the Indians' faces, and as though he could hear the music, the deaf-mute danced and clapped his hands.

After the joiners' shop came the blacksmith's forge, the foundry, the sugar refinery, and the tailor's shop. Everything needed for the life of the community and the service of the church that was within the capacity of the Indians to make, they made.

"And this is where the people come to get their meat", Anselmo explained, as he led the way to a building which backed against the

176

palisade and had a well-trampled yard in front. "The people line up at these windows, and the men inside pass the meat out to them. Every day they kill many beasts for us to eat. The Lord provides well for us. When I meet one of the Indians in the forests, I say to him, 'Why don't you become a Christian, then you wouldn't be hungry.'"

"But what would you say, Anselmo, if the Lord allowed a famine?"

"I would say he allowed it to try our faith and because of our sins, Father. But a heathen doesn't know what sin is. So I tempt him—like the devil—but in the right direction. I am a good angel to him. And I'm not lying, because all my life we've had enough to eat. Now, come this way, Father, and I will show you something special."

He entered the building.

"Please to lower your head", he said over his shoulder as he pushed a dangling carcass to one side. "Your Reverence does not object, I hope. Sometimes it turns the stomach."

Alfonso had a confused impression of raised hatchets, gleaming knives, blood-stained tunics, heaps of offal and dismembered limbs. Then he followed Anselmo out of the back of the slaughterhouse, through a gate in the palisade, across the ditch, and into some trees and bushes which hid the fields from the town. On the far side they stopped in a huge enclosure, half-encircled by sheds and cow byres. The muddy ground churned by the hooves of hundreds of cattle was a mass of little pointed brown waves, like a choppy sea. In a similar enclosure on the right, a man was breaking in a horse.

Alfonso had stopped to watch a group of birds called hangnests quarrelling in the branches of a *quebracho* tree.

"Come and look at this", Anselmo called.

The cacique leaned his arms on the paling that separated the two enclosures. Seeing him, the horse trainer was about to bring the horse to a stop, but Anselmo signed to him to continue. So the Indian gave the lunging rein a jerk, and the horse, which had slackened its pace, continued to circle at a canter.

"All our horses are good," Anselmo said, "but this will be one of the best. The *padre cura*, who can do anything with a horse, taught this man. The horse belongs to the Saint. It's the horse the royal standard-bearer will ride on the Feast of San Miguel."

The horse seemed to know it was being admired, for it suddenly swished its tail, arched its neck, and increased its speed. After it had circled the ring a few more times, the trainer drew in the rein and led it up to the paling.

"Good morning, Captain", he said shyly to Anselmo, and then looked expectantly at Alfonso, waiting to be presented.

"This is Nicolás. He is the son of my sister's husband's cousin."

Nicolás grinned.

"How old is he?" Alfonso asked, patting the horse's neck.

"Two, Reverence."

"And how soon will he be ready to ride?"

"Another month, Reverence."

"He has a good trainer", Alfonso said with a smile.

Nicolás looked down at his bare feet and moved his toes in the mud. The conversation, short as it was, had made him perfectly happy.

Anselmo dismissed him with a wave of his baton.

As they left the enclosure, he pointed out the mill standing among the trees by the river, which ran parallel to the north side of the town. But there was no need to look at that, Anselmo said. He was sure the *padre compañero* had seen many a mill before.

"And that building in the far distance?" Alfonso asked.

"The tannery. It smells strong, so we built it a long way off." For some reason Anselmo suddenly seemed anxious to press ahead.

Outside the north gate, they looked at the pool where the Indians took their weekly bath—the men one day, the women and children another. The bottom and sides were lined with cut stone. At the corners there were steps to make it easier for the old and the small children to get in and out. The pool was fed by a spring which poured itself in a gleaming arc, smooth as glass, from the mouth of a stone mask, and on the opposite side the overflow made its way through an artificial channel to the river. A border of palm trees a few feet from the edge shaded the water from the sun.

"Clothes are washed in the river", Anselmo said laconically. "They must not be washed here, or the offenders will be punished."

Alfonso bent down and put his hand into the water to feel the temperature. As he did so, he was again conscious that Anselmo was anxious to move on.

They returned to the plaza and entered the church where Anselmo's eldest son was at work.

"Dídaco."

"Father?"

The son was crouched on a scaffold against the wall of one of the chapels. At the sound of Anselmo's voice, he took the paint brushes out of his mouth, swung his legs over the edge of the platform, and jumped to the ground.

"This is Dídaco, my eldest son", the cacique said. "Tell the *compañero* what you are doing."

Dídaco explained his painting—St. Leo the Great repelling Attila and his Huns, with the help of St. Peter and St. Paul.

"See!" Anselmo said excitedly. "The Pope was like us. Bad men tried to capture his city and burn it. Here they are over on this side. They were savage and cruel like the Paulistas. They made war on him. And here is the Pope with Rome behind him. He prays, and St. Peter and St. Paul drive them away. Our people love St. Leo very much. When the Paulistas come, the men go out to fight, and the women pray to St. Leo."

Dídaco watched his father gravely. His face was serious and intelligent, and he explained his work in a practical, businesslike way. He was working in fresco, he said. Some of the paints he prepared himself, but a few colours had to be brought from over the sea. Unlike some of the other craftsmen they had talked to that morning, he seemed to have a genuine grasp of the principles underlying the techniques he had been taught. He picked up a book of engravings, open at the page he was copying, and showed it to Alfonso. The original was by Guercino, but Dídaco had altered the picture considerably. The choice of colours was his own, since the engraving was in black and white, but he had also changed the posture of the figures. The result was less suave than the original but more arresting.

"My picture is different, is it not?" Dídaco asked, a smile drawing up the corners of his mouth.

"You are an artist, Dídaco. A true artist always has his own way of expressing himself."

Dídaco put a finger on the engraving.

"In this picture the people are waving their arms and legs in a foolish way. This is not right. You do not see men in those positions. And look. This angel is pulling away a curtain. But they are in a field. Why should there be a curtain? And this angel here ought to be watching what he is doing instead of smiling out of the picture at us."

The old cacique listened, scarcely understanding a word, but much happier than if he had understood, for then his son would have seemed less clever.

"Tell the padre how you mix paints, son. With an egg, Reverence, would you believe it?"

Alfonso saw that Dídaco wanted to get back to his work, so he complimented the painter once more, and they left the church.

"Well, Anselmo, what next?"

"Whatever Your Reverence pleases. There's the school and the cemetery and the pharmacy." He paused and looked upwards, as though searching his memory, then added quickly, "And the arsenal."

Ah, Alfonso thought, that's what he wants me to see so badly. "The arsenal", he said aloud. "I'd like to see that."

When they reached the long, black building, the cacique put his head in at the door of the house alongside.

"Wife", he called.

"You are guardian of the arsenal, then?" Alfonso asked, as they waited under the veranda.

"The *padre cura* does me the honour. I am not worthy of it."

"It is a very responsible post."

Anselmo presented his wife, who was tall and dignified like her husband. Her dress hung in long, straight folds, and she wore a piece of woollen cloth over her head, like a Roman matron. She was strikingly like her son Dídaco, but in a tenderer mode.

Inside the arsenal, four men were sitting at a long table polishing a cannon. Farther down the room was a group of men cleaning muskets and sabres and cutlasses. There was a smell of burned powder and gun oil.

Anselmo pointed the door into the armoury.

"That room is full of weapons", he said. "So many I can't keep all the numbers in my head. But it is full, full. We have to have many weapons. Often the Viceroy sends for us. We fight for the King alongside the Spanish soldiers. We help to protect the frontier. We help to protect the Spanish settlers, as well as ourselves, even though the settlers are not always good to us."

He said something rapidly to the men at the far end of the room.

They disappeared into the armoury and soon returned with some of the prize pieces captured from the enemies of the San Miguel Indians over a period of nearly 150 years: arquebuses with ornate brass fittings, swords with inlaid hilts and heavily chased blades, pikes, halberds, steel caps, breastplates, embossed shields.

"Are they not beautiful?" Anselmo asked, as he handed the weapons lovingly one by one to the priest.

THIRTY-FIVE

The next day Alfonso started work.

Among other duties, he was responsible for supervising the education of the six hundred children in the Reduction. All of them attended the junior school, where they learned to read and write, speak simple Spanish, and do addition and subtraction. The cleverer boys went on to the senior school, where they were taught more advanced arithmetic, bookkeeping, Church Latin, and music. Jacinto Epaguini, the head teacher, presided over both schools.

Jacinto was about sixty. Small and lean, he had a dropped right eyelid which made him look as if he were perpetually winking. The other Indians regarded him as a kind of magician. He could add six-figure sums in fifteen seconds; he could recite the four Gospels by heart; he could read and write in three languages—Spanish, Latin, and Guarani; he possessed books of his own; he knew the history of Paraguay from the first arrival of the Europeans; and he had been many times to Buenos Aires and once, long ago, to Lima. The insignia of his office for solemn occasions was a silver-mounted inkhorn with a wild boar's tooth for a stopper, which he wore hanging from his belt by a chain.

Catechism, a privileged subject, was taught in church. The children sat row upon row, with their light walnut-coloured faces and brown eyes fixed on Alfonso, who stood at the top of the nave holding a white baton. First he read out the questions in a singsong voice. Then he waved his baton, and the children chanted the answers in a psalm tone—a method which, it had been discovered, helped them memorize the words.

Alfonso also had children to prepare for their first Communion, a choir and an orchestra to supervise, thirty altar boys to direct, and the sick of the town to visit. In the evenings, he presided at meetings of sodalities, except on Saturdays, when he and Father Huber heard confessions.

Four sacristans, two carpenters, and a mason looked after the upkeep of the church. They greeted Alfonso's arrival with joy. While Father Huber had been without an assistant priest, they had had to manage largely by themselves, a state of affairs they disliked intensely. With sombre satisfaction, they led Alfonso about to show him the evidence of dilapidation and decay.

"See, Father, the roof is leaking. The men who sit under this part have complained."

"Come and look at the south bell tower, Father. Insects are eating the beams."

"What shall we do, Father? We ordered new glass from Buenos Aires for the windows of the nave. A storm broke them. But they've only sent us half what we need. We don't know where the rest is."

"Please, Father, you must speak severely to the boys. They are cutting marks and letters in the pillars."

As soon as Alfonso had settled one lot of problems, others arose. A hinge on the west door was giving way. Should it be mended or replaced? A moth had eaten holes in one of the best copes. How was it to be mended without showing?

"I used to think buildings were such durable things", Alfonso said to Father Huber. "Now I'm amazed the church stays standing overnight."

Father Huber laughed.

"*Sic transit gloria mundi*. Nothing brings that home to one like having to take care of property."

September came, and with it the rains. Winter turned to summer, with no intervening spring. The bare lapacho trees suddenly burst into pink blossom. As evening came on, armadillos left their burrows and trotted about the plains, looking like small, long-snouted, armour-plated pigs. Christmas was celebrated in a temperature of 95°, to be followed by a scorching January and February. In the first week of Lent, a jaguar was killed in the thickets near the tannery, and a plague of caterpillars destroyed a part of the tobacco crop. In March the cotton and manioc were harvested. Then, just before Easter, a cool wind from the south sprang up. Everywhere, by now, the grass was a pale biscuit colour, and from a distance the forest looked like a wall of dusty felt. In late April rain fell, and everything became fresh and green again.

As Alfonso was crossing the plaza from the senior school to the hospital one day, he suddenly realised that he had been at San Miguel a year.

THIRTY-SIX

A mile from the town, where the fields met the forest, Xavier Tupanchichu was sleeping under a paraiso tree. Twenty other Indians lay round about, as still as stones. They had eaten their midday meal, and the sun was warm. Their tools were heaped at the foot of the paraiso tree.

Only the overseer was awake. He sat plaiting leather thongs to make a belt. After a time, he looked at the sun, raised a horn to his lips, and blew into it. One man stirred. The overseer blew a second blast, and the other men began to wake.

Xavier raised himself on his left elbow and stared sleepily at the field of sugar cane in front of him, which crackled like burning twigs when stirred by the breeze. In the distance there were more paraiso trees, as well as palms, cedars, urundays, and quebrachos. With the sun shining directly down on them, they looked almost black. Apart from his companions, there was no one in sight. Everything was silent and peaceful.

"What are you smiling at?" asked Crisóstomo Gato, who was standing beside Xavier, tightening his belt.

Xavier rubbed the top of his head.

"I had a dream."

"What about?"

"Wait. I shall have to remember."

"Hurry, or Agustín will blow his horn again."

"Go and ask him if we can work together. Then I will tell you."

While Crisóstomo went to ask the overseer's permission, Xavier followed the other men to a chapel that stood on a hillock just behind the paraiso tree. The chapel, dedicated to St. Isidore, the Spanish farmer saint, had adobe walls and a thatched roof.

Inside it was dark. The altar was heaped with flowers. The figure of St. Isidore was just visible. Xavier knelt down.

Lord, he prayed, I offer you my work for the rest of today, and please may everything come about as it happened in my dream. He crossed himself, got up, left the chapel, and went back to the paraiso tree to fetch his tools. Crisóstomo was waiting for him.

"What did Agustín say?" Xavier asked.

"He said yes. But we mustn't be idle."

The Indians were harvesting the sugar crop. They returned to their work, some talking, some singing, and carrying their bows and arrows as well as their tools. San Miguel, being on the northern edge of the Reduction territory, was more exposed to the raids of Indians from the forests and of Portuguese slavers than were the townships to the south.

Working in pairs, the men began cutting the canes in strips six feet wide across the field. When their strips merged with the adjacent ones, they shouldered their tools and moved farther down the field to cut a fresh lane.

Xavier and Crisóstomo went to the spot where Xavier had broken off at midday.

"In the name of the Father and of the Son and of the Holy Ghost", Xavier said, crossing himself and beginning to slice the canes energetically.

"Your dream", Crisóstomo said. "You still haven't told me what it was."

"Why do you want to know?"

"Come on. Tell me." Crisóstomo gave Xavier a push.

Xavier pushed him back. They closed and wrestled, then fell on the ground struggling, laughing, kicking. When they stopped, Crisóstomo was on top.

"Tell me! Tell me! Tell me!" he shouted, pummelling Xavier's chest.

"Stop! Stop! I will. Stop!"

Crisóstomo let him go, and they struggled to their feet. Xavier rubbed his back, which had been cut and bruised by the cane stumps left in the ground.

"San Miguel. It hurts."

Crisóstomo scratched his leg.

"I don't think your dream was worth it."

"Wait till you hear! I dreamed that I was married to Clara and that I played the part of the Archangel on the feast of San Miguel."

"Is that all?"

"What do you mean?"

"There's nothing special about a dream like that. Didn't you have adventures? Everyone knows you're going to be married. As for playing San Miguel, you're too young. It's impossible."

"Why? Anyhow, I'm more likely to get the part than you are."

A voice called from the next lane.

"You boys had better start working. Agustín will be after you if you don't."

"All right, grandfather", Crisóstomo called back.

They set to work, cutting the canes close to the ground and tying them in bundles.

As they moved along, side by side, there was little to distinguish them. Both were of medium height with strong, compact bodies and arms and legs as solid as logs. Crisóstomo had, perhaps, the less intelligent face but made up for the lack by his cheerfulness. Life at San Miguel, for the young at any rate, had few problems. When his stomach was full and his body warm, he had all he wanted. Xavier's face was more reflective-looking, as if he were already aware that things in this world do not always go smoothly.

These differences apart, their outlooks were identical. Their world, the only world that mattered, was a circle of countryside around San Miguel with a radius of about ten miles. On the circumference lay a band of country where the known became confused with the unknown. They were conscious only of forests and plains like those close to home, stretching away without end. Although they had been told that the world was round, the information left their outlook unchanged. Neither of them had considered that the forests and plains must have an end somewhere.

Outside this green and pastoral universe, they knew, apart from the

186

names of some of the other Reductions, the names of only five or six cities. That of the Paulistas was in the direction of the rising sun. Asunción was where the sun set. Buenos Aires was where you looked when you turned your back on the sun at midday. They also knew that somewhere there was a large piece of water called "sea", which they pictured as a river ten or twenty times as broad as the Paraná. Beyond that was more land—similar to their own—where the Pope and the King lived. And Jesus, the Blessed Virgin, and most of the saints had lived there, too. But since Jesus was in the church, and the Blessed Virgin and the saints were in heaven, which was plainly close at hand since prayers could be heard there, they felt no sense of loss in knowing that the earthly home of Christ and his Mother was so far away.

How small, how circumscribed their world! On the other hand, they were troubled by no uncertainty about the purpose of their existence. They were to work for God in this world in order to be happy forever in the next. Working for God meant mainly growing food to support themselves and their families, when they had them, and, once they were married, having children so that God would have lots of souls to fill up heaven and to take the place of the angels who had rebelled.

The shadows giving dimensions to this picture were illness and accident and sin. Illness and accidents meant pain. Big sin, pleasant at the moment of indulgence, meant, if discovered, punishment by the *alcaldes* or *corregidor* and later, if unrepented, hell.

The devils were busy everywhere, and besides the devils, a man had another horde of enemies in his passions. Who could tell which was responsible, the flesh or the devil, when a man found his neighbour's lost tool, bow, or belt and itched to keep it for himself; when, at an insult, the blood raged in his veins and he gripped the handle of his knife; or when at dusk, in a lonely part of the Reduction, he unexpectedly met a woman or girl returning home by herself and had to struggle to pass her by with no more than a greeting?

Fortunately, the angels and saints outnumbered the devils by more than two to one and were quick to bring help. If a man gave way to his passions, the damage could be repaired in the wooden cupboard in the church, where, through the curtained hole in the partition, the padres dispensed the mercy and forgiveness of God.

THIRTY-SEVEN

Xavier and Crisóstomo had already worked their way back and forth across the field several times and were once more drawing near the far side, where the woods grew close to the edge, when suddenly Xavier shouted, "Look out!"

Crisóstomo, who had his knee on a bundle of canes and was tightening the rope around it, turned his head quickly.

"What's the matter?"

But it was unnecessary to ask. Xavier was already snatching up his bow and arrows. Crisóstomo instinctively reached for his own and scrambled to his feet.

About a hundred yards off, at the edge of the forest, just out of the shadow of the trees, stood a man with a spear. Instead of being dressed like the Indians of the Reductions, he was half-naked.

Xavier put an arrow in his bow and pulled the string, ready to shoot. To their surprise the man fell on his knees.

"Stop! Stop!" he shouted in a dialect sufficiently like their own to be intelligible. "Don't shoot!"

Xavier and Crisóstomo approached him cautiously. The man, who was bedraggled and dirty, had long tangled hair with a broken parrot's feather in it. His arms and legs were covered with cuts and bruises. In case the plea for mercy was not genuine, Crisóstomo took away the stranger's spear and made him unfasten the knife at his waist.

The man, still on his knees, pulled it off and forced it into Crisóstomo's hands.

"Take it! Take it! I'm your prisoner. Don't kill me!"

Xavier looked puzzled.

"What do you want?" he asked.

"I'm your prisoner. I want to live here. My people are looking for me. They want to kill me."

Up to this moment, under the influence of their first emotion, Xavier and Crisóstomo had looked hostile and suspicious. But once the stranger had spoken of wanting to live at San Miguel, their attitude changed.

Crisóstomo went off to find Agustín, the overseer. He soon returned with him, followed by the other members of the working party, who, out of curiosity, wanted to see the new arrival for themselves. They surrounded him, touched him, stroked him as though he were a young animal, told him how sensible he was to come and live with them and how good the life was at San Miguel.

"The men who are chasing you," Agustín asked, "are they close?"

"No, no. They will not follow me here", the man answered. "They are afraid of the big guns that run along the ground and fire heavy stones."

As the man seemed close to exhaustion, it was decided to send him back to town with Xavier, whose arm he had not ceased to clutch, on one of the oxcarts that stood ready loaded at the edge of the field. The San Miguel Indians all offered their ponchos to spread on the bundles of sugarcane, and it was some minutes before Agustín could establish which of the ponchos should be used.

When the man tried to stand, it became clear that he had either broken a bone in his right foot or badly sprained it. He gave a sharp cry and sat down again. Carefully, with jokes and encouraging remarks, the Indians lifted him onto the wagon. Xavier climbed up beside him, putting an arm round his back to keep him from falling off. The carter struck his beasts on the flank with his whip, and they set off.

Besides the injury to his foot, the man had an arrow wound in his left shoulder, which Xavier tried to staunch with the hem of his tunic.

"Why did your people want to kill you?" he asked.

"The medicine men are afraid. They want to stop us from running away to join the Christians."

"Why are they afraid?"

"Because if everybody joins the Christians, the medicine men will have no more power. We used to live far away from here to the north. We had never heard about Christians. But there was not enough food. Other tribes, stronger ones, took it all. So we came south. Then we heard about the Christians and the different way you live. Some of us thought, 'If we join the Christians, we shall always have enough to eat, and maybe we won't have to be giving presents to the medicine man all the time.' So my brother and I ran away, but they shot him in the thigh and caught him."

The man started to whimper, but at the sight of the town he stopped and looked about him with awe.

The carter drove his wagon into the plaza. Xavier jumped down and went to look for Father Huber. Some women gathered at a distance. After staring at the man and the wagon for a while, most of them hurried off to tell their neighbours. An older woman advanced a little and beckoned to the carter.

She gave him a pitcher of milk, a loaf of bread, and some meat. The carter passed them to the stranger, who snatched them greedily and, lifting the pitcher, emptied it without removing it from his lips. He then attacked the bread and meat. The women watched with interest and murmured sympathetically when they saw how hungry he was.

"Good?" the carter asked.

The man nodded and kept filling his mouth. When he had finished, he gazed in a stupefied way at his benefactress and her companions, as though coming out of a trance.

"Very good people!" he said.

"I'll tell them you said so", the carter replied. "They're pleased to see you. Here, give me the jug. They won't thank us if we break it."

"Who is the woman on top of the big tree trunk?" The stranger was staring at the top of the column in the centre of the square.

"That's the Mother of God."

"Why is she up there?"

"So that all the people can see her."

The man was silent for a moment.

"Who is God?" he asked.

"Who is God? Why, the Lord. The One who made everything. He who lives above." The carter jabbed a finger at the sky. Then suddenly his voice became sharp. "What are you doing? Take care. You'll have my load of canes on the ground."

The stranger, his eyes still raised toward the statue, was trying to kneel on top of the uneven bundles of sugarcane.

"That's not the Mother of God herself, friend", the carter said, forcing the man to lie down again. "That's a piece of stone made to look like her. She's in heaven. That's the place we go to when we die—if we are good. The Lord lives in that house there." The carter pointed to the church. "But you needn't kneel to him now. We kneel when we go inside."

"What is the Mother of God carrying?"

"The Lord, her son. No. Not the Lord himself. Another piece of stone made to look like the Lord when he was a baby. The Lord is in the church, as I told you. You can't see him because he is hidden. But he is there. A very long time ago the Lord came from heaven and made himself a man, and when he became a man he chose a mother for himself. Later his enemies killed him, but he came alive again and went back to heaven with his own body. Now he lives in many places at the same time. He is in heaven, but he also lives with us."

"Is the Lord's mother God, too?"

"No, she's not."

"Why did the Lord make himself a man?"

"To help us to get to heaven. Do you want to go to heaven?"

The man reflected an instant.

"Are they good to you in heaven like those women there who gave me the food?"

"More good."

"Then I want to go there."

"The *padre cura* will show you how."

At this moment Father Huber arrived with two *regidors* and an *alcalde*. Whenever Father Huber was about, the Indians seemed immediately to see what had to be done and to set about doing it quickly and deftly. The *regidors* climbed on the cart and lifted the man down.

"Gently, gently", Father Huber said. "Welcome, my son. We are very happy to see you. That's right, lower his legs first. Hold on! Xavier, get that poncho and spread it on the ground so they can lay him on it. My poor boy, what a mess you've got yourself into. Now let's see what's the matter." He knelt down and examined the man's shoulder, touching the flesh lightly all around the wound. Then he felt the ankle.

"Does that hurt?"

"Yes, Lord."

"I am called 'Father', my son. Can you move your ankle from side to side?"

The man waggled his foot.

"Good. It's not broken, then. A bad sprain, I expect." He turned to an official. "Take him to the hospital, and tell them to dress the wound and bandage the leg. I will be there shortly to see how he is." He smiled at the stranger. "They will take you to that house over there. It is where they look after the sick. You can spend the night there. Xavier, go with him and keep him company. Tomorrow we will see how you are."

Since first catching sight of Father Huber, the man had kept his eyes firmly fixed on him.

"Will you send me away tomorrow?"

"No. You can stay with us as long as you like. Only you will have to learn our customs and live as we do. Do you think you can?"

The man nodded.

They brought a litter; then Father Huber hastened off to finish the business he had interrupted. On the way to the hospital, Xavier walked beside his charge and encouraged him by telling him how kind the people at the hospital were and how comfortable he would be there. The man listened.

"Is the Father a cacique?" he asked.

"No. He's a priest."

"What is a priest?"

Xavier looked perplexed, never before having had to define the word.

192

What is a priest? Well, the *padre cura* is a priest, he thought, and so is the *padre compañero*. They say Mass and hear confessions. They baptize and put oil on people when they are dying. He began to think of other things the priests did, such as reading prayers out of a black book—far too many things to tell the stranger just now.

"The priest", he said, "does for us what Jesus would do if he were living with us and we could see him." Then he remembered the stranger did not know who Jesus was. He suddenly felt overwhelmed by the difficulty of describing his religion, since it seemed necessary to explain the very words in which the description was couched. "Jesus is God", he said, with a feeling of helplessness.

But the man's attention had wandered.

"Am I a Christian now?" he asked.

"Not yet."

"But the Father said I could live here if I do as you do."

"To be a Christian you must be baptized. The Father will pour water on your head, which will wash away your sins."

"Will he do it tonight?"

"Oh, no. First you must learn about God, what he is like and what you must do to serve him so as to get to heaven."

"I know already."

Xavier smiled, as if a three-year-old child were telling him he could read Latin.

"Yes," said the man, "the Lord lives in that house over there. He has a body like a man. He had a mother who was a woman. To get to heaven I must do as you do and the women who gave me the food to eat do."

Xavier stared at him.

"Who told you that?"

"The man with the cart."

"Oh, that's not all. There's more than that to learn," Xavier said loftily, planning in his mind what he was going to say to the carter later for daring to interfere with his catechumen. Then he noticed that the stranger was gazing questioningly at him, as though asking "Am I not right?" and he felt ashamed.

193

"That's very good", he said, smiling. "The Father is sure to baptize you very soon. But you will have to have a new name." He scratched his thigh with the tip of his bow. "What about Wenceslaus?"

The man repeated the name slowly, pronouncing the syllables one by one.

"Yes," he said, "it is good. I like it. What is it? Is it the name of an animal?"

"It's the name of a saint", Xavier said, looking scandalised. This time he forgot to explain what a saint was.

They reached the hospital. The *regidor* repeated Father Huber's instructions to the guardian, and the stranger was taken into the men's ward. There he was washed, dressed in a cotton shirt and cotton trousers, and given a cot to lie on. He submitted to these attentions with an expression of naïve pleasure. Then his wound was dressed and his ankle bandaged. The two other invalids in the ward sat up on their cots to watch. As the guardian, his assistants, and the two *alcaldes* blocked the view, Xavier gave them, from the bedside, a running commentary on what as going on.

"The wound is as long as my thumb and two inches broad . . . they say it won't be necessary to sew it up . . . it has stopped bleeding . . . now it's being washed . . . there's a lot of mud in it . . . he says he fell down several times . . . there's a piece of muscle showing . . . it looks like bow strings . . . now they are pulling out a bit of metal . . . it's stuck . . . no, it isn't . . . yes . . . no . . . here it comes . . . it's about the size of a fingernail . . . the foot is not broken . . . but it's badly bruised . . . the skin is black . . . he says it doesn't hurt much, but I think it does . . . he's just groaned . . . he says the bandage pinched him."

The two sick Indians listened attentively. When the sufferer groaned, they groaned in sympathy. As soon as the dressing was finished and the newly named Wenceslaus lay back on his cot, one of them, who was smoking a pipe, took it from his mouth and, getting out of bed, crossed the room and placed it between the stranger's lips. Xavier, continuing his role of spokesman, told them Wenceslaus' story.

"He ran away. He was afraid. When he was telling me about it, he cried. Some of his brothers are very wicked. He says he hopes a jaguar will catch them. But I have told him he must forgive them. He would like to be a Christian, but he is still very ignorant."

Wenceslaus puffed his pipe and listened with a contented smile, as if he were being praised for valour. Feeling shy, he was glad to have someone to speak for him, but the experience of being a focus of concern was new and pleasing. At last he fell into a doze, and Xavier, after watching him for some time, said good-bye to the other men and tiptoed away.

THIRTY-EIGHT

It was late afternoon. The sound of singing announced the return of the Indians from the fields, and the streets were full of white-clad figures all moving in one direction, as the artisans and craftsmen, after closing their shops for the night, made their way to church. Among them went Clara, Anselmo's granddaughter, holding the hand of a friend.

They were not late. There was no need to hurry. The sooner they got to church, the longer they would have to wait. Nevertheless, they ran—making a zigzag through the throng—just because they were young and full of energy.

Inside the church, they took their place on the women's side, among the unmarried girls. They knelt down. After a short prayer, Clara's companion nudged her.

"In a few months," she whispered, "you will be sitting back there."

Clara looked round at the benches where the married women sat.

"So will you one day", she replied.

The other girl sighed. She knew the boy she would like to marry, but neither the boy nor his parents seemed to have thought about asking to have her as a wife.

"It will be a long time. How I shall miss you!"

Clara was going to say: "I shall miss you, too", but then she thought it would be silly to do that since it was only in church that they would be separated. To console her friend, she pressed her hand. Then they recollected where they were, took out their beads, and bent their heads.

As usual, the *padre compañero* was leading the night prayers, and, as usual, Clara thought how far he had come and how frightened she would be at having to go so far away from her home, and she thanked God for sending him.

When prayers were over, the two girls made their way through the crowd in the plaza and ran off, each to her own home.

Clara's mother was cooking the supper in an enclosure at the back of the house. Nearby some chickens were scratching in the dust, and a solitary gander, head lowered, was hissing at a rooster parading up and down on the other side of the fence to the left.

"Are you there, my love, my pet, my chick?" she called. "Here, take this to old Angela across the street. She's sick, and her husband is out with the cattle. I've cooked something for her that will give her an appetite." She handed Clara a pot covered with a leaf. "And afterward just run out and give these to Pedro's daughter." She tucked two flat loaves like large pancakes under Clara's arm. "Her husband is a sluggard and a glutton. He neglects his land and eats his wife's share of food as well as his own. She's too good to him—or too soft; I don't know which. Ah, my pet, marriage isn't all beef and sweet dreams. Still, your Xavier is a good boy." She kissed her daughter. It was a wet kiss, which made a sound like a ripe apricot falling on a damp flagstone.

Clara's mother was short and fat, and her wide, good-natured mouth was seldom shut. She had had eight children and possessed that imperturbability usual in women who have successfully brought up large families—who have learned to cook, scrub, and mend and do all the things expected of a mother, with babies constantly crying for attention or getting in their way as they work. She loved all her children, but Clara was her favourite.

Still running, Clara went on her errands. At one point she skipped, until it occurred to her that this was not fitting in a woman soon to be married. On the way back, however, she walked slowly and tears kept coming into her eyes.

Her mother looked up from the fire.

"What's the matter, my chick?"

Clara knelt down and hid her face in her mother's lap. "I don't know. I don't know. It's so sad", she sobbed.

"What's so sad, my pet, my chick?"

"Pedro's daughter."

"But you've often seen her before."

"Yes, but I didn't understand. Her face is so thin, and her eyes . . . when she thanked me, I couldn't look at them. They made me want to cry. Oh, why is she so unhappy?"

Although her last words were a question, she did not want an answer. Everybody was familiar with the story of Pedro's daughter. But Clara had suddenly had an intimation of how much wretchedness there might be in an unhappy marriage. She grieved for the poor wife. But she was also frightened by what she had seen in a different abyss she had just glanced into. Pedro's daughter was good. Why should her marriage be a source of misery? If good people could have unhappy marriages, how could she be sure that her own would not go wrong? Was it possible that life with Xavier, which she had thought was going to be all happiness and contentment, might inexplicably be the reverse?

The mother put a thick arm round the girl and pressed her to her side, while with the other arm she continued to stir the pot.

"There, there, little one! We must all learn sooner or later. Life's full of troubles—like a loaf of bread with grit in it. We must swallow what we can and spit out the rest."

"But Pedro's daughter has so much more to suffer than other people", Clara said.

The mother glanced up at the crucifix on the wall.

"She's not alone", she said. "In heaven she will be a great princess."

"Is her husband very bad?"

"How can we tell? The Lord is his judge. For myself, I think he may be a bit soft in the head. There, now, I hear them coming, and the food isn't ready. Hurry, girl, and give me a hand."

The preparations were not difficult to make. The family ate sitting on the floor and had a bowl and spoon apiece. The men also had their knives.

The house, separated from those on either side by a lath and plaster wall, consisted of two rooms—the living room and a smaller one leading off it where the parents slept. At night the living-room was divided into compartments by rush screens which, during the day, were stacked against a wall. The hides on which everyone slept, and the blankets to go with them, were kept in the inner room. The only solid piece of furniture was a chest in which the family's best clothes were stored. There was a shelf for the cooking pots, a row of pegs for hats, cloaks, belts, and weapons, a broom standing in a corner, a mirror hanging on a nail, and a holy picture. A second shelf, on the wall separating the two rooms, held the private treasures of each member of the family. For the girls it would be a little basket containing needles and thread, a necklace, a pair of scissors, a religious picture or statuette (these last, the work of a friend or a prize for industry or good conduct). For the boys it was, perhaps, a knife, some smooth stones for their slings, a religious medal or two carefully wrapped in a cotton rag, or some natural curiosity like an oddly shaped nut or an alligator's tooth. Hanging from the rafters, along with strings of manioc and lumps of dried beef, was a rush basket in which the youngest member of the family, a baby six months old, was sleeping.

The father, Methodius, a carpenter and captain of the militia, was the first to come in. He was a fine-looking Indian in his mid-thirties, not unlike his father, Anselmo. He was inclined to be silent, letting his wife talk for him. Nevertheless it was he, not she, who was always the final authority in the family.

After the father, the other children tumbled into the house—Clara's elder brother, then two boys and a girl, aged twelve, eleven, and nine, and finally a girl of six and a boy of four, who had been playing together in the street. Before entering, they washed their hands and faces in a wooden tub under the veranda. The father then said grace, and they sat down.

For six or seven minutes there was silence as the nine pairs of jaws worked steadily on the supper. The third boy, having emptied his bowl first, surreptitiously took a piece of bread from the place beside him, while the brother to whom it belonged was looking the other way. Without a word, the father leaned over, boxed the boy's ear, put the bread back in front of its owner and went on with his meal.

Suddenly, the youngest boy, the four-year-old, stopped eating and looked solemnly round the circle of munching figures.

"I have seen the new cabacuma", he announced.

His twelve-year-old brother, the one who had nearly lost his bread, laughed loudly and unexpectedly. The cleverest member of the family, he was being trained to teach in the school.

"You don't say 'cabacuma', stupid. You say 'catechumen'."

"Hold your tongue, boy", the father said. "If studying in school is going to make you conceited, I'll get the *padre cura* to send you to work in the fields. Go and ask his pardon."

The boy got up, knelt beside his brother, and asked to be forgiven. The smaller boy, not having understood what his father was saying but realising his brother was no longer laughing at him, smiled delightedly, put his arms round his neck, and rubbed his nose up and down his cheek.

The father cut an extra lump of beef and gave a portion to each of the boys.

"Tell us about this catechumen, Guerrico", the mother said.

But Guerrico was suddenly bashful.

"That's all", he said.

"Where has he come from, pet?"

Guerrico looked in turn at each of the faces of his brothers and sisters to see if any of them had heard about the catechumen and could answer for him. Then he rushed out the words, "They found him in the forest. Xavier caught him."

"Ah, good boy!" The father looked at Clara. "The *padre cura* has found you a fine man. I'm proud of him. But if he'd been no good, I wouldn't have had him for a son-in-law, no matter what the *padre cura* said. No, our family has always been honest and hard-working; not an idler, not a lawbreaker within memory. Remember that, all of you, and see that none of you is the first to disgrace us."

When the meal was over, grace had been said, the dishes cleared away, and the room had been straightened, the mother lifted the baby out of his basket to feed him. Clara smoothed her hair before the mirror, put on a necklace, and, carrying a sewing basket under one arm, went out to the veranda to wait for Xavier, who was permitted to pay his court to her three evenings a week. She sat down on a stone bench and stitched a piece of embroidery that was to decorate her dress when she was married. As her hand moved up and down, pushing the needle through the cloth and drawing it out the other side, her thoughts flew back and forth from Xavier to Pedro's daughter. When she thought of Xavier, of his having taken a man a prisoner and of the way her father had praised him, she tingled with pride. But when she remembered Pedro's daughter, it was as though she had heard the note of a distant horn playing in a minor key. Her thoughts, like a river that, for part of its course, flows along in the sun, flashing with light, and, in other parts, glides, green and dark under trees, kept alternating between cheerful and solemn impressions, until suddenly they were interrupted by the sound of Xavier's bare feet padding hurriedly toward the house.

Pretending not to see her, he went straight inside—as good manners required—to pay his respects to her parents.

"Hail Mary, most pure", he said, giving the accustomed greeting.

"Conceived without sin", the father replied.

He asked Xavier to sit down, and the mother questioned him about the new catechumen.

By now, Xavier had repeated his story at least a dozen times, and it was both longer and more detailed than at its first telling. In the process, Wenceslaus had somehow grown three or four inches taller, was twelve or fourteen pounds heavier and several degrees fiercer, while his wound was deeper and his condition more serious. Xavier also forgot to mention that Wenceslaus had not really been captured but had given himself up of his own will.

Clara stitched her embroidery and listened from the veranda.

After a quarter of an hour, the father said, "Clara is outside. Would you like to see her?"

"Thank you", Xavier said, as if being told something he did not know. "If I have your permission . . ." And he went outside.

He and Clara greeted each other softly. The three youngest children rushed out of doors to play. The mother followed them and sat down at the opposite end of the veranda, singing to the baby in a low voice. The lamp burning within shone through the door and the light caught the side of her face and the top of the baby's head. An Indian lounging in the door of the next house as he smoked his pipe nodded at them. In the street, people went to and fro to visit their friends. Xavier and Clara sat close together without speaking. Under the trees that lined both sides of the street, they could see the house opposite, and hear voices and laughter.

Clara broke the silence with a sigh—a sigh of contentment.

"And did you do it all by yourself?"

Xavier hesitated for a moment.

"No. Crisóstomo was there."

"All the same, it was very good. The *padre cura* must have been pleased."

"Yes."

Another silence.

"What's the matter?" Xavier asked, seeing that Clara was looking at him strangely.

"I was thinking of Pedro's daughter. I saw her today."

"Which Pedro?"

"The daughter of Pedro, the smith. She is very unhappy."

"That is because her husband is no good."

"If I were bad, you would be unhappy too."

"But you aren't bad."

"But if I were . . . ?"

"Well, what if I were? We should deserve to be unhappy."

"But Pedro's daughter is unhappy, and she is good."

Xavier had not thought of the problem in this light. He pondered it for a considerable time.

"I don't know why she has to be unhappy", he said at last. "But if I am ever bad, you must still be good like Pedro's daughter. And if you are bad, I must be good."

"Yes", said Clara.

She remembered what her mother had told her about Pedro's daughter. "In heaven she will be a great princess." On those terms, she thought to herself, one could bear almost anything.

"But you will not be bad."

"With God's help", he replied.

PART THREE

The Heart of an Absolute King

1765–1767

THIRTY-NINE

One evening toward the middle of October 1765, three mud-splattered carriages drove rapidly across the bridge over the Loire at Tours, down the main street, and into the yard of the town's principal inn.

The postillions reined in their horses, as hostlers and stable boys, shouting and waving lanterns, came running from the surrounding buildings. The first to reach the leading carriage pulled open the door.

There was a pause while the two travellers inside disentangled themselves from their rugs. Then they got out and hurried across the yard to escape the rain and wind. The landlord, who, from the commotion outside, had sensed the arrival of money, met them with bows. The travellers ordered supper and rooms for the night.

"Immediately! Immediately, Messieurs!" The landlord clapped his hands. "Gaston! Maurice! Charles! Henriette!"

As soon as the servants appeared, he sent them scurrying on different errands, called them back, gave them fresh orders, scolded them for hanging about, and generally behaved like a sea captain who has discovered that his ship has sprung a leak. Then he led the way upstairs to the best private rooms.

When supper was over and the waiter had cleared the table and left the room, Monsieur Charville and Rodrigo moved their chairs near the fire. Rodrigo stretched his legs until his shoes were almost in the embers.

"How pleasant and comfortable it all is!" he said. "I shan't find inns like this when I reach Spain—nor a desire to improve the existing ones, either."

Monsieur Charville leaned forward and rubbed his calves. He had put on weight, had more ease of manner, and his clothes, without being showy, looked expensive. On the middle finger of his left hand, where before there had been none, there was now a heavy gold ring.

"If you want good inns, you must set an example by starting one yourself. You could put up the capital and get a man trained in France to run it." He smiled. "You mustn't take me seriously. I'm just preaching a little sermon in disguise. My meaning is that if one wants to progress, one must do something about it oneself, starting with small things."

"Small things?" Rodrigo said, with a grimace. "If we're content with them, our good intentions will come to nothing. We must undertake big things. We must have industries and proper roads. We must plant forests and irrigate wastelands. We must wake people up. We must teach them to respect work instead of despising it. We need men at the head of affairs who understand political economy and have the courage to destroy outworn institutions that hinder reform, like the guilds and the Mesta."

"Moderation, moderation, my overenthusiastic friend! You can't change the world in five minutes—at least, not without doing a lot of damage . . ."

ACTUALLY, what had most struck Rodrigo during his travels, when comparing the rest of Europe with Spain, was not the absence of poverty or inefficiency in the countries they had visited. He had encountered plenty of famished-looking peasants, derelict cottages, poor roads, and incompetent or venal petty officials in France and Italy.

No, it was not the condition of the poor but the condition of the educated, affluent, and aristocratic that had made him feel his own country was backward and "uncivilised". Everywhere he had been impressed by the number of handsome new buildings, the refined furnishings and fittings, the scope and elegance of the libraries, the ease and polish of people's manners. At balls and on excursions, the discussion of love affairs and French fashions had been interspersed with talk of philosophy, geology, physics, and natural history. Young men, whom he would have expected to be interested only in women and horses, had spoken knowingly about *chiaroscuro* and the "three orders". Beautiful girls had asked his opinion of Buffon, Descartes, Newton. Compared with the drawing rooms of Naples, Vienna, and Paris, the meetings of his guardian's Society for the Dissemination of Useful Knowledge in Madrid had seemed like gatherings of country doctors and village schoolmasters. When people had asked him about the state of the arts and sciences in Spain, it had been in a tone never consciously impolite but of the kind they would have used if enquiring about a remote Pacific island. The first six months of his journey had been a continuous humiliation.

There was only one way, he had realised, to gain respect for himself and his country. He must read and master the books and subjects that everyone discussed. He had bought a large selection of the most fashionable authors, taken lessons in mathematics and political economy, attended lectures on Newtonian physics and the possibility of a plurality of inhabited worlds.

However, there are very few books, no matter what their subject, that do not give at least a glimpse of the writer's philosophical principles, and in the mid-eighteenth century, an enlightened author could scarcely write on the properties of gases or differential calculus without bringing in his opinions on man, society, the universe, and God.

In most of what he read, Rodrigo found it taken for granted that monasteries and convents were centres of idleness; that the inmates ought to be usefully employed instead of praying; that priests encouraged superstition; that the Church had contributed nothing to civilisation; and that the past, when the Church was supreme, had been typified by ignorance, violence, torture, and dirt.

These views had been shared by many of the people he had met through the letters of introduction from the Marques and Marquesa de Torrelavega, provided by his cousin Gaspar's wife, Luisa de Montesa.

In Naples, the amusing and gifted Count Belmonte, with the pretty daughters, had told him that the Italian peasants unquestionably regarded the saints as so many gods and goddesses. In Parma, the Marchesa di Sanstefano, a sensitive woman who had praised his taste in pictures, had described her niece's experiences in a convent at Rimini, assuring him that many convents were worse. In Vienna, the Bishop of Ulm, a fatherly prelate, highly respected in Court, had explained that the control of Rome over the local episcopates was excessive, dangerous, and contrary to the practice of the apostles. In Grenoble, the president of the local *parlement* had spent two hours proving to him that it was unnecessary for God to work miracles and that even though he could, he never did.

Could so many intelligent, agreeable, often serious, and high-minded people, Rodrigo had wondered, all be mistaken?

From feeling there was something wrong with his religion, he had begun to wonder if it were true. The crisis had come at Munich.

He and Monsieur Charville had been visiting the church of St. Hedwige, which contained a miraculous picture of the Virgin of Peace. While watching the people praying in front of it, he had suddenly turned to Monsieur Charville and said, in Spanish, "It really is idolatry!"

"Nonsense", Monsieur Charville had said sharply. "How can you tell what is going on in their minds?"

"As an educated man, I have a right to guess."

"As an educated man, you have a duty not to make foolish statements you can't support."

They had argued all the way back to their inn, and the dispute had continued through dinner and late into the evening. With a strained, set expression, Rodrigo had justified his new ideas loudly and aggressively. By ten o'clock he had been expressing doubts about the Resurrection and the Trinity.

Up to their arrival in Vienna, Monsieur Charville had not spent much time in Rodrigo's company, pleading as an excuse the demands of scholarly research. Nor had those pleas been altogether insincere. It is true that, without Rodrigo's knowledge, he had had long and crucial conversations with Tannucci in Naples and Kaunitz in Venice, as well as with lesser figures elsewhere. But he had also spent many hours in libraries and calling on local historians and antiquarians. Since his trip to Spain, his plans for a history of Roman Gaul and Spain had expanded. The work would now cover all the provinces of the western Empire, putting him, he hoped, on the same level, if not above, the great historian of antiquity, Rollin.

Because of these other preoccupations he had been slow to recognise the change in Rodrigo. But before they left Italy it had become impossible not to, and he had realised that he must take action. If Rodrigo returned to Madrid talking like an infidel French abbé, he, Henri-Lucien Charville, would lose Don Maurice's friendship—a friendship that meant money, convenience, and useful connections. To preserve these, the truth of Catholicism had to be firmly fixed in Rodrigo's mind. So he had begun to argue back, defending Christianity and Catholicism with an energy and resourcefulness that would have astonished his Parisian friends.

"My dear boy," he had said, as Rodrigo launched into a diatribe against the worldliness of bishops, "the more you say, the more you reveal your ignorance. Christ laid down that his Church was to be run by men, not angels. Don't you read the Gospels? The wheat and the tares are to grow together in the same field until the harvest. Since Christ has said this himself, it would be proof that the Church was not his Church if we *didn't* find vagabonds in high ecclesiastical positions. So much for scandals. But no institution is to be judged on its failings alone."

"I didn't say it could be. What I meant was—"

But Monsieur Charville was not going to be stopped. "You don't know what you mean. If you did, you couldn't possibly say anything so absurd as that the Church has done nothing for civilisation and progress. How many hospitals, orphanages, schools for the poor were there in ancient Greece and Rome? How many are there today in India and China? None, my dear boy, none. The Church brought them into being. Without her, they wouldn't exist."

"But wait a minute—" Rodrigo protested.

"No, no. You must hear me out." As Rodrigo grew more heated, so Monsieur Charville's way of speaking grew cooler and more cutting. "The other day I listened to you descanting on the beauties of parliaments *à l'anglaise*. Do you know their origin? They started in the ages of 'superstition and ignorance'. So did the universities. How do you explain that? You say there is no need for a Church; that if men are taught to use their minds, they will be naturally good, and everyone will be happy. *Mon Dieu!* Think of all the clever people we've been meeting. Do you really believe that their morals are on the same level as their intelligence? The Church has never been so foolish as to promise to produce a utopia. She knows that even if the whole world were to be baptized, the devil would still be busy and men free to act wickedly. Can you say that her view of human nature doesn't fit reality?"

By this time Rodrigo was like the general of a routed army, flinging into battle any men he can lay his hands on, however incompetent or ill-trained—cooks, orderlies, ambulance attendants.

"But look how the natural sciences have progressed since men began to throw off the shackles of religion", he said violently, wiping away with his cuff the sweat that was beading his forehead.

"Please do get it into your head", Monsieur Charville said, "that progress of the sciences has nothing to do with the spread of rationalism or whatever you like to call this fashionable philosophy everyone has gone mad about in France. Rationalism, enlightenment—give it any name you please—is as much a religion as Christianity. Belief in the omnipotence and infallibility of the human reason demands an act of faith as blind as belief in the Trinity. No rational proof leads one to accept it. But at least there is evidence that the existence of the Trinity has been revealed by God. Whom has the omnipotence of human reason been revealed to? Helvetius on the top of Mont Blanc?"

"But Diderot says—"

"Diderot is, in his way, as much a religious bigot as any mother superior of a convent—possibly more so. The only difference is that he believes in the perfectibility of man, whereas the mother superior believes that man has been permanently damaged by original sin. There can be no doubt, on this point, that Diderot's beliefs are more ridiculous."

Gradually, Rodrigo, with relief and gratitude, had begun to yield to the older man's arguments.

Since I am so good at convincing other people, Monsieur Charville had thought when he had gone to his room and was climbing, exhausted, into bed, why can't I convince myself? If only the Pope could have heard me!

While waiting to fall asleep, he had amused himself with imagining how the news that he had been made a cardinal would be received at Ferney.

FORTY

Rodrigo's faith had been saved. The Church was still the pillar and ground of religious truth. One could be "enlightened" without being unbelieving. But he still could not find a satisfactory reason why the Church's vigour and influence seemed to be declining so steeply, nor why his country, Spain, should be sharing in that decline. The honour of both, with which his own honour and self-respect were bound up, had demanded an explanation.

He had at last found one in Paris, after an evening at Madame du Deffand's. In the middle of a conversation, his blind hostess had suddenly turned to President Hénault and said: "You want everybody to think alike. You have the spirit of Ignatius Loyola. I detest that. It kills initiative and imagination."

The next day, as he sat reading in the Bibliothèque Mazarine, Rodrigo had recalled these words, which had suddenly released in his mind unexpected trains of thought. St. Ignatius! The Jesuits! They killed initiative. They wanted everyone to think alike. That was it! How long had the influence of the Church been dwindling? For about two hundred years . . . just the length of time since the Jesuits had been founded. And St. Ignatius was Spanish. The Spanish would have a predisposition to share his outlook. If the Jesuits could only be driven out of Spain and then suppressed, the Church and Spain would both be renewed and . . .

Objections had suggested themselves. What, for example, would happen to Alfonso? But he had argued the objections down. It was because he loved Alfonso that he wanted his eyes to be opened. Once Alfonso knew how damaging the influence of the Society really was and had been to the prosperity and peace of nations, he would no longer want to be a Jesuit.

The next day he had confided these thoughts to Monsieur Charville, who had gone into battle a second time.

"As if the Jesuits would really have tried to kill the King of Portugal", he had said scornfully. "Not that it would have been such a bad thing if they had. You might as well believe that the Pope is secretly an atheist. A more respectable body of men than the Jesuits doesn't exist."

"But they are always intriguing."

"Who says so?"

"Baron Grimm, Monsieur de Condillac—dozens of people."

"And how many contributors to the Encyclopaedia, may I ask, have given up everything to go and civilise savages? Besides, if these literary gentlemen are so anxious about the progress of the natural sciences, why do they attack a religious order that is outstanding for the number of its mathematicians and astronomers?"

But this time reason and evidence had proved powerless. To preserve his faith and appease his patriotism, Rodrigo needed a scapegoat. Having found one, he had clung to it tenaciously. Monsieur Charville's logic had been expended in vain and after a time he had decided it would be wiser to drop the subject.

However, as they sat in the inn at Tours, warming themselves before the fire and gradually emptying the decanter that stood between them on a little pedestal table, he decided to come back to it one last time. They were to part the next morning.

"Will you allow me to give you a word of advice?" he said.

"I should be a fool to refuse", Rodrigo replied. "If it hadn't been for your help and advice over the last year and a half, I might well have become a complete sceptic by now. I can never repay all I owe you or thank you enough."

"Then I advise you, my friend, to be careful, when you get home, how you speak about the Jesuits in front of your guardians."

"But you don't understand. I'm used to discussing everything with my family . . ."

"Nevertheless, if only for my sake, I ask you not to criticise the Jesuits in front of them. I don't want to lose Don Maurice's friendship, and

I certainly shall if he thinks I'm responsible for these new notions of yours."

"Then, of course, I shan't so much as mention them. I should hate to cause a quarrel between two people who have been so good to me."

Having received this assurance, Monsieur Charville turned the subject to Rodrigo's artistic purchases during their travels. They included some small Graeco-Roman bronzes, several landscapes in the style of Claude and Gaspar Poussin, watercolour views of Rome and Naples, portfolios of engravings, a box of coins and cameos, books. Most of them were presents for his family and friends. To house them he had had to buy an extra carriage. The piece he liked best, a bronze Apollo purchased in Florence, he had given to Monsieur Charville.

At eleven, Monsieur Charville yawned and said he thought it was time for bed. Rodrigo jumped to his feet.

"What am I thinking of! You want to be on the road early tomorrow." He took two candlesticks from the mantelpiece. "And thank you again for coming with me this far. If we'd said good-bye in Paris the journey would have seemed much longer."

"It's been a pleasure. Besides, as I told you, I have some family business to attend to in this area. Then the day after tomorrow I shall return to Paris by the humble diligence, which will help me all the better to appreciate the comfort of your chariot."

The humble diligence! Rodrigo repeated the words to himself as he undressed in his bedroom. It must be hard, with such talents, to have so little money.

The next morning, when he and Monsieur Charville had breakfasted, he suddenly pulled an envelope out of his pocket and laid it beside Monsieur Charville's plate. He was blushing like an awkward fifteen-year-old. Inside there was a bill of exchange.

"My dear friend," he said quickly, "I shall be deeply hurt if you refuse to accept this. I know what a lot of extra expense you've been put to because of me. Uncle Maurice would certainly expect me to make it good. Think of this as coming from him."

At first Monsieur Charville pretended not to understand; then he pretended to be indignant. A dispute followed, with Monsieur Charville rejecting the money and Rodrigo pleading with him to accept it.

"It really belongs to you", Rodrigo said. "It wouldn't seem right for me to take it back. So I shall leave it here over the fireplace."

"Do, by all means, if you want to enrich the chambermaids. I refuse to touch it."

They were interrupted by the landlord with the bill, followed by Monsieur Charville's Dubois and Rodrigo's valet carrying valises and portmanteaus, and everything else was forgotten.

Once more alone together for a moment, they embraced, promised to write, and thanked each other again and again.

The stairs, entrance hall, and yard were crowded with servants, all apparently busy with dusters, buckets, and brooms. Rodrigo distributed tips this way and that and, followed by good wishes and admiring looks, got into his carriage. The other two carriages, now much emptier, were drawn up behind. Monsieur Charville waved until they were out of sight, then he returned to the inn and went quickly back upstairs. The envelope was still in its place over the fireplace. He hesitated for a moment, while his self-respect struggled with his love of money. Then he took the envelope and slipped it into an inside pocket.

An hour later, in a hired carriage, with Dubois up behind, he set out for Chanteloup, the Duc de Choiseul's chateau, a few miles away, near Amboise.

MEANWHILE, Rodrigo's three carriages were bowling along between the straight French trees along the straight French road toward Poitiers, Angoulême, Bordeaux, and the Spanish border.

On his way across France, a year and a half earlier, he had sat hour after hour with his face at the carriage window, watching the landscape go by. Now, for the greater part of the time, he lay back with his head against the red leather upholstery, remembering the things he had seen and done and thinking about the future.

Monsieur Charville's warning had stirred a sense of unease. It was true he had always discussed everything that interested him with his family. But he had never before wanted to discuss anything so sensitive. Was it possible that Monsieur Charville was right, that Don Maurice really would be as upset by his new views about the Jesuits as the Frenchman foresaw? Common sense and his knowledge of his family said "Yes". But, as we have seen, for deeper psychological reasons, he did not want to accept their verdict. For a good hour the two compartments of his mind wrestled fiercely for mastery. As last, however, common sense was floored, bound, and anaesthetized.

A man of such integrity and intelligence as his guardian, he told himself, was bound, in the end, to bow to the evidence of the facts, painful though it might be. Of course, he wouldn't raise the subject at once. He would allow his views to appear gradually. Alfonso, he would point out, could do much more good as a bishop than as a Jesuit. Wasn't it because the Jesuits absorbed so much talent that there was such a scarcity of good and holy bishops?

Satisfied at last that all would be well, his thoughts turned again to his family, and began to picture the welcome his family would be preparing for him.

FORTY-ONE

Rodrigo stood in the hall, alone. Outside, the valet and footmen were lifting the luggage from the carriages.

There was no one to welcome him. The letter he had sent ahead from Pamplona must have gone astray.

Disappointed, he was still glad to have this moment by himself, to adjust present to past and past to present. He looked about him.

Everything was the same, though diminished and less impressive— the stiff-backed chairs, the carved chests, Doña Teresa's sedan chair in a corner, the bust of Cardinal Jiménez, the portrait of Don Maurice's great-grandfather, Don Bartolomé, and, on the stairs, the picture of St. Laurence being roasted on a gridiron, which he had always avoided looking at as a boy when he passed it at night with a candle.

There was no reason to have expected change. But the sight of these familiar things still in their accustomed places momentarily gave him the feeling that everything that had happened to him abroad had been an illusion and that reality, unalterable and timeless, had all along been here.

Suddenly footsteps sounded overhead, then quickened, then multiplied and, as they moved toward the staircase, began clattering on the polished chestnut wood. Within a moment he was surrounded by his family.

After the third exchange of hugs and kisses, he looked around for the cousin who had still been a schoolboy when he went away.

"Where's Jaime?" he asked.

"Didn't you get my letter about him?" Doña Teresa asked. "He's a Jesuit novice, and so happy."

Later, after supper, when they were all in her boudoir, she insisted on reading aloud some of Alfonso's letters from Paraguay. Rodrigo sat with one hand shading his eyes, as though absorbed by what he was listening to.

Oh, God, he was praying, don't let them realise yet what I'm thinking. Don't let me have to argue or differ with them for the present. Please let me have a few weeks of peace before I have to say anything.

The succeeding days passed quietly. Progress, reform, philosophy—somehow they seemed less important, and he avoided thinking about them.

After Mass on Sunday, Don Maurice summoned Rodrigo to the library and told him that he now consented to his marrying Beatriz. When Rodrigo tried to thank him, Don Maurice smiled and said, "You must thank Beatriz, not me. She has made so many novenas to Our Lady of Covadonga that I dare not stand in your way any longer. Go and give her the news."

The betrothal, it was decided, should take place on the feast of St. Silvester and the wedding be celebrated in January.

But before the feast of St. Silvester, Rodrigo had quarrelled with Don Maurice.

IT HAPPENED AT DINNER. Don Maurice's sister, Doña Juana Colmenar, with her husband, Don Enrique, and their three children, Casilda, Ruiz, and Angel, were spending the day with the de Vallecases. The young people were sitting together at the bottom of the table, and Rodrigo, who was next to Casilda, a pretty girl of nineteen, was telling her about his travels.

"After our audience with the Prince-Bishop," he said, "the *maestro di camera* showed us the gardens, which are even more superb than those at Caserta."

"Oh, how wonderful!" Casilda exclaimed. "You must have met all the most famous people in Europe, Rodrigo."

"How do you know he hasn't met some of the most infamous ones, too?" Her brother Ruiz laughed, and winked at Rodrigo.

"Perhaps he knows this Voltaire everyone's talking about", Angel said.

Angel, who was sixteen, knew no more about Voltaire than his name, but he had heard him discussed in low voices and had noticed that if he himself seemed to be listening, people immediately spoke of something else.

"Really, Angel!" Casilda said. "How can you mention such a person."

She was not certain who Voltaire was either but supposed he must be a French criminal.

"Look at Rodrigo!" Angel said. "He's as red as a pomegranate. I believe he actually *has* met this Voltaire."

Angel's voice drew the attention of everyone at the table.

"Come on, Rodrigo," Ruiz said, laughing again, "tell us what he was like."

Rodrigo wiped his mouth with his napkin, so as to give himself time to think.

217

"Voltaire", Don Maurice said, leaning forward and addressing his daughters, his niece, and his nephews, "is a French writer who hates Christianity and the Church. Naturally Rodrigo will not have met him."

They were all looking at Rodrigo, as though expecting him to agree. He realised that this was the moment to turn the conversation to a new subject but was too flustered to think how.

His silence and embarrassment seemed to surprise Don Maurice.

"I am right, am I not?" he asked.

Rodrigo felt his chest contract as if he were being buckled into a steel corset a size too small. He coughed twice and twiddled the stem of his wineglass. He was tempted to lie.

"I'm afraid not."

"You mean to say you *have* met him? May I ask where?"

"At his château. At Ferney."

Don Maurice dropped his fork onto his plate and pushed back his chair. The majordomo signed to the footmen to leave the room, and he himself tiptoed to the door.

"Charville actually took you to this man's house? It's outrageous! What on earth got into him?"

"Monsieur Charville had nothing to do with it", Rodrigo said quickly. "If anyone is to blame—though I can't see that I did anything wrong— I am. I'd heard a great deal about Monsieur Voltaire. People are reading his books everywhere, even in Rome. So when we got to Switzerland, I decided to visit him to find out what he was really like. Monsieur Charville did his best to prevent me, so you have no reason to be angry with him."

"Thanks be to God, someone behaved sanely." Don Maurice turned to his wife. "You heard that, Doña Teresa. We weren't mistaken about Charville." He grew calmer. "I'm amazed, astounded at you, my boy", he continued. "You've been extremely rash and foolish. To put yourself deliberately in the path of a man like Voltaire was to expose your faith without cause to a very grave danger. He is not only extremely clever; he has spent the best part of a lifetime studying how to undermine the Church. You have neither the age nor the experience to stand up to him.

I can only be thankful that you have come to so little harm. Had you returned a sceptic or unbeliever, I should never have forgiven myself. It would have been bad enough if you had come back canting about the Jesuits . . ."

Don Maurice broke off and stared. Rodrigo had lifted his glass to drink some wine, but his hand was shaking so much that when the glass was halfway to his mouth, it began to spill, and he put it down again without drinking.

"You seem to be extraordinarily upset." Don Maurice was kneading the carved knobs on the end of the arms of his chair, and his expression had become hard and fixed. Rodrigo, who had never seen him looking this way, realised what it must be like for a criminal to be sentenced by him. "Does this mean that you, too, have joined the Church's enemies and have become a slanderer and pursuer of Jesuits?" He paused for a moment. "Well?"

"I think that some of the criticisms of the Jesuits are justified."

"Is this a polite way of saying that you think they ought to be suppressed?"

"I believe that both the Church and Spain would be better off if they were." Rodrigo replied in a feeble, hurried way that made him ashamed.

"Oh, you do, do you? So! I see! It's even worse than I first thought. Monsieur de Voltaire", Don Maurice emphasised the "Monsieur" and the particule scornfully, "has done his work well. I suppose he specialises in deceiving the young. They are more gullible and easily flattered."

Up to this point Rodrigo had been feeling in the wrong. To oppose Don Maurice, whom he had always loved and revered, seemed like sacrilege. But this reference to the gullibility of the young touched his pride.

"Monsieur Voltaire didn't even mention the Jesuits", he said. "I formed my opinion about them independently."

"Independently! As if that were possible for a boy of your age. May we ask what facts you discovered to justify this independent point of view?"

"Facts!" Rodrigo almost shouted the word. Only by letting his anger take charge could he overcome his awe and respect for Don Maurice enough to defend himself. "In Spain people are too blind to see the facts. But everywhere else they are common talk. I've even heard cardinals and bishops say that the power of the Jesuits is ruining the Church."

Don Maurice, who had momentarily recovered command of himself, spoke more quietly. The centres of his cheeks, however, were marked all over by little scarlet veins. Everyone at the table, except Don Maurice and Rodrigo, sat with lowered eyes, the young people appalled at the results of what had been meant as harmless teasing.

"Has it ever occurred to you", Don Maurice said, "that there is nothing independent about your opinions—that you are simply echoing fashionable gossip? Not every cardinal or bishop puts the Kingdom of God before the approval of the world."

"Very well!" Rodrigo was by this time so carried away by his anger and misery that he had lost all sense of where he was and to whom he was talking. "If you want facts, why is it that ever since the Jesuits have been running all the best schools, atheism and scepticism have been increasing?" Seeing that Don Maurice could not answer, he hurried on. "Of course the Jesuits like to give the impression that anyone who criticises them is attacking the faith, but no one capable of thinking for himself will be taken in by a trick like that."

"Hold your tongue, sir."

"Why should I? That's what's wrong with Spain. We're frightened of hearing anything unpleasant. And what's the result? Ignorance, bigotry, intellectual stagnation."

Don Maurice pushed back his chair. His face was distorted with the effort of controlling himself.

"Leave the room, sir, immediately. Leave the room!"

"Gladly", Rodrigo said. "What's the use of talking with people who are terrified of new ideas."

He stood up, breathing hard, and, throwing his napkin over the back of his chair, strode to the door and pulled it open. As he disappeared into the hall, it swung back into place behind him with a crash.

FORTY-TWO

An hour later a servant came to Rodrigo's bedroom on the second floor.

"The señora would like to see you, sir", he said. "His Lordship has just gone out."

As soon as the man had left, Rodrigo rushed downstairs.

Doña Teresa was in her boudoir.

"Come and sit beside me", she said, and patted the seat of the sofa. She looked neither reproachful, disapproving, nor angry. Her face was the same as always—peaceful and kind—though graver than usual and deeply sad. "The important thing to remember is that we love each other. If we keep that in mind, we shall see everything else in proportion. Now, you will apologise to your uncle, won't you?"

"Of course. I didn't mean to lose my temper."

"I knew you would." She smiled and took his hand.

An irrelevant thought came into Rodrigo's mind as he looked up at the portrait of Doña Teresa's mother, which hung between the windows on the wall behind her. She's begun to look like that picture—she never has before.

"Then there is the question of the Jesuits." Doña Teresa's smile had faded a little. "Your uncle expects some sort of admission that you are wrong."

"But that's impossible."

"Try to look at it from his point of view for a moment. Is it so unreasonable of him to see a connection between your new opinions and the fact that you have been meeting men like Voltaire?"

"But there isn't a connection. I've heard your cousin the Field Marshal in Vienna say that he hopes the Empress will expel the Jesuits and that the Pope will finally suppress them."

"There's nothing infallible about relations, my dear boy." Doña Teresa let go Rodrigo's hand and revolved her wedding ring slowly on her finger. "Your uncle thinks, and so do I, that the men who are organising these attacks on the Jesuits also want to destroy the Church. There may be Catholics who simply dislike the Jesuits for reasons of their own and, as a result, blind themselves to this. But the fact is that such Catholics are, perhaps without realising it, helping the Church's enemies as well as—in your uncle's opinion and mine—persecuting innocent men."

"But what does Uncle Maurice expect me to do? Say that I think the Jesuits are all saints?" In the intimacy of the family, Rodrigo was accustomed to calling his guardian and Doña Teresa "uncle" and "aunt", in spite of their being only cousins.

"He expects you to consider carefully whether you may not be wrong."

"But I've been thinking about this problem for months."

"The difficulty is this . . . as long as you see things the way you do, I don't see how you and Uncle Maurice are to live in the same house. You will have to meet at mealtimes, if at no other time."

"Can I go on living here only if I agree with everything he says?"

"Of course not, my dear boy. But I don't think you understand how strongly your uncle and I feel about all this. It's understandable. After all, in Portugal, Jesuits have been imprisoned and even put to death. The same thing could happen to Alfonso and Jaime if you had your way about the Society." She was silent for a moment. When she spoke again, there was no longer a trace of a smile in her expression. "I think it would be best if you spent a night or two with Gaspar and Luisa. Maybe, after a day or two, we shall all see things differently."

"Yes, certainly—if that will help. But don't be disappointed when you find that I haven't changed my mind."

"Will you do me a favour, then?"

"What is it?"

"While you are at Gaspar's, will you go and see Father Padilla and talk to him about these ideas of yours? He has known you from childhood. He is fond of you. And he is understanding."

"I doubt if it would be any use. Besides, you can't tell a man to his face that you think the organisation he has dedicated his life to has done more harm than good."

"But you ought at least, in fairness, to hear what he has to say on the Jesuits' side."

Rodrigo sat thinking.

"All right", he said, after a minute. He felt that, by agreeing, he would prove he was not simply a man of prejudice like Don Maurice.

"Will you promise?"

"I promise."

When Rodrigo arrived at the Montesa Palace, Gaspar had already received a note from his mother explaining what had happened and telling him to be kind and to avoid arguments.

"Stay as long as you like", Gaspar said, greeting Rodrigo at the top of the stairs. "Luisa will be delighted." He took Rodrigo into the picture gallery to watch the men who were hanging a newly bought painting by Carlo Maratta.

Before he went to bed that night, Rodrigo wrote to Don Maurice apologising for his rudeness and for having lost his temper, but he did not retract what he had said about the Jesuits. He got no reply, either the next day or on any of the following ones.

When he had been four days at the Montesa Palace, he suddenly remembered his promise to Doña Teresa and about five in the afternoon set out for the Jesuit residence, the Casa San Felipe.

A lay brother answered the door.

"Is Father Padilla in?"

"No, sir. But the Rector is. Would you like to see him?"

Rodrigo hesitated. Why not? he thought. One priest is as good as another. As long as I talk to a Jesuit, I shall have kept my promise. And perhaps it will be easier with a priest I don't know.

The lay brother showed him into a whitewashed waiting room. There were two chairs, a table, and on the wall a picture of St. Aloysius. While Rodrigo was studying the picture, Father de la Cueva came in.

"Can I help you?" he asked.

Father de la Cueva was one of those people who have the misfortune to be less likable when trying to be agreeable than when they are being their ordinary selves. At the sound of his overamiable voice, Rodrigo turned. Tartuffe! he thought.

"Good afternoon, Father", he said. "I'm sorry to trouble you. I wonder if I could ask you some questions?"

"Certainly. Won't you sit down?"

Rodrigo took the chair nearest the window.

"I don't know quite how to explain", he said, playing with one of his lace cuffs. "I had an argument with my family. They think I'm losing my faith. Just because I don't agree with them about everything."

"That often happens."

"Is it a sin to criticise a priest, for instance?"

"Not if there are good reasons to."

"Or a religious order?"

"You may criticise the Pope if you honestly think he has done something unwise or wrong."

Rodrigo looked at his lap.

"So it would be permissible to criticize your Order, Father—the Society of Jesus?"

"Why not, if you see faults in it." Father de la Cueva was glad he could show that he was not like those narrowminded members of the Society who saw every criticism as a malicious attack. "Some of our friends do us more harm than good by their uncritical admiration."

"And if, for some reason, the Society of Jesus were disbanded, would it mean that the Church would collapse?"

"How could it? Christ has promised that his Church will last to the end of the world. He gave no such promise to St. Ignatius about his Order."

This priest is remarkably sensible, Rodrigo thought, forgetting his first impression.

"But haven't I seen you before somewhere?" Father de la Cueva asked.

"I don't think so, Father."

"Yes. I feel sure of it. With Father Padilla. That's right. Aren't you a son of Don Maurice de Vallecas?"

"His ward", Rodrigo said, annoyed at being identified.

"I thought I recognised you. Now isn't that interesting." Father de la Cueva's voice grew even more amiable. "I once had the privilege of conversing with Don Maurice. An unforgettable occasion! What an intelligent man! A gentleman of the old school. I have a great respect for him." Father de la Cueva folded his hands. "So you've had a difference with him? What a pity. Of course, when criticising our neighbour, we have to be careful of our motives. Is their spiritual good our first concern? Or are we giving way to envy and uncharitableness? We don't want to fall into the sin of detraction. Then, of course, there's the fourth commandment. I take it that in your case Don Maurice is *in loco parentis*. We have a duty to honour our parents even when we are no longer bound to obey them, and 'honouring' means respecting their judgment and not lightly disregarding their advice . . ."

Rodrigo listened impatiently, his second, more favourable impression, rapidly dissolving. I might have expected it, he thought. Just what everyone says about the Jesuits. Two-faced. And always making up to the great. This one gives me an honest opinion until he discovers I've quarrelled with Uncle Maurice, whom he's afraid of offending. Then he changes his tune. What luck he didn't know who I was to begin with! He can't deny what he said first, even though he's trying to take back as much of it as he can.

Rodrigo stood up, buttoned his coat, adjusted his shirt-cuff, and tucked his three-cornered hat under his arm.

"Thank you, Father", he said. "I think you've more or less solved my problems for me."

"One is always happy to help bring back harmony in a family", Father de la Cueva said, with another overamiable smile, as he showed Rodrigo to the door. The thought had suggested itself to him that, unworthy though he was, he seemed to have a special gift for helping young men in difficulties. "And you will give my respects to Don Maurice, won't you?"

WHEN RODRIGO GOT BACK to the Montesa Palace, he found a note from Doña Teresa.

My very dear Rodrigo,

I wish I could send you better news, but your uncle absolutely refuses to see you until, he says, you have changed your mind. So we had best go on as we are for a week or two, sad though it is for us all. Do, while you have time on your hands, reconsider seriously these stories you have been told against the Jesuits. With this letter I'm sending you two books: the Bishop of Tarragona's *Reply to the Portuguese Government's Charges against the Society of Jesus* and Padre Osuna's *The Church's True Defenders*. I beg you to read them and try to keep an open mind.

Your affectionate aunt,
Teresa de Vallecas

For about three-quarters of an hour, Rodrigo leafed through the books and looked at random passages. The usual arguments, he thought. Nothing I haven't heard before. There was clearly no need for him to read them from beginning to end. Besides, he thought to himself, Uncle Maurice is bound to take a more reasonable view of things in a day or two. He hasn't yet got used to the idea that I'm a man now and, as such, entitled to my own opinions. But even he knows that there's more than one way of looking at a problem, and he's too sensible not to recognise eventually that there may be some truth on my side. After all, he must be aware that a lot of very intelligent and far-seeing people think as I do.

Having satisfied himself that the quarrel would soon be made up, he went to the nursery to see Tonio, with whom he had promised to play at bulls and matadors.

FORTY-THREE

But when Rodrigo had been a week at the Montesa Palace, he began to wonder whether, after all, Don Maurice was going to be reasonable. And at the end of ten days he decided the answer was no.

For the first time in his life, he let himself consider his guardian's faults. I've often noticed, he said to himself, how carefully Aunt Teresa has to handle him. She can't have had all that easy a life with him.

After a while, however, he felt guilty and made himself remember how much he owed to Don Maurice. Then suddenly he thought, with panic: "Suppose he tries to stop the wedding . . ." He rushed to a desk and wrote a short letter to Doña Teresa explaining that he wanted to see Beatriz urgently.

In her reply, Doña Teresa said that she and Beatriz would meet him at three on the next day outside Madrid on the road to Getafe. "Wait for us", she wrote, "in the valley beyond the hill with the three windmills."

RODRIGO, wearing a riding cloak and jackboots, was first at the rendezvous. After tying his horse to a stunted evergreen oak, he walked impatiently up and down the road. Ten minutes went by. Then a carriage appeared over the crest of the rise and came slowly down the hill toward him.

That's not our carriage, he thought. It's too old. Good God, it's the Colmenars'! What's happened?

As the coachman reined in the horses, Don Enrique Colmenar put his head out of the carriage window.

"They're with me inside", he called to Rodrigo. "We're going to that house."

The carriage turned onto a track that led to a deserted cottage about four hundred yards from the road. Rodrigo untethered his horse and followed. The coachman drove the carriage around behind the cottage. When Rodrigo got there, Don Enrique was helping Doña Teresa and Beatriz to get out.

"You can have a quarter of an hour, children", Doña Teresa said. "And I don't know if I ought to allow you that much. Your Uncle Enrique and I will walk about here while you talk."

Close to the cottage was an orchard gone wild, surrounded by a low wall. Rodrigo led Beatriz through a gap where the stones had tumbled down and lay half-hidden in the withered grass.

"Listen", he said, when they were out of earshot and he had put her arm through his. "There are all sorts of things I can't go into because there isn't time. First of all, I love you. Secondly, I love you. And thirdly, I love you. Fourthly, it looks as if we shall have to get married without Uncle Maurice's consent."

"But Rodrigo—"

"Let me finish. My property at Logrosan is too far from Madrid for us to live there now. But as you know, I have some other property near Segovia. There's quite a reasonable house on it, and I'm going to have it put in order so that we can live there until Uncle Maurice sees things in a more reasonable light. When it's ready—"

"But it's impossible."

"What do you mean?"

"I couldn't marry you without Father's consent. Surely you realise that?"

"So you've turned against me, too!"

"I haven't. I haven't. I love you, and I shall never love anyone else."

"Then why are you more afraid of hurting Uncle Maurice than of hurting me?"

"I'm not. Haven't I disobeyed him for your sake? Haven't I come here, although he's forbidden me to see you?" Beatriz unlinked her arm from Rodrigo's, and her voice rose a tone. "Why do you care for me less than you do for your wretched new opinions?"

"I see. So you're another of these people who put loyalty to the Jesuits before everything else. It's certainly true that they have a remarkable influence over people."

"You're the one who's easily influenced. How can I marry a man who's ready to see my brothers flung into prison and murdered?"

They walked back and forth, arguing and growing more and more vehement and angry. Then they abruptly stopped talking and walked in silence, shocked at having quarrelled.

The shaft of a broken plough lying in the grass caught the edge of Rodrigo's cloak. As he turned to release it, a partridge started up and winged away over the orchard wall.

"What can we do?" he said, in a voice that was no longer angry but despairing.

"If only we could go back to being as we were before you went away!"

"That's impossible. I can't pretend to think what I don't think."

"We must trust God, then; and we must try to be patient."

"Oh, Beatriz, how can I be patient? I love you so much. We've had to wait such a long time already. I can't face waiting any more."

Beatriz put her arm back in his.

"Do you think I don't find it hard to be patient, too?"

"If only I could believe that!"

For an answer she unfastened the top of her cloak, took off the gold chain and crucifix she was wearing round her neck, and put them into his hand.

"Rodrigo! Rodrigo!" Don Enrique was calling from the cottage. "I'm sorry, my boy," he said as they returned, "but we must say good-bye now. Sancho! Turn the carriage round. There, cousins, please be quick." He held his watch in his hand. He was a timid man, in awe of his more successful brother-in-law, and kept glancing toward the road, as if he expected to see Don Maurice come galloping over the skyline. Doña Teresa had had to tell him half a dozen times that Don Maurice had gone for a week to Toledo before he would lend her and Beatriz his carriage or would agree to come with them. "Good-bye, Rodrigo", he continued. "Take care of yourself. I would ask you to come and see us, but under the circumstances it might be awkward, you know . . ." To hide his embarrassment, he turned away and told the coachman to hurry.

Doña Teresa kissed Rodrigo and said, "I'll write." Then she and Beatriz got into the carriage. Don Enrique followed, but, once seated, he began to feel ashamed of the way he had just spoken to Rodrigo. He put his head out of the window and beckoned to him.

"I'll come and pay you a visit", he said. "And if you possibly can, make it up with your uncle. There aren't many things it would be worth losing a girl like Beatriz for. We won't forget you. And remember, all clouds have silver linings."

He would have continued his homely advice had the carriage not started with a jolt and made him withdraw his head for fear of being knocked under the chin by the top of the window glass.

For a long time after the carriage had gone, Rodrigo paced up and down by himself beside the cottage. Then he returned to the road, unfastened his horse, and rode back to the city.

The grey plain, the low clouds, the cutting wind, the withered grass; everything made him feel that "Valley of Tears" did not begin to describe what a dreary, hopeless place the world could be.

About an hour after midnight, Doña Teresa awoke suddenly. For several seconds she lay still, trying to collect her thoughts. Then she sat up and pulled back the curtains on the right side of the bed. A lighted candle stood on the table, feebly showing the outlines of the room. Beside it, Beatriz was sitting in a chair, crying.

"Beatriz, my darling, why didn't you wake me? Quick, get in here beside me." Doña Teresa drew her daughter into the bed and, half-pulling the curtains together, put her arms around her. "There, my darling, there! I understand. There, my pet! There, my sweet!"

"Oh, Mama, Mama", she sobbed. "What has happened? What has made him so different? I shall die if I lose him."

FORTY-FOUR

"Attention!"

"Present arms!"

"Move that coach out of the way, and tell that fool of a coachman to hurry. He's blocking the steps."

"Look out! Stop! *Dios*, that's done it! Don't move! Your wheels are locked."

A long line of coaches was moving slowly up to the main entrance of the Palace. It was January 20, 1766, the King's birthday, and everyone with the right of entry to the royal presence had come to El Pardo to kiss hands.

As each coach reached the steps, the gentlemen got out and gave their hands to their wives and daughters. Before mounting the steps, the women glanced quickly down at their jewels or touched their hair, while the men patted a sword into place or smoothed the ribbon of an Order. Then the coachmen, flipping the reins, drove on to find somewhere to wait.

Inside the Palace, the galleries, stairs, halls, and antechambers were crowded with majordomos, equerries, gentlemen-in-waiting, chamberlains, officers and soldiers of the Guard, pages, footmen, and the stream of nobles and functionaries of state flowing to and from the audience chamber.

In the suite of the French Ambassador was a tall young man with a puglike face, who strolled along staring at the ceilings, pictures, and statues as coolly as if he were in a museum.

The Chevalier de Savin had been in Madrid for three years as an honourary attaché at his Embassy. A junior member of a famous French family, he was known in society as "the little ambassador" because of the way he never stopped pointing out, no matter what the occasion, the virtues, achievements, and beauties of his country. Next after France, his special enthusiasm was for political economy, about which he had exchanged some letters with Quesnay and Condorcet. If he happened to go into a church in Madrid to admire the architecture and saw poor women praying, he would immediately start calculating how many hours of work could be gained if all the praying poor women in Spain could be set to weaving cloth. He would picture them in a vast factory and, with a feeling of satisfaction, add up the amount of money that could be made by their labours.

During the ceremony of kissing hands, the Chevalier de Savin amused himself by noticing facial resemblances between members of the royal family and various grooms, footmen, gardeners, and serving-maids at his father's château in Burgundy, while on the way back through the state rooms, he criticised to himself the stiff and awkward dresses of the women, comparing them with what would be worn in Paris.

In the last of these rooms, which was filled with minor officials who did not have *entrée*, he suddenly saw a face he recognised. He halted abruptly, causing the gentleman behind him to run into his back.

"My dear Don Rodrigo," he called, ignoring the gentleman's indignant complaint, "what on earth are you doing here? I thought you were still abroad."

The Chevalier's penetrating voice easily dominated the general hubbub. Rodrigo was standing at the edge of the crowd. Suddenly finding himself being stared at from all directions, he tried to look unconcerned. The Chevalier occasionally attended the meetings of the Society for the Dissemination of Useful Knowledge, and it was there they had met. For Rodrigo, at that time, the Chevalier had represented all he most disliked about France and Frenchmen. He was not sure he was going to like him any better now that their views were more likely to coincide.

"As you can see, I have returned", he said. "I've been back for three months."

"Three months!" The Chevalier continued to block the gangway down the centre of the room and talk over the heads of the people nearest to him. "Why haven't I run into you sooner? Were you at the Lirias' the other evening?"

"No."

"Well, you didn't miss much. I beg your pardon, madam." He bowed to a woman whose foot he had just stepped on. She stared coldly, and the gentleman with her scowled. "I seem to be making myself unpopular", he said, in a tone implying that nothing could be more unlikely. "By the way, Don Rodrigo, if you're free, I'd like to hear about your travels. Why don't you come back to my rooms with me?"

Realising that this would be the easiest way not to be questioned in front of strangers, Rodrigo edged through the crowd and joined the Chevalier. They made their way down the stairs together. The rest of the French Ambassador's suite had already left, taking all the carriages, so they had to cross the congested courtyard on foot. In a few minutes they reached the village at the edge of the Palace grounds.

ACCOMMODATION, for those who had to live at Court but did not have an apartment at the Palace, was poor, expensive, and hard to get—even though the inhabitants of the village rented every square foot of floor space and themselves retired to their attics and haylofts. Gentlemen envied each other the use of a single room, while a bed with hangings was a luxury.

But the Chevalier de Savin was one of those people with a gift for looking after themselves—in a desert he would have been first to find a bush and some shade—and the lodgings he had discovered in a house at the end of the principal street were among the best in the place.

He took Rodrigo upstairs to the sitting room. Although shabby enough, the Chevalier had transformed it by the skilful placing of a few valuable objects—the miniature of a pretty woman framed in brilliants and set at an angle on the windowsill, some finely bound books on top of a chest, a travelling writing desk with gilt fittings which lay open on a table.

Rodrigo looked about him enviously. He himself had arrived at El Pardo after the Court had already been there for some time, and he had only been able to rent an attic room, which he had to share with a Galician lawyer. He was sorry for the lawyer, who was trying to get a post as an auditor in a provincial court, but the man's conversation, which was all about his grievances, depressed him.

"Now make yourself comfortable—or as comfortable as you can", the Chevalier said, as he tossed his hat into a corner and started to unbuckle his sword. "And you'll stop and dine, won't you?"

Rodrigo was about to refuse but then changed his mind. "I'd be delighted to", he said. "Thank you."

Earlier, at the palace, he had caught sight of Don Maurice, Doña Teresa, and Beatriz in the distance, talking to a young guard's officer whom he had recognised as Diego de Torrelavega. Seeing him in a gold-encrusted uniform talking to Beatriz, when he himself was prevented from going near her, had suddenly made him feel lonely, rejected, and jealous. He did not want to dine alone or with the lawyer.

The Chevalier went off to give orders to his valet about the meal. When he returned, he had changed his wig for a turban and was wearing a silk dressing gown.

"Well, how did Paris strike you?" he asked, standing beside the brazier and rubbing his hands.

Rodrigo began to describe his travels. The Chevalier listened—with coolness to praise of Italy and Germany but with quickened interest when the beauties of France were extolled.

Before Rodrigo had finished, several of the Chevalier's friends came in. They stayed for an hour talking about politics, Court gossip, and people they all knew. When they finally went, the Chevalier took a deep breath and pulled the lapels of his dressing gown aside as though he needed air.

"What's wrong?" Rodrigo asked. "They seemed quite agreeable."

"Oh, they're agreeable enough. But did you hear one of them express an original thought about the state of society, about literature, about the arts or sciences? Were you struck by their capacity for rational discussion?"

"I suppose they didn't feel in the mood for that sort of conversation."

"My dear Don Rodrigo"—the Chevalier picked up a letter from Turgot that was lying on the table and dropped it again so that the signature was showing—"you are too indulgent. These people have appetites and passions but no minds. For instance, time and time again I've tried to interest them in canals. Have you ever thought what canals mean? When moulding the geographical features of a country, Nature, as you may have observed, often makes mistakes. The rivers, which ought to be the veins and arteries of a nation, along which the lifeblood of trade, can move from district to district, are too often irregularly spaced, or flow in the wrong directions. Man must therefore correct these defects in Nature's work by linking his country's waterways with canals and allowing the vital sap of trade to pulse into every part. To have attempted this is one of the glories of the modern age. But, alas, how little is its importance understood!"

He clapped his hands and ordered the valet to serve dinner. During the meal he made up for the intellectual incapacity of his recent visitors by discoursing on the beauties of philosophy and by explaining how if men listened to the voices of Reason and Nature they would everywhere be happy, virtuous, industrious, and at peace.

Suddenly, he broke off.

"But my dear fellow, if you don't mind me asking, what exactly are you doing at Court?"

"Trying to get a post in the Ministry of Finance."

"What do you mean by 'trying'? Surely you just have to ask?"

"There happen to be about 150 other people applying for the same posts, that's all."

"But, my dear fellow, don't be ridiculous. People like you aren't expected to stand in line, waiting with the herd."

"I've quarrelled with my family. I have nothing to do with them any more."

The Chevalier, who had just put a spoonful of pudding into his mouth, swallowed quickly to avoid choking.

"How very unfortunate", he said, when he had recovered from his astonishment at learning that a man actually existed who could allow a family row to disturb his convenience or advancement. "Can't the quarrel be made up?"

"I'm afraid not. You see . . ." Rodrigo hesitated. Could he trust the Chevalier? He hated to think of his troubles being gossiped about to strangers. He decided to take the risk. This decision was not the result of any very favourable judgment of the Chevalier's discretion but of his having for weeks had no one to open his heart to and of feeling that he could no longer keep all that was in it to himself.

235

The Chevalier not only heard the whole of Rodrigo's story from his departure for France to his falling out with Don Maurice. He also learned how, exasperated by his family's attitude, especially Beatriz's refusal to marry him without her father's permission, Rodrigo had left the Montesa Palace and was now living by himself in rooms near the Retiro. Since then, he had been hardening his heart against his guardian more and more. What had perhaps contributed most to this process was the memory of the way Don Maurice had spoken to him at the time of their row in front of his much younger cousins. How it rankled. He had allowed Don Maurice to treat him like a schoolboy. And, worse still, he had responded like one.

"If people like my guardian weren't so infatuated by the Jesuits," Rodrigo said bitterly, "every bit of this trouble could have been avoided."

"Ah! *Les bons pères jésuites!*" For a minute or so the Chevalier sat tapping his teeth with a gold toothpick. "Look," he said suddenly, "leave it to me. I'll get my Ambassador to arrange for you to see Don Manuel Roda."

"But it's Squillacci I'm trying to get an audience with."

"You don't want to serve under a man like that. Not with your views and ambitions. You say you want to help your country, to bring it up to date. Then first things first. You must attach yourself to a minister who will follow the lead of France in regard to the Jesuits. They are the magnet that attracts everything old-fashioned and behind the times. Once they are out of the way, then will be the time to think of modernising your institutions, developing your commerce, and all the rest. Besides, you still want to marry your cousin, don't you?"

"Yes. But what has that got to do with it?"

"A lot. When your uncle finds that your point of view is shared by the King and his ministers, he'll be forced to admit that he's been in the wrong. The sooner the Jesuits go, the sooner you'll be able to get married. Yes, Don Manuel Roda is the man for you. He detests the Society. Of course, he's not a gentleman. In fact, I believe he was educated as a charity scholar. But does that matter? I despise people who judge others by the length of their genealogies. Leave it to me. I'll arrange for you to see him. If anything is going to be done about the Jesuits, as Minister of Justice, he is bound to play an important part.

THE FOLLOWING MORNING, the Chevalier and Rodrigo were at the Palace, waiting alone in Don Manuel Roda's anteroom. After half an hour, the door to the minister's study opened, and the minister himself came out, still in conversation with the French Ambassador.

As arranged in advance by the Ambassador and the Chevalier, the Ambassador started, as though surprised to see the Chevalier there. The Chevalier then handed the Ambassador a letter. The Ambassador, who had met Rodrigo for the first time the night before, presented him to the minister as a friend and then, after asking permission to open the letter, withdrew to one side to read it.

Rodrigo flushed with embarrassment, feeling sure that the minister must see through such an obvious subterfuge. Don Manuel looked annoyed, and because he felt socially insecure, resentfully suspicious. Was he being treated with sufficient respect? Ought he to have allowed the Ambassador to read his letter? Turning away, he stared vacantly at a tapestry depicting the triumph of Liberality over Parsimony.

The Chevalier was unabashed.

"What a strange coincidence!" he said, laughingly. "My friend here, Don Rodrigo Logrosan, has been trying to obtain an audience with the Marquis Squillacci, when he meets Your Excellency instead."

Before the minister could answer, the Ambassador rejoined them.

"You would be wise, Excellency, to snatch Don Rodrigo away from the Minister of Finance while you have the chance", he said. "My young friend has every qualification necessary to make him useful to Your Excellency. I can recommend him highly."

Rodrigo was still unworldly enough to be shocked by the Ambassador's recommendation. The Ambassador had spoken to him the night before for a bare ten minutes. How could he conceivably know what he was really like?

For his part, Don Manuel was wondering whether Rodrigo could in some way be a relation of the Ambassador's. He tried, with an unconvincing smile, to hide his lack of enthusiasm for advancing the Ambassador's obscure Spanish connections.

"I didn't quite hear your name", he said to Rodrigo.

"Logrosan."

"Do you live in Madrid?"

"Yes, Excellency."

"And where were you educated?"

"The Collegio Imperiale."

"With the Jesuits?" An unintentional but convincing coldness replaced the unconvincing smile. "A first-class education. Unfortunately, I can't oblige the Ambassador by offering you a position at present. Every post in my Ministry is full."

The Ambassador drew the minister aside and whispered in his ear. Don Manuel glanced at Rodrigo, this time with a look of curiosity.

"Well," he said aloud to the Ambassador, "if he cares to come and see me tomorrow morning, I will talk with him further. But I can't promise anything."

He drew the Ambassador's arm through his own, and together they walked on toward the apartment of Don Jeronimo Grimaldi.

THE NEXT DAY, Rodrigo went alone to the minister's anteroom. This time it was crowded. On giving his name to an usher, he was at once led through the minister's empty study and into his dressing room.

The minister stood in front of the fireplace, in which newly lit sticks were crackling and flaming. Above it, a French clock ticked hurriedly. Through an open door opposite, a canopied bed was visible, with sheets and blankets tumbled about.

The valet kept bringing up different clothes and circling around his master, now crouching, now kneeling, now standing, as he fastened a button or did up a strap.

On Rodrigo's entrance, Don Manuel, in contrast to his previous coldness, nodded affably and pointed to an empty chair. Several gentlemen were sitting round the room. One of them, who kept fingering his watch fob, was holding forth about Montesquieu's *De l'esprit des lois*. His neighbour, an elderly man who might have been a judge, listened disapprovingly.

Occasionally, Don Manuel interrupted the speaker. But after a quick burst of words, he would break off to say something to the valet or to look in the mirror that the man held first in front of him so that he could straighten his cravat and then behind so that he could see whether his waistcoat lay smoothly across his back. He reminded Rodrigo of a horse being currycombed.

When the minister was dressed, the valet put a towel round his shoulders and led him to a chair in which he sat to have his hair powdered. Another servant brought him a cup of hot chocolate and buttered rolls on a silver dish.

"That's all very well", he interrupted again. "But Montesquieu wasn't a fool. When he was writing, the English constitution hadn't taken its present form. Theoretically, the executive and legislature in England are still separate. But they have ceased to be so in fact, because parliament has usurped more and more of the Crown's authority."

Rodrigo, although still smarting from the minister's rudeness the night before, began to have a higher opinion of his intelligence.

A few minutes later a secretary entered the room and stood meaningfully by the door. The gentlemen rose and, one by one, began to take their leave. Each, as he bowed to the minister, said a few words in a low voice—the real business for which he had come.

So this is all I'm going to get, Rodrigo thought. This is Don Manuel's way of not giving the Ambassador a direct "No". He rose to leave with the rest, but the minister signed to him to stay.

"So you decided to come?" he said, when they were alone.

239

"Yes, Your Excellency." Then he added, "But I had half a mind not to."

Don Manuel smiled. It was not a particularly radiant smile, suggesting, rather, a wan gleam of sunlight in the courtyard of an orphanage. But it was warm enough to show that he was amused.

"I don't know if the Ambassador told you about my ideas", Rodrigo said.

Don Manuel frowned.

"Ideas? We don't have ideas at Court. We are His Majesty's servants." He paced about for a few seconds, then his smile returned. "But I think I can use you, all the same. I'm going back to Madrid this afternoon. Come with me in my carriage, and we can talk on the way."

FORTY-SIX

The winter of 1765–1766 was long and hard. The cold seemed to penetrate everywhere—through the thickest shutters, curtains, hangings, bedclothes. The toes and fingers of Court ladies were swollen purple with chilblains, like those of Poor Clares and servant girls. Food was scarce and prices were high because of a bad harvest the summer before. But toward the end of Lent, the weather grew milder, and people's spirits rose. It was like escaping from the rule of a tyrant.

On the afternoon of Palm Sunday, Jean-Paul Houdin was sent by his new master to deliver a note at a house near the Guadalajara gate.

After leaving Monsieur Laborde, two years before, he had worked for five other French business houses but in each case had been dismissed after a few months without explanation. Eventually he discovered that Monsieur Laborde was responsible. So, finding that he could not get work as a clerk and, by now, not having enough money to remain idle for more than a fortnight, he had taken a post as a valet. His new master, for whom he had been working since the previous summer, was Diego de Torrelavega.

On his return from his errand, Jean-Paul was walking slowly along the Calle d'Atocha, thinking of nothing in particular, when he saw a crowd at the other end of the street moving rapidly toward him. It filled the street from side to side and gave off a sound like rapidly boiling water. For a moment he thought it was a religious procession, but he soon heard angry shouts and cries and saw that the men at the front were brandishing sticks, mattocks, sickles, scythes, and the odd sabre and musket.

Respectable citizens out for a Sunday stroll hurried into side streets or, where there were none close enough, pressed themselves as far back as possible into the doorways of houses. Jean-Paul found himself wedged between a middle-aged gentleman and his wife in the entrance to a shop. A minute or two later the torrent of human bodies was sweeping past. Many wore the slouch hats and flowing cloaks beloved by the more turbulent elements of the city's working class. Others seemed to be artisans and small shopkeepers. Above the shouting, he heard cries of "Down with Squillacci!" and "Long live the King!" Toward the rear, the crowd was less dense, and people were moving about confusedly in different directions. Some, who had just heard of the riot, were running to join it; others, who had been swept into it against their will or who had begun to lose heart, were running away.

Curious to know what the uproar was about, and not being sufficiently settled in life to think of reasons why it might be wiser not to get involved, Jean-Paul stepped from the shop entrance.

It was like jumping into a millrace. He felt himself pushed and shoved, first this way, then that, and for a few seconds had difficulty keeping his feet. Being so short, his head was on a level with the shoulders of most of the rioters, and he could not see, in any direction, more than a few feet. Soon he found himself hurrying along beside a tall artisan wearing a battered shako. There had already, it seemed, been a clash with the military.

"What's going on?" Jean-Paul shouted.

"Down with Squillacci!"

"Why Squillacci?"

241

"Because he's the one who's been making food so dear. He's the one who's been selling the bread of the poor to monopolists and swindlers. He's the one who's been putting lights in the streets so that his agents can spy on honest men. Down with the Food Commission! Down with foreigners! Down with spies and traitors!" In spite of his furious cries, the man looked about him laughing and grinning, as though out for a day's holiday.

The man on Jean-Paul's other side nudged him with his elbow. "Where the devil do you come from, friend? Haven't you heard about the new law?"

"Which law?"

"Squillacci thinks our cloaks are too long and the brims of our hats too wide. His spies can't see us properly. So we must all have our hats and cloaks trimmed to the new size. We've got to wear wigs and cocked hats like the blasted French and Italians. May they rot in hell! As if a Spaniard is going to let a dirty Italian tell him what clothes he's to wear. We're on our way to his house to teach Señor Squillacci a lesson."

Just at this moment they were forced to slow down. Jean-Paul heard cheers and stood on tiptoe to see what was happening. After a minute or two the crowd moved on again, veering to the right to pass a heavy carriage drawn up half across the street. A man with a scarred face, bloodshot eyes, and a broken nose was leaning out of the window urging the rioters on. In the shadow behind him, Jean-Paul caught sight for a moment of another face which he instantly knew he had seen before. But when? Where?

As he was trying to remember, the man with the broken nose suddenly withdrew his head and shoulders from the carriage window, and a few seconds later what looked like a rolled-up cloak, came flying through the window of the carriage and soared into the air. At the peak of its trajectory the bundle burst, and printed sheets of paper fluttered to the ground. Jean-Paul just had time to pick one up as he was hurried forward by the rioters behind him.

The paper was an open letter to the "Loyal and Patriotic Citizens of Madrid". Most of it was devoted to abusing foreigners, particularly the two unpopular ministers, who were blamed for the five years of bad harvests, the icy winter, the rise in prices, the unpopular street lights, and the new edict banning overly large cloaks and wide hat brims.

Turning over the sheet, Jean-Paul saw a sentence which read: "Spaniards, we want a Spanish King, a King who drives out foreigners and traitors, a King who listens to the cry of the poor, a King who protects and defends the religious orders against heretics and infidels." Since the King had no Spanish blood in him, this sentence, he realised, was patently seditious.

By this time the crowd was approaching the Guadalajara gate, which Jean-Paul had left not long before. Here they met half a dozen coaches moving briskly toward them.

The King, with a party of courtiers, was returning from the country-side, where he had been shooting. Seeing the road ahead blocked, the driver of the leading coach stopped, and the King, on being told why, sent word to his Master of the Horse, the Duke of Medina-Celi, who was in a separate coach, to go and speak to the rioters and get them to disperse.

The Duke told his coachman to drive forward, and in a few seconds he, his coach, mules and all, had disappeared into the seething human mass. Only the heads and shoulders of the coachmen and grooms remained visible.

After trying unsuccessfully to address the crowd from the window of the coach, the Duke was made to get out and was lifted onto the shoulders of two hefty labourers. As he came into view, swaying a little in his unaccustomed position, the chorus of shouts broke out again. "Down with Squillacci!" "Long live the King!"

The Duke held up a hand, his manner suggesting a bailiff sent to tell a particularly large and rough-looking crowd of trespassers to get off his master's property.

While the crowd was listening to the Duke's speech, Jean-Paul wriggled his way clear and made off down the Prado. Home, he said to himself. Then suddenly he thought of the unpopular minister and of what might happen if the rioters caught him. The man is probably the scoundrel they say he is, he thought. Somebody must have been lining his pockets for food to be the price it is. All the same, he ought to be warned. He may be murdered.

He ran though the empty streets toward the minister's palace, which he had often passed on his errands for Monsieur Laborde.

"Is anyone there?" he called, after hammering on the great doors into the courtyard with both fists. "I'm a friend. His Excellency is in danger. They'll be here in a few minutes." But there was no reply. Every door and window was shut.

He ran down a side street and in the wall of the palace garden found a gate, which opened when he pushed it. Crossing the garden, he made his way into the palace and mounted a great staircase to the first floor. Every room was empty. In one of the drawing rooms a table had been knocked over in the occupants' haste to escape, and a smashed china shepherdess lay near it on the floor.

The flight of apartments ended in a great bedchamber with a high canopied bed and, next to it, an open door leading to a closet beyond. Jean-Paul crossed the room and peered inside. Against the far wall stood a wardrobe with doors flung wide, and dresses hurriedly dragged from it and then discarded trailing across the carpet. The half open drawers of a chiffonier nearby disgorged equally tumbled contents. He trod on something hard; it was a ring.

Just as he was wondering what to do with it, he heard a movement, and turning saw a girl crouched in a corner like a frightened animal. She looked up at him and shrieked.

"It's all right, señorita", he said. "I'm a friend. I've come to warn the minister. He's in great danger. Where is he? He must escape."

The girl stared at him—first in terror, then, seeing that he was in livery and was small and looked well-disposed, with hysterical relief.

"They've gone, all gone", she said, in broken Spanish.

"Where to?"

"To the convent."

"What convent?"

"The convent where the Signora Marchesa's daughters are at school. The Marchesa was out walking in Las Delicias when they came to tell her that wicked men were coming to kill the Signor Marchese. Immediately she came home to collect her jewels. Then she went to the convent where they will protect her."

"But what are you doing here?"

"Just as they were getting into the carriages, she sent me back to look for a bracelet. But when I'd found it, they'd all gone."

"Leaving you alone? What a mistress! Never mind." He felt at ease again now he knew she was a maid and therefore someone of his own sort. "I'll look after you. Do you know where the convent is?"

"I couldn't find the way alone. But you won't leave me here, will you? The Holy Madonna has sent you."

"Of course I won't leave you. But my master's house is a long way off, and I'm wondering if there's any place closer where you would be safe. I know. Come on. We must be quick."

Ten minutes later they were standing at the back of Monsieur Laborde's warehouse. Jean-Paul told the girl to wait under an archway and then went gingerly into the courtyard. It was empty, and he crossed it, unobserved, to the back entrance. Finding the door locked, he was wondering what to do when he saw Madame Laborde at an upstairs window. She signalled that she would come down and let him in.

Since leaving Monsieur Laborde, Jean-Paul had paid regular monthly visits to his wife and daughter, first taking care to ensure that the merchant was out. His purpose, it was understood, was to find out whether the ladies had any commissions for him or if there were some other way in which he could be useful. But this was just a pretext to enable them to hide their real motives from themselves.

Jean-Paul paid his visits because he was in love with Madeleine and wanted to see her. Madame Laborde enjoyed having somebody sympathetic with whom she could talk in French. And Madeleine looked forward to his coming because he was the only young man, apart from her father's clerks, she ever had a chance to talk to.

Did Madeleine feel more than this? She did not know. Her thoughts and feelings were tangled, and her inability to separate them prevented her from understanding the state of her own heart. Several times a week she told herself that of course Jean-Paul was not really a valet, that he had been forced by misfortune to become one, and that he was capable of far better things. Then her pride reminded her that Jean-Paul was only a foundling, while the Labordes were among the leading merchants of Lyons. At other times, in a despondent mood, she would say to herself: He only comes here out of kindness—there's sure to be some girl of his own sort with whom he's in love.

The sight of Jean-Paul with the Marchesa Squillacci's Italian maid seemed to confirm this final surmise. Immediately she felt miserable, recognising at last that she was longing for Jean-Paul to propose to her. Now, however, she felt sure he never would.

When Jean-Paul had explained the girl's story, Madame Laborde kissed her and said she would be safe with them until she could go back to her mistress. "And wouldn't I have a thing or two to say to that Marquise if I met her", Madame Laborde said indignantly. "Deserting a poor girl to the fury of a licentious mob! I'd tell her she was a selfish, godless, heartless, over-painted hussy. Which is what she is, I'll be bound. Italians are no better than Spaniards. Do you think there's much danger, Monsieur Jean-Paul?"

"You've nothing to be afraid of, madame. They're only interested in Messieurs Grimaldi and Squillacci."

"Well, that mob won't get in here without paying for it. The maid is heating all the olive oil we've got, and there's boiling water ready, too."

"I wouldn't use that, madame. It would only infuriate them. But they won't come this way. They're too busy elsewhere."

Before he left, Madame Laborde took him aside.

"Madeleine has promised her father that if no one else has asked for her hand a year from now, she will marry Mesnier." She shrugged her shoulders. There were tears in her eyes. "What can we do?" But she did not expect an answer; she only wanted to relieve her mind.

"Don't lose heart, madame", he said. "A year is a long time. I

246

shouldn't be surprised if providence found a way out for you sooner than you expect."

As soon as he had left Monsieur Laborde's, Jean-Paul began to run again. It was three hours since Diego had sent him to deliver the note near the Guadalajara gate. By this time the mob had broken into the Palacio Squillacci, all the windows were wide open, and every few seconds a shower of miscellaneous objects—silver dishes, hats, shoes, cushions, pieces of china, musical instruments—came flying out, to be caught and carried off by the looters' friends waiting below. The less quick-witted or acquisitive members of the mob stood cheering a man in a flounced nightdress and an enormous lace cap who was dancing a seguidilla on the roof.

FORTY-SEVEN

While the Duke of Medina-Celi was trying to calm the rioters at the Guadalajara gate, the King and his party of courtiers had driven off by back streets toward the Royal Palace.

One of the gentlemen-in-waiting made a timid effort to put an encouraging interpretation on what was happening.

"I'm sure they're really devoted to you, sir. I heard them shouting 'Long live the King!' It was only . . ."

The King turned his head and stared.

Who, his face seemed to say, gave you leave to make excuses for my rebellious subjects? The gentleman fell silent and fumbled in his pocket for his snuffbox. But, as he took it out, he dropped it, and a shower of snuff fell over the King's legs.

Gaspar de Vallecas, who was also in the coach, leaned forward to dust the royal knee and calves. Although loyalty prevented him from criticising his royal master's choice of ministers, he did often wish the

King did not sometimes give the impression of having been happier as King of the Two Sicilies and that he would put his confidence more in the Spanish nobility rather than in men of obscure origin whom he had raised to high posts.

From time to time he glanced sideways to see how the King was reacting. If the eyes had not blinked, he could have been a waxwork. What self-control, Gaspar thought. But the expressionless face was only a mask, hiding royal perplexity and outraged royal pride. Where a different prince might have said to himself: "Perhaps there's something in these charges against my ministers; I ought at least to investigate them", for King Charles the rioters were simply ungrateful children of a good father. And since his mother was Italian, the agitation against "Italians" was an added insult. There could be no question of "Father" having been at fault.

The coach lurched into the Palace courtyard, and the great iron gates, which had been hurriedly opened, were as hurriedly shut again. The guards had been trebled, and extra detachments could be seen waiting in an inner courtyard.

After alighting with the help of a gentleman-in-waiting, the King went straight to his private apartments, and soon afterward sent word that for the present he wanted the Duke of Montesa to remain in the Palace. So Gaspar dispatched one of his servants with a message for his wife and then, having nothing else to do, joined one of the groups of courtiers discussing the events of the afternoon in the hall of Apollo and Diana.

Don Pedro Stuart was explaining in a knowing way how the trouble had started.

"I have it at firsthand—from one of my servants. The whole thing was deliberately provoked by a party of *majos*."

"Who are they?" asked a young attaché from the Bavarian Embassy.

"Who are the *majos*?" Don Pedro exclaimed in amazement, then, seeing who his questioner was, smiled graciously. "The *majos* are the plebeian dandies of Madrid. They set the fashions that the rabble follow.

How could anyone expect the *majos* to let their beloved hats and cloaks be trimmed to reasonable proportions. You might as well ask women to shave their heads and wear breeches. Squillacci should have had the sense to see there was bound to be trouble. The whole thing was folly from start to finish."

"I don't see why it was folly", said a gentleman who was engaged to one of Squillacci's nieces. "If we want Madrid to be a place where people can walk about safely, it's sensible to make it easier rather than more difficult for the police to catch criminals. It looks to me as if someone is deliberately stirring up anti-Italian prejudice."

"I'm not anti-Italian", Don Pedro said quickly. "I fully recognise that the Marquis has some good ideas, but he doesn't understand our Spanish people. Anyhow, as I was saying, one of these *majos*, wrapped in his long cloak, with his hat pulled down over his eyes—in fact, deliberately defying the edict—parades up and down in front of the barracks. The guards probably think the edict is nonsense, too. But, after all, they are soldiers. Soldiers can't have opinions; they have to obey orders—so, they start to arrest him. Instantly a group of roughs, who've been waiting in a side street, set on them with sticks and knives. They knock down one of the guards, overpower and disarm the others, and suddenly the streets are filled with men and women shouting 'Down with Squillacci!'"

"When you say the riot has been deliberately provoked . . ."

"I simply mean that the people have had a hard time. The edict is the last straw, and the *majos*, being the aristocracy of the populace, have determined to show they've had enough. I see not the slightest grounds for excitement or for dramatic measures. Distribute more food, and the whole thing will melt away. That, at least, would be my remedy if I were responsible."

Gaspar wandered to another group. There the Prince of San Martino was saying that the quickest way to restore order would be to hang the ringleaders. He turned away. What business is it of San Martino's, he thought indignantly. This is a Spanish affair. A foreigner ought to have tact enough to keep his mouth shut.

Feeling troubled and restless, he decided to go and see the Duke of Losada, the King's closest friend, who had also been a friend of the old Duke of Montesa, Luisa's father.

"Good", Losada said, as soon as he saw Gaspar. "We can play chess. I'm forbidden to leave my rooms in case His Majesty needs me." But they had barely finished setting out the pieces when the door burst open and a dishevelled, terrified-looking lackey rushed into the room. After staring wildly about for a moment, the man dropped into a chair. "Water, water," he cried, gasping and panting, "get me some water."

The two dukes looked at him in astonishment.

"Good God", Gaspar said. "Squillacci." He rang for a servant. "Water for His Excellency. Quickly!"

"What on earth are you doing in that outfit, Marquis?" Losada said. "I was about to take you by the collar and kick you downstairs."

The footman came hurrying back with a carafe and a glass.

"My God", the minister said, still panting as he swallowed the water. "You don't know what I've been through . . . I was out of town . . . they sent a man to warn me when I was on my way back . . . if I hadn't had time to change clothes with my groom, I'd be a dead man by now . . ."

"And your wife and children . . . ?" Gaspar asked.

"It's not my wife and children they're after. They'll be safe enough. The curs, the ungrateful curs. After all I've tried to do for them. I've worked only for the good of His Majesty and Spain, and they want to murder me. But the people are not really to blame. They've been misled by my enemies, who are jealous of my influence with His Majesty. They are using the people to ruin me with His Majesty."

He glared at the two dukes as though they were the enemies he had in mind; and the glare was not without effect. Neither had intrigued against him, but neither liked him, and both had felt a momentary pleasure at his misfortune. They looked away.

"Who's that?" he cried sharply, starting up at the sound of a knock on the door and running to hide behind a screen.

But it was only a servant—this time a real one.

WHEN THE MINISTER HAD RECOVERED sufficiently to go to his own quarters, Losada asked Gaspar to stay to supper. During the evening visitors came and went, bringing contradictory reports about events in the city. First it was said that after sacking Squillacci's palace, the mob had set fire to Grimaldi's, then that it had only broken Grimaldi's windows. About midnight a servant reported that the crowds were in the Calle Mayor smashing the hated streetlights.

As Gaspar did not have an apartment of his own at the Palace, and the King had still not given him permission to go home, Losada had a servant make up a bed made up for him in the room where they were sitting. They parted for the night, telling each other that by morning the whole thing would probably have blown over.

But when Losada's valet woke Gaspar the next day, he told him that, far from dispersing, the rioters were gathering in front of the Palace. Pulling a blanket around his shoulders, Gaspar went into Losada's bedroom. Losada, in a nightcap and still half-asleep, was sitting on the edge of his bed, gulping hot chocolate. His hairy legs showed under the bottom of his nightshirt and his feet were thrust into Turkish slippers.

"Have you heard?" Gaspar asked.

"Yes."

"It's more serious than we thought. It looks like the end of our two Italian friends."

"You don't know His Majesty, if you think he'll be dictated to by a rabble," Losada replied. "Some firmness and a shot or two over their heads, and they'll soon disperse." He shouted for his valet and began to pull on his breeches.

Having dressed, the two dukes made their way quickly to the suite of rooms overlooking the Palace forecourt. In the Hall of Ambassadors, courtiers were already stationed at the windows watching the mob surging against the railings that separated the forecourt from the street. Most of them were rather enjoying the scene. The riots were not directed against them.

"Good God!" Gaspar said. "They've put the Walloons on guard." The Walloons were recruited in the one-time Spanish Netherlands.

"Haven't they got sense enough to keep them out of the way? Don't they realise how unpopular they've been ever since they accidentally killed those people two years ago at the Infanta's wedding? Look! Just as I thought. They're in trouble already . . . over there on the right . . ."

He pointed to where some of the rioters were climbing the railings. The Guards on the outside were trying to stop them by hanging on to their legs, while those on the inside were poking at them with their bayonets through the bars. In spite of this, three of the rioters managed to reach the top, and their success encouraged others to emulate them.

Suddenly, two detachments of Walloons just below the windows where the courtiers stood watching marched forward and halted in the middle of the courtyard. An officer shouted a command. The men of the left-hand detachment raised their muskets and fired.

Losing their grip, three of the men who had been clinging to the top of the railings fell backward, and a howl like the cry of a single, gigantic wolf rose from the crowd.

In the Hall of Ambassadors, a moment of absolute silence had followed the musket shots. Then everyone started speaking at the same time.

"What's happened?" "They've killed someone." "But they were firing over their heads." "The idiots!" "Who on earth gave the order to shoot?" "About time they were frightened . . ." "They were getting out of hand . . ." "This will bring them to their senses . . ."

Meanwhile, the Walloons outside the railings were desperately defending themselves, and, as the courtiers watched, one of the guardsmen fell and vanished from sight under the rioters' feet.

Gaspar pulled at Losada's sleeve. "Quick! We must see His Majesty."

FORTY-EIGHT

In the royal apartment etiquette was by now largely in abeyance. The King was sitting in the principal drawing room surrounded by a group of nobles and statesmen who, when they were not addressing him directly, argued among themselves about the best way of handling the situation, while lesser functionaries bringing news or carrying out orders came and went without ceremony.

Since all authority lay with the King, each noble was bent on enticing or pushing the royal will in the direction he wanted it to go; and each was convinced that the most effective way of achieving this was, not by providing convincing arguments, but by alternately playing on the King's fear and pride.

The King listened with a flushed face.

Eventually, having heard Gaspar's and Losada's account of events in front of the Palace, he once again sent his Master of the Horse to try and reason with the crowd.

Accompanied by the Duke of Arcos, Medina-Celi rode out to the railings, where the guardsmen on the outside had managed to fight their way back through the gate.

"My good people," he shouted, standing up in his stirrups, "if you will all go home, His Majesty will . . ."

A roar of abuse drowned the rest of the speech. In ordering the troops to fire, authority had put itself in the wrong, and the rioters imagined they could now force it to grant their demands.

"We're not going home till we get justice, fair prices, and no street-lights and cocked hats", one of the leaders shouted.

Two men near the gate lifted up the dead body of a woman, accidentally shot by one of the Walloons, to show there was now a new grievance.

After several unsuccessful attempts to make themselves heard, the two dukes turned their horses about and rode back to the Palace. At the same time a group of rioters, dragging the dead woman's body with them on a cart, headed for the centre of the city where the sight of it had the intended effect. The crowds there set on the detachments of the Walloon and Italian guards stationed in the Puerta del Sol and Plaza Mayor. The soldiers in the Puerta del Sol fended off the attackers with the butts of their muskets. But in the Plaza Mayor, the officer in command lost his nerve and ordered his men to shoot. In the ensuing skirmish the soldiers were forced to retreat. Several were caught and killed and their mangled bodies paraded up and down the Calle Mayor and the Calle de Alcalá. Meanwhile, outside the Palace, priests from the neighbouring churches and monasteries were trying to get the crowd to disperse.

"This is no time for preaching", a voice shouted. "We're good Catholics. We'll only listen to the King."

At this, Father Yecla, the Prior of San Juan en la Mancha suggested that the leaders put their grievances into a petition, which he promised to present to the King on their behalf. Being uncertain, like the King and the courtiers, what to do next, the rioters approved the idea. As many as could packed into a nearby tavern, where, after a great deal of argument, the petition was drawn up. It demanded the banishment of Squillacci and his family, the formation of a ministry of Spaniards, the dissolution of the food commission, the withdrawal of the Walloons, liberty for people to dress as they pleased, lower prices for staple commodities, a general pardon for all that had occurred, and it ended with a threat that if the people's demands were not met, they would burn the Palace and the city. At the bottom came a list of barely legible signatures.

The Prior, who, in the meantime had returned to his monastery now reappeared dressed as a public penitent, with a crucifix in one hand, ashes on his head and a rope around his neck. Taking the petition, he made his way to the gate in the Palace railings, and was let into the courtyard.

His arrival in the royal presence immediately silenced the babel of argument and recrimination that had been surging uninterruptedly around the King for the past two hours. He walked slowly down the room, stopped within a few paces of the King, and fell on his knees.

"Your Majesty, your people have asked me to be their spokesman. They have done wrong. But they are your children, and now they are sorry, and, on their behalf, I beg Your Majesty to pardon them. They have been disobedient and rebellious only because they are hungry and unhappy. So they turn to Your Majesty, as to their father, asking you to redress their wrongs. Your Majesty will, I beg, allow me to read the list of their entreaties." The Prior's head was bowed and his voice was low and hesitant—as much from the strain of having to calm the crowds as from nervousness at finding himself the focus of so many grand people's attention.

The King moved slightly in his chair. "You have our permission."

Without looking up, the Prior started to read from the smudged sheet of paper, here and there stumbling over a word. Several passages he had to rephrase impromptu to make them sound more like the entreaties of repentant children and less like the demands of rebels. The threat to burn the Palace and Madrid he suppressed.

When he had finished, he moved forward on his knees and gave the petition to the King, who handed it to the Prince of San Martino.

"Your Majesty," the Prior said, "if Your Majesty would graciously consent to speak to them in person the people's fears and anxieties would be calmed, and I am confident they would go home without causing further disturbance."

His humble manner seemed to soothe the injured royal pride. But just as the King appeared to be about to give way, the Neapolitan favourite, who was standing behind his chair, leaned forward, holding out the petition so that the King could read it for himself.

"Look at this, Sir," he said, pointing to the sentence about burning the Palace and city. The King's expression changed.

"You may go, Father Prior", he said. "We shall have to consider this further."

As soon as the Prior had left, another battle between the courtiers began. The Duke of Arcos and the Counts of Priego and Gazzola led the party in favour of force. The Marques de Sarria, the Counts of Onate and Revillagigedo, and the Duke of Montesa headed the opposition in favour of clemency.

Which of us will he listen to? Gaspar wondered. A movement of royal will in one direction, and Madrid would be in turmoil—lives lost, families bereaved, destinies changed, hopes cut off, hatred festering

255

for years. A movement in the opposite direction, and they all, King, courtiers, and people, would be sleeping peacefully that night as though nothing had happened.

The King, too, was conscious of these alternatives but with a difference. As a Christian prince, he had an obligation to show mercy. Also, injudiciously handled, rebellions might end anywhere—*had ended* in the loss of thrones. But now there was this threat. To grant the petition might look like weakness—could even be interpreted as cowardice. He had already changed his mind once. A second change would be an admission that he had twice been wrong. In his thoughts the scales went up and down.

Suddenly he announced that he would speak to the people after all and moved toward the stairs. Gaspar went to a window and watched him ride out toward the railings where the kneeling Prior presented him with another copy of the petition. The roar of cheering a few seconds later announced that the petition had been granted, the people began to sing, and a procession formed. In the middle a statue of the Virgin of Almudena, carried shoulder-high by four Dominicans, moved unsteadily above the throng. The uprising seemed to be over.

FORTY-NINE

The same evening, Beatriz de Vallecas was sitting near a window in the Queen Mother's apartments writing to her cousin Casilda Colmenar. Too innocent to realise that rulers open and read their subjects' letters, she described the effects of the riot on the Queen Mother's entourage without the prudent circumlocutions that a woman like Doña Ana would have employed.

> Her Majesty was in a furious temper . . . it was the rioters shouting "Down with the Italians" that made her so angry . . . she pulled Doña

Dolores' hair . . . when the Walloons opened fire, Doña Inmaculada screamed like a madwoman . . . all the ladies said we would be murdered . . . I was terrified . . . this morning they were sewing jewels into their underclothes . . . I don't know why . . . if we were going to be murdered, what would have been the use of jewellery . . . ?

The alarms of the last twenty-four hours, together with her own private troubles, had combined into a single monstrous worry that weighed on her spirits like an immense boulder.

The letter continued:

Do you remember my telling you how kind one of the royal governesses, Doña Elvira de Quiroga, had been to me and about the mysterious person whose conversion she asked me to pray for? Well, last week she revealed that he was none other than that uncouth young man Diego de Torrelavega. Can you believe it? All this time, Doña Elvira has been playing a trick on me. The mystery she has made about Don Diego was simply a way of getting me interested in him. Of course, he isn't as bad as he used to be. Since General Pradanos and his wife more or less adopted him, he's improved a lot. People even say they have made him their heir, which means he won't be short of mothers wanting him to marry their daughters. All the same, he's not the kind of young man I could ever really like, much less love. So you can imagine what I felt when, shortly afterward, Papa— dear Papa, who I thought would always understand me—told me with a serious face that the Marques de Torrelavega had asked for my hand for his son. And Papa said he hoped I would consider the proposal seriously. Oh, dear Casilda, you can't imagine how Papa has changed since Rodrigo left! In the past he would never have pressed me to marry a man like Don Diego, whom he must know I can never care for. Dreadful as it is to say so, I feel that this is his way of punishing Rodrigo. How I wish you hadn't all gone away to the country. The whole world seems to be falling apart . . .

Suddenly a door opened and Doña Ana swept into the room, closely followed by the Mayordomo Mayor, the Marques de Montealegre.

"I shall count on you, then", the Mayordomo was saying. "Her

Majesty and her household will be ready to leave as soon as I send word."

"You can count on nothing of the sort", Doña Ana replied. "You know Her Majesty, and you have heard what she said."

"Her Majesty must be persuaded to change her mind."

"In other words, you are telling me to storm a fortress that you know to be impregnable."

The Mayordomo Mayor smiled.

"Is there such a thing as an impregnable fortress, Doña Ana? And besides, with your wisdom and understanding of Her Majesty's character, I'm sure this particular fortress will surrender quite quickly."

"Flattery, my lord! Pure flattery!" But Doña Ana was not unpleased and curtsied as the Mayordomo Mayor withdrew. Just as she was about to leave the room, she caught sight of Beatriz.

"What are you doing here?" she asked sharply. "Of course, of course," she went on in a gentler tone, "where else should you be? Well, you may as well know what's going on. You heard what the Mayordomo Mayor said. We are leaving tonight for Aranjuez."

"Leaving? But what for?"

"Don't ask me 'what for?' The longer I live at Court, the less I understand why things are done the way they are done. What's more, we're leaving secretly—as though such a thing were possible at Court, which is necessarily made up of the most garrulous and indiscreet persons in the kingdom." The prospect of having to make the Queen leave against her will had ruffled Doña Ana's usually well-controlled temper to an exceptional degree.

"But I thought the riot was over. Surely we're not leaving because of that?"

"What other reason can there be?"

"Oh, if only His Majesty would trust the people", Beatriz said earnestly. "I'm sure they don't really mind Italians in the government. But they're hungry. If they only had enough to eat, they would never give His Majesty any trouble."

The sumptuous meals she had to eat at the Palace often made her unhappy, and, when unobserved, she frequently removed cakes and fruit from the table in her napkin for her maid to take to the poor.

But Doña Ana had decided that criticism had gone far enough. "That will do", she said. "I suppose you think you know better than His Majesty and all his ministers how to rule the country. Go and collect your things. Only what you can carry yourself, though. Then wait here. You will be told what to do when the time comes."

Later that night, Beatriz found herself with the other ladies, all wrapped in cloaks and furs, waiting while, behind closed doors, Doña Ana stormed the last strongholds of the Queen's will.

Doña Ana's victory was announced by the appearance of the Queen herself—leaning on the arm of the lady least liked by Doña Ana. The Queen was talking as she came into the room, and her face was red and blotchy. Doña Ana's face expressed nothing.

"We're running away!" the Queen said excitedly. "We're running away! That's the modern method of doing things. That's the new idea of courage. Did Don John of Austria run away from the Turks? Did Charles of England run away from Cromwell? But we're running away from a handful of beggars. It's magnificent! Superb! Real Spanish courage. Well, Italians would be ashamed of such cowardice. I'm ashamed myself." Her half-blind eyes flashed as she turned them on her ladies. "'Down with the Italians', eh? Well, it's time the Spanish had a taste of their own medicine. Do you think we haven't had more than enough of Spanish rule in Italy? Over two centuries of it. So don't be mistaken. You are hated in Italy. More deeply than the Turks in Greece, or the English in Ireland. Hated for your pride and arrogance, your brutality and rapacity. And if the people of Italy knew what was happening today, they would not only hate the Spanish—they would despise them."

There was a splendour and impetuosity about the old woman's fury that made her ladies inwardly cringe and assent to what she was saying.

Only when Doña Ana had manoeuvred the Queen into the sedan chair that was to take her to the coaches, and stood ready in the centre of the room, was the spell broken. As the ladies followed the chair and its four porters downstairs, they reminded themselves indignantly that Italians were notoriously more cowardly than Spaniards, that Her Majesty was losing her mind, and that if Italians had suffered under Spanish rule, then they had only had what they deserved.

On reaching the ground floor, the porters prepared for a further descent. The Queen stuck her head out of the sedan-chair window.

"Don't these blockheads know which way to go? Or are we to spend the night in the cellars?"

"There is a way out underground, ma'am", Doña Ana said, moving forward. "They have orders to use that. We shall be less noticed."

"*Dio!* What's everyone afraid of? Aren't there guards? If King Philip were alive, this wouldn't be happening."

In the underground passage the air was cold. Halfway along the sedan chair got stuck where the passage turned a corner, and fifteen minutes passed while one of the porters went back to the Palace for a saw to shorten the handles.

As the Queen's ladies stood whispering and shivering, and wondering fearfully whether bats were going to get into their hair, they switched their indignation from their mistress to the gentlemen of the Court. Why hadn't they arranged things better? Why couldn't everyone have left the Palace in a dignified fashion, properly protected? Where were the captains of the guard, the Master of the Horse, the chamberlains and ushers? What were men for, if not to look after women in situations like this? Probably they had all fled.

When at last they reached the end of the passage, they found carriages waiting and soldiers. Beatriz looked about, expecting to hear the shouts of the rioters and see the sky red with the flames of burning buildings, but there was nothing to see except shadowy figures and the huge motionless coaches; or to hear, apart from the stamping of a horse, the jingle of harness and the whispers of the officers and attendants. She was helped into a coach with five other ladies; an officer gave a muffled order, and they set off.

During the first half hour the ladies continued to talk and argue acrimoniously, then, one by one, they fell asleep. Only Beatriz, who was in the middle of the back seat, remained awake. The head of the lady on her left was resting on her shoulder, and the heels of the lady on her right were digging into her instep. In spite of her discomfort, she had not moved for fear of waking the two exhausted sleepers and becoming herself the victim of their bad temper.

She wondered where Rodrigo was and what he was doing. It hurt her to think about him, since to think about him meant to dwell on his loss. But she could no more keep his image out of her mind than she could have controlled a headache.

First she pictured him in various heroic situations, addressing the rioters, rescuing people in danger, ordering the Walloons not to shoot. Then she began to go over, for the many hundredth time, the quarrel between Rodrigo and her father, trying to think of ways in which, if they had all acted differently, it could have been avoided, and of the ways in which it could now be made up. But, as always, she ended by feeling, with a sense of weariness and despair, that in human terms there was no solution. Her father and Rodrigo had pitted their wills against each other, and neither was the kind of person to give way. What conceivable circumstance would make them change? She could think of none.

But just as she was thinking that life was unbearable and that she might as well have been killed by the rioters, she suddenly understood that although humanly the situation was hopeless, she had been brought to realise this only in order to help her understand that God alone could end her troubles: for the future she must depend entirely upon him. Momentarily her heart was filled with peace, and although the sensation faded, the memory of it revived her courage.

They had been driving for about an hour when there was a jolt, a lurch, a crash, and the carriage came to a halt, tilted heavily to the right. The ladies woke up and shrieked. Beatriz heard footsteps and whinnying horses. Doña Dolores de la Pena put her head out of the left-hand window.

"Where are we? What's happened?" she demanded.

"There's a wheel come off, milady", a voice replied.

"Then stop the other coaches. They'll have to make room for us in them."

"They've all gone, ma'am."

One of the younger ladies began to laugh and sob hysterically.

"If you would care to alight, ladies," said an officer in a long military cloak, "there's a house just up the road where you can wait while the wheel is mended." The unruffled masculine voice seemed to reassure them.

"Are we alone?" Doña Dolores asked.

"The rest of the party has gone ahead, señora. But they've left two of us here, with a dozen men to look after you."

After the ladies nearest the door had clambered out of the carriage, Beatriz felt herself being helped to the ground and a few seconds later was walking up the road on the arm of the other officer. They soon outstripped the rest, making for a house on the top of a rise, where it stood out black against the stars.

"Would you mind going slower?" Beatriz asked. "The others won't be able to catch up with us."

"That's just what I want to avoid, Doña Beatriz", the officer said. "I have something I must tell you, and this may be my only chance."

Beatriz, recognising Diego de Torrelavega's voice, inwardly uttered what was more a reproach than a prayer. "Holy Mother of God, how could you let this happen? You know I'm almost at the end of my tether, and only a few minutes ago I was feeling sure God was going to make everything right." At the same time, the thought that Diego could take advantage of such a situation to press his attentions on her gave her a worse opinion of him than ever.

"I'm sorry," she said firmly, "but I can't listen to you. We must wait here until the others have joined us."

"Please hear me," he said, "if only for a minute. You'll be glad when you know what it's about. Truly. Our families are trying to arrange a marriage between us. Well, I wanted to tell you that nothing will induce me to marry you, no matter what they do. They tried to make me a monk once, and they couldn't. I shall stand up to them this time, too. But now I've offended you. I never know how to say things properly. Please understand that, of course, if you were willing to marry me I should die of happiness. But I know you don't want to. And even if you were to say you would, I should be forced to refuse, because you could only be doing it out of kindness and because you didn't know the kind of person I am."

As the meaning of his words became clear to her, Beatriz let herself be drawn forward again, and they walked for some seconds in silence.

"I don't know what to reply", she said at last. "I have been so unjust to you in my thoughts, and now you have been so generous. I wish I could make some return. Not that I think the proposal your parents have made on your behalf anything but a compliment, but . . . but for the present I have decided not to marry, and you have saved me the pain of giving a refusal."

"There *is* something you can do for me."

"If I can, I will."

"I was wondering . . . is it possible . . . do you think your sister, Doña Isabel, has any special regard for me?"

"You were thinking of Isabel?"

"Of course, it's foolish I know, but . . ."

"It's not. Why should it be? But I admit that I hadn't considered the possibility. Isabel is still so young, and besides, sisters don't confide all their secrets to each other. She certainly talks about you quite often."

"Is that really so?" Diego asked excitedly.

I oughtn't to have said that, Beatriz thought. It's not strictly true. At least Isabel doesn't talk about him in the way he imagines. I must stop her. She ought to be more understanding. He may be a little different from other people, but he's kind, modest, and considerate; much more so than Angel or Ruiz for instance.

"There's one thing I don't understand", she said with a smile. "Just now you made yourself out to be the sort of man no woman would want to marry. I don't believe it. But if it were true, how could you expect me to think you would make a good husband for my sister?"

"I meant I wasn't the sort of person to marry you. Doña Isabel is different. With her I wouldn't feel so ashamed of myself."

"You ought to have more self-confidence, Don Diego. You worry too

263

much about your failings. After all, everybody has them. Many people have more than they let appear. They are just better at hiding them, and I'm not sure that this is a virtue. Will you promise me to have a higher opinion of yourself in the future?"

"I will promise anything you ask", he answered happily.

They had reached the farmhouse and went into the kitchen, where Diego left Beatriz in the care of the owner's wife. A few minutes later the other ladies joined her, and for several hours they sat on stools, dozing uncomfortably round a smoking brazier. At last a soldier came to say that the wheel was mended.

It was long after daybreak when they finally reached the escarpment at the edge of the Tagus valley and saw, in the distance below them, embedded in its oasis of plane trees and elms, the roofs of the Palace of Aranjuez.

FIFTY

As the news spread that the Court had left Madrid, the rioters, realising they had been tricked and afraid that the concessions extracted the day before would be withdrawn, again appeared on the streets.

To calm them, the President of the Council of Castile, Diego de Rojas, Bishop of Cartagena, offered to drive to Aranjuez with a new petition. The leaders approved and the Bishop composed a memorial in which the greater part of the blame for the people's sufferings was once again placed on the unfortunate Squillacci, who, no matter what happened, was now almost certain to be dismissed. The Bishop saw no point in making enemies unnecessarily by implicating other people.

He climbed into his carriage, thankful that he, too, was soon going to be out of Madrid, beyond the reach of the mob.

However, he had not yet crossed the Toledo bridge before the rioters changed their minds and decided to keep him in the city as a hostage. He was made to return to his palace, and an escaped convict was sent to Aranjuez with the petition in his place. The mob passed the rest of the day raiding the arsenals, sacking houses and breaking into shops. The tumult only began to subside when the convict returned late in the afternoon with the royal reply, in which the King assured the people that he would keep his promises provided they give up their arms and restore peace and order.

Once again it looked as if the party favouring clemency had been proved right. But within a day or two, reports were coming in that riots had broken out in Saragossa, Barcelona, Salamanca, Murcia, and Corunna. The whole country seemed about to burst into revolt. The King had a seizure and was bled twice. On recovering, he at last yielded to what was now the majority opinion at Court. For whatever reasons, good or bad, just or unjust, Squillacci had to go. The minister was ordered to leave the country and was taken under escort to the coast.

Squillacci's departure meant another bad day for the Queen Mother's ladies-in-waiting.

"The cowards! The miserable cowards!" the Queen cried, striking out blindly with her ebony stick, and catching Doña Ana across the ankles. Doña Ana bit her lip but otherwise stood as though untouched, a heroine of palace etiquette.

"They've dismissed the only man to get anything done", the Queen continued. "Grimaldi, Arriaga—what are they worth? Nincompoops and sycophants. But *I* know why certain people are determined to ruin Squillacci. Not because he's an Italian. No. Because he's a good Catholic. They want to destroy the Jesuits, the way the miserable French and Portuguese have done. But Squillacci stood in their path. They were afraid the King would listen to him. Ah, what has happened to my son? If he'd listened to his mother, there wouldn't have been any riots. Nothing like this happened when King Philip and I were ruling."

BY THE END OF THE WEEK, although the riots in the provinces had subsided, unemployed workmen from the countryside were reported to be pouring into Madrid, and the capital was still restless. What should be done? Everyone, from the King down, knew that none of the existing members of the government was strong enough to reestablish the royal authority. Where was a saviour to be found?

The chief contenders for the role were the Duke of Alba, the Marques de la Ensenada, the Marques de Torrelavega, and Count Aranda. While Alba was known to be hostile to the Jesuits, Ensenada was considered their friend. The King vacillated like a nervous driver wondering which of four fiery-looking steeds to harness to his chariot.

During this period of uncertainty, the courtiers attached themselves first to one contender, then to another, according to the rumour of the moment.

On the Monday after the feast of St. Isidore, for instance, word went around that the King had sent for the Marques de Torrelavega. Within minutes, people were crowding into his apartment to congratulate him. But on Tuesday his rooms were deserted; the King was said to be closeted with the Duke of Alba.

Gaspar de Vallecas, who by nature was drawn to people in need of friends rather than to those oversupplied with them, went to call on the Marques. His apartment, not having been attended to since the influx the day before, looked as if it had had a visit from the rioters. Chairs had been pushed into corners, a curtain had been half-pulled from its pole, and snuff was still strewn over the carpet, which had been kicked into ridges and stained with wine and hot chocolate.

The Marques was sitting at a table, writing a letter with one hand while, in the other, he held a fork which he kept dipping into a plate of chicken and rice. He seemed barely aware that he was eating, and bits of food kept falling on his open portfolio and on the front of his silver-laced coat. His pen moved across the page in rapid jabs.

"Good morning, Duke", he said, without putting down either fork or pen. "You're a true friend. Take that chair there, please. There's plenty of room today, as you can see." He smiled sardonically. "Forgive me if I go on eating. This is the first meal I've had since yesterday. At all costs we must stop His Majesty from choosing Alba or Ensenada. Alba's in his dotage, and Ensenada will start a war with the English."

"Can I help in any way?"

"Indeed you can. Aranda and I will have to form an alliance to keep the other two out. Can you go and see him for me? Tell him if he will support me he can have any post he likes."

A servant appeared in the doorway, and bowed.

"His Excellency the Marquis Grimaldi to see your Lordship."

Torrelavega glanced at Gaspar. "The great trimmer", he whispered. "The tide must be turning in my favour again. Tell Aranda. He'll know what it means."

However, when the King at last made up his mind, he chose, not the most vicious, but the strongest horse. On April 11, Count Aranda, who had been Captain General of Valencia, was appointed President of the Council of Castile and head of government with special powers to deal with the rioters. The Marques de Torrelavega was given a seat on the Council of Castile and made Captain General of Burgos.

Gaspar hurried to Torrelavega's rooms to commiserate with him.

"Victory!" the Marques said in a triumphant tone, intended to hide his defeat.

"I hoped it would have been you."

"The important thing is to have outwitted Alba and Ensenada."

"There's one consolation", Gaspar said. "Aranda will soon put a stop to the stories that the Jesuits started the riots. I happen to know he's particularly fond of them. His old tutor, Father Martinez, is always at his house."

As SOON AS the new chief minister had kissed hands, he set out for Madrid, where he immediately had one of the leaders of the riot hanged and gave orders for all vagrants and outsiders to be expelled from the capital. He then sent for the mayor, the city councillors, the magistrates, and the heads of the guilds. He wanted them, he said, to ask the King to withdraw the concessions to the rioters. He did not raise his voice or scowl or sound rude or imperious as Torrelavega would have. Yet after two minutes in his presence, the dignitaries felt that they would rather risk a new riot than refuse his request.

On receiving this third petition, the King, who had remained at Aranjuez, ordered the Council of Castile to declare the concessions null and void and a short time afterward instructed its new President to set up a special commission to investigate the cause of the riots.

FIFTY-ONE

You ran away. You know you did. That's what they're all saying.

The King was fishing in La Ria, a channel in the grounds of the Palace that connected the two sides of a loop in the Tagus. The island thus formed had been laid out as a garden nearly two centuries before by Philip II. The avenues were lined with enormous elms, rising eighty feet into the air, whose topmost boughs swayed as a breeze from the north brushed them in its passage. But on the ground, in spite of the shade cast by the trees, the heat was so great that the King felt the sweat trickling down his arms, legs, and chest. Seated on an oak stool, with his back against the pedestal of a statue of Hercules clasping Antaeus, he held his rod over the water and watched the float drifting in the current. As a background to his thoughts, he could hear the splashing of a fountain from beyond the shrubs and evergreens that grew beside the path.

A bored gentleman-in-waiting farther along the bank waved his arms at a group of courtiers advancing down a convergent alley and signed them to turn back.

You ran away. You know . . .

If the King argued with the voice, it argued back. If he tried to concentrate on fishing, it returned to its first refrain, repeating the accusation with the persistence of a cuckoo.

You know you did. That's why they're all . . .

I wonder if the bait has fallen off the hook, the King said to himself with deliberation. I'd better reel in the line and see.

That's what they're all saying . . .

No, the bait is still there, he thought. But perhaps it needs a fresh piece. He removed the dead worm, took from the silver canister on the ground beside him one that was alive and wriggling, and carefully impaled it on the hook. Then he threw the line, hook, and float back into the water. In the distance he could hear the rushing of the Tagus as it plunged over a weir.

. . . as soon as you're out of earshot.

I didn't run away, he retorted, his patience suddenly snapping. Everyone knows I'm not a coward. My Italian campaign is there to prove it. I left Madrid because it was necessary. If I had stayed, I would either have had to grant the people's petition or else use force against them. I didn't want to use force because I'm a merciful ruler, but it would have been mad for the people to have had their petition granted. They ought not to think that they can get favours by being disobedient.

The voice, which had begun to sound drowsy, was suddenly alert again.

But you'd already granted the petition.

I hadn't. Not properly. My consent was extorted from me under compulsion.

That's casuistry. You must have picked it up from the Jesuits. First you granted the petition, then you broke your word by withdrawing your consent.

That's untrue, the King replied fiercely. I withdrew my consent on the recommendation of the guilds and the city council. I have a duty to listen to the advice of my principal subjects.

Ha! Ha! Ha! Ha! Ha! I wonder if you'd have listened to their advice if they'd said something you didn't want to hear.

The King realised that it had been a mistake to argue. It was better to put up with the voice. In argument he was defeated. He fixed his attention on the patterns made by the current and watched two sticks being sucked from eddy to eddy.

You ran away. You know you did. That's what . . .

The King riveted his eyes on the sticks. He wouldn't answer. He wouldn't answer. But suddenly it was too much.

I didn't run away, he began again, this time furiously, though anyone watching him would have noticed nothing but a slight knotting of the eyebrows apparently caused by his concentration on fishing. I had sound reasons for leaving Madrid. I've explained them enough. And events have proved that I took the right course. The disturbances are over. But that doesn't mean the situation wasn't dangerous . . .

He paused, as if waiting to see what the voice would have to say in reply. Unexpectedly, it said nothing. He had actually won a point. And a very good point. The seriousness of the riots. The danger he had been in. He dwelt on this, considered it, reconsidered it, magnified it. The thought of this very great danger was consoling. He hadn't run away. There was no question of his having run away. The danger and the seriousness of the situation had been sufficient grounds for leaving secretly and by night.

How hot it was! His skin prickled all over. He opened his coat and undid a button on his shirt. A breath of cooler air touched his ribs and glided round his sides and back. The sensation was like drinking iced lemonade after a dusty journey.

There could easily have been a civil war, he continued to himself. I no more ran away than Charles of England ran away from Cromwell. No one accuses him of having run away. But he left London in just the same way that I left Madrid. My mother doesn't know what she's talking about. And I have done far better than Charles of England. I have prevented a catastrophe. There was much more behind the riots than high prices and a dislike of Squillacci.

I wonder who started them? This time the voice had an ingenuous, almost captivating sound.

The special commission I have had the Council set up will decide that, the King answered, with more assurance this time. It seemed possible to dominate the voice.

Perhaps it was the Jesuits?

I didn't say it was the Jesuits, the King replied sharply, involuntarily giving his rod a jerk. I don't know who it was; that's for the commission to discover. But we were in danger. Great danger. My mother and my children might have been massacred. It was a plot against the throne, and whoever was behind it must be punished.

Suppose your mother were dead. Would you admit that the Jesuits were behind it then? They're the most likely people. And think of the support you'd get from their enemies.

What's that got to do with it, the King asked, frightened. No one can ever say I act unjustly. In questions of justice I am impartial. God is my witness. No one shall suffer unless I'm convinced they are guilty. My mother's life or death will have no effect on the verdict. There are many people who could have instigated the riots. It's for the commission to find out. I shall abide by its verdict. But the kingdom was in danger, great danger. That's what the world must know.

The voice was silent.

The King felt battered but triumphant. He took a deep breath and looked upward. An opening in the canopy of leaves overhead revealed an oval of blue sky that seemed to have the texture and consistency of the thinnest porcelain. At one side, a stone leg projected into his line of vision—the right leg of the figure of Antaeus kicking in midair as he struggled to free himself from the arms of the stone Hercules.

Meanwhile, the float had drifted across the stream and had caught in the roots of an alder. The King called to the gentleman-in-waiting, and soon a gardener in a rowboat appeared from around a bend and, pulling toward the alder, released the float and disentangled the line.

The King went on fishing. He felt calmer now and more sure of himself. Supporting the rod between his knees, he pushed back his hat and wig and wiped his forehead with a handkerchief. A different string of words unwound through his mind; words that did not worry or frighten him or have to be argued with.

. . . grave danger . . . very grave danger . . . we might all have been massacred . . . plot against the throne . . . the world must know.

As the summer went by and the Queen Mother's health grew worse, her fondness for Beatriz increased. Week after week she insisted on Beatriz remaining at Aranjuez, letting her leave the room for only a few minutes at a time.

She spoke almost entirely about her girlhood in Italy. Then, as the days passed, she began referring to her own death. She seemed to be trying out the idea to see how it sounded, or to make herself realise that it actually *was* going to happen. She would say of some future date: "That will be when they've put a marble slab over me" or, more briefly: "when I've gone". One day, after talking about Parma, she added: "where I'd like to be buried, if queens could do as they pleased", and another time: "where my ancestors lie—would that I could lie with them." Sometimes her remarks were lighthearted. "Aren't I fortunate," she said one morning, as she was having the pillows of her bed arranged, "to be called after a saint who was a queen too? St. Elizabeth of Hungary, *ora pro nobis.*" And a few weeks later: "What *am* I going to say to poor Madame des Ursins, whom I treated so badly, when we meet in heaven?" But when she thought of the Judgment, a mournful look crossed her face like a cloud shadow over a landscape, and her voice sounded anxious. After mentioning Pope Benedict XIV, who had died seven years earlier, she paused for a moment, then said, "Our Italian policies caused him and his predecessors much anxiety. What a lot I shall have to suffer to make up for it!" Another time she exclaimed: "Ah, how much we rulers shall have to answer for! May God have mercy on us!" But toward the end, after several conversations with Father Bramieri, her confessor, she became serene. "I have put all my confidence in the Blessed Virgin", she said to Beatriz. "She will know how to plead for me."

Elizabeth Farnese died on July 10 while in another room Beatriz was writing to her parents that the Queen seemed better.

FIFTY-TWO

Halfway along a narrow street near the Plazuela de la Cebada, in a district that families of rank had long abandoned, stood a sixteenth-century building whose long low front was decorated, between the irregularly spaced windows, with rows of carved stone bosses that from a distance looked like a multitude of doorknobs.

Such was the home of the General Count de Pradanos and of his wife, Doña Mercedes. Being childless, and having been converted in middle life to a love of the poor, they had been content to continue living in an old-fashioned house, and an area that was fast becoming a slum.

At all hours of the day, the people of the neighbourhood were accustomed to seeing Doña Mercedes, enclosed in an old sedan chair, on her way to comfort the sick at the Hospital de la Latina or the Hospital de la Pasión, or, dressed in mantilla and basquina, flitting through the streets, followed by a manservant carrying two great baskets, toward the house of one of the many poor whom she befriended. Doña Mercedes was a member of the Third Order of St. Francis.

The General, a tall, large-boned man with a narrow, rectangular face, a forehead like a wall, and very straight black eyebrows, wore his unpowdered grey hair tied at the back with a plain dark ribbon. Having retired from the army, he was writing a history of the Spanish conquests in Italy and belonged to the Brotherhood of Our Lady of Refuge and Pity. His identity hidden under a smock and hood, he helped to carry the sick to the hospitals, toured the streets by night searching for the destitute, whom he took for shelter to the Brotherhood's hospice, and assisted at the funerals of the poor. He was a member of the Third Order of St. Dominic.

On the Feast of St. Francis, the General gave a dinner for Doña Mercedes, and on the Feast of St. Dominic, Doña Mercedes gave a dinner for the General.

However, in the spring of 1764 their tranquil existence had been dramatically changed when, at the suggestion of Father Padilla, they had asked Diego de Torrelavega whether, while he was in Madrid, he would like to make his home at the Palacio Pradanos. After introducing his new penitent to them, Father Padilla had privately explained to them how unlikely it was that the young man would persevere in his good resolutions if he continued to live in his parents' house with the example of his brothers continually before him. He was asking them for an act of charity, he said, as he would ask for alms for a destitute child.

Diego's father was more than satisfied with the arrangement. Diego was going to be provided for at someone else's expense, while he himself would be relieved of the annoyance of his presence. His mother, realising how much it would contribute to her son's happiness, had welcomed the arrangement out of love.

The friends of the General and Doña Mercedes, on the other hand, had predicted disaster. Diego, they said, was scarcely civilised, possibly a little mad, and the Pradanoses, never having had children of their own, would not know how to control him.

At first it had looked as if the friends were right. Diego's change of heart after his meeting with Father Padilla, though genuine, had not immediately produced very noticeable results. The General and Doña Mercedes had had their kindness well tested. For at least a year Diego had continued to drink too much, to lose most of his money at cards, to have unsatisfactory friends, and from time to time to vanish for several days without explanation. Each time he would be contrite, but each time his resolutions of amendment quickly snapped.

In other, less serious ways, he had been a trying member of the household. He had several times accidentally set fire to his room, had used a painting in a back passage as a target for pistol practice, and had nearly caused the old majordomo heart failure by putting a dead snake in his bed.

If the General and Doña Mercedes had been inspired by anything less than the love of God, they would have made him leave after a week, but their goodness enabled them to bear with him calmly. And in the end, after loving him for God's sake, they had come to love him for his own, finding, under the disordered habits and riotous impulses, a heart longing for affection and capable of great generosity. Helped by the discipline Diego had to submit to in the guards, they had gradually guided him into different ways, and life at the Palacio Pradanos had flowed again in its former tranquil course. The majordomo had decided that he need not ask the General to pension him off after all.

But while the General and Doña Mercedes and their staff appreciated the change, to everyone else, since they judged by superficial signs, Diego had remained much the same Diego as before. He was still far from having the polish people expected in a young man of his position.

Then one day his valet had disappeared—taking with him from the General's bedroom a bag containing several hundred reales intended for the poor—and he had engaged Jean-Paul Houdin in his place.

Within a month, those who had been prophesying that Diego would never change were telling each other how remarkably he had improved. He was on time for engagements, remembered to offer women his chair, no longer put his feet up on sofas or spattered the front of his coat with food. In the past, he had either worn the wrong clothes or chosen loud, unsuitable colours or forgotten to put something on or gone out without doing up straps and buttons. Now he was always properly dressed, and there were no more frenzied last-minute searches for his hat, cloak, gloves, or sword.

These lesser improvements, which the world put most store by, were the work of Jean-Paul, who had been startled to find in his new master a young man so ignorant of ordinary social behaviour. Touched by Diego's helplessness, he had tried, whenever he could, to show him by hints and suggestions why his manners gave offence and how he could avoid affronting people in the future.

"Excuse me, sir," he would say, "but I've noticed that gentlemen of your sort always stand back to let older gentlemen go first." Or, "If I might suggest, sir, I think Doña Clara was displeased by the way you said good-bye to her. Perhaps, another time, a somewhat lower bow . . ." And Diego, who had very little pride and quickly became attached to anyone who showed an interest in him, had followed his new valet's suggestions as unquestioningly as if they had come from God.

FOR ALMOST TWO YEARS Jean-Paul had worked for Diego, showing every sign of being contented and happy. He was always whistling and singing when not on duty or when polishing his master's boots and buttons. But about nine months after the riots, he began to lose his brightness and briskness.

"What's happened to Houdin?" the General asked at dinner one day. It was just after New Year's Day 1767. "He's been looking very preoccupied recently."

"Preoccupied?" Diego said. "Has he? Yes, now you mention it, I can see he has." Then anxiously: "I hope he's not thinking of leaving."

At the end of the meal he sent for Jean-Paul and questioned him. At first, Jean-Paul pretended not to understand what Diego was getting at. No, he said, he was quite satisfied. He had nothing to complain about; he was happy in his work. But when Diego continued to press him, he confessed that he was worrying about Madeleine Laborde. If no one else had asked to marry her by Easter, he said, she was going to accept Mesnier. Time was running out. He could not bear to think of her married to a man she disliked so much.

"And you would like to marry her yourself—is that it?"

"I wasn't really thinking in those terms, sir. I was only one of her father's clerks. Some day she will be rich."

"All the same, you would marry her if you could."

"Yes, sir", Jean-Paul said after hesitating for a moment. "I would if I could. It's not as if I'm uneducated."

Diego rushed off to the General and repeated what Jean-Paul had told him. He was not a lucid narrator, and it took time for the General to disentangle the substance of the story from the irrelevant details with which Diego encumbered it.

"Here's Jean, one of the finest fellows in the world, longing to marry her," Diego said, red in the face from excitement and waving his arms about, "and the father's selling her to some low moneylender. We must get the mother and daughter away at once. I could go and fetch them tonight. Then tomorrow I could take them to your estate at Getafe; the priest there could marry her to Jean, and the whole thing would be settled."

"I don't think that would do", the General said. "It's easy to interfere in people's lives. But to help them, one must go carefully."

Nevertheless, the next day the General sent his steward to make enquiries. The man made friends with one of Monsieur Laborde's clerks, and the story he brought back confirmed what Jean-Paul had told Diego. Reassured, the General got Doña Mercedes to write to Madame Laborde asking her to call on them.

When she received Doña Mercedes' note, Madame Laborde decided that Jean-Paul must be in trouble. Had he been accused of stealing something? Monsieur Laborde was out, so she hired a sedan chair, and on the way to the Pradanos Palace prepared herself to act as her young compatriot's defending counsel.

The porters set her down in the courtyard, at the bottom of a handsome but crumbling flight of stairs. By the time she had mounted them under the eyes of the doorman and had been led by the old majordomo up a gigantic staircase and through a large number of rooms with coffered ceilings from which much of the gilt and paint had flaked away, to Doña Mercedes' private sitting room, she was feeling intimidated and defiant. Not on any grounds, she told herself, was she going to let a poor innocent French boy be unjustly treated by a lot of rich, insolent Spaniards.

"We're so grateful to you for coming", Doña Mercedes said when Madame Laborde was shown in. The General smiled benevolently. The ramparts of Madame Laborde's hostility subsided.

After asking Madame Laborde how she liked Madrid—a question that severely tested the Frenchwoman's good manners—Doña Mercedes explained why they had asked her to call. They understood that her daughter was contemplating marriage with a man she did not care for.

"Forced into it by her father, señora", Madame Laborde said promptly.

Doña Mercedes indicated that this was what she had been told and then continued. She and her husband had a solution to offer. They did not want to trespass or interfere, but they realised that Madame Laborde and her daughter, as strangers in a foreign country, perhaps without many friends, might be in need of help. If, therefore, they would like a temporary refuge from which to negotiate with Monsieur Laborde, so as to persuade him to behave more reasonably, they were welcome to rooms at the Pradanos Palace. Alternately, if they wanted to return to their relations in France and needed money, she and the General would be happy to advance it to them.

Madame Laborde, who had listened in astonishment, took out a handkerchief and cried. In two seconds, all the care she had put into arranging her hair and powdering her face, the work of a good half hour, was undone.

"Oh, señora, you don't know what it means . . . just your sympathy . . . more than I can bear . . . all this time in Madrid and hardly knowing a soul . . . no one to help us . . . and now this . . . may the good God bless you . . . and to think of all the times I've said the Spanish were heartless and horrible."

When Madame Laborde was composed again, Doña Mercedes said that they had a further offer to make. They were interested in a young man who was in love with her daughter and who, they believed, would make her an excellent husband—Monsieur Houdin.

The General and Doña Mercedes had realised that this suggestion would sound less agreeable to Madame Laborde, and they had discussed carefully beforehand the best way of putting it to her. According to plan, the General now interrupted the discussion.

"Madame, before you say anything, I want to tell you a little of what we think of Monsieur Houdin. In the first place, it is only misfortune that has forced him temporarily to do work incommensurate with his qualities and education. He is capable of much better things. Apart from his education, he has an excellent mind and an even better character. I've watched him for two years. Almost any other man in his position would have made it plain that he thought the work he was doing was beneath him. But not Jean-Paul."

"He is always so cheerful and friendly", Doña Mercedes said.

"But what has won our admiration and gratitude", the General continued, "is the way he has looked after Don Diego de Torrelavega, going far beyond the terms of what such a relationship demands. In a man of his age and situation, his tact and selflessness have been extraordinary."

"We should like him to stay with Don Diego always", Doña Mercedes explained. "But it wouldn't be fair. He would be wasting his gifts."

"So with Don Diego's approval," the General said, "we intend to advance him a sum of money with which to set up in business in France. In doing this, we feel that the debt will still be on our side. And if your daughter wishes to marry him, we shall settle enough on them so that they can live in the way she has been accustomed to."

In coming to the Pradanos Palace to discuss Jean-Paul's affairs, Madame Laborde had seen herself as, if not exactly a social equal of its owners, at least far above being offered one of their servants as a son-in-law. Never had her pride been so humbled. She felt as if she had been invited to a ball, only to find that she was expected to wash the dishes in the kitchen, and for a few moments she was on the point of leaving. But the General's tact—his avoidance of the difficult word "valet", his references to "Monsieur Houdin", his allusion to Madeleine's different social position—this, added to his generosity and her own common sense, helped her to see past the promptings of vanity and to recognise that providence was offering her a way out of her troubles that she could never have found for herself.

She reminded herself that there was nothing wrong in being poor; that as a Christian she was meant to regard poverty as more blessed than wealth; that she had always liked Jean-Paul, who was decidedly poor, whereas she detested Mesnier, who was unquestionably rich. She remembered that Monsieur Laborde's grandfather, when a child, had begged in the streets of Lyons, and she told herself that poor men often rose to great positions.

When she had strengthened herself with this concoction of heavenly and earthly wisdom, she thanked the General and Doña Mercedes again and again, shed more tears, told them how dreadful her husband was, let herself be comforted, and, after saying that she would talk to Madeleine, was taken home in the Countess' sedan chair a grateful and less self-confident woman.

Madeleine, during recent months, had entirely given up reminding herself that she came from one of the leading merchant families of Lyons and had spent more and more time thinking how happy she would be as Jean-Paul's wife—even though that might be an absurd daydream. When she heard her mother's news, she looked almost frightened. It was as though a fortune-teller's prediction had come true.

"General and Countess de Pradanos think very highly of him, my dear", Madame Laborde said anxiously, having misinterpreted her daughter's expression.

"So do I, Mother", Madeleine said, to her mother's astonishment. "There's no need to worry. I love him."

MADELEINE AND JEAN-PAUL were married early in February in the chapel of the Pradanos Palace. The General had convinced the Vicar General of the archdiocese of Toledo that Madeleine was being subjected to unlawful pressure by her father and that only by this marriage, without his consent, could her rights be protected. On these grounds, the necessary dispensations had been granted.

After the wedding, Jean-Paul continued to work for Diego, and Madeleine went on living at home. Accompanied by Madame Laborde, they were to leave secretly for France at the end of March, when the better weather arrived.

But before the better weather arrived it would be Jean-Paul who went to France on his own.

FIFTY-THREE

"Sir! Sir!"

"What's the matter, Jean?"

"We're on the wrong road."

Diego stopped his horse and peered about. Nothing was visible but a darkness of varying intensity. An icy rain beat against his face, and the wind blew his cloak out behind him like a flag.

He had just come off duty at El Pardo after obtaining two months' leave of absence from his commandant in order to accompany General de Pradanos on a tour of his estates. He was returning in a hurry to Madrid, where he was to spend the evening with the Vallecases. This meant he would be able to sit beside Doña Isabel, and he had been looking forward to reciting to her one of Gongora's sonnets that he had learned by heart in order to prove he was not as boorish and ill-educated as she thought him to be.

"We must have missed the way after we passed that carriage", he said.

They turned back. But instead of finding the highroad again, they were soon lost in a maze of cross-country tracks. Here they wandered for over an hour, cold, wet, and increasingly hopeless.

At last they saw a light and quickly rode toward it. Suddenly the light went out. But by this time they could distinguish the outline of a building, apparently a farmhouse, and beyond it the shapes of lower buildings that seemed to be barns and cattle byres. Diego vaulted off his horse, ran up to the door, and knocked on it with the handle of his whip. There was no answer. Dropping the whip, he started to hammer with his fists.

"Take the horses and see if you can make anyone hear at the back", he shouted to Jean-Paul. Somebody's here, he thought, or there wouldn't have been a light. I'm going to get in, even if I have to batter the walls down. After kicking the door several times, he began to charge it shoulder first.

Suddenly the door opened, and his own impetus carried him into the house and headlong against a man with a lantern, who staggered backward. When they had both recovered their balance, they stood staring at each other in amazement.

"Manso!" Diego said. "What the devil are you doing here? And why didn't you open sooner? Don't you realise what it's like outside?"

The man had the battered-looking face of a professional boxer; he pressed a forefinger to his lips.

"Please, sir! Not so loud. Santa Maria de la Cabeza, what a mess! If I were you, sir, I'd get out of here right away. For your own good."

"In this weather? Are you mad? What's all the mystery about? I don't suppose you're up to any good—but that's your business. All I want is somewhere for myself and my man to sit and warm ourselves until the rain's stopped."

A light showed under the door of a neighbouring room. Diego made a movement toward it, but Manso stepped agilely in front of him.

"Look, sir," he said, still in a whisper, "if you don't want to get yourself in trouble, and me too, you'll keep away from that door. There's a gentleman here, an extremely powerful gentleman, and he's got a lady with him, and they wouldn't want to be found out. Now you stay here, and I'll see what can be done."

"You mean my father?"

"Now, that's a nice question for a young gentleman to ask", Manso said. "A much more powerful gentleman than your father." He opened the door just enough so he could squeeze between it and the doorframe and disappeared.

Left to himself, Diego examined the room by the light of the lantern that the man had put down on the floor. It looked derelict and unused. There were only two pieces of furniture—a bench and, opposite it, a table. The walls were covered with damp marks.

Just then Jean-Paul came in, with rainwater streaming from his hat and down his cloak.

"There's something going on here, sir", he said. "There are a whole lot of soldiers outside. One of them stopped me but let me pass when I told him my master was inside. He'd been sleeping under a lean-to and only woke when one of our horses whinnied. I've tied them up in the barn. There must be half a dozen soldiers or more in there, too, and twice as many horses."

"Not so loud, Jean. There's somebody important here. I can't make out who it is. But he's got a woman with him."

"The Prince of the Asturias, I should think, sir, if he has to bring a regiment along! Don't you believe a word of it, sir. I looked through a crack in the shutters into that room next door, and . . ."

But before he could say what he had seen, Manso, carrying a lighted brazier, edged his way around the door and, not having a free hand, pulled it shut behind him with his right foot. Then he put the brazier near the bench, dragged the table in front of the door, and sat down on it cross-legged.

"Now, sir, the gentleman says you can stay here till the rain stops, but you're not to leave this room, and I'm to see that you don't."

As the minutes accumulated into quarter hours and as, outside, the wind and rain went on buffeting and drenching the house, Manso smoked his pipe, polished his brass coat buttons with his cuff, and examined the pistols and knives that he drew from time to time from the pockets of his greatcoat. From the next room came the murmur of talking; but the thick walls and heavy door made it impossible to hear what was being said or to identify certain other sounds that occurred at regular intervals.

For a while Diego listened intently, but then he dozed, leaning back against the wall. Jean-Paul stayed awake.

After what seemed a long time, the door into the next room was opened from the inside.

"Manso," a voice said irritably, "where are you? And what the devil's this?"

Diego woke.

The lantern had gone out, and the speaker, a tall man, stood peering into the room from the partly opened doorway, holding a candle level with his face and trying to push past the table on which Manso had fallen asleep. As the table rocked underneath him, Manso woke too, scrambled to his knees, and sprang to the ground.

"Oh, God!" the man in the doorway said. "I forgot. Haven't they gone yet?" And, retreating into the other room, he slammed the door.

Aranda! Diego thought as he stared into the darkness. Count Aranda! No, it can't have been. But it was. Holy saints, I don't want to get mixed up in his affairs! He fumbled his way toward the other door and looked out.

"Thinking of going, sir?" Manso asked, as he relit the lantern.

"Yes."

"That's right, sir. And if you'd like some advice, keep anything you may have noticed to yourself. When gentlemen in great positions spend the evening with ladies they're not married to, they don't like it talked about. Sometimes you hear of nasty things happening to tale-tellers. Why, the wind's dropped, and it's almost stopped raining. I'll find someone to put you on the right road."

"Excuse me, sir," Jean-Paul said, when they had reached the highroad again and had dismissed the guide, "but how did you come to know that fellow called Manso?"

"He's a sort of agent of my father, who uses him for all kinds of . . . oh, I don't really know what. But he's always been around. I hate him. He used to make my life miserable when I was a boy, though he's been more respectful since I've lived with the General and the Countess. Everyone has. I suppose they think I'm going to inherit their money."

"I saw him last year, sir, at the time of the riots. He was in a carriage with another man . . ." Jean-Paul broke off suddenly. "I've got it! Sir, I've got it!"

"Got what, Jean?"

"Who the other man in the carriage was. I only caught a glimpse of him, but I knew I'd seen him before. It was Charville. A Frenchman, sir, called Charville."

"That's a coincidence. I met a Frenchman of that name about two years ago, and I ran into him again the other day when I was visiting Don Maurice de Vallecas and his family."

"You mean he's in Madrid now, sir?"

"I imagine so, Jean, unless he's gone back to France in the meantime. But there's probably more than one Frenchman called Charville."

"Not in Madrid at a time like this. He's been sent back here to make trouble. I know it for a fact."

He told Diego about Monsieur Charville's letter—the way he had

284

come by it, what was in it, how he had given a copy to Father de la Cueva, and the Jesuit's reaction to it.

"When I saw Charville with this fellow Manso during the riots, Manso was egging the people on. Then he threw a bundle of printed papers into the crowd. I picked up a copy. I'll show it you when we get home."

"But what's that got to do with this evening?"

"A lot, sir. How many women do you think were in that room?"

"I've no idea, Jean. I suppose there was only one."

"None, sir."

"None? Then what was going on?"

"There were six people in all—three gentlemen and three others. One of the gentlemen was your father. He and the tall gentleman who opened the door just now were talking. The third gentleman was writing. The other men were setting up type and working a printing press."

"A printing press? What on earth would Count Aranda be doing with a printing press in a place like this?"

"Count Aranda? Was the tall gentleman Count Aranda, sir?"

"Yes."

"Look, sir, let's stop a minute. We can talk better over there out of the wet, and this is important." They guided their horses off the road into a clump of cork trees.

"Now, sir," Jean-Paul said, as the rain dripped from the twisted branches above them, "if a gentleman of Count Aranda's importance is having something printed in a lonely farmhouse guarded—or supposedly guarded—by soldiers, and if he comes in person all the way from Madrid on a night like this to supervise it, then it's about something which, if it got out, would cause a sensation. In view of the presence of Manso and of his connection with your father and Charville, and of what we know about this gentleman from his letter and of the rumours going around Madrid about the secret commission inquiring into the cause of the riots, I suspect that what I saw being printed was either the secret commission's report putting the blame on the Jesuits or an order for their expulsion. Whatever it is, as soon as we get home, we must tell his Excellency the General. And please, sir, don't say a word about it to anyone else."

On reaching the Pradanos Palace, they changed into dry clothes and then went at once to see the General, who was reading in his study. He put down his book and listened to their story in silence. Jean-Paul then handed him the original of Monsieur Charville's letter and the printed paper picked up during the riots. After reading them twice, the General asked some questions.

Early next morning, he took Diego and Jean-Paul with him to the Church of San Francisco Borja to see the Jesuit Provincial, Father Idiaquez. They were shown into a parlour, but, on hearing of their arrival, the Provincial came downstairs and took them up to his room. On his desk a ginger cat lay asleep between a skull and an inkwell.

"I knew about this letter", the Provincial said, when Diego and Jean-Paul had repeated their story. "Father de la Cueva, the Rector of San Felipe, passed it on to me. I showed it to her late Majesty the Queen Mother, and I believe she gave it to the King. Since then we have heard nothing more of it. Unfortunately, I was given to understand that the source from which the letter came was suspect and that it was almost certainly a forgery."

"But after what Jean and I saw last night . . ." Diego broke in.

"Are you sure it was Count Aranda?"

"Positive, Father. I've seen him lots of times at the Palace."

The Provincial's face had the shadowed look of a man who realises that a long-dreaded disaster is suddenly close at hand. He turned to the General.

"What do you think?" he asked.

"Father, I'm convinced this letter is genuine", the General said. "I met this man Charville when he was in Madrid two or three years ago. I understood that he was a French savant. We met at one of the Duchess of Montesa's soirées. Afterward we had several conversations, and I asked him to write down his theories about Caesar's campaigns in Gaul for

286

me, which we were both interested in. I've compared those sheets of paper with this letter, and the handwriting is the same on both."

The Provincial was silent.

"I wonder what you would do in my position", he said at last. "On the one hand, I am continually being warned that an attack on the Society is about to begin. There are people, among them our Father Lopez, a priest of great judgment and shrewdness and with connections at Court, who believe that the special commission of the Council of Castile has already reached a decision unfavourable to us. On the other hand, we have friends who assure me that His Majesty has never looked on us so favourably, and the Marquis Grimaldi has told the Nuncio we have nothing to fear. The fact that only a few months ago more than thirty of our missionaries were allowed to sail for the Americas and that two of our Fathers are educating His Majesty's children seems to confirm this second, more favourable estimate of the situation."

He stopped speaking for a moment to remove a quill pen that the ginger cat, suddenly awake, had begun to play with.

"Now you come with evidence in support of the first view", he continued. "And very convincing evidence it is. Yet even if I let myself be convinced, what can I do? Had I known for certain a year or more ago that the letter you've shown me was genuine, we could perhaps have outwitted our opponents. But now, if I take any positive steps to forestall an attack, our opponents will use this as additional evidence that we are always intriguing and stirring up trouble. You see, General, we are caught in a net of misrepresentation, and any movement we make to get free only entangles us more inextricably."

"I pity you, Father. But 'blessed are those who suffer persecution for justice's sake.'"

"That is true, General. And, in a sense, if the whole Society were suppressed it would be possible to say that it would be our gain and the world's loss. I'm not boasting; as a group of men, we are nothing. But I think of all that God has been pleased to achieve through our Society and of all that will be ruined if it is destroyed. As individual priests, we shall not miss our reward if we are faithful. But shall we all be faithful?

I have to think of the many souls I am responsible for. How shall we act when the test comes? No one knows this province of the Society better than I do. Thanks be to God, the lives of our Fathers are none of them a scandal or reproach. But not all are equally fervent. At present that is more or less hidden. But in disaster the man whose soul is given to God will be distinguished from the one who is keeping a part of himself back; 'The secrets of many hearts will be revealed.'"

"Forgive me, Father," the General said. "I was talking foolishly."

"Our friends will have to fight for us. If the Holy See can provide solid evidence that His Majesty has been misled, that the riots were deliberately provoked by the Jesuits' enemies, and that his ministers have been acting in collusion with the French government, it is just possible that His Majesty will change his mind and, more important, that the Empress will stand firm. If the Empress refuses to expel the Society from her dominions, it will be much easier for the Pope to resist the pressure of Portugal and the Bourbon courts to have the Society suppressed altogether."

"Then you will let me take this matter into my own hands?"

The Provincial smiled slightly. "I have no way of stopping you, General."

"How much time do you think we have?"

"I'd say two or three months. Perhaps longer. It took several years to suppress our French province. Here in Spain there will surely have to be some show of a public inquiry. Even in Portugal, the Court first petitioned Rome for a Visitor to investigate the affairs of the Society. Letters to and from Rome take time."

"The longer the better", the General said, rising to go.

Back at the Palacio Pradanos, he told Diego and Jean-Paul to get ready for a journey of several weeks, leaving that night on horseback.

288

The General slept in a small, whitewashed room next to his study. It had been a powdercloset and was now furnished with some of the equipment he had used on campaigns—a camp bed with a palliasse and two coarse blankets, a folding chair, a trestle table, and a collapsible metal stand supporting a jug and basin. One end of the trestle table was next to the head of the bed, and on it stood a crucifix discoloured by the many candles of poor quality that had once lighted his tent.

Here he often went when he had difficult decisions to make. The absence of things seemed to make it easier to see principles and essentials. After the interview with Father Idiaquez, he was not in doubt about what ought to be done, only about whether he had the right to involve Diego and Jean-Paul in it. He was as loyal a subject as Don Maurice, but unlike Don Maurice, he did not believe that a king—or, at any rate, the present King—could never do anything seriously wrong just because he was religiously inclined.

For a quarter of an hour he remained kneeling silently in front of the crucifix. Then he fetched ink, pen, and paper from the study and began to write at the trestle table.

MANY YEARS AGO, as a young man, he had fought in the Spanish campaigns in Italy, including the campaign of 1734, which had placed the then eighteen-year-old Charles III of Spain, hitherto Duke of Parma, on the throne of the Two Sicilies for twenty-five years. At the end of this last campaign, he had spent several weeks in Rome. There, while walking one evening among the ruins on the Palatine, he had met and made friends with a Monsignor Rezzonico, and they had not been talking together for half an hour before they discovered they had a common interest in Greek and Roman coins. The Monsignor had invited Captain de Pradanos to come back with him to his apartment in the Palazzo Lambruschini, where they spent the next two hours examining the Monsignor's treasures. On leaving, the Captain had taken with him, as the first of many such presents, a gold coin of the Emperor Trajan. After his departure from Rome, he and the Monsignor had corresponded, and over the years they had continued to do so, telling each other of recent discoveries and mentioning the still-missing coins they hoped to find.

Monsignor Rezzonico, however, had not been destined to remain all his life an Auditor of the Rota. In 1737 he had been created a cardinal-deacon and in 1743 had been consecrated Bishop of Padua. Finally, on July 6, 1758, he had been elected Pope, taking the name of Clement XIII.

In his long and affectionate reply to the letter of congratulation sent to him by General de Pradanos, the new Pope had written:

> This friendship, so precious to Us, begun among the coins of imperial Rome, will, We trust, flourish the more now that We command the coinage of Papal Rome. Beloved Son and dear Friend, see in these first coins struck to inaugurate Our Pontificate a pledge of that devotion which you only have to call upon to give Us the warmest and most sincere pleasure. Remember, you have always a friend here.

Clement XIII, the General knew, would trust any messengers he sent him. So the course to follow was plain. Diego and Jean-Paul must go immediately to Rome with a letter from him to the Pope. In that letter the General explained who Diego and Jean-Paul were, his reasons for sending them, his grounds for trusting them, the nature and value of the evidence they were bringing, and how they had come by it.

> I have given here only a brief summary of their story, Holiness. We are pressed for time. They will fill in the details and answer any questions that may suggest themselves to you. Your Holiness will, I hope, place in them the same confidence I do.

He signed, sanded, and sealed the letter, rang a bell, and sent for Diego and Jean-Paul to come to him in his study.

"I want you to understand", he said, "the nature of the risks you are taking. They are considerable. Great functionaries of state do not like their policies interfered with. As for the account they will one day have to give to God for the way they achieve them, they believe the end justifies the means. You will be in most danger between here and the coast; but the powers have their agents in Rome, so you will have to be vigilant there, too. Are you willing to go through with it?"

Diego, who, unlike Jean-Paul, knew from experience what it was like to live under the displeasure of a great "functionary of state" who didn't like his policies interfered with, gulped. "Yes," he said, after a moment's hesitation.

"And you, Houdin?"

"More than willing, sir."

The General divided the money for their expenses between them equally, in case they got separated. He also gave Jean-Paul a bill of exchange, saying it was nothing in view of what they owed him, and told him to send his address when he got to Lyons.

When they came to say good-bye to Doña Mercedes, she put her arms around Jean-Paul and embraced him like a mother.

"If it had pleased God to give me a son," she said, with emotion, "I could have wished him no different. May it not be good-bye for good. You will never be forgotten." On letting him go, Jean-Paul pressed his lips to her hand.

Since Madeleine could not remain in her father's house later than Easter—the day she had set for agreeing to marry Mesnier—and since Jean-Paul could not safely return to Spain to fetch her even if there had been time for it, the General said he would arrange for Madeleine and her mother to travel to France in the care of one of his stewards.

At two o'clock the next morning, after the servants were all in bed and, it was hoped, asleep, the General helped the two young men to saddle and load their horses. There were three horses; one for each of them to ride and a spare. He had sent the night watchman home, insisting that, since his wife was ill, she would need him to look after her.

Then, with a few last hurried and whispered good-byes, the General let them out of the stable yard, through an arched gate, into a side street.

Realising that if Diego had been recognised by his father's retainer,

Manso, he was probably being watched, he had told them to start as if for Valencia but to turn east at Tarancon, about forty-five miles southeast of Madrid, and make their way across country via Cuenca and Teruel, hitting the coast farther north. From Barcelona they could either go direct by sea to Civitavecchia or, if no ships were sailing to the Papal States, try for a passage to Genoa and go on from there by land.

The weather was bad all the way. At a little place called Morella, halfway between Teruel and Tortosa, a groom from the Pradanos Palace caught up with them. He brought a letter from the General saying that the day after they had left, two men had called at the palace, wanting to see Diego and asking where he was. "You have a good start", the General wrote, "even if they are following you. But don't delay."

After this they rode part of the night as well as by day.

PART FOUR

The Flight of the Archangel

1765–1766

FIFTY-FIVE

Not long after the episode that had ended in the new catechumen, Wenceslaus, joining the community of San Miguel, an *alcalde* called one evening at the house of the Tupanchichus. Xavier was at the back of the house, splicing together two halves of a broken spade handle.

"The *padre cura* wants to see you", he said.

"You mean now?"

"Yes."

Xavier threw down his spade and ran to the college, trying on the way to remember what he could have done wrong.

Tarcisio, who was sitting on a stone beside the door, nodded to him to go inside.

"Good evening, Xavier", Father Huber said. "I want to talk to you about Wenceslaus. Tomorrow he will be leaving the hospital, and, since he seems to like you, I've decided to put you in charge of him. You will live and work together, and you will be responsible for teaching him our rules and customs. Remember to set him a good example. That's the best way of explaining our religion. Do you think you can do it?"

Xavier looked at Father Huber, dumbfounded at being offered a position of such responsibility. Still unable to speak, the boy nodded.

"Good. And now, tell me when you are to be married."

"In four months, Reverend Father."

"I see. Well, by that time, Wenceslaus should be able to manage on his own. Meanwhile, I've arranged for you both to live with Jacinto, the schoolmaster, and his wife. There won't be room for an extra man in your parent's house. But you don't have to do this if you don't want to, you know."

"Reverend Father, I would like to do it."

"Thank you, my son."

Xavier went home and told his family what the *padre cura* had said. They were incredulous, and he had to insist on his story before it was believed.

"See you don't start boasting", said his father, foreseeing that other families were going to be jealous.

Xavier's mother caressed him and then began to torment herself with the possibility that Jacinto's wife would not give him enough to eat. His brothers and sisters spoke to him hesitantly and respectfully, as if addressing the *corregidor* or the *teniente*.

For a long time that night the mother and father lay awake behind the rush partition, discussing the matter in whispers. In the end they agreed that the *padre cura* could not possibly have chosen Xavier simply on the boy's merits. His choice was evidently intended to honour the whole family.

The next morning Xavier moved, with his bow, knife, spare tunic, and poncho, into the schoolmaster's house and established himself there with Wenceslaus. Then they were sent to help the shepherds who were grazing their flocks on the higher ground near the town. The more distant pastures were waterlogged after the rains.

For a week, Xavier and Wenceslaus spent each day with the shepherds, but at night, instead of sleeping out with them on the plains, they returned to San Miguel so that Wenceslaus could learn from the schoolmaster how to read and write.

At first Xavier was a strict and exacting instructor. Scarcely half an hour went by without his finding something to fault in his pupil's behaviour or ideas. A less docile man would have been driven to rebellion by this continuing barrage of correction and solicitude. But Wenceslaus was anxious to learn, and Xavier, remembering what the *padre cura* had said to him about setting a good example, kept a no less careful watch on himself.

After a few weeks, however, the effort of having to practice all the virtues at a high level day in, day out, became too much. The honour of being Wenceslaus' instructor had lost much of its glitter, and his vigilance began to slacken.

One day they were alone on the plain, about a mile from San Miguel, watching some ewes with their lambs. Xavier was teaching Wenceslaus to play the *tatapuca*, a kind of flute. In front of them a pot was simmering on a fire inside a circle of stones.

A party of Indians from the Reduction came by, heading for the forests. "Look at those lazy shepherds", one of them shouted. "Nothing to do all day but sit and play tunes."

"Where are you going?" Xavier shouted back.

"Fishing. Didn't you know? Tomorrow is Friday."

"Of course he didn't know. Shepherds don't have brains. They need looking after more than their sheep."

The men laughed and continued on their way. But Xavier's friend, Crisóstomo, who was one of the party, lagged behind.

"Why don't you come along with us?" he asked. "It doesn't need two of you to look after a few lambs. Wenceslaus can take care of them for an hour or so." Then he ran off after his companions without waiting for an answer.

Xavier followed him with his eyes until they had all but disappeared into the forest. Why not go? There's no harm in it. Yes, there is. I have to set Wenceslaus a good example. Well, suppose I go for a short time, just to see how they get on. I shall be back before I'm missed.

He looked sideways at Wenceslaus and glanced wistfully again after the retreating fishing party. The call to join them was loud and strong; the call to duty, faint as a distant bell. He put down the flute and clambered to his feet.

"I won't be gone long. Stay here till I come back. If the sheep stray beyond those bushes, drive them back this way."

"Where are we going?" Wenceslaus asked with a frightened look. Ever since his arrival he had obstinately refused to go near the forests.

"You're not going anywhere. I'm going after those men. You're to stay here."

"Yes, I stay here." Wenceslaus spoke eagerly. "You go."

Xavier picked up his bow and ran after the fishermen. When he looked back, Wenceslaus was blowing into the flute with all the force in his lungs without getting a sound out of it. Xavier laughed out loud and ran faster, swerving now and again to avoid an anthill and going out of his way to jump over a palmetto bush. He suddenly realised how irksome the responsibility of looking after Wenceslaus had become. Soon he caught up with the fishing party.

Crisóstomo, who was in the rear, looked round. "Xavier!" He sounded scandalised. "What are you doing here?"

Xavier felt hurt. "Didn't you tell me to come along?"

"That was just a joke. Do you mean you've left Wenceslaus on his own. You won't half catch it."

"No, I won't", Xavier said stubbornly, feeling that if he turned back now he would look foolish. "The shepherds are my friends. They won't tell. Anyway, it's time Wenceslaus learned to be by himself for a while."

"Oh, well, as long as you know what you're doing", Crisóstomo said, without much conviction.

They tramped along in silence. Xavier struggled with his conscience, which had been roused into activity again, and Crisóstomo brooded over what he took to be Xavier's perfidy. He does something bad, Crisóstomo said to himself, and then pretends it was I who made him do it.

But soon, the sights and sounds of the forest and the thought of the sport they were going to enjoy distracted them, and they began to chat as if nothing had happened.

The fishing party crossed a tract of forest, silent and still, and on the far side came to a swamp, now transformed after the heavy rains into a necklace of lakes and ponds stretching away to the north. Clumps of enormous water lilies floated on the surface of the nearest lake, and jabiru storks waded in the shallows. Here the men separated into fours and started unfastening their nets and preparing their spears.

Xavier, who had intended only to watch for a few minutes, was soon working along with the rest. Then the leader of the party, assuming he had been sent to help by the head shepherd, gave him the end of a net to hold while he himself advanced into the water. He walked gingerly forward, unrolling the net as he went and exploring the bottom with a pole for fear of alligators.

The method of fishing at San Miguel was like the method for shooting game birds in England, with a net taking the place of a line of guns. The net was stretched across the end of a pond or a section of a lake, and the Indians, acting like beaters, then waded in a line through the water, driving the fish into the trap ahead of them. If anyone saw a fish escaping, he killed it with his spear.

After the first catch, Xavier stayed for a second one, then for a third and a fourth. The sun was hot, the water cool, and the muddy bottom of the swamp soft under his feet. The Indians shouted and called excitedly to each other across the water. The fish wriggled and flashed silver in the sunlight. Several hours went by, and an Indian on the bank shouted that it was midday and time to eat.

While they had been at work, a wagon had arrived from the Reduction to carry the catch home. The fish were counted and packed with leaves in baskets, which were then stored in the shade. Two of the men had lit a fire and were grilling some of the catch. Xavier sat down to eat with the rest. Afterward they slept.

When they returned to work, they moved to a different part of the swamp. At their approach, hundreds of water birds, which had been basking undisturbed, rose into the air with outraged cries, wheeled overhead for several minutes, then abruptly turned northward into the sun and dropped down on a distant stretch of water, like particles of falling dust. The Indians worked on for several hours more. The catch was even better than in the morning.

"At least a quarter of the fish will have to be salted", the leader of the party said proudly, as the last basket was being loaded. He patted Xavier on the shoulder.

"It's a good thing they sent you along. I never saw a fellow so quick with his spear."

On the way home the men all talked at once, each one boasting of some trick or feat by which he had personally increased the size of the catch.

Suddenly, at the top of a rise, they came in sight of the place where Xavier had left Wenceslaus in the morning. But instead of the patient Wenceslaus sitting by himself near his flock, they saw ten or twelve Indians shouting and gesticulating. A thick column of smoke was rising from the fire, and the sheep were scattered about the plain in twos and threes.

Xavier's heart sank. He felt giddy. I might have known it, he thought. He looked at Crisóstomo. He could have run back and hidden in the forest. Instead, he ran forward.

An *alcalde*, who had been arguing with one of the shepherds, swung round and glowered at him.

"Ah! Here he is!"

This time Xavier felt as if his heart were in his throat and about to choke him. The *alcalde*, he knew, had a grudge against him. He had overheard him saying to a neighbour, "That boy is too empty-headed to be looking after the new catechumen." He had a son for whom he coveted the position.

"Why did you have to go and leave Wenceslaus alone?" the head shepherd said in a voice that was reproachful but not unfriendly. "You ought to have known better."

"What's happened?" Xavier asked.

"Can't you see?" the *alcalde* asked sarcastically.

On the edge of the group, between two Indian constables, stood a terrified-looking Wenceslaus. A short distance away were the remains of a fire—a much bigger fire than the one by which Xavier had left Wenceslaus playing his flute. The grass was burned and littered with charred sticks for several feet beyond the original circle of stones. The smoke came from the smouldering wool of a dead, partly skinned sheep that lay on its back with its legs sticking stiffly in the air like extended tent pegs. The left hind leg had been cut off, and pieces of roasted meat and bits of bone were lying among the embers.

"You're going to have a lot to explain to the *padre cura* when we get back to the pueblo", the *alcalde* said.

By this time the fishing party had come up. When they heard from the shepherds what had happened, they stared at Xavier. Two of them laughed; but others looked sympathetic. To kill a domestic animal was a serious offence. Had it not been, the herds on which the whole town depended would have been rapidly depleted.

"You men wouldn't be laughing if you had done this, I can tell you," the *alcalde* said angrily. He turned to the leader of the fishing party. "Now clear off. And you," he said to Xavier, Wenceslaus, and the two constables, "you follow me."

The *alcalde* led the way; after him came a constable, then Xavier and

Wenceslaus, and at the back the other constable. The prisoners were much too dejected to run away, and even had they not been, there was nowhere for them to run except the forests, which, considered as a refuge, were about as useful as the open sea. But the *alcalde*, who had been chosen for that office for the first time at the last elections, was intent on proving his zeal and efficiency.

"What will they do to me?" Wenceslaus whispered to Xavier as they went along. "Will they put me in prison?"

"No. You're a newcomer. You don't know any better. It's me they'll punish."

There was neither irony nor bitterness in Xavier's voice, but he sounded so deeply sad that Wenceslaus felt guilty.

"I am bad. Very bad", he said simply. "I am sorry."

Xavier said nothing. He trudged along, wondering how he could have been so foolish. It was not the beating he had earned that daunted him; it was the shame and disgrace he had brought on himself. Worse still, he had brought disgrace on his family and Clara. He remembered his conversation with Clara on the night Wenceslaus had arrived at San Miguel. How easy it had been to judge and condemn the husband of Pedro's daughter! But who was bad now? He saw everything vanishing in an instant—love, honour, self-respect.

"Ah, why did you do it, Wenceslaus?" he said.

Wenceslaus, who had been watching him sideways and trying to read his thoughts, dropped his eyes.

"I was hungry. You were such a long time."

"But you had food to eat. Why did you have to kill a sheep?"

"The lambs looked too little."

"But haven't I told you we mustn't kill any of the animals belonging to the Reduction?"

"I know. I'm bad. It was my belly." To emphasise the point he rubbed his stomach. "I was lying on the ground just where you left me, and suddenly I felt as if I could eat a cow. It was as if there were another man inside me shouting at me to get up and eat. There wasn't a cow, so I killed a sheep and ate that. Afterward I fell asleep. When I woke up I saw men coming after me. I was afraid. So I put the rest of the sheep on the fire to burn it."

Xavier was about to explain that the voice which had ordered him to get up and eat was the devil's, but, remembering that he had been the first to fall and that his fall had been more blameworthy, he sighed and said nothing.

"Halt!" called the *alcalde*.

They had reached the plaza. The *alcalde* went into the college to report to Father Huber. A few minutes later he reappeared.

"You", he said to Wenceslaus, "will go back to Jacinto's house. And you", he said, turning to Xavier, "will spend the night at your father's. The court sits tomorrow. You will come here to the plaza so that the justices can hear the case against you."

FIFTY-SIX

The prayers invoking the assistance of the Holy Ghost resounded through the Church. Then the choir began to intone the "Veni Creator Spiritus". With the second verse, organ and congregation took over, playing and singing at full blast, and so the hymn proceeded, with choir and congregation singing antiphonally.

In the front row of the congregation sat the justices and officials who were to give judgment on the disputes and offences that had accumulated since the last session of the court.

Just before the final, roof-raising "Amen", which the descant of the choirboys' treble voices seemed to lift higher and higher until it was absorbed by and vanished into the sky, the chief justice, wearing a magisterial wig, put out a bare foot from under his scarlet robe and squashed a cockroach with his heel as it was scurrying to take refuge in a confessional. Then he stood up and moved into the aisle. The others formed a line behind him.

"Procedamus in pace", Father Huber sang in his cracked baritone.

"Amen."

Preceded by the marshall of the court carrying a coloured staff, the procession passed, slowly through the west door into the plaza. Grey clouds, impressed with a quiltlike pattern, covered the sky, and the grass, after the rain, was the fresh translucent green of lettuce leaves. The furniture of the court—heavily carved chairs for the justices, lesser ones for the auditors and amanuenses, solid tables covered with velvet cloths —was set out in the centre of the plaza at the foot of the column topped by the statue of the Mother of God.

As the procession advanced, the marshall left his place and ran ahead.

"Shoo! Shoo!" he said, waving his arms at a turkey sitting on the crimson and gold cushion in the chief justice's chair. It stood up, gobbled, and spread its tail.

"Get away, you old devil", the marshall said, picking up a footstool and holding it out like a shield. He grabbed the purple-faced and hysterical bird by the neck and carried it off to the bushes at one side. Then he chased away a flock of chickens.

On reaching their chairs, the justices turned and sat down. Father Huber took a seat at one side. Justice in the Reductions was administered entirely by the Indians with the *padre cura* supervising to see that the law was correctly applied and punishments were not excessive.

The accused, in the charge of four constables, moved to the left of the auditors' table. Their faces registered a spectrum of emotions from stoic resignation to despondency. The witnesses were grouped on the opposite side behind the table of the court clerk. The public was not present, in order to avoid attempts to sway the judges' decisions and keep family ill-feeling and resentments to a minimum. The men were in the fields, and the women in the workshops or at home.

When everyone was in his place, the chief justice felt inside his robe and drew out a pair of spectacles, which Father Huber had bought for him in Buenos Aires. The other Indians watched respectfully as he fitted them on his nose and tucked the sidepieces under his wig.

"Silence in court", shouted the marshall, beating three times on the pillar with the end of his staff. The auditors dipped their quills into the

303

ink, and their faces turned expectantly toward the justices like runners waiting for the signal to start.

"Adeodato Catapachu", called the clerk of the court. A short Indian with a short nose stepped forward and mounted the dock—a stand like a pulpit without a pedestal.

"Your Honour," said the prosecutor, a tall man in black robes with a melancholy face, "on the twenty-sixth of last month the accused was drunk and beat his wife. I will call the first witness. Nepomocin Ninguru."

The witness was sworn in and gave his evidence.

Xavier stood among the rest of the accused, with hunched shoulders and drooping head like a stork in the moulting season. As the proceedings continued, he heard nothing—except, in his mind, the reproaches of his relations, which had gone on late into the previous night and had started again as soon as the family had awoken in the morning. Was his fault that bad? Why were they so unmerciful? If only the trial were over and he could have a chance to show that his crime had been an accident and that he was still responsible and trustworthy.

A constable took his arm; his name was being called. He straightened himself and walked unsteadily to the dock. Everyone was looking at him. All these eyes fixed on his face felt like muskets pointed at his chest.

He listened to the prosecutor reading the charge against him and swearing in the witnesses. Opposite, on a stand like his own, the *alcalde* who had arrested him began to address the court.

Xavier could not deny that what the overseer said was true. Yes, he had abandoned his post. Yes, he had set a bad example to a catechumen. Yet somehow Xavier felt that the overseer's evidence was unfair. Everything he had done was being presented in the worst light.

"Your Honour," the *alcalde* concluded, "in my opinion Xavier Tupanchichu is not fit to have charge of the catechumen Wenceslaus. This is not the first time he has set a bad example. Last month, in front of the catechumen Wenceslaus, he kissed the daughter of Benito Xapuchu, who is betrothed to another man."

"That's a lie", Xavier cried. "Your Honour, this man hates me because he wants his son to look after Wenceslaus. He is jealous of me."

"Jealous of you!" the *alcalde* sneered.

"I didn't kiss Benito Xapuchu's daughter. But your son Gregorio went trapping monkeys last month when he was meant to be working in the tobacco fields."

"It's you who lie now", the *alcalde* said furiously. "Your Honour, I demand . . ."

"Why should I wish to kiss Benito Xapuchu's daughter?" Xavier shouted excitedly. "She is ugly, whereas my Clara is beautiful!"

The clerk of the court jumped to his feet, knocking his chair over backward as he did so.

"She's not ugly! She's my niece."

"Silence! Silence! Silence!"

The marshall was beating his rod on the back of the chief justice's chair.

Father Huber leaned forward.

"We must stick to the case we are trying. The court does not want to hear whether Xavier Tupanchichu kissed Anastasia Xapuchu, nor whether Gregorio Oco went trapping apes."

"The *padre cura* has spoken wisely", the chief justice said. "The accused does not deny that he left his work without permission. There is a more serious charge—that the sheep in his care might have been seized by the Indians of the woods. Call the next witness."

The head shepherd climbed onto the stand. While he was giving his evidence, Wenceslaus, from among the accused, watched without comprehending. Noticing, however, that the chief justice resembled the picture in the church of St. Leo the Great, who also had long white hair, he fell to wondering what could be the connection.

When all the witnesses had been heard, the justices whispered together as they considered the verdict. Then they sat back, pulling their robes together and smoothing the folds.

"Xavier Tupanchichu," the chief justice said, "the court finds you

305

guilty of desertion, bad example, and serious neglect. The sentence is ten *azotes*." An *azote* was a stroke with a leather thong. "Where is the catechumen Wenceslaus?"

A constable pulled the terrified Wenceslaus forward like a rider pulling an unwilling horse by its bridle.

"Wenceslaus," said the chief justice, "you are a newcomer. You do not understand our ways yet, so we cannot blame you for what has happened. But do you understand why Xavier will have to be punished?"

Wenceslaus answered in one sentence without pauses.

"Yes, because he ran away from his work, and I must not kill or eat cow, sheep, chicken, horse, dog, if I do I am very bad."

"That is right. The accused will now receive his punishment."

Xavier pulled off his tunic and lay face down on the pavement. The strokes began. One, two, three, four. Thud, thud, thud, thud. He grunted and clenched his teeth. Five, six. He lost count. Thud, thud, thud, thud. The strokes stopped. A voice said, "That's all." Someone helped him to get up. He shook himself like a wet dog getting out of a river and put on his tunic again.

How it had hurt! But no one could have told from his face. He was proud of that. His enemy, the *alcalde*, hadn't been able to gloat over him. And now that his fault was paid for, it couldn't be held against him any more.

A scarlet and turquoise macaw flew across the plaza and settled, screeching, on the shoulder of one of the stone apostles decorating the roof line of the church. There were six more cases to try. Xavier, now among the "just", moved to the witnesses' side of the court and looked on. Giles Avarendi had stolen a cutlass from the armoury and used it to skin a wild boar. Ignazio Abiazu had quarrelled with a neighbour and had tried to set fire to his house. He, like Xavier, received ten strokes.

Not as hard as the ones I got, Xavier thought with the detachment of an expert. And I didn't wriggle.

FIFTY-SEVEN

Toward evening Alfonso left the school where he had been teaching Latin to the older boys and went to the cemetery to say his Office. The cemetery was nearly always deserted at this hour, and the thick glistening leaves of the orange and lime trees bordering the paths shut out the noise of the town.

Rain had threatened again most of the afternoon, and a little had fallen, leaving the earth on the paths just wet enough to take a footprint and bring out the smell of the few orange flowers that persisted in blossoming despite the season. Heavy clouds tumbled westward across the sky as Alfonso walked back and forth under the trees reciting the psalm "Quam dilecta habitatio tua."

In turning at the end of the path, he noticed a man crouched on the ground twenty yards away. He was not surprised, as the Indians often came to the cemetery to attend to the graves of their dead and pray for their souls. But something about this particular Indian made him look a second time.

"Good evening", he said, while still a short distance off. "They'll be saying rosary in the church in a few minutes. Perhaps you should be making your way there, too."

Xavier looked up, showing a tear-stained face.

Alfonso came closer. "What! More trouble? I thought it was all over."

Xavier remained kneeling. His attention was turned inward on his troubles, and he peered up at Alfonso like a man with short sight.

"Come," Alfonso said, "tell me what's the matter. Perhaps I can help you."

Xavier continued to gaze at him as though trying to make out how sympathetic he was likely to be. Then he bowed his head and pressed his forehead against the sleeve of Alfonso's cassock.

"My Clara. They won't let me see her. They say I can't marry her." He sobbed convulsively.

"Who are they? Do you mean the *padre cura*?"

"N-no."

"Who, then?"

"Her father."

"Anyone else?"

"Her grandfather, her uncle, her cousins."

"I see. But the *padre cura* did not say you couldn't marry her?"

"N-no." Xavier looked up again. His face was still troubled, but now there was a look of hope in it, which came and went like a wavering pulse, drawing life from the tone of Alfonso's question.

"What did your own family say?"

"They are sorry, but they said I can't expect anything else."

"Well, go into church now, and afterward I will speak to the *padre cura*. I expect something can be done. Pray hard, and don't forget to say a prayer for me, too."

XAVIER WENT OFF. High in a tree a toucan was hammering a hole in the bark. Alfonso looked up and watched it for a few seconds before following Xavier to the church.

"I'm afraid there's more trouble", Alfonso said after Benediction, as he helped Father Huber take off his cope in the sacristy.

"Trouble is the coin with which we buy our way into heaven", Father Huber said with a smile. "What's the matter?"

Alfonso repeated what Xavier had told him.

"I can't exactly say I foresaw it", Father Huber said. "But I'm not surprised. Some of our sheep are as vain about their good name and their unspotted family records as Austro-Hungarian families with pedigrees stretching back to Attila. Respectability is the vice the devil catches them with when he fails with the seven deadly sins." Father Huber opened the door to the kitchen. "Tarcisio, supper will be delayed. Please tell Anselmo I would like to speak with him. Anselmo, the cacique. We shall be ready in about three-quarters of an hour." He shut the door, and then had an afterthought and reopened it. "And tell him, please, to bring his son Methodius with him."

The two priests crossed the courtyard to the office. After a few minutes Anselmo arrived, panting and looking anxious.

"Good evening, Anselmo", Father Huber said. "Come in. Sit down. Is it true what I hear, that your son Methodius has told Xavier Tupanchichu that he can't marry his daughter?"

"I believe so, Reverend Father. But my son did not consult me."

"And do you approve of what he has done?"

Anselmo shifted in his chair. He wanted to think what the *padre cura* thought and would have preferred to hear exactly what that was before giving his own opinion.

"Reverend Father, after what has happened . . ."

"Have you spoken with your son?"

"Yes, Reverend Father. I mean, no. Everything at his house is in an uproar. The men are shouting and arguing, the women are running about blaming each other, the children haven't been fed and are crying. I had just gone to see if I could put things straight when your message came that you wanted to see me."

"With whom are they arguing?"

"Xavier's relations, who say—what isn't true, Your Reverence—that fifty years ago one of our family was beaten for stealing. It is shameless, Your Reverence . . ."

"The *regidors* had better go and make peace."

"I have already told them, Your Reverence."

There was a knock on the door, and Clara's father, Methodius, appeared. His cheeks were flushed, and his eyes still flashing at the accusation just levelled against his forbear.

"Ah! My son!" Anselmo spoke with relief and eased his chair backward into a corner.

"I hear", Father Huber said to Methodius, "that you have told Xavier Tupanchichu that he can't marry your daughter Clara. Don't you think you should have consulted me first?"

"Reverend Father, forgive me. I forgot. I was thinking of my daughter. I did not wish her to marry a man who has had a public beating."

Methodius' face twitched, and he kept his eyes on the wall behind Father Huber's chair.

"I see", Father Huber continued. "Of course, we were all disappointed that Xavier acted irresponsibly. But now that he's been punished, I have no doubt you have regretted your hasty words and are going to let the young couple marry after all."

"No, Your Reverence."

"No? Did Xavier tell you that I have reinstated him as instructor to the catechumen Wenceslaus?"

"Yes, Reverend Father."

"Then you realise that I trust him and have no further fault to find with him?"

"Yes, Reverend Father."

"And you still do not want him as a son-in-law? Do you think I am wrong to trust him?"

"Oh, no, Reverend Father."

Anselmo in his corner made a noise with his tongue. The *padre cura* mistaken? Impossible!

"Then what objection do you have to the boy?"

Methodius glanced round, trying to catch his father's eye so as to get him to answer. But Anselmo was suddenly preoccupied with trapping a spider that was running up his arm.

"I suppose", Father Huber said, "it is because you are ashamed of what your friends and neighbours will say?"

The Indian's face lit up. He had not expected the *padre cura* to be so sensible. With both feet, he jumped into the trap.

"That's it, Reverend Father. We're a respectable family. No one can remember when one of us last appeared before the justices. If Clara were to marry this young man now, he would bring disgrace on us."

"That's right, Your Reverence", Anselmo joined in. "What my son says is true. People would think: 'They used to have the best record in the town, but now they have let their daughter marry a man who has had a public beating.'"

Father Huber was silent. The seconds went by, but he continued to gaze at his hands folded on the table in front of him and to say nothing. Methodius and Anselmo looked at each other anxiously.

"I am ashamed of you", he said at last. "Both of you. Deeply ashamed."

The Indians' expressions were a mixture of amazement and insulted innocence. They looked like children who had just heard themselves sentenced to bread and water after correctly reciting the Ten Commandments and the Eight Beatitudes. Perhaps the *padre cura* was joking. How could such praiseworthy sentiments get such a poor reception? But no. The *padre* looked very much as if he were in earnest. He was now sitting with his elbows resting on the table and his head in his hands.

"Yes, deeply ashamed", Father Huber repeated. "You call yourselves Christians. Indeed, you are Christians. And in spite of this you care more for what your neighbours think of you than for what God thinks. God has forgiven this boy. But you both feel you are too good to welcome him into your family. Perhaps your neighbours will say: 'This family has the best record in town.' But God will be saying: 'This family is the most proud and hardhearted in the town.'"

Methodius blinked and scratched his side.

"I have to think of my daughter, Reverend Father", Methodius said. "I beg Your Reverence to find another wife for Xavier Tupanchichu."

Father Huber turned to Alfonso.

"Do you hear that, Father", he said angrily. "Here's a man who thinks he knows better than God."

Anselmo again clicked his tongue disapprovingly. Methodius looked scandalised.

"How can you say such a thing, Reverend Father!"

"Certainly I can say such a thing. Didn't St. Peter run away and desert the Lord when he needed him most? And didn't the Lord forgive him and make him head of his Church in spite of it all? But you know better than the Lord. What Xavier has done is nothing compared to what St. Peter did. Yet you won't forgive Xavier and let him marry your daughter. You obviously think the Lord was wrong to forgive St. Peter."

Methodius stared at the floor. There was a long pause. The croaking of frogs and the chirruping of crickets seemed, in the silence, to double in volume.

"Son, His Reverence is right", Anselmo said at last. "Let the boy have Clara."

There was another pause, then Methodius moved swiftly round the end of the table and knelt by Father Huber's chair.

"Father, I am a sinner. The boy shall marry her."

Through the window, by the light of the lantern burning outside the college gate, Alfonso had noticed a figure moving fitfully against the shadows.

When Anselmo and Methodius had gone, he went to the gate and looked outside.

"Xavier", he called.

"Reverend Father!"

"All is well. You can marry Clara. The *padre cura* has spoken with Methodius. He has changed his mind."

"Ah, Father!" Xavier seized Alfonso's hand. It was some moments before Alfonso could calm the young man or control his expressions of gratitude.

"Go home now, and get something to eat", he said at last.

Xavier ran headlong, first to his parents' house to tell them the news, then to Jacinto's house. As he rushed through the door shouting, "Wenceslaus! Wenceslaus!", the frightened Wenceslaus, who was eating his supper, jumped to his feet. It's that beating, he thought. He's going to take his revenge. He crammed a piece of fish in his mouth and backed against the wall, covering his face with his left forearm. But instead of being hit, he felt himself seized by the waist, pulled into the middle of the room and whirled around and around in a wild, ecstatic dance.

FIFTY-EIGHT

Athenagoras, the pharmacist, lived alone in a hut beyond the cemetery. It stood by itself outside the pallisade, under an ombu tree. In front the ground sloped down to the thickets along the river.

Inside the hut was dark and smelled of herbs. Fresh herbs were steeping in crocks on the floor. Dried herbs hung in bunches from the roof or, reduced to powder or liquid, stood in jars on shelves round the walls. Each jar was labelled in Athenagoras' careful script: *Lignum Vitae*, Jesuit Bark, Balm of the Missions, *Sangre de Drago*, Sarsaparilla, Camphor. At the back of the hut was a room like a cupboard where Athenagoras slept.

Alfonso, when on his way to visit the sick, often stopped at the hut to watch Athenagoras pounding leaves or seeds in his mortar and tending to the pots that were always simmering on the fire. The pharmacist had the ruminative calm of a domestic animal. Nothing flustered him, neither a jar breaking and spilling nor a pot boiling over and filling the hut with steam. He seemed completely content and at peace.

Once a week Athenagoras would leave the Reduction to hunt for plants, taking with him a donkey saddled with two panniers. The donkey was old like its master and, if not walking or munching grass, dozed with half-shut eyes and drooping head. When it was young, Athenagoras had asked Father Huber what he should call it, and the priest had named it "Aesculapius".

Alfonso sometimes accompanied Athenagoras on his expeditions. They would set out before dawn and proceed along the river through a landscape that, like a faintly inked print, was still all grey and silver. Then, entering the forest as the sun rose, they would spend the day picking the leaves of shrubs and plants and searching in the undergrowth for roots. They would return across the plains at dusk, when the earth glowed red like dried blood and the woods were a black silhouette and the flowering grasses gleamed white against the shadows.

One morning, when they were together in the hut, Athenagoras said, "A baby in the Gato family has measles." He was extracting the seeds from a jarful of dried pods by rubbing them between his hands over a shallow bowl. Alfonso was looking at a manuscript bound in gazelle skin. It was Athenagoras' chief treasure—a work on the flora of Paraguay by a Hungarian Jesuit, Father Asperger.

"In Europe most children catch measles at some stage", he said. He turned a page and began to study a coloured drawing of the copaiba balsam; but as he was admiring the beauty of its execution, he became aware that Athenagoras had stopped rubbing the seed pods. He looked up.

"Here, measles is serious", Athenagoras said. "Many Indians die of it."

Later in the day, Alfonso told Father Huber about the Gato baby. The older man frowned and sucked in his lips over his bare gums.

"Athenagoras is right. For the Indians, measles is as bad as smallpox is for us."

The baby and its mother were taken to the hospital. The next day there were two more cases, the following day ten, and in a week, thirty. Then there were no cases for three days, and everyone said to themselves: "Thank God. It's over." But suddenly there were fifteen new cases, then twenty-seven, then forty-six. Soon the hospital was full. After this, anyone who fell sick had to stay at home, so that the disease quickly spread to the other members of the infected family.

For six weeks the epidemic raged, continually growing worse. Only a third of the men in the Reduction were left to do the work.

Father Huber and Alfonso slept when they could. Day and night, in addition to their ordinary tasks, they were doctoring the sick and bringing them the sacraments. Alfonso learned how to handle leeches, open a vein, and bandage it afterward so as to stop the blood. He also became practised at cupping. The sick preferred him to the Indian nurses. He could apply the cups deftly to the back and chest so that the lighted whisp of tow inside did not burn the skin.

Athenagoras was given six assistants to help him prepare his medicines. There were always fifty Indians praying in the church. Banks of candles burned in front of the statues of the Blessed Virgin, St. Joseph, and

St. Michael. The *corregidor*, the justices, and the caciques led penitential processions and the public recitation of the rosary.

By the seventh week sixty Indians had died. Then the number of new cases each day started to dwindle. Hope returned, and the Indians once more began to smile.

Among the last to fall ill was Xavier. For five days he was delirious. All day, when she was not at work, Clara hovered outside the house.

"You can do nothing. You must go home and sleep", Jacinto's wife, Débora, would say when it began to grow dark. Clara would go a short way down the street, then creep back and hide in the shadows of the veranda, where she stayed for as long as she dared remain away from home, listening to Xavier's heavy breathing and starting up when he cried out or groaned.

On the fifth day, Father Huber came to anoint him. Clara watched from behind a tree. If he dies, I shall die too, she said to herself.

She ran to the church. There were several representations of the archangel St. Michael, carved or painted, in different parts of the building —driving Satan out of heaven, appearing on Monte Gargano before a kneeling bull, coming to the rescue of a variety of suppliants, including a man being vomited up by an alligator. But the one most favoured by the Indians was a quarter-life-size statue on a five-foot pedestal against a column near the entrance. It was the first statue at San Miguel to have been carved by an Indian and had been placed there a hundred years earlier so that the "prince of the heavenly host" would seem less remote from his petitioners.

Pushing her way through the kneeling crowd, Clara stood on tiptoe and grasped the statue by the ankles.

"Great Saint, Holy Archangel, listen! You must cure him. You have only to ask God, and he will listen." She gave the statue a shake. It rocked slightly on its pedestal. There were disapproving cries from behind her, but she disregarded them. "Listen!" she continued, "You are happy up there. But we are suffering. Have pity on us. I shall stay here, and I shan't eat until you cure him. If I die it will be your fault."

Releasing the figure, she knelt down. The minutes went by, the half hours, the hours; but she was still there. She was conscious of shuffling feet as people came and went. She could feel the heat of the candles burning in the archangel's honour and hear the wax falling on the flagstones. At moments she leaned forward and rested her head against the statue's base. Sometimes she swayed and nearly fell sideways. A mosquito bit her neck and flew away, droning triumphantly. The bells chimed midnight, then one o'clock, then two o'clock. Her prayers were a confused jumble. "Hail Mary . . . is he still alive? . . . San Miguel, pray for us . . . if he gets well, we will have four, five, six children . . . blessed art thou among women."

The Indians kneeling nearby nudged each other.

"She's been here since vespers."

"Xavier Tupanchichu is dying."

"She must have taken a vow."

When just before dawn, Rebeca, Xavier's sister came looking for her, Clara was lying in front of the statue, asleep. Rebeca shook her.

"Xavier is better. He understands what we say to him. He wants to know where you are. Come."

The next morning, when Alfonso entered the church to say Mass, the statue had all but disappeared under garlands of red and yellow lianas. Only the face was showing.

XAVIER AND CLARA were married just before Advent and were given a house on the other side of the street, opposite to Jacinto Epaguini's.

FIFTY-NINE

"We had no celebrations in honour of St. Michael last September because of the epidemic", Father Huber said, soon after the New Year. "This September we must do something extra special for him. Seventeen seventy-six is the 150th anniversary of the Reduction's foundation."

Traditionally, all major feast days were celebrated with a public banquet followed by games and a mock battle or tournament, sometimes in canoes on the river. Father Huber organised these with the help of the military commanders and town officials. Everything religious fell to Alfonso.

For the feast of St. Michael, the principal religious feature was the staging of a drama—part opera, part play—acted by the men and boys, called "Captain of the Heavenly Host". The original libretto and score had been written fifty years earlier by a Bavarian lay brother using music from Masses and oratorios popular in South Germany at the time. The play now required nearly two-hundred actors.

Late in January, Alfonso called his assistants to a meeting in the sacristy. He repeated what Father Huber had said about marking the occasion in some special way.

"We must add something to the play that will astonish everyone", Jacinto Epaguini said.

After a number of suggestions had been discussed and rejected, Longinus, the head sacristan, whispered something into the ear of Agustín, the tanner, who in turn whispered it to his neighbour. In this way the message went from one to another until it reached Alfonso. The Indians looked at each other, then at Alfonso to see what his reactions would be. When he hesitated, they all began talking at once.

"Impossible."

"It would be too difficult."

"No, no. The idea is good."

"Yes. No one will expect it."

"Reverend Father, is it not a marvellous idea?"

"We shall have to consult the builders and carpenters first", Alfonso said. "It may be too dangerous."

The "builders" were the maintenance men who looked after the fabric of the church and knew about pulleys and scaffolding. When consulted, they were equally enthusiastic.

"Brother Florian will help us", they said. "Brother Florian will know what to do."

Brother Florian was attached to the nearby Reduction of Trinidad but travelled around the townships as needed. Before entering the Society as a lay brother, he had worked as a foreman under the Bavarian architects the Asam brothers, and earlier still behind the scenes at the Vienna Court Opera.

The next step was to choose the cast. For this Father Huber had laid down certain rules. No one could play the same role two years running. Those who had had major parts the previous year would have minor parts this year. Families who had not had a member in one of the principal roles for the longest period must be considered first. At the same time, ability must be taken into account, and as many boys of the right age as possible must be used.

Applying these rules was like trying to work out a problem in Leibnizian mathematics. Now here is the Nyandu family, Alfonso said to himself, as he sat up late at night studying the list of actors from previous years. They had two important parts three years ago. How do they compare with the Papagayus, who had had four major parts five years ago?

Having drawn up the cast, he next had to combat the family loyalties of his assistants, who would secretly cross out names and substitute those of their sons, brothers, and cousins. When reproached for their perfidy, they laughed unashamedly, and he knew they were thinking: "It was worth trying."

Rehearsals began in February and went on through the spring and summer. Even with the help of Brother Florian, the novelty suggested by Longinus proved so difficult to stage that it was nearly abandoned. First they tried one contrivance, then another. At last, with a different system of cogwheels and pulleys, a solution was found. By the end of August, Alfonso was thinking: All our worries are over now.

But about a month before the feast, Longinus came running to him to say that a fire had burned the wings and badly scorched the costumes of the three principal archangels.

"Reverence, they are finished."

"Why can't they be repaired?" Alfonso asked.

"It is hopeless."

"Then new ones must be made."

"There is no time, Reverend Father."

"Yes, there is, if enough women work on them."

"Where shall we get all the feathers?"

"But the forests are full of birds."

"Who is to shoot them all?"

Longinus seemed to want the disaster to be irremediable.

"I don't know," Alfonso said, checking his impatience, "but it must be possible."

He called his other assistants. They agreed with Longinus.

"The Saint is perhaps displeased with us, Reverend Father."

"There will have to be new frames for the wings, and it takes time to prepare the osiers."

"Even if we could get enough feathers for St. Raphael and St. Gabriel, we still wouldn't have the feathers for St. Michael."

It seemed that St. Michael *had* to have the feathers of a Santos parakeet on his breastplate. It was a rare bird, not easily found.

"In that case," Alfonso said, "we shall have to use the feathers of a different bird."

"Oh, Your Reverence, it would be noticed."

"It has never been done."

Alfonso contemplated the twelve faces confronting him. They appeared not so much downcast as expectant. "How is he going to solve that?" they seemed to ask as they raised each new objection. At the same time, he was sure that no matter how many suggestions he made for repairing the costumes, the Indians would undermine them.

"I see", he said firmly. "*You* want to give up. I am determined to go ahead—if necessary with different assistants."

"Oh, no, Father, that is unthinkable. We should be disgraced."

"Very well then. We are going to try our best to put things right in time. Are we all agreed?"

"Of course, Reverend Father."

Once the Indians recognised that, having made up his mind, Alfonso was not going to change it, their opposition ceased. They went back to their work laughing and chatting as if they had only made difficulties for the pleasure of seeing how the *padre compañero* overcame them.

SIXTY

At six in the morning of September 29, Wenceslaus woke suddenly to the sound of cannon fire and musket shots.

He had been dreaming. In his dream he was back in the forests where he had been captured by a rival tribe and was being forced to undergo their trial of manhood. Four elders were crouched round him in a circle. One was piercing his tongue with a bone needle. The other four were flaying skin from different parts of his body with sharp stones. All this he must endure without moving or showing any sign of pain. None of it had happened to him in reality. His own tribe had no such ritual, but he had heard of it from men who had been captured by and then escaped from the Abipones of the Chaco.

Paulistas! he thought, as the cannonade continued. They're attacking us. What shall I do?

He lay staring in terror at a bunch of corncobs hanging from the rafter overhead and did nothing. Then memory began to work. The salvos, he realised, were for San Miguel.

Behind the partition, Jacinto was talking in a querulous voice to his wife, Deborah.

"I put it on the shelf when I took it off last night."

"Well, here it is under the cowhide. You've been sleeping on it."

Jacinto grunted, but not a grateful or apologetic grunt. He sounded put out. How could he have been wrong? Whatever it was he had lost ought to have been on the shelf.

Wenceslaus sat up and pulled aside the blanket that acted as a substitute for a door. The light outside, soft and misty, looked as though it had been filtered through milk. On the opposite side of the street, Xavier was washing himself in front of his house. As he bent forward, pouring water over his head from a jug, it ran down his neck, scattered over his body like mercury against his skin, and trickled in rivulets to the ground where it was soaked up by the dust.

The cannonade, which had stopped for a few minutes, started up again.

"Hurry!" Xavier called. "We'll be late."

Five minutes afterward, Wenceslaus and Xavier were walking with Jacinto toward the church.

Major feast days began with an early Mass at which everyone who could received Holy Communion, followed by a solemn High Mass with singing later in the morning. The streets were already crowded with Indians going in the same direction. Most of them walked in silence with lowered eyes, intent on the amazing fact that the God-Man who had died for them was about to come into their bodies and souls. For several weeks the *padre cura*'s sermons had been preparing them for the event, and everyone had been to confession. But now that it was close at hand, its awesomeness struck them with full force. The pealing of the church bells seemed almost frivolous. It somehow belonged to later, when the marriage of God to their souls would be complete.

Inside the church, garlands hung between the pillars and festooned the sanctuary. Xavier and Wenceslaus knelt in the south aisle.

As a catechumen, Wenceslaus remained in his place when the other men went up to receive Communion. The file of white-clad figures flowed slowly toward the altar rails, then back down the nave. Within the sanctuary, the *padre cura* and the *padre compañero*, assisted by two visiting priests, moved back and forth, each carrying a silver-gilt ciborium.

Wenceslaus watched intently, unconscious of anything but the line of kneeling men raising their heads as the priest approached to place the consecrated wafers on their tongues.

When Xavier, carrying the mysterious Bread in his body, returned to his place and knelt beside him, the thought that the God-Man was so close started a slight trembling in the calf of his left leg. The first time he had seen the congregation receiving Communion just over a year ago, he had got up when Xavier came back from the rails and had prostrated himself in front of him. But this, it had been explained to him, though well intended, was not appropriate; it could lead to misunderstanding. So now he shut his eyes and remained as still as he could, while the women went up to the altar and the choir sang a Monteverdi motet.

After Mass and breakfast, it was time to prepare for the procession that preceded High Mass. Xavier, who was in the militia, swallowed his food quickly, strapped on his weapons, peered into the basket where his recently born son, Belarmino, lay asleep, and rushed off to the plaza.

Across the street, Jacinto put on the academic gown and hood that Father Huber had designed for him for feast days. It was in blue silk with a white lining. With it went the chimney-pot hat of a doctor of the Sorbonne. The hat did not fit very well so Deborah stood behind him on a stool and hammered it into place with a stick. Wenceslaus, as a catechumen, wore a white alb with a green cincture.

When they returned to the plaza, *regidors* and *alcaldes* were running this way and that, trying to marshall the procession, but no one was paying much attention. Groups of officials in gala dress were strolling about showing off their clothes or chatting self-consciously with the equally richly dressed visiting officials from the Reductions of El Trinidad and Santa Rosa. Musicians were tuning their instruments, men with banners and flags were comparing notes about the best way to control them in a wind, while children darted around the adults and under the horses. The bells were pealing again and at every second stroke soared through the belfry arches as if, in an ecstasy of joy, trying to fling themselves into the sky.

Jacinto approached a stately Indian in a red cloak.

"Good morning, Captain. It's good to see you again. This is one of our catechumens, Wenceslaus Aroyu." He turned to Wenceslaus. "The Captain is from Santa Rosa."

The Captain inclined his head slightly.

"Do you have many catechumens?" he asked.

"What the Lord chooses to send us", Jacinto replied, but without mentioning a figure.

"I can say the same for us."

"We are blessed with a good day."

"We are blessed indeed."

They bowed again and moved off to greet other acquaintances.

"The Captain is a great soldier", Jacinto explained to Wenceslaus. "He commanded the militia three years ago when our soldiers went to help the Governor of Asunción defend the town against a big band of Toba Indians."

Suddenly, and as if spontaneously, the chaos of moving bodies began to fall into order, and the shouting and talking died down. Those not taking part because of their responsibilities for other aspects of the festivities, fell back to the edge of the plaza, and the procession moved off, headed by an Indian wearing the wide-brimmed hat of a seventeenth-century cavalier and riding a black charger. A heavy cavalry sword, attached to his body by a pale blue sash, hung down the charger's right flank, and strapped to his bare heels he sported a large pair of silver-gilt spurs. A detachment of militia followed, and after them musicians, a choir, a troop of dancers, and a man leading a panther cub. The mayor and councillors came next, in scarlet satin with white lace neckcloths and shirt cuffs, and in their wake another detachment of militia, three men leading ostriches on gold cords, more musicians, choristers and dancers, preparing the way for the chief justice, the *alcaldes* and *alguacils*. A crossbearer preceded the heads of sodalities, the sacristans and beadles, and farther back came a group of children leading six gazelles on red strings, then the schoolmasters and catechists and the masters of the different crafts. The banners with their bearers, scattered up and down the procession, looked like the sails of galleons tossing on a flooded river. In the subtropical landscape the ribbon of bright colours looked natural rather than artificial.

After passing down the main street under arches of greenery, the procession moved out of the town and across the fields to a chapel dedicated to San Miguel standing in a grove of terebinths and cedars. Here, when the choir had sung a hymn in honour of the Archangel, the mayor dismounted and went into the chapel, followed by six boys carrying horizontally, like a section of a ship's mast, a ten-foot long wax candle. The boys fixed the candle in a bronze holder. The mayor mounted a ladder and lighted the wick. Then, after he had said a prayer asking their patron to protect them from famine, the procession moved on between the fields where the new crops were beginning to show green through the ploughed earth.

Having circuited the town, stopping at other chapels along the way, they returned through the south gate.

"Where are we going now?" Wenceslaus asked. He was walking next to Jacinto, a place of honour. Because of the dramatic circumstances of his arrival, he was still regarded as a kind of trophy.

"To fetch the *alférez real*", Jacinto said. "He carries the royal standard. He represents the King. He is waiting for us now."

The procession stopped in front of the *alférez's* garlanded house. The mayor and councillors dismounted and went inside, reappearing a few minutes later with, what seemed to Wenceslaus all but impossible, an individual even more superbly dressed than those he had already seen. It was difficult to imagine that a man could be more loaded with lace, galloon, gold braid, and feathers without disappearing altogether under the accumulation. His breeches and shoes had paste buckles, his sword a gilded hilt, and he was carrying gloves.

"But it's Justino", Wenceslaus said suddenly, after gazing open-mouthed for a minute at this symbol of royal authority and power. Justino was the foreman at the slaughterhouse.

"Of course. Justino is *alférez* this year."

In Wenceslaus' mind, two unrelated ideas came together in irregular wedlock.

"Does he wear the best clothes because he gives us our meat?"

"No. I told you. It's because he carries the King's standard. He's like the King himself, you could say. Look, he has shoes and stockings."

Wenceslaus looked first at the standard-bearer's white silk stockings and scarlet-heeled shoes, then at Jacinto's bare feet.

"The *regidors* don't have shoes and stockings either", Jacinto said defensively.

"Have you ever been *alférez*?"

"Why should I want to be *alférez*? I am schoolmaster."

"The schoolmaster ought to wear shoes and stockings, too; he knows more than anyone except the Fathers", Wenceslaus said after a pause, and was astonished by the grateful and affectionate look he received in exchange.

A boy dressed like a court page came forward, leading a white stallion with bows and ribbons in its mane and tail. Under the silver-encrusted saddle, a crimson cloth embroidered with St. Michael's monogram and the royal arms covered its back and sides.

The *alférez* mounted, an attendant brought the standard from under a canopy outside his house, the drums rolled, the trumpets blew a fanfare, and the procession moved off, this time circling the inside of the town.

Outside the church, the *padre compañero* was waiting to bless the *alférez* and his standard before the beadles and sacristans led him to his place at the head of the nave, along with the other officials and their visitors.

With all the visitors, there was not room for everyone in the church, so the doors had to be left open for the worshippers outside.

During High Mass, Wenceslaus wanted to listen to the singing, but Jacinto kept up a whispered commentary. Instructing people was his vocation, and, as so often happens, he could no longer tell the difference between "in season" and "out of season".

"Look," he said, "now they are carrying the book of the Holy Gospels, which tell about the life of Jesus. The deacon will read from the book. You see, a lighted candle is carried either side of it to show how holy it is." Wenceslaus felt insulted. I know that already, he thought.

After the Gospel came the sermon.

"Do you understand what the *padre cura* is saying?" Jacinto asked. Wenceslaus nodded, in the hope of silencing him. But Jacinto's question had been rhetorical; ignoring the nod, he proceeded to paraphrase the sermon point by point.

"He's telling us San Miguel is a great angel, and we should pray to him a lot."

I know that, too, Wenceslaus said to himself, realising at the same

325

time that there was no need to listen to what Jacinto was saying. If he nodded from time to time to keep his instructor happy, he could let his thoughts wander about where he pleased.

By now the sermon was over, and it seemed to him that his thoughts were like the smoke from the incense burner that an acolyte was holding ready for the incensing of the altar. It started in a compact stream rising in a straight line, then as it got farther and farther from its source, it started to float about in clouds in all directions, growing more and more diaphanous until it reached the roof and drifted down again.

But with the Consecration, his mind again became fixed on the altar. The trumpets blew, the soldiers lining the aisle held up their bows in salute, the hundreds of kneeling figures bowed like grass in the wind and, for the second time that day, Wenceslaus said to himself: "Yes, He is there."

Toward the end of Mass he began to feel tired and wondered how long it would be before they could eat. He would have liked to scratch and stretch his legs, but, wanting to behave like everybody else, he kept still in his place until the priests had left the altar and people began to move outside.

During Mass, some of the women had been setting out the food for the banquet. Most of the Indians sat on the ground to eat. There were jars of maize beer; bowls of roast beef and mutton with manioc bread; roast wild fowl and ape's flesh cooked with oranges; baked iguana; sweet dishes made with honey and jam—all laid out in lines under the trees. The men went to the north side of the plaza, women to the south. The dignitaries joined the priests at a long table in the middle of the west side, facing the church. Father Mayer, the *padre cura* of Santa Rosa, said grace, and the company set to eating. Each Indian carried his own knife and a dried gourd to drink from.

When no one could eat any more, and the *regidors* and *alcaldes* judged from the noise and laughter that enough had been drunk, the dishes and tables were cleared away, the priests retired to the college, and most of the company stretched themselves out under the trees to sleep. The officials, however, had their gala clothes to consider and retired to their houses, taking their guests with them.

For the first time since early morning, silence fell on the town. Finches and parakeets, which had been watching their opportunity from the surrounding trees, fluttered down, first in ones and twos, then, when the courage of a few had emboldened the rest, in dozens, and hopped among the motionless bodies, clearing up the remaining fragments of the feast.

SIXTY-ONE

At two o'clock the church bells rang again. One by one the sleeping Indians stirred, rolled over, stretched, and rubbed their eyes. The frightened birds rose in a flock and settled, chattering, in the trees. Soon everyone was running about to get ready for the tournament.

Pastimes like the tournament took place in a long rectangular meadow outside the town to the east. Here two stands with coloured awnings and pennants at the corners faced each other across the lists. In the middle the carpenters had erected a striped pole, topped by a statue of the Archangel, with a projecting arm on either side from which hung a rope with a ring on the end of it.

The Indians competing in the tournament ran off to get their horses, and the rest sat down in long lines stretching the length of the meadow. The men were nearly all first-rate horsemen and therefore keen critics.

When everything was ready, the *alférez* appeared with his escort of officials and guests and took his place in the booth on the far side. A few minutes later, the priests came from the college and, with the rest of the officials and visitors, seated themselves in the booth nearest the town. The talking, which had died down at their appearance, grew louder and more excited, breaking into cries and shouts as the contestants and their horses appeared at opposite ends of the field. The contestants were divided into two teams, the reds and the blues, distinguished by their sashes, with twenty-five men to a team.

At a sign from the *alférez*, a drum rolled and a rider from the red team trotted forward on a bay gelding, whose coat had been groomed until it shone like polished chestnut. Impatient at being held in check, the animal advanced with short, springing steps and kept throwing up its head and jingling its harness.

The rider set his teeth, tightened his grip on his lance, and put his horse into a canter, then a gallop. As the tip of the lance moved rapidly toward the ring, there was another moment of silence, then a burst of laughter and shouts as it hit the cord, sending the ring dancing wildly in the air and leaving the rider to canter on disconsolately to the far end of the field, where the first competitor from the rival team was waiting his turn.

Crisóstomo, Xavier, and Wenceslaus were sitting together near one of the booths, eating nuts left over from the banquet.

"Wait till I'm allowed to ride in the tournament", Crisóstomo said. "I'll soon show them how easy it is."

"Listen to him!"

"He thinks it's easy."

"He couldn't hit the ring if it was as big as a cartwheel."

"I could hit a smaller ring than this one", he said. "Now look at the little fellow coming along now. That's not the way to sit a horse. He looks like a monkey on an ostrich. You can tell he's afraid of falling off by the way he's gripping his reins."

The rider cantered past them and carried off the ring on the end of his lance. When the applause had died down, Xavier and Wenceslaus turned on Crisóstomo. Laughing and jeering, they pushed him over, threw a poncho on top of him and pummelled his back and thighs.

"Who said he would miss?"

"Tell us what the next one's going to do."

"Did I say he wouldn't hit the ring?" Crisóstomo said, grinning as he struggled from under the poncho. "I said he sat on his horse like a monkey . . . and he does."

Spears and harness glinted in the sun, the pennants fluttered, the tops of the trees rocked in the breeze, and the crowd rippled with little movements, as heads turned and arms and hands changed position.

THE RED TEAM WON, twenty-three hits to nineteen, and went forward to receive their prizes from the *padre cura*.

After the tilting came Spanish riding.

"It is a speciality of our Reduction", Father Huber said, leaning sideways and addressing Father Fields, the Irishman who had travelled out from Spain with Alfonso and was now assistant priest at El Trinidad. "We once had a lay brother who had worked in the imperial stables in Vienna. He taught our Indians."

A string orchestra was playing a gavotte, and a team of horsemen in buff-coloured breeches, bottle-green coats, and cocked hats came cantering down the course. As they approached the booths, they divided into two columns, stopped on either side of the tilting pole, and turned inward. Then, at a command from the leader, the twenty stallions sank back on their haunches, raising their front legs in salute to San Miguel.

"This position is called the *levade*", Father Huber explained to Father Fields.

The word carried Alfonso back to his childhood. He was sitting on a stool beside his mother's chair. On her other side sat Gaspar, aged six. Doña Teresa had a big book open on her lap with brightly coloured pictures of prancing horses.

"Why isn't it called Austrian riding, Mama?"

"Because it was invented in Spain. Spain and Austria were once ruled by the same Emperor."

And now, thirty years later, the once diminutive Gaspar, who had asked the question, was the stately Duke of Montesa, ruling a household of two hundred or more. How difficult it was to connect the two Gaspars —boy and man. Alfonso was reminded of his philosophy courses before his ordination, when he had first learned to distinguish between "being" and "becoming". Certainly there had been a lot of becoming in Gaspar's life. The continuity of being was superficially harder to discern; it was something each man could be sure of only by looking into himself.

Alfonso returned from his daydream to hear Father Huber saying, "And now they are going to do *caprioles*."

This time horses and horsemen were drawn up, line abreast, farther down the course. Then each in turn cantered forward, and as they came opposite the booths, at a sign from the rider, the horse bounded into the air with its forelegs neatly curved under its body and its back legs stretched out to the rear. The musicians had stopped playing, and the only sounds were an occasional snort as the animals gathered themselves together for the upward spring and the thud of their hooves on the grass as they came down.

The display ended with a dance. To the music of a tarantella, the horses moved in a circle, sometimes one behind the other, sometimes in pairs, pirouetting on themselves or their partners as they went. As they galloped off the course, the riders raised and waved their cocked hats.

Next, troops of children came dancing onto the field dressed as ancient Greeks and Romans, Dresden shepherds and shepherdesses, Turks, Cossacks, Chinese, and Scots. At first, the young unmarried men pretended to be bored, but once they began to recognise their brothers and sisters and cousins, interest became general. Some of the costumes were a confused mixture of countries and periods, having been made according to the instructions of successive generations of Jesuits, who had often had to depend on their memories of paintings and engravings seen long ago in Europe.

The dances were equally varied in origin. There were slow dances and fast dances, court dances and peasant dances, German, Scottish, Italian, and Spanish dances. But a Hungarian gypsy dance performed by six Cossacks and six Chinese received the longest and loudest applause.

The afternoon ended with a series of mock battles in which teams from San Miguel and El Trinidad took on teams from San Miguel and Santa Rosa. The weapons were poles with padded ends, and the aim was to unseat as many of the opposing side as possible. The battles were the most popular of the entertainments, at least among the men. Two mounted *alcaldes* acted as referees. Anyone convicted of trying to do malicious damage was liable to ten days in the lock-up.

Afterward, when the victors had received their prizes and the wounded had had their cuts and bruises attended to, everyone left the field and made their way to the church for vespers and Benediction, at which groups of altarboys danced in front of the Blessed Sacrament.

In the half hour before the play, most of the Indians went home to eat again, taking any visitors with them.

Clara, who had Belarmino fastened to her back in a sling, shuffled along in the crowd beside her mother. Suddenly, seeing a tall girl she knew a short distance ahead, she let go her mother's hand and pushed forward to speak to her.

"Is it true, Perpetua, that you're going to marry the catechumen, Wenceslaus?" she asked.

"Yes. It's true."

"But he isn't baptized."

"He will be baptized on All Saints Day."

"I am glad. He is a good man. He is Xavier's friend."

Perpetua smiled, showing two exceptionally fine rows of white teeth. She peered over Clara's shoulder and touched Belarmino on the forehead.

"Your baby is beautiful", she said.

They walked for a few minutes in silence, drawn together by the exchange of compliments, since, unlike many compliments, theirs had the merit of being completely sincere. They had been uttered without any special desire to flatter or please.

"I will ask my father to speak to the *padre cura*", Clara said. "If he gave you and Wenceslaus a house close to ours, our children could grow up as friends."

"That would be very good", Perpetua said. "And one day some of them might marry each other." For Perpetua the world was still beautifully predictable.

"Let's sit next to each other at the play."

331

The stage had been set up on the west side of the square, with the audience sitting with their backs to the church. It was like a large, oblong house with two floors, open at the front, the whole raised five feet above ground level. Steps at the sides descended in baroque curves from the upper floor to the lower floor and from the lower floor to the paving stones of the plaza. At ground level, walls projected to left and right, each with an arched gateway in the middle. The gate on the left was surrounded with painted flames and surmounted by a cartouche bearing the word *Infernum*. The gate itself was studded with bones. The cartouche over the right-hand gate carried the word *Coelum*, the gate being framed in painted birds, fruits, and flowers. The chairs for the orchestra were on the ground in front. The painted tile roof over the upper stage had a flat top with pinnacles at the four corners, while immediately below, painted clouds and cherubs filled the corners and broke the right angles of the upper stage itself to leave no doubt that this was heaven.

For the Indians, the only unfamiliar feature was a pair of cables running overhead from the church roof behind them to the rear of the stage, where they were attached to two posts with wheels and pulleys. Only the Indians at the back of the audience could see the upper part of the posts, and there was much argument about what they could be for until their attention was distracted by the arrival of the town dignitaries and the clergy.

The sun was now in the west, and the whole plaza lay in cool and luminous shade. While waiting for the play to begin, Clara amused Belarmino by rattling a dried gourd. Then a bell rang. There were cries of "Quiet! Quiet!" and a child near the front cried shrilly "It's beginning." The curtains of the upper stage drew aside and, to a roll of drums and solemn chords from the orchestra, revealed God the Father and God the Son enthroned, with the Holy Ghost suspended by a chord from the ceiling between and a little above them.

IN NORMAL LIFE, God the Father was an assistant blacksmith. He had been chosen for the part because of his stature—he was the tallest Indian in the Reduction—and for his singing voice. A towering papal tiara added a good two feet to his height, and a white beard like a cloud covered his chest and solar plexus. God the Son, shorter and slighter, had a Titian red wig and beard.

In a three-part hymn, the three Divine Persons sang of their mutual love and perfect happiness, a singer backstage taking the part of the Holy Ghost.

"Our happiness cannot be increased", said the Father, when the hymn was over. "But let us share it, nevertheless."

"Let us make spirits in our own image", said the Son.

"Let them be called angels", said the Holy Ghost.

"Let them be free", said the Son.

"But some will rebel", said the Holy Ghost.

"Then we will make man to take their places", said the Father.

"Man shall be small and weak," said the Holy Ghost, "to make it easier for him not to fall into the sin of pride."

"We will make time and space for him to live in", said the Father.

"When he rebels, I will redeem him", said the Son.

The audience murmured excitedly.

The Father stood up and sang an aria, summoning the spirits into existence: angels and archangels, thrones and dominions, principalities, virtues and powers, cherubim and seraphim. Troop by troop, in tight-fitting feathered suits, each with a broad smile to indicate his state of beatitude, they came running up the stairs from the lower stage and knelt before the Trinity. At the appearance of St. Michael, immediately recognised by his special feathers, the cheering sent all the birds in the town wheeling into the sky.

Having been created, the angels had to be tested.

In a dramatic recitative, the Father explained to them that, having seen his Son in glory, they must now see and adore him as he would appear at a future time for reasons not yet to be revealed to them.

Half turning, the Father gestured to the curtains at the back of the stage, which parted in heavy loops to show a life-size Christ on the Cross, his flesh covered in wounds and blood. A groan rose from the audience, ending in a single giant sigh.

The obedient angels prostrated themselves. But Lucifer, furious and trembling, ran to the front of the stage.

"Non serviam", he shouted, turning to shake his fist at the crucifix.

"Non serviam", echoed the rebel angels. "We will not serve."

The hissing and booing that greeted this second "non serviam" sounded as if all the snakes, bulls, and bullocks in Paraguay had assembled to express their horror at the blasphemy.

Meanwhile, St. Michael had jumped to his feet, crying, "Quis ut Deus?" and the faithful angels replied, "God is supreme."

A duet and chorus followed, with St. Michael and his angels praising God's greatness and goodness, and Lucifer and his followers extolling their courage and independence. At the conclusion Lucifer and his followers ran howling down the stairs to the left, while St. Michael and his supporters marched singing down the stairs to the right.

While the armies were preparing for battle, two cherubim and two seraphim sang a quartet on the roof. When Lucifer and his army reappeared, they were wearing black tights and had horns, tails, and bats' wings.

The battle was fought on the lower stage in the form of a ballet. After various advances, retreats, *mêlées*, and flank attacks, St. Michael and Lucifer met in single combat. At one point, Lucifer seemed about to overcome his opponent. Forgetting he was watching a play, a man in the front row dashed forward to help the archangel. His friends, catching him by his tunic, pulled him back to his place.

At last Lucifer fell. The devils were disarmed and driven, shrieking, into hell. Goggle-eyed monsters and reptiles were looking down from the top of the wall, and sulphurous smoke was pouring from the open gates. When the last devil had vanished inside, St. Michael locked the gates with a foot-long key.

On the other side of the wall the devils, carried away with enthusiasm for their parts, continued to shriek and howl and throw smoking brands in the air until stopped by a message from Alfonso.

The act ended with the heavenly army singing a triumphal chorus on the lower stage, while St. Michael mounted to the upper stage, handed the key of hell to the Father, and was crowned captain of the heavenly host with a coroneted helmet.

WHEN THE CURTAINS PARTED for the second act, they revealed the Queen of Heaven—played by the twelve-year-old son of one of the shepherds—seated on a low stool between God the Father and God the Son. She was dressed like a Tiepolo princess. Her gown of lemon and aquamarine satin was roped about with imitation pearls and diamonds, and a spiked crown, set far back on her head, held in place a white veil embroidered with stars. Her ladies stood in groups at the edge of the stage; martyrs in red to the left, widows and virgins in white and gold to the right. Each carried a basket of flowers.

After a short cantata the Queen of Heaven rose. The Son embraced her.

"Where are you going, Mother?" he asked.

"To earth, my Son, to be close to men", she replied and, followed by her ladies, descended to the lower stage. Here she seated herself on a damask cushion, and the ladies arranged themselves round her in a semicircle. The effect of a garden was suggested by pots of flowering shrubs.

In the song that followed, each of the ladies sang a verse about one of the flowers in her basket. The flowers were the prayers of people on earth. A white flower was the prayer of a pure soul; a purple one, the prayer of a sorrowful soul. St. Agnes, who looked like a Watteau shepherdess and was holding a live lamb with a red ribbon round its neck, sang a verse about a small blue flower, which represented the prayer of a humble soul. To keep the lamb quiet, she had removed her gloves and was letting it suck one of her fingers. St. Monica, who

335

was nervous and kept her black lashes lowered, held up a wilted flower representing the prayer of a sinner.

At the end of the song, the ladies discussed their petitioners on earth while the Queen of Heaven listened, gently waving her silk and ivory fan.

"My clients", said St. Rose of Lima, who had gold roses in her powdered hair, "are always asking me to take away aches and pains or find lost beads, knives, and weapons. But they hardly ever ask me to make them better people."

There was laughter, and the visiting Indians from Santa Rosa cheered.

"Yes," St. Cecilia said, "and as soon as they've got what they want, they stop praying. They never remember to say 'thank you.'"

St. Monica took off her shoe to scratch her foot but quickly put it back on again when she saw St. Veronica frowning at her.

"The other day," St. Catherine said, "a woman, whose name I won't mention, asked me to cure her son. Then as soon as she was off her knees, she was quarrelling with her neighbour."

After every lady had had her say, the Queen of Heaven sang an aria about God's mercy to sinners. She had barely finished when St. Michael reappeared, bowing respectfully as he approached.

"Most Holy Virgin," he said, "a soul that bears my name is in danger. Please will you intercede for him?"

"We will go at once. Is he young or old?"

"Young, Holy Virgin. But old in sin."

"Alas! Alas! But my Son will hear me. And you, Michael, hold Satan off in the meantime. Make haste now. I am on my way." And, followed by her ladies, she mounted to the upper stage.

The curtains of the lower stage had been drawn the moment she left. When they reopened a few minutes later, a small hut, open at the front, occupied the centre of the stage. Inside, an Indian lay on a cot tilted at the back so that the audience could see him better. His wife and children knelt on either side. The man moaned; the children sobbed; the women kept peering out of the hut, crying, "When will the *padre* come? Oh, when will the *padre* come?"

Immediately, three panting youths arrived one after the other, like the messengers of Job. The first said the priest had gone to a distant part of the Reduction and could not be found. The second, who had been sent to a neighbouring Reduction, said that the priest there was on his deathbed. The third arrived limping and with a bandaged head—he had been attacked on the road by robbers. The woman sang a lament to music by Monteverdi.

As the last note died away, the children screamed. Two devils, one with a cow's head, the other with a gigantic cock's comb, were looking into the hut through a window at the back. The children turned their heads away so as not to see, only to find other devils making faces at them from in front. Then all the devils joined hands and danced around the hut, singing about the torments they were going to inflict on the sick father once he was dead.

At this moment, the gates of hell flew open, and Lucifer appeared, followed by his chief demons. Advancing angrily toward the hut, he broke up the dance, kicking one devil, cuffing another, pulling a third by the hair.

"Lazy curs! Amusing yourselves instead of working! Have you made a list of this man's sins? He is not ours yet. We can't be certain till the last moment. To work!"

He delivered another round of kicks, cuffs, and hair-pullings. The lesser demons, after capering about and howling with pain, came cringing to their master, kissed his hands, licked his feet, and lay on the ground for him to trample over them. But as soon as he turned away, they jumped up, pulled long noses, and stuck out their tongues at him. Then they all started tormenting the family. Lucifer went to the bedside. His largest and blackest follower stationed himself by the mother; the other devils took charge of the children. They whispered first in one ear, then in the other, and drove home their suggestions with pinches and punches.

The dying Indian rolled his eyes and threw out his arms.

"I'm lost! I'm lost! My sins drag me down. I see fire."

"Pray, children, pray!" the mother cried. "St. Michael, pray for us! St. Michael, help us!"

The orchestra began to play, and everyone on the stage began to sing, with the soprano voices of the boys rising in long curves above the staccato basses and baritones of the demons like silver streamers unfurling above a turbulent sea.

As the song ended there was an explosion, followed by a flash of light. Every head in the audience turned as if jerked from behind by the hair.

"Holy Mother of God!"

"Look! Look! San Miguel!"

With outspread wings and a flaming sword, the Archangel stood poised on the apex of the pediment at the top of the front of the church. In other years at this point in the play, he had always appeared tamely through the door on the right of the stage marked *Coelum*. But how was he to reach the man in the hut?

Suddenly, with a roar, the audience answered its own question.

"He's flying! He's flying!" a thousand voices shouted, as with beating wings the Archangel came sailing through the air forty feet above the audience and landed on the roof of the upper stage in a cloud of pink smoke, which enabled him to recover his balance.

At last the mystery of the cables stretching from the roof of the church to the back of the stage was explained.

"Again! Again!" the audience shouted, as St. Michael stood smiling and bowing. And before the play could continue, he had to make two return journeys and two more descents.

The audience would have been for three, four, a dozen—they did not know how many repeats, but Brother Florian, his round, homely red face beaming with satisfaction, explained from the front of the stage that he was afraid of straining the machinery, and the play was allowed to go on.

"Depart, hellish fiend", St. Michael commanded, as he entered the hut. "That man is mine."

"Not so", Lucifer replied, and opened a scroll containing a list of the man's sins. He allowed one end of the scroll to fall from his hand so that it unrolled across the floor. "You can see from this that he belongs to me."

St. Michael replied by reading from a list of the man's good deeds.

338

"You'll never find enough good deeds to match all his sins", Lucifer gloated. "You might just as well let me have him without any fuss."

"None of your tricks", St. Michael said sternly. "You know the law. No matter how many sins he's committed, if he repents, a million million sins will be forgiven."

"But he won't repent. My demons have told him his sins are too black to be forgiven—that there's a limit to God's goodness. And he believes them. Look how he tosses about."

St. Michael bent down and whispered in the wife's ear. Lucifer was about to kick her in order to distract her attention, but a watchful angel darted forward, caught his hoof in midair, and gave it a twist. With a curse, the rebel archangel fell to the floor, and, before he could get up, the woman snatched the crucifix from the wall and held it in front of her husband. The man took it. For a moment he seemed to waver between conflicting impulses while the angels sang words of encouragement and the chorus of devils urged him to despair. Then slowly he raised the crucifix to his lips, kissed it, and fell back dead.

FOR THE FINAL ACT, the back of the lower stage was covered with tombs looking like white tool chests, while, up above, the Father and Son sat surrounded by angels and saints, with the Blessed Virgin once again on her footstool between them.

After a quartet and chorus, angels appeared on the lower stage and ran about among the tombs, blowing silver trumpets.

"Look! It's Xavier!" Clara said, tugging Perpetua's sleeve, as one of the angels sped along the front of the stage. But she had no time to admire him, for the dead were waking up and throwing back the lids of their coffins. Some jumped joyfully out of their graves; some sat up, rubbing their eyes as if they had been asleep. A few peeped over the edge, then cowered back inside; these the angels hauled out by the hair.

The "dead" each had a weapon, tool, or headdress to show what they had been in life—caciques, captains, herdsmen, smiths, scribes, farmers. Mothers held babies or cooking spoons.

When the angels had gathered everyone together at the front of the stage, angels and men sang the "Dies Irae" from Victoria's 1605 Requiem. Judgment and sentence were given in mime.

At the conclusion, the damned, their faces buried in their hands, were driven, sobbing, toward hell, where they were pulled inside by the devils, and the saved were led off through the door marked *Coelum*, to return after a few minutes wearing white robes and gold crowns. As they mounted the upper stage in two columns, St. Michael, his sword once more aflame, appeared on the roof. The audience jumped to their feet, and, to the ringing of the church bells, actors and audience together sang at the top of their voices the final thunderous chorus.

SIXTY-THREE

When Alfonso and Brother Florian, their faces streaked with sweat and dust, their cassocks smudged with charcoal and gunpowder, entered the college living room, the other three Jesuits stood up and cheered.

"Don't know how many times I've seen that play", said Father Mayer, whose huge, powerful body, worn by years of rough living, suggested a crumbling fortress. "Never shed tears before, though. Deeply moving."

When stirred emotionally or carried away by his subject, he tended to talk in one-clause sentences without definite or indefinite articles, like a man jotting down his thoughts in a notebook, a habit contracted during the long periods in his life when he had had no one to speak to but himself. He and Father Huber had been friends as boys in Linz.

"Congratulations on your flying machine, brother", Father Fields said. "It was superb. I can't wait to have a ride on it tomorrow."

"I'm sorry," Alfonso said, "you're too late. The Indians were beginning to have the same idea, and we foresaw accidents. So we've told the carpenters to start dismantling it."

Father Huber nodded approvingly.

"Now isn't that just my luck", Father Fields said. "You'll book me for a ride next year though, won't you?" He turned to Father Florian. "At least I hope you'll show me how it works before we go home."

"With pleasure, Father." Like most good mechanical engineers, Brother Florian was always glad to explain how anything he had made worked.

"I've only one criticism to make of the production as a whole", Father Mayer said, contracting his thick white eyebrows above his startlingly blue eyes. "A doctrinal matter."

"Not serious, I hope."

"Very serious. The devils looked as if they were enjoying themselves more than the angels."

Everyone laughed, and Alfonso and Brother Florian went off to wash and change their cassocks. When they came back, Father Huber said grace, and they sat down to supper.

It was dark outside, and behind the five chairs the candles burning on the table cast five long shadows that spread starlike across the tiled floor, stood upright against the walls, and bent inward over the ceiling like four genies hovering in attendance on their masters. When the candle flames moved in the air from the open windows, the shadows wavered from side to side across the portraits of the long-dead priests with their high-cheekboned faces and tilted eyes.

Tarcisio and Cayetano, carrying dishes and plates, circled the table, in and out of the shadows, like moths around a lantern. In their scarlet coats, white breeches, and leather slippers, they looked like retired field marshalls fallen on bad days. The uniforms had been designed by Tarcisio. He had told Father Huber that if everyone else with a position of importance in the Reduction had a uniform, except the college servants, the people would not have a proper respect for their priests. Father Huber had therefore given them permission to wear the uniforms on great feasts, but never before the Bishop, the Governor, or any other visitors outside the Society. He wanted to make Tarcisio and Cayetano happy, but he did not want to start rumors that the Jesuits were being waited on by liveried servants.

At the far end of the room, beyond the reach of the candlelight, a lamp winked before a flower-crowned statue of the archangel draped in a gold cloak. Tarcisio would have thought it disgraceful to wear gala clothes and not provide them for the Reduction's patron.

During the meal, Father Huber guided the conversation, tossing the lead first to one guest, then another, and only interrupting to fill a glass or say, "Try some of this, Aloys . . . Tarcisio does it to perfection", or, "Come, Father, take some more . . . you must be hungry, I know."

With each course, Father Mayer put on a pair of rusty spectacles and peered at the dish he was being offered to see if it were something new or familiar. After tasting a mouthful or two, he would growl his approval and nod at Tarcisio. "Excellent," he said, "I congratulate you", or, "This is different from last time—but even better." Only a slight trembling of the dish in Tarcisio' hands betrayed his gratification.

"Ah, Johan," Father Mayer exclaimed with a sigh, as he helped himself a second time to a special goulash Father Huber had taught Tarcisio to make, "it's well for my soul that no one at Santa Rosa can cook like Tarcisio. And if I didn't know that as soon as our backs are turned, you'll be living off beans and bread crusts, I'd be beginning to worry about your soul, too."

"Nonsense! Nonsense, Aloys! Eat up." Father Huber turned to Father Fields. "Did you know that Father Mayer is one of our great missionaries? He converted a whole tribe of Moxos Indians single-handedly. Tell them about it, Johan. It will encourage them."

"I'll be butchered first. Tell them about the number of converts I made in the Chaco, if you like."

"Father Mayer worked for many years in the Chaco", Father Huber said. "He knows more about the Chaco and its Indians than anyone else alive."

"And a lot of good I did there. A great missionary, eh? I'll tell you a story. I once chased a tribe of Chaco Indians up the Pilcomayo for six weeks. That's a river, in case you didn't know. Chaco Indians most unstable people. Can't hold on to an idea for more than two minutes. In one ear and out the other. Fierce, too. At the mercy of their passions. And wrapped in darkness. You can't conceive it. Revolting habits, too. But God understands. Ignorance scarcely blameworthy. Lovable to him. All a profound mystery. Six weeks I was chasing them, and it rained all the time. I hate wet feet, always have. Expect you do, too. There were three of us—myself and two Indian guides. Couldn't trust either. Nothing to eat but dried beef. Not dry for long. Waterlogged. Full of worms. Disgusting. Just the sight of dried beef still makes me sick."

"And did you find the tribe?" Father Fields asked.

"Yes and no. Truer to say they found me. Chief got fed up with having me on his trail. Seen enough of me. Devil at work in him, too, I suspect. Had me trussed like a chicken and left in a tree. Thought I was done for at last. No one for miles. Shouting in vain. Two days go by. I pray. I grow weaker. 'The end', I say to myself. But no. A Spaniard comes by, a soldier, a deserter from Asunción. Can you believe it? There's no understanding God's providence till you experience it. The man had me down in a twinkling, unfastened me, carried me on his back to his camp, looked after me like a mother. In return I got him a pardon and made a good Christian of him. The only one I made in four years."

"Father Mayer has forgotten to mention that he discovered whole tracts of the country that Europeans had never seen and came back with priceless information about plants and animals."

"That's enough, Johan. Now I'll tell them a story about you. What a holy man, eh?" He winked at Brother Florian and the two younger priests. "Meek, gentle, affectionate." He dropped his shoulders, imitating his friend's stoop. "Always thinking of others. Never seems to have any wishes of his own. Devoted heart and soul to his flock. God bless me, how he loves them. Not like me, sinner that I am. Often want to knock their heads together. Most of them good as gold of course. Not for me to find fault with them. One of them worth ten of my sort. But cultural differences, you know. Different way of looking at things. Makes you feel isolated sometimes. Want to shut myself in my room. Fed up with palm trees, brown faces, ants, manioc, and Christmas in the middle of summer. Long to see Europe. A great missionary, eh? Always repent afterward, when I feel that way. Ashamed of myself. Deeply touching, their affection for one. If one weren't a priest, affection would be utterly misplaced. Lord have mercy on us. What was I talking about?"

"About my superior", Alfonso said with a smile.

"Father Johan! Ah, yes! I'm warning you. Don't be taken in. He's less

343

mild than he looks. We were lads, and we were out riding. He had a new horse, a present from his Dad. Immensely proud of it. Crazy, too, at that time, about weapons and firearms. Carried four or five on him whenever we went out. Soon to join a regiment, but more often looked like a cutthroat. Along we go, then. Come to fence. He puts the new horse at it. Over it goes. Admirable. I applaud. They jump another and another. Then we come to a brook. The horse won't jump. Father Johan tries again. Horse still refuses. 'Look, there's a bridge over there', I say. He won't listen. Horse must jump the stream. But horse won't. What's he do? Gets off, takes out pistol and shoots horse dead. That was before he was converted. Makes you think, eh?"

Father Huber nodded.

"Quite true, quite true. I remember it well. Father Aloys can be depended on to tell the truth about me."

"There, listen to him. He ought to be hanging his head with shame, and instead he's looking as pleased as if I'd said he was fit to be Pope."

After this the conversation ran on the affairs of the Reduction and finally came to rest among the doings of forty and fifty years before and the war in which both the older priests had played a part as young men. This was a subject they could never agree on, and Father Mayer enjoyed nothing so much on his visits to San Miguel as fighting over the rights and wrongs of it. His particular bugbear was Father Huber's hero, Prince Eugène.

Father Mayer's eyebrows came gradually together in a Jehovah-like frown.

"It's no good", he said. "I can't forgive your precious Prince. Allying himself with that scallywag Marlborough, a heretic into the bargain."

"But, my good Aloys," Father Huber said mildly, "the origin of the war had nothing to do with religion."

"Nonsense. King William and the Protestants were delighted to see the Catholic powers scrapping like cats and dogs. King Louis and the Emperor should have been forced to get on together."

"But that's begging the question. It was the vacancy of the Spanish

344

throne that set them at loggerheads. Who can say which of them ought to have given way?"

"I still say Eugène had no right to ally himself with that . . ."

Father Huber leaned over to Alfonso.

"I think I hear the fireworks beginning. Would you go and see that everything's all right? The balcony of the church is a good place to watch from. Take Father Fields and Brother Florian with you."

They got up and went out. Father Mayer was too busy unhorsing Prince Eugène to notice. The last thing they heard as they went down the cloister was the old priest's fist striking the table and Father Huber's voice saying, "But, my good Aloys . . ."

THE BALCONY was bathed in flickering light. They leaned on the balustrade and looked down at the plaza. All around, lanterns winked and shone in the trees and windows of the houses, while near the middle two bonfires were sending up jagged sheets of flames. Hundreds of little figures, casting stilettolike shadows, swarmed on the ground. Many were dancing, and the music of the mandolins mingled with the confused murmur of voices and laughter. The dancers twirled and jumped, joined hands and parted. The rest of the Indians looked on, gazed at the flames, or stared at the sky, waiting for the rockets that went up with a rush and a whistle and burst with a pop-pop-pop. Against the moonless sky, blacker by contrast with the fiery light below, the rockets burned doubly bright.

After watching for twenty minutes, they climbed one of the towers. Here, the glow from the bonfires was less fierce, and they could see over the fiery plaza with its girdle of twinkling lights to the featureless darkness of the empty fields and silent forests. But for the stars, it would have been impossible to say where the horizon lay or where sky met earth. Suddenly a rocket burst high above them, casting a lurid simulacrum of daylight over the countryside. Distant objects—a chapel, a herdsman's hut, a cluster of sleeping cattle—leapt into life as though that instant summoned by the power of God out of nothingness. Then the last of the burning globes lost its fire, and the night, like the returning waters of the Red Sea, closed once more over the landscape.

"I wonder what it will all be like in another hundred and fifty years?" Father Fields said musingly.

"If we can get enough priests," Brother Florian said, "all the tribes between here and Lima should have been converted and civilised by then. That will mean more than a hundred new Reductions. Think of it."

"And after that?" the Irishman asked.

"What do you mean, Father? After that?" Brother Florian's face, redder than usual from the glow of the fires below, looked perplexed. In his simplicity and goodness, he found it hard to imagine any situation that prayer and practical good sense could not set right. Had he not successfully been using both for more than forty years—as theatre technician, architect's assistant, lay brother—just for that purpose.

"I mean," Father Fields said, "how are we going to integrate the Indians with the Europeans. It will have to happen sometime. We can't keep them apart forever. But once they mix, all our work with the Indians is going to be undone."

Brother Florian chuckled. "That's when the really hard work begins, Father. I'll be dead. You'll be in your eighties, and you're going to have to start converting and civilising the Europeans."

"If we're allowed to survive that long."

"If you're worrying about the future of the Society in Spain," Alfonso said, "there's no need to. I had a letter from my father recently. He says the King is more attached to our Society than ever and that the manoeuvres of our opponents have been completely unsuccessful."

They felt their way down the stairs and crossed the plaza in a zigzag through the dancing Indians.

In the college living room all was peace. Father Huber and Father Mayer were playing chess, while the mingled smoke of their pipes, like an embodiment of the harmony in their hearts, drifted about the ceiling in a blue-grey cloud.

PART FIVE

Into the Wilderness

1767–1772

SIXTY-FOUR

The gale had been blowing for three days. Scraps of paper, rags, dust, dead leaves, and pieces of orange peel hurtled along the streets or flew through the air to the confusion of the gulls. From time to time the heights of Montjuich vanished behind slanting veils of rain, while the more distant hills seemed to have disappeared permanently into the clouds. The ships in the harbour tossed up and down on the green-grey water, which had been whipped into jagged waves that looked like broken bottle glass and, farther out, the rollers broke against the seawalls in explosions of surf. Later, whenever Jean-Paul thought of Barcelona, he associated it with the sound of banging doors and the shriek of the tempest.

After roaming the deserted quays for an hour, looking in vain for a ship that was sailing to Italy, he returned, hustled along by the wind, to an inn in a back street near the city ramparts, which he and Diego de Torrelavega had chosen as being the kind of place where their pursuers were not likely to look for them.

Diego was in their room sitting at a table, building a house of cards. The draught, as the door opened, blew the flimsy structure flat.

"Damn! That was nearly a record, Jean. Four stories. Had any luck?"

"No, sir."

"I didn't think you would. Nobody's going to put out to sea in this gale." He swept the cards together, and his face began to look troubled. "I wish I knew what to do. If anyone is following us, they'll soon be catching up with us. Not that they're likely to find us in a hole like this. All the same, it makes me nervous to think of them possibly being in the same city."

"I'm afraid it's not a question of 'may be' any more, sir. I saw your father's man, Manso, just now. He was coming out of the Custom House."

"Manso? Oh, my God. Did he see you?"

"It was difficult to tell. But to be on the safe side, I came back a roundabout way. I'm fairly sure I wasn't followed."

Diego bit his finger, then stood up and moved restlessly about the room.

"I wish I knew what to do", he said again.

"Fortunately, sir, we don't have much choice. But first you'd better have your dinner. We're more likely to make the right decision on full stomachs. I'll go and see to it."

Momentarily, Diego looked more cheerful. "You always have such sensible ideas", he said.

While Jean-Paul was downstairs ordering the meal, Diego tried half-heartedly to distract his mind from its anxieties. He stared out the window, threw himself on the bed, got up and tried building another card house, poured out a glass of wine, looked vacantly at himself in the looking glass, took off his shoes, and pulled on one of his riding boots. Suddenly he got down on all fours and peered under the bed. Then, blushing, he stood up hastily and glanced toward the door.

"I've been thinking", he said, when Jean-Paul reappeared carrying a tray with two plates on it. "You remember what they did in Portugal to those people who were supposed to have been friends of the Jesuits eight or nine years ago . . ."

"Now, sir, come and eat your dinner and forget about things like that."

"I can't help it, Jean. It keeps coming into my head. A man I know was in Lisbon at the time and saw it all. They tied them to wheels and broke their arms and legs with hammers, and then burned them while they were still alive. If they catch us and do things like that to us, Jean, I shan't be able to stand it. I know I shan't. I'm afraid, Jean. I ought to be ashamed to tell you, I know. But I'm not. Apart from Father Padilla, the General, and the Countess, and, in her own way, my mother, you're the only person who has ever really cared for me. I wish to God you'd been my brother. You're much kinder to me than a brother, and I don't mind what you know about me."

Jean-Paul took Diego's arm and drew him to the table.

"Try to think of something different, sir. I'm just as scared as you are at the thought of being smashed to bits like a piece of old crockery.

It's natural. One can't help it. But it's no use dwelling on what may never happen. What's this, though? You've got one of your boots on. You won't need that for an hour or so. Let me change it . . . there now, that's better."

Jean-Paul spread a cloth, opened a napkin, and uncovered the dishes, which were heaped with rice and some not very appetising fish. Diego looked on passively.

"Eat with me, Jean."

"If you want me to, sir."

"Do you know, Jean, I'd almost rather be killed by a hammer than fall into Manso's hands again."

"No fear of that, sir. He's just been sent along to identify us."

"It's an awful thing to say, but when I think of him, I have no difficulty in understanding why God had to create hell. You can't think how clever that man used to be, when I was a boy, at inventing ways of making my life miserable . . ."

"Well, I shouldn't waste time worrying about him", Jean-Paul said. "If they were to catch us, we should be the King's prisoners, not your father's or Manso's."

When they had finished eating and Jean-Paul had cleared away the plates, they considered what to do.

"I suggest, sir," Jean-Paul said, "that we ride as fast as we can for the French frontier. If we stay on here waiting for a boat, we shall have to go down to the port from time to time, and that's just where they'll be waiting to catch us."

Diego agreed.

As soon as it was dark, they left the city by a gate on the west side and, after riding a mile or so, doubled back around the northern ramparts, past the citadel of Philip V, and on to the road running northeast toward Blanes. But after a few miles, instead of following the coast—as their pursuers, if they learned of their departure, would probably expect them to do—they turned inland and made their way toward the frontier by a cross-country route.

SIXTY-FIVE

At the beginning, they rode almost continuously, and when they stopped at an inn it was just to eat, feed their horses, dry their clothes, and rest for an hour or two. They allowed themselves only enough sleep so they could keep awake for another stretch in the saddle, as they pushed on, heavy in the head and sore between the thighs.

Once beyond Gerona, they felt safer. The frontier was only thirty miles ahead, and, if they were still being followed, they had a good start. Turning off the road a little before Figueras, they looked for an inn where they could take a longer rest. They found one near a water mill on the outskirts of a village. After ordering a meal and hiring the one private room, they went to bed.

When Jean-Paul woke after several hours, Diego was sitting in his shirt on the edge of the bed.

"How do you feel now, sir?"

"I've been doing some planning, Jean."

"It would have been better to spend the time sleeping, sir."

"Are you awake enough to understand what I'm going to say?"

Diego sounded unexpectedly resolute. Jean-Paul sat up and pushed his hair out of his eyes.

"Our money is in these bags", Diego said. "And here are the letters to the Pope and the other papers. From now on, you are going to carry them. If we find they're overtaking us, I shall give myself up so that you can escape. You must ride as hard as you can. If necessary, go into hiding for a time. Once they've caught me, they won't worry about you. They'll think you've run away because you're scared."

"That's ridiculous, sir", Jean-Paul protested. "They won't catch us, but even if they do, I'm certainly not going to run away and leave you."

"You must, Jean."

"Why, sir, what do you think his illustrious lordship, the General, would say when he heard about it?"

"He'd say you did right. It isn't a question of your safety or my safety but of getting to Rome with these papers."

"In that case, sir, I'll give myself up, and you can escape."

"It wouldn't do, Jean. I'm the one they're looking for and will most easily recognise. And I'm the one they'll expect to find carrying letters."

Jean-Paul got out of bed and began to pull on his coat.

"Look, sir, you did me the honour two days ago of saying you wished I'd been your brother. Don't you think your safety means anything to me?"

"I know it does, Jean. You've been a true friend. But we're not going to leave this room until you've promised to do what I've told you to do."

It was a quarter of an hour before Jean-Paul reluctantly gave in, and then only because he saw that Diego had the better case and that he had no alternative. He was also subconsciously influenced by the new authoritativeness with which his master spoke.

When they set out again it was growing dusk and a stiff wind was racing the clouds across the sky. They rode all night, making for Llansa, a town on the coast, five miles from the frontier. Jean-Paul, already regretting his promise and wondering if he could argue Diego into letting him take it back, was silent and gloomy. Soon after Figueras, they left the valley and entered hilly country that gradually grew rougher and steeper. About midnight, the wind dropped and the sky cleared. A low-hanging moon showed up a crest of peaks to the left. Then, shortly before dawn, the road began to descend again. Soon cottages and farms were coming to life, and they were passing labourers on their way to work.

Outside Llansa, where their path rejoined the coast road, Jean-Paul lost a stirrup and dismounted to pick it up.

"I'll go and find the inn", Diego said, "and see what they can give us to eat."

The road turned several corners, winding between stone walls, sheds, small fields, and leafless olive groves. Whistling, and with his hat on the back of his head, Diego trotted his horse into the straw-littered yard of a small tavern. He was about to dismount when the tavern door opened and a sleepy-looking man with rumpled hair came out. He looked up at the sun, blinked, and scratched himself under the armpits.

Diego's whistling stopped. He wheeled his horse round, kicked it in the flanks, and galloped back the way he had come.

353

"Quick! Quick!" he called breathlessly, when he came in sight of Jean-Paul, who had mounted again and was riding slowly downhill toward him. "They're here. Manso. He saw me. You must go."

Jean-Paul started to object. Diego seized his horse by the bridle, pulled its head around, and hit it hard across the crupper. The animal snorted, reared, and then bolted up the road. Jean-Paul, hanging on by the mane, turned to wave before vanishing around a corner.

"Good-bye, Jean!" Diego called. "Good-bye! God be with you."

He turned his horse and walked it slowly back toward the town. Two hundred yards down the road he nearly collided with Manso, as he came galloping around a corner in pursuit. Three other men, whom Diego also recognised as servants of his father, followed close behind.

"What's this, master?" Manso cried, reining in his horse. "Running off like that, I thought you must be afraid of me."

"I was coming back to find out what you were doing here", Diego said, trying to sound casual.

"Ah, that's a good one!" Manso winked at the other men. "I think you know pretty well what we're doing here."

"Well, I'm hungry", Diego said. "I'm going to get some breakfast."

"Certainly, master, and we'll go along with you, if you don't mind." Manso winked again. "You didn't expect to find us ahead of you, did you? That's what comes of being too clever. If you'd followed the coast, we would never have caught up with you."

The tavern had a small room at the back where Diego was given breakfast. Manso sat with the back of his chair against the door, singing songs, taking snuff and laughing, half under his breath, from time to time.

Impudent bastard! Diego said to himself. But the longer you go on gloating over having caught me, the longer it will be before you remember about Jean.

When he had finished, Diego yawned and stretched his arms. "I'm ready now. You can go and tell the officer who's been sent to arrest me that I'm ready to give myself up."

"You see him before you, master."

"Stop playing the fool."

"God have mercy on us!" Manso said, pretending to be afraid. "What a high and mighty tone your lordship takes." He got up, crossed the room, and, leaning over the table, thrust his dark, battered face close to Diego's. Diego instinctively drew back. "You can come down off your perch", he said roughly. "Your protectors, the General and his wife, have been arrested. You're all under suspicion of treason. I'm the only officer in charge here, and I've been sent to take you into custody."

"You? What authority have *you* got?"

"All the authority I need. A letter from the Minister of Favour and Justice to 'whomsoever it may concern' in any town in the country, ordering the magistrates to provide me with men to find and catch you. But I'm only to use it in an emergency. His lordship, your father, doesn't mean to let his son be arrested like a common criminal. He has too much respect for himself."

Diego felt his courage waver. "Show me the letter", he said.

Manso opened a piece of paper and dangled it in front of Diego, just out of reach. "Satisfied, master?"

Diego turned away.

"Your lordship's horse will be ready in half an hour", Manso said, and went out, locking the door behind him.

SIXTY-SIX

Five minutes later, Manso burst into the room again.

"Hey, master, where's that man of yours?"

"What man?"

"You know who I'm talking about. There's no need to look so pleased. We'll catch him all right, and when we do, by God, I'll make him pay for giving us this extra trouble."

This time, when he left, he slammed the door.

From the window, Diego watched Manso's men mount their horses and gallop off in search of Jean-Paul. It was long after dark when they returned. Diego ran to the window; he could hear Manso yelling at them.

"You bastards! Haven't you caught him? Get back on your horses and look some more. I don't want to see any of you until you've found him."

Twenty-four hours later, the men returned a second time, still without Jean-Paul. When Manso brought Diego his supper, he looked worried. Diego could not keep himself from smiling.

"Ah, master, you'll be laughing on the other side of your face soon", Manso said angrily. "You're the one they want. They're not going to trouble themselves about a valet."

The next morning, after breakfast, Manso told Diego to go downstairs and get on his horse. In the yard, six men were already mounted; five others stood by the stable door.

"All right, you five," Manso said, "scour every nook and cranny between here and the frontier. There's two hundred reales for whoever catches the man. And now, master, no tricks. I don't want to have to shoot that horse if it starts to gallop."

The journey to Madrid took five days. They rode in a bunch; two in front, three behind, and Diego in the middle with Manso on his right and a man called Tereceno on his left. Manso and Tereceno spent much of the time talking about executions, hangings, and torture.

"Did you see Garrido swing?"

"The forger? Yes. But give me an execution any time. I've known the blood to spurt as much as ten feet."

"For high treason, you know, they pull out the man's guts while he's still alive."

"Brrrrrrrrh! It makes you think."

Diego clenched his fingers around the reins and compressed his lips.

Whenever they stopped for the night and Manso brought Diego his supper, he would first let his prisoner see what was on the tray and then throw half of it out of the window. Later, when the young man had fallen asleep, he would wake him roughly and tell him to get dressed because they had to ride on. Sometimes he did this two or three times a night. If Diego refused to get up, he would say that, unless he obeyed, the General and Doña Mercedes would be made to suffer. The threat always worked. On the third night, Manso took away Diego's hat and cloak. For the rest of the journey he was either cold or wet, and often both.

To begin with, Diego had kept looking for a chance to escape. But after the third day, he gave up. Worn out and frightened, he relapsed into the apathy that had been habitual to him in boyhood. It was useless to struggle; his father would always be stronger and cleverer—he would never be able to outwit him.

THEY RODE INTO MADRID late on the afternoon of March 23 and went first to the Torrelavega Palace. Then, after dark, Diego was put into a carriage and driven across the city to a building he did not know. There he was taken upstairs and, after waiting for an hour in an antechamber, was shown into a large room hung with crimson damask. The room was lighted by a pair of candelabra at either end of a table covered with a brown cloth. Three men dressed in black were sitting in a row on the opposite side. On the wall behind them was a painting of the dead Christ supported by angels.

Diego recognised the man in the middle. He had recently seen him with his father, but he had no idea what his position was and knew him only as Don Ricardo. The other two men were speaking to him in tones of discreet flattery.

"I see with regret that my fears have been fulfilled", Don Ricardo said majestically as Diego entered. "Sit down. We are here to investigate your case. Answer when you are spoken to."

Diego remained standing. His eyes moved restlessly to and fro.

"What right have you to question me?" he said abruptly and vehemently. "I suppose my father has arranged it all. First, I'm arrested by his servants. Then I'm brought here before a private tribunal made up of his friends. He acts as if all Spain were his private estate. I protest against it. I am an officer in the royal bodyguard. If I'm to be interrogated, I demand a court-martial."

Don Ricardo, who had begun to write on a piece of paper, looked up.

"You are still, I see, as I had been warned, an extremely rebellious young man. There's no need to excite yourself. We have all the authority we need from the Supreme Council of Castile. Do as you are told and sit down."

For an hour the three men questioned Diego, trying to catch him out in his answers. Suddenly the youngest of them leaned forward with the abrupt movement of a large bird about to peck a smaller one.

"You say you weren't carrying any letters. You are lying."

"I said you can search me, and you won't find anything."

"On the contrary," Don Ricardo said, "your luggage was examined, and this was found." He held up a letter addressed in a hand Diego had not seen before.

"That's got nothing to do with me", Diego said excitedly. "I gave all the letters to . . ." He stopped. Oh, God, what a fool I am, he thought.

"So you admit you were carrying letters?" the youngest man said.

The third man, who had been lolling back, tickling himself under the chin with the end of a quill, interrupted.

"Don't you think you ought to tell us whom you gave the letters to?"

"Whoever it was," Diego said, "he's over the border by now and out of reach."

The man raised his eyebrows.

"I wouldn't be too sure. I wouldn't be too sure."

Don Ricardo impatiently shook the paper he was holding.

"We don't need to know about any other letters. This one is more than enough to establish a case of treason."

He began to read it aloud.

The letter, supposedly written by the Provincial of the Jesuits to the Pope, explained that King Charles of Spain was not really the son of Philip V, but the illegitimate child of Elizabeth Farnese and Cardinal Alberoni. After giving his grounds for believing this, the writer asked the Pope to dispense the Spanish from their allegiance to the King.

"Well?" Don Ricardo said, when he had finished reading.

"Someone planted that in my bags," Diego said.

"You're trying to tell us that you didn't know what was in this letter?"

"I deny knowing anything about it or having had anything to do with it."

"Why were you trying to leave the country secretly, then?"

"I wasn't. May I not travel abroad if I want to?"

"We have other evidence, apart from this letter, to prove that your journey was not undertaken merely for pleasure, and it all points to your having been an accomplice in a plot to have His Majesty assassinated. If you are convicted, you will be subject to the death penalty. Only an act of mercy on the part of His Majesty will be able to save you." Don Ricardo paused and sat back in his chair to let his words take effect. The wick of one of the candles needed trimming, and a thin thread of blue-black smoke rose quivering toward the ceiling. "No doubt," he continued, "you now realise the seriousness of the charge against you. However, out of consideration for your father and his exalted position, and also because you were possibly unaware of the purpose you were being used for, His Majesty has graciously given permission for you to remain in your father's custody until your case has been more thoroughly examined."

The next day, without having seen any of his family, Diego was put into a carriage and, with Manso beside him, driven away to the Marques de Torrelavega's estate at Sala de los Infantes.

SIXTY-SEVEN

It was nearly midnight, and most of the community at San Felipe's were asleep. Only Father Padilla was still up, sitting beside the bed of an eighty-year-old fellow Jesuit named Father de Salcedo, who had an earache.

Father de Salcedo lay propped against his pillows with his left ear over a jug of steaming water, which Father Padilla was holding for him. Every minute or two the tassel of his nightcap slid sideways and would have fallen into the jug if Father Padilla had not caught it just in time.

"How does it feel now?" Father Padilla asked.

"Easier, thank you, Simon."

"But it still hurts?"

"Just a little."

In an effort to distract Father de Salcedo's attention, Father Padilla began to talk at random.

"Such an aggravating thing happened yesterday. I dropped the small telescope and cracked a lens. I shan't get it mended this side of Easter. To think it's just a year from the Palm Sunday riots . . . how quickly the time goes. . . . They say Count Aranda was at the bullfight again yesterday. What a good thing we have him for our protector! I was talking to our Father Martinez, who used to be his tutor. He's in and out of the Count's palace all the time."

But Father de Salcedo was not listening.

"Simon, the Provincial is going to send me to our house at Guadalajara", he said suddenly.

"He's not!"

"Father Rector told me yesterday. It's reasonable. My rheumatism is so bad now; I can hardly walk or use my hands. I'm in the way here."

"You aren't. It does us all good to be able to come and talk to you. Anyhow, I don't think it's right the way they push us off to a backwater when we get old."

"No, no. I shall be better at Guadalajara . . . with all the other retired warhorses of the Society. They need my room here for an active man. It's strange to be old, Simon. Outwardly, one looks so different—missing teeth, white hair, wrinkles, and the rest. One doesn't seem at all the same person one was as a boy or a young man. But inside, one feels very much the same person. It's like standing in a building and watching it fall to bits all around you. I've had a happy life, though. God has been good to me. How I used to love the missions in the countryside! I used to meet such strange characters on the road as I went from village to village. It's good to think of our many fine young priests carrying on the work. What's that?"

"What's what?"

"A noise outside, Simon."

"Well, your right ear is sound enough. I heard nothing."

"There's someone at the street door. It may be a sick call."

Father Padilla put the jug down on the floor, went to the window, and pushed back one of the shutters. For about a minute he remained gazing down into the street. His mind both understood what he saw and yet refused to understand it. Then, softly, he pulled the shutter to.

"You were right. There is someone there. I'd better go and see what they want."

But before he could move, there was a loud knocking and then a bell rang inside the house.

"Hurry, Simon", Father de Salcedo said reproachfully. "It must be urgent."

Father Padilla came slowly back to the bed and sat down on the edge. "Father," he said gently, "can you prepare yourself for some bad news? It looks as if Count Aranda wasn't our protector after all. The street is full of soldiers."

For some moments they sat looking at each other in silence. In that time, they lived imaginatively through many existences. Father Padilla was the first to speak.

"What ought we to do?" he asked in a whisper, as though the soldiers were already outside in the passage. "Ought I to go down and let them in?"

"Certainly not. Make them take the first step and put themselves in the wrong."

"I wonder what the ecclesiastical penalties are for breaking into a religious house?"

"Automatic excommunication at least, I should think. Not that that will stop them. Unfortunately our rector is hardly the man to handle a situation like this."

"Listen! Somebody is opening the front door."

"The idiot! What's the point of making things easier for them? You'd better get my clothes, Simon, and help me to dress. I can't go to prison in a nightshirt."

"There's no reason to think they're going to take us to prison. They probably mean to search the house and take away our papers."

"I want to be prepared, all the same. Tear a piece of this handkerchief and push it in my ear."

Father de Salcedo's limbs were so stiff that getting him out of his nightshirt and into his clothes was like dressing a chair. Father Padilla was only half finished when a young lay brother appeared. He looked frightened.

"Father Rector says that everyone is to go to the refectory", he said breathlessly.

"I'll be down in a minute", Father Padilla said.

"He says you're to come at once, Reverend Father."

"Then stay here and help Father de Salcedo to dress."

"I daren't, Father. The *alcalde* told me to come back as soon as I had given the message."

"You go, Simon", Father de Salcedo said. "I shall be all right."

"What a hurry they're in!" Father Padilla said. "Surely they're not planning to put us on trial before daylight."

The lay brother followed him down the stairs.

"What will they do to us, Father?"

"I'm no wiser than you are, Brother."

"It's a great privilege to go to prison for God's sake, isn't it, Father?" The lay brother's voice was eager and trembling.

"Yes, Brother. But it may not be easy. Don't forget to pray for the grace to stand firm."

The community was in the refectory, gathered along one side, some sitting, some standing. At the far end, near the door, a detachment of soldiers stood at ease. In the middle of the room, the Vicar General of the Archdiocese of Toledo was talking in a low voice to an *alcalde*, while,

362

a little apart, and silently watching them, stood a second *alcalde* and an officer.

As Father Padilla took his place, Father de la Cueva broke off a conversation with a priest beside him. "We are all here now," he said to the senior *alcalde*, "except for the old priest I mentioned."

What a spineless way to talk, Father Padilla thought. Why doesn't he stand up to these officials and tell them what he thinks of them? And what's the Vicar General doing here? I thought he was a friend.

The *alcalde* held a rolled-up parchment. His fingers played with it nervously.

"Reverend Fathers," he began, "I am here by His Majesty's command. My instructions are to read this decree to you and see that it is carried out. I regret that it will not be pleasant to listen to."

He then unrolled the parchment and began to read. At first his voice was hurried and indistinct, but it gained in loudness and clearness as he went on.

"Charles, by the grace of God, King of Spain, of Castile, of León and of Aragon, Duke of Brabant and Milan, Count of Barcelona, and Lord of Biscay and Molina," the *alcalde* read, "relying on the memoranda of His Extraordinary Council and of other highly placed persons, moved by weighty reasons, conscious of His duty to uphold obedience, tranquillity and justice among His people, and for other urgent, just, and compelling causes, which He is locking away in His royal breast, hereby decrees that all members of the Society of Jesus who have taken their first vows and novices who refuse to secede from the said Society are banished forthwith and forever from His realms and dominions both in Spain and the Indies . . ."

The community of San Felipe listened in silence to the end.

"Your Reverences," the *alcalde* said, rolling up the decree and thrusting it into the pocket of his coat when he had finished. "You will please go to your rooms and collect your clothes. You may also take your breviaries and any tobacco and chocolate. Everything else, including articles of value, money, papers, or letters, you will leave. They now belong to

His Majesty. You will then come back here and proceed to the carriages which are waiting outside."

His last words were drowned by the cries of the protesting Jesuits.

"It's a plot."

"The King hasn't done this."

"Somebody must tell the cardinal."

"They can't banish us without a trial."

"Why didn't the Provincial foresee this?"

"Even in Portugal, they had a pretence of legal proceedings first."

The *alcalde* waved his arms in an attempt to get silence.

"If you question my authority," he shouted, "the Vicar General here will confirm that my commission is genuine."

Father de la Cueva shouted at the community, too.

"You will do as this gentleman commands. I order it under holy obedience." He turned to the *alcalde*. "But understand, sir, that though we submit to His Majesty's decree, we protest against the injustice and illegality of these proceedings. As priests of God, we are forbidden to meet force with force. But we deny that His Majesty has the right to condemn us without trial or that we are guilty of any crime."

The *alcalde* shrugged his shoulders.

How I have misjudged our rector, Father Padilla thought. As he moved toward the door, he felt someone touch his arm. It was the Vicar General.

"They've sent me to take an inventory", he whispered. "Aranda's orders. I refused. But the cardinal told me to inform the Nuncio and, if he did not object, to carry the orders out."

"What did the Nuncio say?"

"He gave me authority to obey Aranda. What can one do? The Nuncio is more interested in making up to his cousin Grimaldi and to the King than in serving the Holy Father."

Father Padilla pressed his hand.

"You can't help it. God be with you. And pray for us. We'll need it."

A soldier accompanied each priest and brother to his room. As Father Padilla collected his clothes and made them into a bundle, words from the Gospels kept running though his mind: "You have come out to arrest me with swords and clubs as if I were a robber, and yet I used to sit teaching in the temple close to you, day after day, and you never laid hands on me." They were being arrested by night for fear of the people.

Suddenly a different thought came into his mind. My books, my papers, my instruments! A large part of my life's work is going to be lost or ruined. Perhaps I could dash up to the observatory and put the notebooks together in a pile under the table. Then I could ask the Vicar General to take care of them until it's safe to send them to me. But this soldier here will think I'm trying to escape. Maybe I could bribe him. What with?

Father Padilla looked quickly about. His eye fell on a small box—his collection of coins. That! he thought. I'll offer him that. What, and give him a bad conscience? No. There's no way out. Oh, my God, help me detach myself from these things you have given me the use of for so long. You know how weak I am, how hard I find it to part with them and follow you into the wilderness.

On the way downstairs, he passed the open door of Father de Salcedo's room. The old man was sitting, still half-dressed, on the edge of the bed.

"What does it matter who's relation I am?" he was saying, and his cracked voice shook with indignation.

"Out of consideration for your cousin the Duke of Sotomayor," the senior *alcalde* replied in a voice suitably modulated for the member of a powerful family, "His Majesty is pleased to make an exception in your case. The decree of banishment does not apply to you. You may live anywhere you choose in Spain, and the Duke has undertaken to support you."

"Am I guilty or innocent?"

"Reverend Father, that isn't a question I can discuss."

"If His Majesty has persuaded himself that we have committed some crime, why should I get off? Because I have powerful relations? Do you call that justice? But if we are innocent . . ." He caught sight of Father Padilla in the doorway. "Ah, Simon, come and help me finish dressing."

The *alcalde* tried to repeat his offer.

"Go away, sir, go away", Father de Salcedo said impatiently. "You have done your duty. Now leave me in peace to do mine."

As the *alcalde* had been instructed to act with prudence, he watched in silence while Father Padilla helped Father de Salcedo put on his shoes and cassock.

Meanwhile the junior *alcalde* was staring about him, wondering where all the gold and treasure were hidden.

When Father de Salcedo was dressed, two soldiers carried him downstairs.

"Don't hold this against us, Father, will you?" the soldier on his left asked.

"Say a prayer for us, Father", the one on his right added.

Father de Salcedo patted the tops of their three-cornered hats. "May the Lord bless you! And remember to think of your souls sometimes."

The two soldiers carried Father de Salcedo into the refectory. Father de la Cueva quickly counted the community to see that everyone was there.

"We are ready", he said, addressing the senior *alcalde*. "But I repeat that we are innocent and go under protest. I must also remind you that one day you will have to give an account before the Judgment Seat of God of what you are now doing."

The *alcalde* made an angry movement with his hand, as though wiping out something written on an invisible slate, then pointed to the door. Led by Father de la Cueva, the Jesuits filed out to the street. The oldest of the lay brothers was crying. The *alcalde* had refused to let him pay a last visit to the sacristy where he had worked for forty years. Father de la Cueva took the lay brother with him into the first carriage. The rest of the community got into the others. Soon they felt the carriages move. They could not see out because the blinds were drawn and the edges nailed to the window frames. After a time the rumble of the wheels changed key; they were crossing a bridge. Few spoke. Sitting in silence and darkness, they thought of their families and friends whom they were never to meet again; remembered familiar places they had looked at for the last time; regretted this or that trifling but valued thing—book, holy picture, or tin snuffbox—which they had either been forbidden to bring or had forgotten or had been unable to find at the last minute; pictured the future only to find it uniformly sombre and threatening; tried their best to see it in a hopeful light; made frequent acts of resignation to God's will, which almost immediately had to be renewed as their minds filled with indignant thoughts about their enemies; fell unconsciously into rambling speculations about the causes of their banishment, its part, on the supernatural plane, in God's plan and how, on the level of the world, it had been engineered; countered these thoughts by praying for their persecutors; and, as the long journey continued, begged for help to get through the days ahead.

SIXTY-EIGHT

On the night of April 1, the scene that had taken place at San Felipe's and the other Jesuit houses in Madrid was repeated all over Spain. Wherever there was a Jesuit church or community, troops surrounded the house shortly before midnight, the priests and brothers were assembled to hear the decree of banishment, and then, sick or well, were ordered into carriages and wagons and carted off. So carefully had the undertaking been planned that only in one instance, at Saragossa, did the Jesuits receive any warning of what was about to happen.

Most of the Spanish people, however, did not share their rulers' view of the sons of St. Ignatius. As the vehicles passed through towns and villages on their way to the coast, the inhabitants frequently marched alongside, asking the Jesuits for their blessing and even cutting off bits of their clothing to keep as relics.

"Ignorance and superstition!" Don Manuel Roda exclaimed angrily, when he read the reports of these incidents. "Just what the Jesuits have always encouraged." No one had ever cared enough about *him* to snatch a hair out of his wig or a piece of braid off his coat for a keepsake.

"And now, Antolinez," he said, turning to the official of his ministry who sat waiting for instructions on the other side of his tortoiseshell-inlaid desk, "there is the question of the novices. His Majesty has temporarily excluded them from the operation of the decree. He wants them to have complete freedom of choice. If they renounce their membership of the Society, they can stay in Spain. If not, they will be sent into exile along with the priests and brothers. However, they must be encouraged to use their freedom wisely. We need to cut off the supply of future Jesuits. Moreover, if the novices are known to have abandoned their vocations, it will diminish the Society's prestige. So I want you to make these young men see reason. You will have your work cut out. All young religious are fanatics. But I count on you to get results. They are at present locked up in their noviciate outside Toledo. Take Espa and Cancela along to help you."

IN THE NOVICIATE at Toledo, Jaime de Vallecas was sitting at a table with his head resting in his hand. It was now thirty-six hours since the priests and lay brothers who ran the noviciate had been taken away and the novices confined in separate rooms. The room was in half-darkness, the shutters of the window being closed and barred, and they had had nothing to eat since noon the day before.

"Good morning", a voice said. "I have come to talk about your future." Jaime turned his head and looked at the speaker suspiciously. The man standing in the doorway was slight, almost delicate, with features that suggested Arab blood. The dark, intelligent eyes were set close together, and the lips, thin at the edges, were, at the centre, full and red as if pouting. "My name is Antolinez. Señor Antolinez."

"Why are we here?" Jaime asked heatedly. "Why weren't we arrested with the others?"

"Wouldn't you rather stay in Spain?"

"I am a Jesuit. His Majesty, apparently, has no more use for Jesuits."

"His Majesty has great use for loyal subjects. And it is because he believes that the son of his good servant Don Maurice de Vallecas cannot be other than loyal that I have been sent to talk to you."

Señor Antolinez stayed arguing with Jaime for an hour. His manner was pleasant and matter-of-fact, no matter how biting or contemptuous Jaime's replies.

"It seems a pity that a young man of your intelligence should throw away his gifts on a lost cause. After all, the Pope is expected to disband the Society altogether quite soon."

"I don't believe it."

"I'm afraid it's true. Besides, if you choose exile, how are you going to live? The priests and brothers are getting pensions. But novices will get nothing. In the Papal States, where they are sending you, there will be no work for you. You will merely be a burden to the others."

"God will give bread to anyone who asks for it", Jaime said. But sensing that he was losing the argument, he added in an exasperated voice, "You're wasting your breath. I shall live and die a Jesuit."

Señor Antolinez frowned slightly and, with a quick movement of the tongue, moistened his lips. "Then in fairness," he said, "you ought to know the consequences of your decision. If you reject His Majesty's clemency, you can never come back to Spain, you can never see any of your relations again, you may not write to them, nor they to you, and if, while in exile, you do anything to displease His Majesty further, it will have unpleasant results for your whole family. Think it over. I'll come and see you again tomorrow. After a night's sleep we often see things in a different light."

Señor Antolinez left, and Jaime heard him go into the next room. The murmur of voices rose and fell. After what seemed like another hour, the door opened and shut, and the footsteps went farther down the passage. Perhaps what he said is true, Jaime thought. What use shall I be to the Society without work or money? For the rest of the day he considered and reconsidered what he had been told until his mind felt like a rug that had been tramped over by an army in steel boots.

But a night's rest had the effect Antolinez had predicted. By morning he saw the issues more clearly. If "they" wanted him to renounce his membership of the Society, obviously that was what would harm the Society most, and therefore he must at all costs resist.

THE NOVICES remained locked in their rooms for ten more days, under-fed and, most of the time, in darkness. After Señor Antolinez and his assistants came members of the higher clergy—bishops, abbots, canons —offering ecclesiastical benefices and positions at Court for the com-pliant, and threatening prison for the obdurate. Where these methods failed, they tried working on the novices' consciences. His Majesty, they were told, had made it clear that he considered the Jesuits a danger to the state. To side with His Majesty's enemies would be a serious sin.

They were followed by the novices' relations; those, at least, who could be trusted to say the right thing. Jaime was astonished by the number of remote cousins suddenly anxious about his welfare and keen to give advice. The only thing he feared was seeing his father and mother, but, to his relief, they did not come. Instead, the Duchess of Montesa arrived, followed by Gaspar.

"You poor, poor boy", Luisa said, rushing into the room and throwing her arms around Jaime's neck. "What a time you've had! Never mind, it's all over. We've come to take you home. Your parents are longing to see you."

Jaime disentangled himself and stepped back. His face was pale, and the skin round his eyes was a brownish purple from lack of sleep.

"Please take her away", he said to Gaspar. "I'm not going to change my mind."

"Now do be sensible", Luisa said coaxingly. "We're not asking you do to anything wrong. You're not yet bound to the Society by any vows."

"I've made a private promise to God."

"We can get you dispensed."

Jaime shook his head. Luisa's expression and tone of voice changed abruptly. "This is schoolboy pigheadedness", she said shrilly. "Have you thought of the trouble you're making for us. We shall be ruined."

Jaime turned to Gaspar, who was standing apart. "Is that true?"

Gaspar, who had lost much of his usual air of authority, glanced quickly at his brother and quickly away, thinking how disconcertingly youthful and valiant Jaime looked. Obviously no considerations about his position in the world or the respect of his friends caused him to hesitate between opposing courses. By contrast, he, Gaspar, felt like a heavy coach loaded with gold plate, spattered with mud, and incapable of motion, except on the broad highway of worldly success.

Although convinced that the expulsion of the Jesuits was unjust and had been engineered by their enemies, he could not reconcile himself to the loss of royal goodwill and, perhaps worse, social ostracism, confiscation of property, or prison. Had it not been for Luisa and the children, he told himself, he could have faced anything. But he had to think of his family. It was to clear himself of the suspicion of secretly sympathising with the Jesuits that he had agreed to see Jaime. Now he felt ashamed.

"It would make things easier if you stayed in Spain", he said, still avoiding his brother's eyes. "You're welcome to live with us, if you'd like to."

"Where's Rodrigo? Is he involved in all this?"

"Not so far as I know. There's a rumour that he's been sent on a diplomatic mission abroad somewhere."

"And Father and Mother? Why haven't they come?"

"Don't imagine it's because they approve of the way you're acting", Luisa interrupted. "They were too upset to come."

Jaime ignored her.

"They think I'm right not to leave the Society, don't they?"

"They didn't want to put pressure on you", Gaspar said, glancing uneasily at his wife.

Luisa began to sob hysterically.

"Go on! Take his side. Encourage him to ruin us." She turned on Jaime. "Do you care only about yourself? Don't you realise that if you have your way, we may all be executed?"

"Keep quiet, Luisa!" Gaspar said. "You know that's not true."

"Wait and see! Wait and see!"

"Why did you let her come?" Jaime said. "Please take her away and leave me in peace."

"I'm sorry." Gaspar spoke humbly. "You're right. We shouldn't have come. You must follow your conscience."

He pushed his wife, still protesting and scolding, toward the door. Then he embraced Jaime quickly, muttered, "Forgive me", and, with his head down, as if running the gauntlet through a hostile crowd, made his way into the passage.

SIXTY-NINE

Father Padilla gazed around the crowded courtyard of their temporary prison. The hundreds of priests and lay brothers of the Castilian province of the Society were being temporarily housed in the one-time Jesuit College at Cartagena. It's like a honeymoon, he thought. How considerate misfortune has made everyone!

In a nearby corner, Father Diaz, who rarely smiled, was laughing with a group of the younger priests. In another, under a moping ilex tree, Father Alkon, the taciturn professor of philosophy, was playing a makeshift game of draughts with one of his pupils. Father Larios, the rector of the Collegio Imperiale, was reading to a sick brother who lay on a truss of straw in the shade. And Father de la Cueva, transformed since the night of their arrest, was washing Father de Salcedo's shirt in a bucket beside the well.

If only I were more like them, Father Padilla thought. No matter what he was doing, his mind kept picturing his observatory at San Felipe's as he imagined it must look after having been ransacked by the soldiers, and he realised with sorrow and shame how much less he loved God than he had thought he did.

What do my theories and calculations matter? he said to himself reproachfully. It's not as if God didn't understand his own universe and was waiting for me to find out about it and then tell him. He has other work for me now. Oh, my God, teach me to love your will, not my own.

A voice behind him said, "Father !" He turned.

"Jaime!" he cried. It was the first time they had met since Jaime had entered the noviciate a year before. The young man looked so pleased to see him that immediately Father Padilla felt better. "When did you get here?"

"Just now. What a journey! Our carriage must have lost its springs twenty years ago. And they made us keep the windows shut all the way. We nearly suffocated." Jaime was laughing. Although a prisoner, he now felt happy and free.

"I thought they weren't going to allow the novices to leave", Father Padilla said.

"They did their best to persuade us not to, but after a while they saw it was hopeless. How long are they going to keep us here, do you think?"

"Until the ships are ready to take us to Italy, I suppose."

"I wish they were sending us somewhere like India or Japan, so that that we could suffer even more for our Lord."

Father Padilla looked at him in silence for a moment. Does he really mean that? he wondered. Or is it the kind of pious phrase our novices so easily pick up from each other? No, he said to himself, the boy is sincere. At his age, when they really love God, they do it without reserve. The holiness of some of our older priests is probably more meritorious. They've been thoroughly tested. But when the young are good, they make you think of what Adam must have been like when he came fresh out of God's hands. And the best thing about them is that they've no idea they're in any way unusual.

Two days later, the imprisoned Jesuits were awakened at three in the morning. They were sleeping in rows on the floor all over the college. The soldiers came tramping in, shook them by the shoulder, and ordered them to assemble in the courtyard below. Their lanterns gave the only light.

Half-stupefied with sleep, they put on their shoes, gathered together

373

what possessions they had—comb, brush, breviary, spare shirt, hat—and, huddled in their cloaks, fumbled their way downstairs.

Ten minutes later they were moving along through the dark, empty streets to the sound of the soldiers' rhythmic marching and their own disorganised shuffle. They came out into the open space surrounding the harbour. Lamps shone feebly in the rigging of the ships tied up along the quay.

"Halt!" an officer shouted. The long column of priests, lay brothers, and novices stopped parallel to the water.

"I've never been on a ship before", whispered Millan Nunez, a novice standing next to Jaime.

"Neither have I", Jaime said.

The officer moved down the column, dividing prisoners into groups. His face, lit from below by his lantern, started out of the night like a portrait with a dark background. "You lot here will go aboard this ship in front of you." He walked on. "And you lot here . . ."

The cloaked figures began to file across the gangplanks. One of the priests still waiting on the quay said, "The last time we shall stand on Spanish soil."

Once on deck, Jaime looked about with bewilderment at the partly lighted scene—tumbled sails, ropes, capstans, bollards—and then, raising his eyes, he peered up at the tangle of masts, spars, and rigging that soared into the darkness above.

"Into the hold, Fathers", a sailor shouted. "This way." One by one the Jesuits lowered themselves through an open hatch.

"My God, it stinks in here!" the novice Millan said, as he climbed down the ladder into the darkness below. Jaime followed, feeling for the rungs of the ladder with the toes of his shoes. A single overpowering smell, like the concentrated stench of a hundred privies, struck him. He wrinkled his nose and held his breath. Even so, he thought he was going to vomit.

At the bottom was confusion. By the light of a single lantern hooked to a nail in the ceiling, stooping figures moved about searching for a place to sit that was not covered with filth.

The head of a sailor appeared in the opening overhead. "Move along, Fathers", he shouted. "You can't stop here. There's more to come."

The group at the foot of the ladder groped their way forward to a farther hold, where tarry water trickled down the walls onto the floor. There were thirty of them in a space meant for ten. They peered about hopelessly.

"Holy Angels of God! I can't stand this. I'm going back on deck."

"They won't let you. It's forbidden."

"Does anyone know how long it takes to get to the Papal States?"

"Only three or four days, I think."

"Three or four? One hour will kill me in a stench like this."

"Courage, Father. Think of the poor wretches who've had the pleasure of using it before us."

"What wretches?"

"It used to be a prison ship—so one of the sailors said."

"They could at least have cleaned up the place a bit first."

"Well, we shan't have to stay so long in Purgatory, that's certain."

A cheerful voice had spoken, and at once it had an effect. The tone of the remarks changed.

"That's true. There's nothing like this in Dante."

"Look! Here . . . in the corner . . . palliasses. Every luxury provided. You see, Fathers, I knew Count Aranda was our friend."

"Yes, and a supply of water that drips from the ceiling. They say that tar is good for the throat, too."

A tall young priest began pulling the palliasses off the pile. Soon they were arranged edge to edge along the sides of the hold and across the end, which left in the middle an unoccupied strip of floor two feet wide. Some of the priests lay down and tried to sleep. The rest sat talking in low voices.

After an hour, the noises overhead multiplied and grew louder. Voices bellowed, chains clanked, hawsers rattled, running footsteps drummed across the deck above. The slapping of the water on the outside of the hull changed to a drawn-out gurgle and hiss.

"I believe we're off." Millan sat straight-backed and cross-legged in the middle of his palliasse. His cropped hair stood up in quarter-inch black bristles. His eyes were woebegone, and his up-turned nose twitched. "How do you feel, Brother?"

"I don't know", Jaime said. "How do you?"

"I don't know, either. It's strange, isn't it? Do you think they'll ever let us back?"

"They may. You can't tell."

Millan lowered his voice. "I wish I hadn't come."

"You don't really wish that . . . you know you don't", Jaime said, trying to sound encouraging. A similar thought had come into his own mind. "Think how proud your family and friends must be of you, and what a reward God will give us in heaven."

Millan shook his head. "I meant to be a missionary. This is different."

"God will look after us", Jaime said, distrusting his own words of comfort even as he spoke. He did not doubt God's providence. Nor would Millan. But God's providence did not exclude suffering and loneliness.

Millan put a hand over his mouth. "I'm going to be sick", he said thickly. Jaime got him to his feet, walked him down the strip of floor, and held him while he leaned over the empty bucket that stood next to the bulkhead. Between paroxysms, Millan raised his head and looked dolefully at Jaime. "And I thought it would be fun to go on a boat."

As soon as all the ships in the flotilla were out at sea, the Jesuits were allowed on deck in groups for half an hour twice a day.

During the rest of the twenty-four hours, they lay on their palliasses, which were now sopping wet. It was too dark for them to read and too cramped for them to walk about. Morning and evening a sailor appeared carrying a basket and, with dirty hands, doled out to each a portion of salt-beef and a biscuit. The drinking water, which hung in a skin from the roof, tasted of sour wine and pitch. They were unable to wash, and when they wanted to relieve themselves they had to use buckets that were seldom emptied and spilled when the ship rocked.

On the third day the flotilla ran into a storm. In Jaime's hold everyone was sick except the tall young priest called Ibañez who had handed out the palliasses. He crawled about from palliasse to palliasse, cleaning up the vomit, bringing cups of water, coaxing and comforting: "Try some biscuit, Brother. It's not so painful if your stomach's got something to get rid of . . . Here, Father, rinse out your mouth with this. You'll feel all the better for it."

Father de Salcedo, in the next hold, had developed an abscess in his ear, and his groans could be heard through the partition. Father Padilla, who was nursing him and who, like Father Ibañez, did not suffer from seasickness, came several times to see Jaime.

"How glad I am", said Jaime, between a groan and a hiccup, "that we're only going as far as Italy."

Father Padilla smiled.

"No more longing for India and Japan?" He gestured toward the bulkhead. "Say a prayer for Father de Salcedo. He's in a bad way."

AFTER TEN DAYS, the flotilla approached the Italian coast, and the Jesuits, released from the holds, crowded the decks and gazed landward at the long, flat, pine-clad shore and, gradually growing more distinct, the houses, campaniles, seawalls and fort of Civitavecchia, port for the city of Rome.

Millan and Jaime leaned on the taffrail beside Fathers Padilla and Ibañez.

"I never thought I'd be so glad to see Italy", Millan said. Seasickness had cured him of homesickness, and his peasant face looked hopeful and expectant again.

"Neither did I", Jaime said. "Think of sleeping in a dry bed and eating ordinary food."

And this, Father Padilla thought, is how we are brought to desire what we have not desired but what in God's providence it may be necessary for us to have.

"I know what I'm longing for", Father Ibañez said. "To shave off my beard." They laughed. The beard was already long, thick, and curly, and everyone in their part of the ship had been making jokes about it. "And you, Father?"

"I?" Father Padilla said. "I'm almost ashamed to admit it, but I'm looking forward to leading a regular life again, with definite occupations at definite hours."

"Well, it won't be long now before we all have our wish."

The harbour was already crowded with ships—other transports carrying other Jesuits from other parts of Spain. When their flotilla had anchored, the captain of the flagship went ashore, where he disappeared into a building on the quay. After half an hour the ship's boat returned for Father de Salcedo, who was now delirious. The Jesuits watched him being rowed to land. Then they went below to get their few belongings and came back on deck so as to be ready to follow.

The afternoon dragged by. A few days before when the first transports had arrived, the townspeople had lined the quays talking and gesticulating excitedly. But today, although anti-Spanish feeling was still running high, most of them were going about their usual business. Ordinary life! To the watching Jesuits, how beautiful and poignant it seemed, even in its details, now that they were deprived of it. Night came, and the reflections of the stars were like phosphorus in the water. They went below again, disappointed but not anxious.

But the next day, and the following one, they were still waiting to land. On the evening of the third day, as, with diminished excitement, they stood watching the activity on the waterfront, a lay brother suddenly shouted, "Look", and pointed to the other side of the harbour. There, near the entrance, one of the ships was hoisting its sails and turning about to put to sea.

Father Idiaquez appeared from the captain's cabin. He climbed on a capstan.

"Fathers! Brothers!" he shouted, so as to be heard above the noise made by the sailors as they ran about the deck, pulled on ropes, and climbed up and down the rigging. "The Holy Father asks a further sacrifice of us. He has forbidden us to land."

Thirty or forty voices spoke at the same time.

"Impossible."

"He can't have."

"There's a mistake."

"What have we done to deserve this?"

"Where are they going to take us now?"

Father Idiaquez motioned with his hands for silence.

"I can't tell you where we are going. But we know the Holy Father has always defended us. Therefore, what he has done must be necessary for the good of the Church. Let us sing the Magnificat: 'My soul doth magnify the Lord, and my spirit rejoiceth in God, my Saviour.'"

After the first few bars, the words were caught up by the Jesuits on the neighbouring ships, then by those crowding the decks of the ones beyond, and so on across the harbour until, as the great, decrepit, half-rotten fleet moved slowly seaward, the air resounded with the voices of the exiles praising God for the good things he had done to them.

SEVENTY

At Bastia, on the northeast tip of Corsica, Count de Marbeuf, commander of the French forces helping the Genoese to reestablish their authority over the rebellious island, sat breakfasting in his headquarters.

The contentment with which he ate was relative to the discontent, discomfort, and annoyance he experienced during the remaining fourteen or fifteen hours a day. Breakfast was the only time he felt in a good temper.

The campaign was not going well. Almost all the Corsicans seemed to side with General Paoli and his rebels, whose methods of fighting broke every recognised rule of war. The French and Genoese troops held only the coastal towns and were low-spirited and underfed.

Accommodation in Bastia was atrocious. Although the best house —the Palazzo Galbo—had been requisitioned for Count de Marbeuf,

379

it was scarcely better than a dirty farmhouse. Baron Galbo's manner was servile and untrustworthy, and the Baroness, whenever she had the chance, bored the French commander with long discourses on the antiquity and nobility of her husband's obviously insignificant family.

But what exasperated the Count most were the instructions he received from Paris. Not only were these at cross purposes with the demands made on him by the Genoese Republic, but they showed a frivolous indifference to the difficulties facing the French forces on the island. Often they sounded as if they had been jotted down by the minister while at the card table or in his mistress' boudoir. Sometimes the Count wondered whether they had not been composed by the mistress herself.

On this particular morning, he had finished eating and was smoking a pipe while he watched a pretty servant girl, down in the courtyard below, hang up washing on the boughs of a fig tree. But the sound of someone running up the stairs warned him that the worries of the day were about to begin.

The sentry on duty in the passage stamped to attention; then there was a knock, and Count de Marbeuf's aide, Lieutenant de Sèze, stood in the door. He saluted.

"Sir, the ships with the Spanish Jesuits are here."

"What? Impossible! I told Paris not to let them come."

"You can see the ships from the other room, sir. They are already in port."

The Count leapt up from the table and hurried into the next room, which overlooked the harbour. Two staff officers, who had been lounging against a table covered with maps, came to attention.

"Damn those fools in Paris", the Count said furiously, as he returned to his own room. "Are you certain you sent those despatches?"

"Yes, sir."

"Well, they can't land—neither the Jesuits nor the crews. The Genoese must take the Jesuits. Tell the captains to turn their ships around and sail for the coast."

"I spoke to one of them, sir. He said they have authority to land both from Versailles and from the Signoria."

"The Signoria can go to hell. If they want me to reduce their miserable subjects to order for them, they'll have to do as I want. I'm in authority here."

"Yes, sir."

The Count turned his back and stared out the window at the wall of houses mounting the hillside.

"The Spanish Ministry", he said angrily, "is obviously made up of madmen and idiots. Why waste time bullying a lot of relatively harmless priests, when the real danger comes from the English? Our people at Versailles are no better. They ought to put some sense into the Spanish instead of supporting this nonsense."

"Personally, sir," Lieutenant de Sèze said, "I don't see why the Pope shouldn't have taken them."

"Why should he?" the Count snapped. "They're not his subjects. What would King Charles say if the Pope dumped several thousand unwanted people from the Papal States on the shores of Spain? If the Jesuits are criminals, as the Spanish pretend, the Pope doesn't want them. And if they're not criminals, they should never have been banished. The Pope isn't a fool. If he lets the Spanish unload their Jesuits onto him, the other Courts—Vienna, Berlin, St. Petersburg—will follow suit, and he'll have fifteen to twenty thousand unusable priests on his hands. What will he do then?"

"Surely there aren't that many, sir."

"Not yet. But this is only the beginning. There's not enough food for the people of this island as it is. Even two hundred extra mouths, even fifty, will be too much. I'm going out. Tell Major de Sparr that by the time I return I expect all the ships to have gone."

"Very good, sir."

Count de Marbeuf spent the morning with his second in command, the Vicomte de Cheverny, touring the defences. Later they rode out to inspect a village that had been captured from the rebels. On his return he found the captain of the Spanish flotilla waiting on the steps of his headquarters.

The Count stopped. "Do you understand French?" he asked curtly.

The man nodded.

"Very well. You will remove yourself and your ships from this harbour at once. It doesn't matter to me where you go. You can dump your passengers on the Grand Duke of Tuscany, for all I care, but you're not going to stay here."

"But I have orders," the Spaniard said excitedly in broken French, "orders from His Majesty's representative in Rome. The Jesuits are to be landed here." He pulled a paper out of his hat.

The Count snatched the paper away, tore it up, and scattered the pieces on the ground.

"I have yet to hear that the King of Spain rules Corsica", he said. Turning abruptly, he went into the house.

The captain, after telling the Count, who was no longer there to hear, that he was a lousy, pox-consumed son of a whore, returned to his ship. But he did not sail away. And the Count, who knew that he had gone to the limits of his authority, and perhaps a bit beyond, did not try to force him.

For over a fortnight, the Count and the captain of the Spanish flotilla remained at a deadlock, while, on the shadeless decks of the ships, and in the airless holds, the Jesuits waited, sick, dirty, unshaven, hungry, and verminous.

Then, one evening, after he had spent the day riding up and down stony mountain tracks, the Count came back to his headquarters and saw, through the open door of the map room, a priest in conversation with his staff officers.

"Who's that?" he asked his aide-de-camp.

"Father Pignatelli, sir." Lieutenant de Sèze spoke in a whisper. "One of the Jesuits. I've been talking to the Spanish commander about him. He's a brother of their ambassador in Paris and a cousin of Count Aranda."

The Count pulled off his hat and wig and threw them to his servant.

"My orders are still the same", he said, angered by the suggestion that he could be affected by the importance of anyone's relations. Looking around, he noticed that the priest was now standing in the door. He turned away. Then, as though to emphasise that he was not going to change his mind, he went and sat down behind a table covered with plans and reports. "No, Father", he said loudly, without looking at the priest and taking up a pen. "Your priests cannot land. There's no shelter for them on the island and no food. I suggest you try to get them ashore at Genoa."

"Of course, Count." The words were spoken in a slightly husky voice. "I understand exactly how you feel."

The Count looked up, surprised. The priest, a youngish man, tall and erect, with a strange nose, long, thin, and hooked, between a pair of fine eyes, was standing immediately in front of him on the other side of the table. Although his clothes were torn and dirty and he was unshaven, he still, somehow, had an air of distinction.

"What do you suppose I feel?"

"That it is an outrageous imposition on a general for him suddenly to have a large body of useless civilians thrown on his hands in the middle of a difficult and dangerous campaign. Please don't think we want to disobey you. I'm sure you will appreciate that obedience is something we are trained to respect."

"You are more understanding than they are in Paris, then", the Count said.

"When superiors are at a distance, their orders are often confusing. But it's rarely because of stupidity, don't you think? They just can't picture what's going on."

The Count's expression relaxed, and he began to smile.

"You are a very good apologist for authority, Father. But then it's your business to be charitable."

"Why my business any more than yours, Count?"

Monsieur de Marbeuf was immediately on guard.

"Now, Father, it's no good trying to get around me that way. I'm certainly sorry for you. Your ships look anything but comfortable. But I have to think of my men and the people of this island. I'm thinking of you, too. There's no food, no shelter, and the place isn't safe. Fighting goes on all the time, and you must have seen for yourself on the way up here what happens when they start bombarding us."

"We will do exactly as you wish, Count. But may I, on behalf of our provincials, ask you a favour."

"That depends on what it is."

"Will you come with me to the ships and explain in person to our priests and lay brothers why they can't land? I'm sure that if they were to hear the reasons from you, they would more easily accept this new disappointment. They know how to take orders, but as you are the commander responsible for the island, your word would have a special force. You are busy and overworked, Count, I know. But it would be a real charity, and our Lord will bless you. They have had a lot to put up with in these last two months, and they have nothing very pleasant to look forward to in the future."

The Count sat for a while, frowning at his pen.

"All right, Father", he said abruptly, standing up and adjusting his sword. "But don't deceive yourself. My orders will have to stand. They can't come ashore."

Two hours later, Count de Marbeuf was back in his headquarters, giving instructions to Major de la Tour, the officer in charge of the port and the provisioning of the town. "Have I made myself clear? You will arrange for the Fathers to come ashore in rotation for half an hour at a time. But on no account are they to eat or sleep on land."

As the major saluted and left, the Count glanced through the door to the room with the maps and saw his aide-de-camp exchanging a glance with one of the officers.

"De Sèze."

"Yes, sir."

"Come here." The Count waited for the young man to appear. "You think that Father Pignatelli must be an exceptionally clever man to get me to change my mind, don't you?"

"That's what the Jesuits have a reputation for, sir", de Sèze said with a smile.

The Count stared gloomily at the Lieutenant as though depressed by his superficiality.

"Father Pignatelli's persuasiveness is not the kind that can be learned in a class, or even of the kind that people are born with. Do you know what sanctity is?"

Lieutenant de Sèze looked embarrassed, as though he had found His Most Christian Majesty's Commander in Corsica on his hands and knees playing with dolls.

"Tomorrow morning," the Count continued, "you will go to the ships with Major de la Tour to see about supplying them with water. While you are there you will inspect as many of the holds as you have time for. If you are not too young and vain to profit by the lesson, you may perhaps learn from what you see how to bear hardships bravely and cheerfully. You will also give my compliments to Father Pignatelli. Should you, after talking to him again, still not be able to understand why, for his sake, I have countermanded my orders, you are incapable of making the most elementary judgment of character and are quite unfit to be on my staff."

SEVENTY-ONE

As the summer advanced, the humped hills of the island lost their colour: the dark tones turned dull and dusty, the light tones faded until they were paler than the sky. A perpetual haze hid the horizon and spread the sunlight in a even glare. The sea, mauve at midday, shone with coppery glints.

Early in July, Monsieur de Marbeuf received new orders from Paris. This time it was impossible to misunderstand them. The Jesuits, the despatch said, were to be landed immediately and given a permanent home in Corsica.

The Count leaned out of his window. "De la Tour", he bellowed at the Major, who was talking to a maid in the courtyard below. "I want you. Come here."

Half a minute later, the Major was standing in front of the Count, who tossed him the despatch.

"Do the best you can", he said. "It's impossible to take them all here at Bastia. Two hundred at the most. Have the rest shipped around the coast to Ajaccio and anywhere else you can find room for them."

Jaime de Vallecas was in a shipload put ashore at Calvi, where, with Father Padilla, Millan Nuñez, and fifteen others, he was assigned to a ruined barn on the outskirts of the town. At the end of three weeks, a cannon ball carried off part of the roof during a skirmish between the rebels and the French, which the French only just won. The next day, they were ordered to evacuate the barn, which was turned into a redoubt, and were shipped down the coast to San Bonifacio, at the southern tip of the island. The Aragonese Jesuits had already been at San Bonifacio for nearly a month.

The Aragonese Provincial welcomed the Castilians as they landed.

"Don't worry, Fathers", he said, as they gathered around him on the quay. "If you don't mind being split up, we can easily find room for you."

They were taken, some here, some there, to cellars, to sheds, to a disused chapel, to a prison, to a boatbuilder's loft. A Castilian priest in his eighties was given a bed in the local Dominican friary. Jaime and Millan joined the Aragonese novices in the crypt of the church of Santa Pelagia.

At San Bonifacio the Aragonese had managed to organise some kind of regular life for themselves with definite duties at specified times.

After hearing Mass at seven each morning, the novices and scholastics attended lectures. Under the olive trees or in the shadow of a rock on the seashore, their attention lulled by the shrilling of the cicadas and the beat of the waves, they listened to their professors discoursing on essence and existence, the sacramental system, or the general councils of the Church. Later there was work: foraging, chopping wood, laundry, cooking. In the evening, since they had neither pencils nor paper, they helped each other to memorize what they had learned earlier in the day.

And all this order and regularity, so the Aragonese novices explained, was the work of Father José Pignatelli of the Aragonese province.

Father José's sister, the Countess of Accerra, had sent him two shiploads of food, along with medicine, money, and books. Father José had bought a herd of cows to provide them with butter and milk. Father José was going to have dormitories built for them. Although Father José was ill and often had haemorrhages, he had travelled into the mountains to see General Paoli and ask for his protection should the French be driven out. Father José was only thirty, but the Aragonese Provincial consulted him about everything. Father José was a second St. Ignatius.

"I'm rather sick of hearing about Father José", Jaime said to Millan after they had been at San Bonifacio a week. It was early in the morning, and they were busy at their first task of the day—collecting sticks in a chestnut wood two miles from the town. To make the work easier, they had hitched their tattered cassocks above their knees, tucking the ends under their belts.

"But look what he's been able to do for us", Millan said.

"That's true, but it's only because his family is rich and powerful."

"Isn't that a good thing?"

"For us, in the present circumstances, yes. But it's not sanctity."

"I suppose not." There was an element of uncertainty in Millan's voice. Having been born on a farm, it was difficult not to be impressed by titles and riches.

They shouldered their sacks and began to trudge downhill by the way they had come.

"I don't mean to be ungrateful", Jaime went on. "I'm sure he's a good man. But I believe in keeping a sense of proportion. It's easy for a person of his birth, with a brother who is ambassador in Paris, to intimidate generals and officials. If Father de Salcedo hadn't fallen sick and been left behind at Civitavecchia, he could have done the same for us."

"Of course", Millan said, suddenly seeing the discussion in a new light—Castile versus Aragon.

By this time they had left the wood and were following a path along the top of a ravine. From inland, a breeze brought the scent of the *macchia*. Ahead and below, where the opposing hillsides interlocked, they could see a violet-coloured triangle of water.

About half a mile from the town, Millan stopped and said, "Let's have a rest."

They threw down their sacks and sat on a boulder. Millan took off his shoes and, after shaking out the pebbles, examined the soles, which were coming apart from the uppers.

Far below at the bottom of the ravine, a man in a tattered grey shirt and greyish breeches was picking his way up the waterless river bed. In one hand he carried a terracotta jar, in the other a small sack. Just below the point where Jaime and Millan were sitting, he stopped, turned, and, pulling himself up by the bushes growing between the rocks, climbed the opposite face of the ravine until he came to a natural platform halfway up. He put down the jar and sack and stood still, breathing heavily. Then he disappeared into a hut half embedded in the hillside at the back. The sheep and goats, which had scattered at his approach, came quietly back and continued nibbling among the dried tufts of grass.

When he reappeared, he was carrying in his arms an old man with straggling white hair and beard, whom he set down on a stone. From across the ravine, Jaime and Millan could not make out what he was saying, but they could hear his querulous voice, and it was clear from his impatient gestures that he wanted to be moved somewhere else. So the younger man picked him up again and carried him to the edge of the platform where he could look at the sea. But this did not appear to please him either. Only when half a dozen places had been tried and rejected did the old man appear satisfied and allow himself to be established on a sheepskin in the shade of a fig tree. Here the younger man helped him light his pipe, and, opening his sack, pulled out a basket and a wine bottle which, with the water jar, he set within the old man's reach. Between puffs, the old man continued his plaintive monologue, while the younger man listened, only occasionally learning forward to say something in reply.

Eventually, the younger man stood up and pointed to the sun, whose rays had just reached the top of the fig tree. Then he pointed westward, as though saying, "I'll be back when it gets there." A few moments later he was clambering down the side of the ravine. At the bottom, he glanced around, and pulled a black bundle from under a bush. It was a rolled up cassock. He shook it open, put it on, and looked up at the sky, screwing up his eyes as he did so. Afterward, he turned, and moved off down the ravine, stepping from rock to rock and pushing his way through the oleanders that choked the course of the dried-up river bed.

Jaime and Millan looked at each other.

"Did you see?"

"Yes?"

"You couldn't mistake that nose."

"God forgive me", Jaime said.

SEVENTY-TWO

The honeymoon with misfortune was over. The weeks on board ship had been appalling, but now that their existence was less intolerable, the exiles found it harder to bear.

It was worse for the priests than for the novices. When each priest had said Mass, read his Office, and done his share of sweeping, foraging, and cooking, there was nothing more to do. San Bonifacio already had, besides its impoverished house of Dominicans, an equally impoverished Franciscan friary and a large number of secular priests, and even had it been otherwise, only a few of the Spanish Jesuits spoke Italian.

The only relief from monotony was fear. When the French and Corsicans fought, they showed little interest in the fate of civilians.

Then winter came. Homer's wine-dark sea turned the colour of old dishcloths. The winds blew. The rain beat down. During the long evenings, priests and lay brothers sat shivering in their dilapidated, ill-lit, furnitureless shelters, which let in both wind and rain, and wondered:

"Is it for life?" Fuel, as well as food, was short and the townspeople charged high prices.

The words "Escape! Escape!" sounded ceaselessly in Father Padilla's mind.

"You are different from the others", the Tempter said. "They are serving the Church by their sufferings and sacrifices here. But you are needed elsewhere. Your vocation is to commend religion to men of science who have lost their faith. Think of the good you could do in correspondence with a man like d'Alembert. It is your duty to escape and leave the Society. You can easily get dispensed from your vows. Then, as an ordinary secular priest, you can continue your astronomical studies in peace."

He tried to picture Christ on the Cross but instead saw himself seated in a comfortable library, the protégé of some scientifically minded prelate or noble.

Then late on a December afternoon, as he was walking by the harbour, he met Coronel, one of the Spanish commissaries who had been sent to Corsica on the orders of Count Aranda, supposedly to look after the Jesuits' welfare.

"Good evening, Father."

"Good evening."

"At last we're getting some better weather. Looking at the boats?"

"Yes."

"Stout little craft. And fast, I imagine."

"Are they?"

"Have you ever thought how long it would take to cross to the mainland in one of them?"

"No."

A pause.

This, Father Padilla thought, is a conversation to be ended. Instead of ending it, he heard himself asking: "How long?"

"A day and a half. Two days, perhaps. And very little risk. You can't beat a Corsican at navigation, even in the roughest sea."

Another pause. The sun, appearing suddenly through a rent in the clouds near the horizon, scattered its last fierce rays, flame on grey, over the dead landscape. With dwindling self-respect, Father Padilla continued to stand where he was.

"You know, Father," Coronel went on, "it isn't His Majesty's wish that you should be suffering all this vexation and discomfort. If he had his way, you would all be living quietly in the Papal States by now. So should any of you want to try to get to the mainland on your own, His Majesty is anxious that you should be given the wherewithal."

"Money, you mean?"

"More than money. I myself will hire the boat and sailors and, if necessary, provide suitable clothes. We don't want any of you to be victimized by your fellow priests."

Father Padilla felt a momentary strengthening of his will.

"This, I suppose, is His Majesty's way of trying to embarrass the Holy See and break up the Society from within—at least its Spanish provinces."

Coronel shrugged his shoulders.

"If you insist on looking at it that way . . . but what future for you as a community is there in Corsica? And as long as you remain together in a community, no other country will let you in."

"And afterward?" Father Padilla's voice was almost a whisper.

"Oh, you wouldn't be forgotten. You could count on His Majesty to be generous."

This time, weighed down by the shame of his cowardice and disloyalty, Father Padilla was silent.

"Think about it, Father", Coronel said. "You know where I live." He pointed to a house facing the water. "Any time you care to call, I'll be glad to help you."

"FATHER, FATHER, WAKE UP!" Jaime de Vallecas whispered, shaking Father Padilla by the shoulder.

Father Padilla groaned and rolled over on his back. He had been dreaming that he was on top of a mountain where he was receiving the congratulations of the Empress of Russia for having established the correct position of the North Pole. He peered bleakly into the gloom. A lantern on the ground cast spokelike shadows; between the shadows, triangles of light showed the other priests rolled up asleep in their blankets along the floor of the cellar.

"Who is it?"

"Me. Jaime de Vallecas. You must come at once."

"What's the matter?"

"I'll tell you outside."

They climbed the steps and came out into the air. The clouds had been blown away, the moon shone from a clear sky, and the piazza, which by day was a desolate rectangle of scuffed earth, looked like a pool of pale blue milk. At another time they would have been awed by the beauty of the night. As it was, they noticed nothing.

"Who did you say? Father de la Cueva?"

"Yes. You must speak to him. You must stop him."

"What made you think he is planning to escape?"

"What else would he be doing at this time of night leaving the town disguised as a fisherman? The other day I saw him talking with the commissary, Coronel. It must be Coronel who arranged this."

"Was he alone?"

"There were two others. I expect they were the fishermen in charge of the boat."

"Quick, then, or we shall miss them. Which way did they go?"

"Over there."

In a few minutes they were out of the town and climbing a headland.

"Don't go so fast, Father", Jaime said breathlessly. "You'll hurt yourself." But Father Padilla pressed on, holding up his cassock in front and jumping from boulder to boulder.

From the top of the headland they looked down on a ring-shaped bay. A boat with furled sails was drawn up on the moonlit beach.

"Thank God! They're still here." Father Padilla was panting. "You can go back now."

"I'll wait", Jaime said. Without stopping to reply, Father Padilla plunged on, half-running down the hillside.

In the shadow of a rock, Father de la Cueva stood arguing with the two boatmen. At the last minute they had decided to raise the price. Hearing the sound of rolling pebbles and snapping twigs, they abruptly stopped talking and looked to see where the noise was coming from. As they did so, Father Padilla came stumbling out of the undergrowth and limped toward them across the sand.

"Father, I must speak to you", he said, ignoring the sudden look of hatred in Father de la Cueva's eyes. Taking the former rector's arm, he walked him away along the beach. "Father, if you leave us like this, you will always regret it."

"What shall I regret?" Father de la Cueva said in an angry hiss. "The Pope has abandoned the Society. Refusing to let us land amounts to saying he no longer regards us as having any legal existence. It's up to each of us to look out for himself."

In his knitted cap, old striped tunic and pantaloons rolled up to the knees, he looked less like a boatman than an opera singer playing the part of a boatman. The supposed disguise was so ridiculous and undignified that Father Padilla found it painful to look at him.

"You know the Pope hasn't abandoned us. He couldn't let us land. How could he have possibly provided for us all?"

But Father de la Cueva was not to be persuaded.

"Ricci's policy has been disastrous. He should never have been elected Father General. We were always so busy imagining enemies everywhere that finally people got tired of us and we made ourselves real ones."

"Do you honestly believe that?"

"Yes, I do", Father de la Cueva said, working up his anger. "Ricci ought to be made to resign. He never knew how to handle men of the world, kings and statesmen. He was unworldly in the wrong sense. He should have forced the Pope to let us land at Civitavecchia. He should have reminded him, if necessary, that he has a duty to harbour the harbourless. I don't know how he has the face to continue in office after what's happened. And our provincial is no better."

"What could Father Provincial have done?"

"For one thing, he could have stopped Father Isla from publishing

393

that ridiculous novel of his, *Fray Gerundio*. Haven't we enemies enough without antagonising the Franciscans?"

"He only made fun of the style of some of their preachers."

"Only! What could be worse? Especially when the King happens to have a Franciscan confessor."

"Yes, it was imprudent, I agree." Father Padilla said in a conciliatory tone. "But sermons did improve after his book was successful."

"That's small comfort now. Who's paying for his success? Or, rather, for his literary vanity. Yes, that's what it was—literary vanity. Trying to imitate those cynical French authors. Well, look at the result. We're supposed to be so clever. But what's really ruined us is our stupidity."

They had wandered close to the water, which at intervals gathered itself into a wave, but one so feeble that when it broke it advanced only a few inches up the sand. As they walked, shells and gleaming fragments of cuttlefish crunched under their shoes.

"Father, change your mind and come back with me", Father Padilla said. "We can slip into the town without being noticed. You don't know how much we all admired the way you spoke to the *alcalde* when they came to arrest us in Madrid. We shall miss you. Stay with us, please. Look, I'll tell you something. I know just how you feel. For weeks now I've been tempted to escape myself."

Father de la Cueva mistook his meaning. "You'll have to find another boat", he said quickly. "There isn't any room in this one. Besides, they'll make more difficulties about the price if I try to bring you along, too."

"I'm not asking you to take me, Father. I was trying to say that I understand the strength of the temptation you've been under. I honestly do."

When he realised his blunder, Father de la Cueva was angrier than ever. "Let go of my arm", he said. "No one is going to force me to stay."

"I wasn't trying to force you. I wanted you to feel you had a friend— somebody who sympathised."

The two figures moved back and forth in the moonlight. Jaime, watching them from the top of the hill was shivering with cold. After

394

three-quarters of an hour, they suddenly parted, and the taller figure crossed the sand to the waiting boat. Two other figures appeared from the shadows, and all three pushed the boat into the water and clambered aboard. Soon the sails were up, and, blown by the night breeze, the boat was moving across the bay toward the open sea.

Twenty minutes later, Father Padilla joined Jaime, and they plodded back to the town.

After a long silence, Jaime said, "If he wants to go, perhaps it's just as well. A man who gives in as easily as that isn't much use to the Society."

"Hold your tongue", Father Padilla said. After another silence, he added, "It's easy to be heroic at twenty. Wait till you're fifty. You'll discover then that to be a little above mediocre is a victory."

FATHER DE LA CUEVA'S FLIGHT led others to follow his example. During January, February, and March 1768, numbers of priests and brothers, encouraged by the Spanish commissaries, escaped from the island, landed in disguise on the mainland, made their way to Rome, and there, having been dispensed from their vows of poverty and obedience, left the Society and tried to make new lives for themselves as secular priests or laymen.

SEVENTY-THREE

Six months earlier, on June 7, 1767, after a journey of two and a half months, Rodrigo Logrosan had arrived in Buenos Aires, carrying with him the decree banishing the Jesuits from the Spanish possessions in the Americas and Count Aranda's instructions for carrying it out. Rodrigo had been recommended for the job by Don Manuel Roda.

The change in his manner and expression over the last year was striking. The eager, enthusiastic youth had been replaced by a hard, purposeful-looking adult. It was not, however, the hardness and purposefulness of the ordinary hard man bent merely on getting ahead without any second thoughts about it. It was the hardness and purposefulness of a man gripped by a fixed idea based on a mistaken intellectual choice that he is constantly trying to justify to himself; an idea, moreover, adopted at the cost of something infinitely precious.

To be hard when you have grown up among tough, hard people is a kind of natural development. To become hard when you have known goodness and love involves a laceration of spirit that can only be healed by the rediscovery of goodness and love. That is why, through the everyday hardness of Rodrigo's expression, there often appeared something tormented and tragic. The fixed idea and the lost love and goodness could not abide together, yet he wanted both.

As soon as he landed, he had reported to the governor, General Don Francisco Bucareli, who received him at his palace in a room overlooking a garden filled with palms, laurels, and acacias.

"An emissary from Count Aranda? You are very welcome. And how is His Excellency? Flourishing, I hope." The Governor smiled as he took the package that Rodrigo held out to him. Still talking, he ripped off the outer cover and examined the envelope inside.

"A Matter of State . . . with the utmost secrecy? What *is* the trouble now? Well, we'll look into it shortly. Come and see me in the morning." The Governor opened a drawer of his writing table and was about to put the papers into it when Rodrigo interrupted.

"Excuse me, Your Excellency, but I am under orders not to lose sight of those papers until I am certain Your Excellency has read them."

The Governor raised his eyebrows.

"I see. Sit down then, while I find out what's the matter."

He opened the envelope and began to read the covering letter. While doing so, he drummed his fingers on the writing table and wrinkled his nose as though the letter had a bad smell. Exile the Jesuits! He foresaw months of difficulties and being blamed for anything that went wrong whether or not he was responsible for it.

The letter ended with praise of Rodrigo, who was commended for his reliability. "He has the confidence of His Excellency Count Aranda",

Don Manuel wrote, "and will be useful to Your Excellency in seeing that the accompanying orders are carried out in accordance with the wishes of His Majesty."

In other words, Bucareli thought, they send a man to spy on me and then expect me to be polite to him. He looked at Rodrigo with dislike.

"I take it you know what these instructions are about?"

"Yes, sir."

"Then see that you keep them to yourself. This is like gunpowder. We must act with the greatest prudence."

AFTER TAKING THE ADVICE of his council, the Governor decided to carry out the instructions from Madrid in two stages: to arrest the Jesuits in the Spanish-speaking parts of the colony immediately and those in the Reductions the following year.

Having been in the colony only a short time, he pictured the Reductions as fortresses guarded by hymn-singing warrior savages under the command of priests wearing breastplates over their cassocks. His military advisers all assured him that the Indians, if not the Jesuits themselves, were certain to make trouble. Having often campaigned alongside them in the service of the crown, they knew from experience what intrepid fighters they were. Obviously, to subdue them, a full-scale military campaign would be necessary.

By the end of September, the first part of the Governor's plans had been successfully completed. The Jesuits of Buenos Aires, Córdoba, Corrientes, Santa Fe, and Montevideo were somewhere out in the Atlantic on ships bound for Europe.

During the following months, Rodrigo journeyed about the colony helping to wind up the affairs of their residences and colleges. With the help of his assistants, he made inventories of their property, arranged for its sale, and searched their papers for evidence that could justify the measures already taken against them. He worked with an almost frenzied energy. For was he not at last going to be proved right? Was not Don Maurice soon going to be forced to admit that the Jesuits were traitors, ask his forgiveness, accept him back into his family, and allow him to marry Beatriz?

But to his surprise he found no incriminating papers, and when he did come on a document that he set aside to send to Madrid, he was conscious that he had to strain the sense to put a bad interpretation on it. Nor were there any secret stores of money.

I suppose it was to be expected, he thought. Obviously the Jesuits keep their riches in the safety of the Jesuit state. And that's where we shall find evidence of their plans for extending their power and dominating the world.

THE EXPEDITION against the Reductions was finally ready to set out at the end of May 1768. By boat and barge, the Governor and his troops journeyed up the Uruguay as far as the town of Salto, where he divided his army into three parts.

Rodrigo was attached to the force, commanded by a Captain Herrera, that was to capture the Reductions along the Paraná. With it went the secular priests and civil commissioners who were to replace the Jesuits.

For a month they travelled through a maze of rivers and marshes. Rain fell continuously; much of the baggage was swept away during the crossing of a flooded stream; and pagan Indians ambushed some of the cavalry and captured their horses.

By the end of the second week in July they were approaching the Reduction of San Fernando. Herrera sent forward a patrol to find out how strongly the town was defended. The rest of the party pitched camp. They caught and slaughtered some cattle that were grazing nearby and had their first good meal since leaving Salto. Afterward, they sat round the fires drying their sodden boots and uniforms.

"Personally," Rodrigo said to a lieutenant called Morenos, who was stretched out beside him with his back against the inside of an upturned saddle, "I wonder if it was necessary to bring such a large force. I wouldn't be surprised if we didn't see the Indians come running out to welcome us once they learn we are in the neighbourhood."

"What makes you think that?" Morenos asked.

"If you were oppressed, wouldn't you want to be liberated."

"What makes you think that's how the Indians see their situation?"

Rodrigo leaned forward to push one of his boots nearer the fire.

"It stands to reason", he said.

"Perhaps to your reason", Morenos said. "Not to mine."

SEVENTY-FOUR

When the news reached San Miguel that the Governor's troops were only a day's march away, Father Huber summoned his flock to the church. As he slowly mounted the pulpit, his shoulders seemed to slope more steeply than ever, as if the invisible yoke he always appeared to carry might at any moment pull him to the ground.

"My children," he said, "this is the last time I shall be speaking to you. I need not say much, because most of what I have to tell you we have already talked about before. Tomorrow the Governor's men, who, as you all know, have been taking away the Fathers from the Reductions farther down the river, will be coming to arrest Father Alfonso and me. In our place they will leave another priest to look after you. The King has been told evil stories about us. That is why he is taking us away. But if you obey your new priest and the men the Governor sends to rule over you, then the King will know that the stories he has been told about us are untrue."

He spoke against a background of sobs. Every Indian in the Reduction was present. They filled the nave from the altar rails to the west door. In the past, when a priest had spoken, they had always been still and attentive. Now they moved restlessly like corn stalks before a summer storm.

"The last year has not been a happy one", Father Huber continued. "We have all been anxious about the future. Work has been neglected. There has been talk of fighting the Governor's men. Some of you have stolen swords and muskets from the arsenal. A few have run away to the forests. Now all this must stop, and those who have stolen arms must bring them back this evening if they want to remain my friends."

He leaned forward and held out his arms.

"You know that I love you and can never forget you. I have been your father, and you have been my sons and daughters for over thirty years. To say good-bye to you tears my heart. But there is something that will grieve me even more—if, after we have gone, I hear that you have disobeyed the Governor's orders or have returned to the forests. My children, you cannot be Christians if you live in the woods without a priest. Stay in your town and follow the laws and customs you are used to. My children, I love you with my whole soul. Remember, we shall all meet in heaven. Life lasts only a short time."

Suddenly, Clara's father, Methodius, who was sitting close to the pulpit, jumped to his feet.

"Father, if you go away, the Europeans will make us slaves. In the Reductions we are free, but when you are no longer here to protect us, we shall be like the Indians who work on the estates of the Europeans." He turned his head this way and that, as if looking for support.

All over the church other men stood up, shouting and gesticulating.

"Father, stay with us. What he says is true."

"They mean to kill you."

"Stay with us, and we will defend you."

"We will hang the Governor."

"We will march to Buenos Aires and destroy all your enemies."

"The King wants to make us slaves. Be our king instead."

By this time, half the congregation were on their feet, surging toward the pulpit. Uncertain what they meant to do, Alfonso, who was in the sanctuary, ran to the pulpit and blocked the way up the steps. Father Huber was shouting and waving his arms. But no one listened.

"Stay with us! Stay with us! Stay with us!"

For five minutes the Indians kept chanting the words until the whole church reverberated like a giant sounding board. Half a dozen men clambered up the outside of the pulpit. Holding on by the heads of the mongol-eyed cherubs cavorting round its gilded panels, they leaned over the rim and plucked at Father Huber's cassock. He put out his hands as though pushing them off and retreated to the back of the pulpit; then he turned away from them toward the altar and covered his face with his hands. This movement of rejection frightened the Indians. The shouting died down a little. Jacinto, the schoolmaster, elbowed his way to the front.

"Father, please hear us", he pleaded. "We are your children, and we are unhappy."

Father Huber remained with his face toward the altar.

"No. No. You are not my children anymore." With his right arm he made a sweeping movement behind his back. "You are rebels, murderers. I cast you off."

The words were repeated from mouth to mouth. The Indians looked afraid.

"Father," Jacinto said entreatingly, "we don't mean any wrong. We were carried away; it is because we are confused. We love you, and we are afraid."

Father Huber turned round. There were tears running down his cheeks. This time the Indians were aghast. They had not supposed he was capable of crying. What must they have done to produce such an effect? Feeling like parricides, they pushed and stumbled over each other in the rush to get back to their benches. There was a pause while the old priest mastered himself.

"That's better", he said at last. "And now, if you are to remain my children, you must promise that when the Governor's men come tomorrow you will not molest or injure them or in any way try to prevent them from carrying out their orders."

There was a long silence.

401

"Do you promise?"

The answer came like a sigh—desolate and heartbroken—of a single person.

"We promise."

BY NIGHTFALL the arms stolen from the arsenal had been piled outside the door of the college.

Father Huber and Alfonso spent the evening getting the records and archives ready to show the new civil commissioner. When they had finished, Alfonso got up and knelt beside Father Huber's chair, resting his forehead on the old man's knees.

"Father," he said, "you must help me. Everything inside me is confusion. How can we abandon them? For myself, I can accept being arrested. But not if it means that they must suffer. And they will. When I tell them they have nothing to fear, my conscience protests. I know I'm deceiving them. Surely in the circumstances we ought to resist . . . for their sakes. They are just children."

Father Huber took Alfonso's hands and held them between his own.

"My dear son, do you suppose I haven't felt exactly the same? Do you imagine that I don't realise how many rapacious wolves are waiting to devour them?"

"Then let us fight. We have a good chance of winning."

"No. No. We may not do evil that good may come. Were the Reductions, as has so often been pretended, really an independent state, it would be our duty to defend them against outsiders. But we are merely delegates of the King of Spain, and if he wishes to withdraw us —whatever we may think of his motives—he has the right to do so. Moreover, resistance, even justifiable resistance, would be useless. Our Indians might be able to drive out the Governor with his present force, but he would return with a bigger one and punish them harshly."

"I feel like a traitor", Alfonso said. "It seems so cowardly to leave them without a struggle."

Father Huber put his hand under Alfonso's chin and raised his head so that he was compelled to look up at him.

"You love them, yes. But do you think you love them more than Christ loved his apostles? Yet when the time came for him to die, he had to leave them at the mercy of his enemies. History is not something straightforward, not something men will ever be able fully to understand or control. It is the unfolding, the working out of the mystery of evil, grace, and free will. We shall be helping the forces of evil if we try to take our own way, rather than God's, through this labyrinth."

THE NEXT DAY Captain Herrera and his men rode into San Miguel. Father Huber and Alfonso met them at the foot of the column in the plaza.

After handing the captain the keys of the town gates and the principal buildings and greeting the priest and commissioner who were to replace him, Father Huber presented the leading Indians to him. Then he took them on a tour of inspection—the church, the college, the hospital, the orphanage, the workshops. The priest and civil commissioner glanced nervously at the sullen crowds silently watching wherever they went.

On their return to the college, they found a deputation of Indians waiting by the wellhead in the courtyard. Dídaco, who was leading it, came forward and knelt in front of the embarrassed captain.

"What does this mean, Dídaco?" Father Huber asked. "Have you forgotten your promise?"

"No, Father. We only want to ask a favour." He clasped his hands and raised his streaming eyes to Herrera's. "Honourable Captain, we have written a letter to His Majesty. Please leave us our priests. When His Majesty reads our letters, he is sure to tell you to send them back, so why take them away? We have promised that if you leave them with us we will work twice as hard as before and will pay more taxes."

"But I have brought you a new priest."

"It is not the same, Captain. We are sure the new Father is a good

403

man. But the Jesuit Fathers have been with us for many generations. They understand us. We cannot be happy without them."

Captain Herrera made a movement with his hand, and Dídaco realised that he was dismissed. Looking grieved and hurt, he got to his feet and stood back. The Governor's men moved on.

"I bet the two Jesuits put them up to it", one of the officers whispered to the civil commissioner.

"More than likely."

"The old one looks cunning. I wonder what other tricks he's got up his sleeve."

In the plaza, a herald read the decree of banishment. It was followed by the Governor's proclamation. In future, authority in the Reductions would be divided. The commissioner would look after temporal affairs. This would leave the priest free to attend to the souls of his flock. Under the previous system, it seemed to be implied, there had been too much attention to business, and souls had been neglected.

After the proclamation, the herald read an order that had just come from the Governor's headquarters on the Uruguay. Don Francisco, it appeared, had been scandalised by the immodesty of the Guarani women, which exposed his soldiers to temptation. The women must make themselves dresses with longer sleeves, higher necks and more voluminous skirts.

The Indians listened to the herald with bewilderment and incomprehension. Never before had anyone suggested that their clothes were immodest. If the soldiers were so easily tempted, why hadn't the Governor left them behind in Buenos Aires?

To avoid demonstrations, the captain confined Father Huber and Alfonso to the college for the rest of the day.

The following morning, Father Huber asked if he and Alfonso might say Mass before leaving. The captain, who had just got out of bed, was smoking a pipe under the veranda. After hesitating a moment, he refused. It was not harshness; he was troubled by the unaccustomed nature of the situation in which he found himself. He understood how to treat priests, and he understood how to treat prisoners. Priests who were also prisoners were a new experience. The word "sacrilege" stirred unpleasantly in his mind. It did not frighten him enough to make him disobey the Governor's orders. He would not have to face God, so he hoped, for a good many years yet, whereas he would have to face the Governor quite soon. But he felt that in refusing to let his prisoners carry out their priestly functions he would somehow be diminishing the sacrilege. They would be less priests if they were not acting as priests.

He sent for his officers, who were still at breakfast. They came out into the courtyard, wiping their mouths and buttoning up their tunics.

"You, Morenos," the captain said, "will stay behind with a dozen of the dragoons to keep order until things have settled down. The rest of you, form up your men in the plaza. Lieutenant Lopez, you will be responsible for the two Fathers. They will remain in the college till we are ready to move. See that you treat them with respect."

He turned to the new priest and the civil commissioner, who were waiting to speak to him. Both looked nervous, and the commissioner asked for extra soldiers to be sent from Candelaria as soon as they could be spared.

Half an hour later, Captain Herrera rode out of San Miguel with Father Huber and Alfonso in the middle of his now depleted force. Hundreds of Indians, who had been waiting in the plaza since before dawn, ran beside them. After several miles, the captain ordered his men to drive them off.

"Don't hurt them", Father Huber cried. "I will talk to them." He removed his battered straw hat and stood up in his stirrups. "My children, I bless you all, your houses, your fields, your families for all generations to come. And now, go home, my dear ones, and may the Lord in his mercy go with you."

The Indians stood still, wailing and crying. Captain Herrera and his party rode on. Father Huber and Alfonso turned in their saddles and waved. When at last the trees of the forest had hidden the Indians from view, Father Huber bent his head, and the tears fell fast on the pummel of his saddle.

405

"The Lord gives," he murmured brokenly, "the Lord takes away. Blessed be the name of the Lord."

SEVENTY-FIVE

A week had gone by.

Clara was sweeping the house. Through the open door she could see the morning sun streaming down on the same street, the same buildings, the same trees, the same bright-coloured birds and flowers as before. But now they might as well have been dead trees, dead birds, dead flowers, gutted buildings. San Miguel was dead. The trust and love that had animated it for 150 years had gone.

A long-drawn-out cry, piercing and agonised, made Clara drop her broom and hurry to the door. Up and down the street women peered from their houses. But instead of running to see what had happened, they quickly retreated inside, succumbing to the dread that, since Father Huber and Alfonso had been taken away, lay continuously at the edge of their minds.

When Xavier came back from the fields in the evening, he said that Crisóstomo's brother, Damián, was going to be hanged. He had caught a soldier raping his wife and had killed him.

Next day, when it was time to go to the fields, Xavier picked up a bundle of osiers, sat down on the steps under the veranda, and started to make a basket.

"What are you doing?" Clara asked. "You'll be late."

"I'm not going."

"But you'll be punished."

"Let them try. Do you think I'm going to leave you alone with all these dirty Europeans about."

Soon more and more men were refusing to work. Not knowing what else to do, the commissioner used the soldiers to drive them to the fields, threatening to shoot them if they resisted. But for the time being, he kept Damián in gaol; he decided not to hang him until the Governor sent the extra soldiers he had asked for.

A FEW DAYS LATER, Clara and some other women went down to the river to do their washing. With her she took her fourteen-year-old cousin, Melania. For some time they worked side by side in silence, pounding the woollen tunics with stones. Then Melania stopped, pulled a silver bracelet out of a pocket, and showed it to Clara.

"Where did you get that?" Clara asked, suspiciously.

The girl tittered.

Clara sat back on her heels and stared at her.

"Not one of the soldiers?"

Melania nodded.

"Before he goes away," she said, "he's going to marry me and take me with him to the city. He will give me lots of bracelets and necklaces to wear and beautiful clothes. He says the Jesuit Fathers were bad men, who kept us poor so that we would work for them."

"And you listened to lies like that?"

"They aren't lies. It's the truth. Manuel said so. If I can find out for him where the gold mines are, he is going to give me a necklace of jewels like the ones on the chalice in church."

"Where is a soldier going to get jewels like that?" Clara said angrily. "He probably means to steal them from a chalice. Don't you dare listen to him, Melania. How do you know he hasn't got a wife already? There aren't any gold mines. He will make you his whore, and then he will go away and leave you."

"How dare you call me a whore!"

Melania flew at her. Clara defended herself. There was a struggle, and they fell to the ground. The other women ran up and separated them.

"What's the matter. Why are you fighting?"

"Let me get at her", Melania shrieked, trying to wrench herself free. "She called me a whore. I'll teach her."

407

"Run off home while we hold her", one of the women said to Clara. "She'll have forgotten all about it in a little while."

Clara picked up her half-washed clothes, thrust them into a basket, and ran, sobbing, back across the fields. Her tears were not so much for herself as for Melania's treachery and disloyalty.

In the pueblo, visitors and speculators from Asunción and Villa Rica, the nearest European town, were wandering about staring at the buildings and making critical remarks. Some of them laughed at the sight of Clara's scratched, bleeding, terrified face. One or two tried to stop her to find out what was the matter. But imagining them to be slave dealers, she pushed them aside and ran on. She spent the rest of the day with her mother, who had been looking after Belarmino for her.

When she went back home to cook Xavier's supper, she found him talking with some friends under the veranda. The Governor had issued another decree. None of the land was to be held communally any more. It was already being divided.

"The Catapachus have been given the best fields", Xavier said.

"They must have bribed somebody", Leo, the blacksmith, interjected, spitting out a pellet of chewed tobacco.

"Have you got any?"

"Some sandy ground near the tannery."

"I know the piece I want", Sixtus, the carpenter, said. "If it's been given to someone else, he'll have to fight for it."

"Those greedy herdsmen have been slaughtering the cattle as though they already belonged to them."

"We're sure to get the worst animals."

"Well, I'm not going to be cheated. If I don't get a fair share, I shall help myself where I can."

The rancour in their voices sickened Clara. She felt as Eve must have felt when the earth was cursed, and Cain murdered Abel.

When the others had gone, Crisóstomo looked in. Clara had finished cooking and was sitting under the veranda rocking Belarmino's hammock. For a time Crisóstomo said nothing. Then he glanced sideways at Xavier, as if gauging his mood and state of mind.

"One of those Europeans from Asunción asked me just now where the gold mines are."

"What did you say?" Xavier asked.

"Oh, I don't know."

"Didn't you tell him there aren't any?" Clara interrupted.

"How do I know there aren't? He gave me this coin and said he would give me a lot more like it if I could tell him where the mines are."

Xavier took the coin and examined it. Suddenly he felt it snatched away and saw Clara run into the open and hurl it with all her might across the street. It rose in an arc and fell behind the houses on the opposite side.

"Curse you!" Crisóstomo said. "What did you do that for?" And, jumping to his feet, he ran off to search for his lost treasure.

"We don't want their money." Clara said passionately, coming back and going into the house. "It's evil, evil, evil." Xavier followed her. He looked embarrassed and ashamed.

"There's nothing wrong with money. You never know. We might need it some day."

"Have we needed it up to now? No. God has looked after us. Oh, what are they doing to us? What is happening to us?" She turned away from Xavier, crying. "Everything has changed", she sobbed. "It will never be the same again."

SEVENTY-SIX

The illusions with which Rodrigo had been deceiving himself for nearly three years had dispersed like tobacco smoke within an hour of his entering the Reduction of San Fernando. It had taken him only that long to realise that the story of a tyrannical Jesuit state, which he had so passionately believed and so eagerly repeated to all who would listen, was a lie, that in fact the Indians loved their priests, and that here, if anywhere, was that utopia celebrated by the Chevalier de Savin in which could be found men who were happy, industrious, virtuous, and at peace.

Almost out of his mind with remorse, he had at first thought of returning to Buenos Aires alone. He would find an Indian who, for a few reales, would take him there by river. But in the end, he had decided to stay with Captain Herrera and his soldiers so as to make sure that the arrested Jesuits were properly treated and in this small way to make a beginning of amends for the evil he had done.

From San Fernando they had proceeded up the Paraná to the Reductions of Cosmé, Itapua, and Trinidad, adding at each in turn to their group of prisoners. Nowhere had the Indians or the Jesuits resisted. The military campaign, prepared with so much trepidation, had turned into a cross-country ride. The soldiers joked about it. The officers, feeling they had been made to look foolish, began to cold-shoulder Rodrigo.

At last they had approached San Miguel. Captain Herrera had halted on the high ground overlooking the Reduction, which lay two miles distant, peaceful and undisturbed beside its river.

"The usual routine", he had said. "Arlandes, you will stay here with the same thirty men as before and the prisoners. Tomorrow you will meet me three hours after sunrise on the other side of the valley where you can see that road going into the forest."

Rodrigo had urged his horse close to Captain Herrera's. "I shall stay with Lieutenant Arlandes", he had said in a low voice.

Captain Herrera had given him a curious, inquiring look. "Do as you please", he had answered at last, shrugging his shoulders, and, turning his horse, had ordered his men to move on.

I can't avoid seeing Alfonso tomorrow, Rodrigo had said to himself. But I'm not going to be present when he's arrested. For hours that night he had lain awake, thinking of the meeting that lay ahead.

Next day, Lieutenant Arlandes and his party, after skirting the Reduction, had arrived first at the meeting place on the edge of the forest. When Captain Herrera and his men were still at a distance, Rodrigo had been able to pick out Alfonso by his copper-coloured hair. Afterward, and for the rest of the day, he had avoided looking in his direction. But it had not saved him from the torture of imagining what Alfonso must be thinking.

That night the little army had bivouacked beside a lake. While the horses were being unsaddled, Rodrigo told Captain Herrera that he wanted to question Father de Vallecas in private.

He approached the little group of Jesuits and their guards. "I have some questions to put to you, Father", he said coldly to Alfonso. "Follow me, please."

This time their eyes did meet. In the twilight it was difficult to read Alfonso's expression, but Rodrigo imagined it to be saying, "So this is how you repay the love lavished on you by my family and the debt you owe to your teachers. Who would have thought you could sink to be so vile."

Stumbling in the half-dark, Rodrigo led the way along the shore of the lake until the camp was out of sight. He stopped where the path was blocked by a fallen tree smothered with creepers. The white flowers shone in the dusk like phosphorescent moths. Alfonso stopped, too. As though unconscious of Rodrigo's presence, he stood staring at the strip of saffron sky just above the horizon and its saffron reflection in the water.

"I want to explain . . . ," Rodrigo began in a shaking, half-audible voice. "I have no right to ask, but I beg you to hear my confession."

HALF AN HOUR LATER, by which time it was completely dark, they were sitting side by side on the ground. Rodrigo's face was pressed into his hands, and he was sobbing uncontrollably, as he had not done since the age of six. Alfonso, with an arm round his shoulders, waited till the paroxysms died down.

"You mustn't cry that way. You mustn't. Of course I forgive you. But, much more important, God has forgiven you."

"I can't forgive myself. I can't forgive myself."

"You must. It's pride not to."

"But I think of all the people whose lives I've ruined."

411

"You ought not to exaggerate your responsibility. There can be pride in that, too. Even if you had never set foot in Paraguay, we would still have been banished. Some other man would have been sent to do your work."

"I suppose so. I hadn't thought of that." From the more distinct sound of the words, Alfonso could tell that Rodrigo had taken his hands away from his face. "But I feel so . . . so appalled that it was I who did it. How could I have been so blind? It was all my conceit, my vanity, my obstinacy." And the young man's shoulders began to shake again.

Alfonso fumbled for his hands and took hold of them.

"Listen," he said, "there's something you have got to understand. Otherwise you are going to make the future miserable for yourself and for everyone around you. Remorse and sorrow are two quite different things—one bad, the other good. We feel remorse because we can't bring ourselves to accept our own weak and sinful nature. But that is just what we must do if we are ever to have peace. I have explained the ways in which you can or should make reparation. But we can never fully make up for the consequences of our offenses against other people. Only God can do that. But neither has any man the right to hold our sins against us, once we have repented, since he is capable of acting as badly or worse. What God wants is not that we should torment ourselves because we have fallen below our own ideal, but that we should have confidence in his love and mercy and accept patiently and humbly the discomfort of having to have a low opinion of ourselves."

WHEN ALL THE JESUITS north of the Paraná had been arrested, Captain Herrera led his force back to Candelaria. There the Governor was busy issuing regulations to remedy the chaos into which the Reductions had already fallen; regulations that, so it seemed to Rodrigo, were simply a restatement in verbose form of the policy already pursued by the Jesuits.

At the end of August, General Don Francisco set sail down the river with his ninety prisoners, leaving the majority of his forces at Candelaria. Rodrigo, who, in spite of Alfonso's words of consolation,

412

was still tormented by the sense of his responsibility for all the misery and harm that had been caused, went with him.

They reached Buenos Aires at the end of September. On the day of their arrival, the Jesuits were transferred to ocean-going ships ready for the journey to Europe, their captors still maintaining the pretence that they were desperate men who might at any minute break loose and start a rebellion.

Two days later, Don Francisco sent for Rodrigo.

"I suppose you'll be wanting to get back to Spain", he said.

"If I have Your Excellency's permission."

"I should be afraid to refuse it", Don Francisco said, "for fear of depriving Don Manuel any longer of your valuable services." He paused. Had he meant it ironically? Then, with a just perceptibly ingratiating note in his voice, he added, "You will be able to tell him what a neat little campaign we had."

The rest of the day Rodrigo spent arranging for his servant to travel back to Europe separately with his luggage. Then, at eleven that night, he left his lodgings alone and on foot, carrying only a bundle tied with a cord. When he reached the harbour, he picked his way through the refuse and stacks of merchandise to the far end, where, in the shadow of a pile of kegs and barrels, he took off his coat, undid his bundle, and put on a cassock and cloak. Before he had finished changing, he was joined by a sailor who waited in silence a few feet away. They crossed to the quay side. At the bottom of some steps, slippery with seaweed, another man sat in a row boat. Rodrigo and the sailor got into it, and a few moments later the boat was moving steadily out into the estuary. After ten minutes, the boatman pulled close to a ship at anchor.

"Are you sure this is the right one?" Rodrigo asked.

"Yes, sir", the sailor said, as he stood up, steadying himself against the ship's hull. "Ahoy there!"

A head appeared high above them, silhouetted against the stars. "What is it?"

"Do you have any Jesuits on board?"

"Yes."

"We've got another one for you. He got left behind."

"Who are you?"

"The Governor's men. You're to take him on board. The orders are here, written and signed by one of His Excellency's assistants."

"Wait a minute." Presently something was lowered down the side. "Put the paper in the bucket", the voice called. A few seconds later the bucket was drawn up to the deck, carrying with it a sealed paper weighed down with a block of wood.

"I'll find the captain. Stay where you are."

They waited a quarter of an hour. Rodrigo handed the sailor a bag of coins and thanked him in a low voice. The boatman looked up as the bag changed hands.

The voice came again from the ship's deck. "Watch out for your heads!"

There was a scraping, rattling sound, and the end of a rope ladder hit the water a few feet ahead of them.

"Send the prisoner up", the voice called. "He won't be lonely. We'll put him with his friends."

The sailor eased the boat slowly forward. Rodrigo caught hold of the ladder and, gripping his bundle with his teeth, began to climb the side of the ship.

SEVENTY-SEVEN

In the summer of 1768, the Marques de Torrelavega left Madrid for his estate near Sala de Los Infantes in the diocese of Lerma. His favourite mistress, Doña Ana Mariano, had gone ahead of him the week before and was already settled in the house he had given her there next to the Jesuit college.

It was more than a year and a half since the Marques had visited Sala de Los Infantes, so busy had he been with affairs of state, an expression which, with him, covered not only the actual business of ruling—of attending meetings of the Council, of receiving people in audience, of dictating orders and reports—but also his efforts to maintain his position against the intrigues of his enemies.

Although disliked as much as ever by most of his colleagues, it was difficult to get rid of him because of his involvement in the events leading to the expulsion of the Jesuits. Indeed, he was said to have threatened that if he were denied the posts he wanted, he would give the Papal Nuncio certain papers in his possession that would disclose the real nature of those events.

Among the affairs of state that had been occupying the Marques during the past months was the disposal of property belonging to the Society of Jesus. Nearly everyone at Court had been astonished by how little the Jesuits owned. The chests of gold, the enormous investments in trade, agriculture, and real estate, which so many courtiers had hoped to discover and to use, so they said, to finance philanthropic projects like the cutting of canals, the building of workhouses, and the paving and lighting of streets—all this long-looked-forward-to wealth was found to have no existence. However, there had been nearly five thousand Jesuits in Spain, and the buildings that housed them, together with their schools and the endowments given over the years to support them, were worth a sum which, if disappointingly less than what had been expected, was still large enough to interest even the richest grandee.

The Extraordinary Council, a special committee of the Council of Castile, had been made responsible for any business connected with the defunct Society, and the Marques, who was a member of it, had had himself appointed administrator of the Jesuit houses in the diocese of Lerma. However, to avoid the scandal of a layman disposing of ecclesiastical property, he had been forced to accept the Bishop of Lerma as his coadministrator. Since the Bishop was his cousin, the same who had dispensed his son Diego from the canonical impediments to being an abbot at seventeen, the Marques did not expect him to give any trouble. However, he believed in the usefulness of being certain about such things beforehand, so he stopped in Lerma on the way to his estate and called at the episcopal palace.

The Bishop was in his library, preparing a translation of the odes of Horace for the press. When his chamberlain announced the visitor, he jumped with fright. The movement caused his pen to splutter, ruining an entire page of the fair copy. Although only twenty-nine, his stomach already protruded noticeably under his violet sash.

"What a delightful surprise", he said, crossing the room to greet the Marques and masking the look of vexation on his face by an overly large and nervous smile. He half held out his hand in such a way that if the episcopal ring were not kissed, it might seem that he was simply making a gesture of welcome.

The chamberlain was still in the room, so the Marques knelt and brushed with his lips the large amethyst that symbolised the Bishop's marriage to his much-neglected diocese.

"I want your agreement to the transfer of some of the property at Sala de Los Infantes", the Marques said as soon as they were alone, cutting short the Bishop's questions about the health of the Marquesa.

"The Jesuits' property?"

"If it were anyone else's there would be no need to discuss it with you."

"But, my dear cousin, we can't go about disposing of it in bits and pieces. We must first talk it over systematically. We must have a policy. What about Tuesday next?"

"If you like. But there's nothing to stop us deciding about the land at Sala de Los Infantes right away."

"I never heard that they had much land there. I think there is just the church and the college."

"It's a question of the garden. I want it granted to Doña Ana Mariano."

The Bishop, who knew as well as anyone the nature of the Marques' relations with Doña Ana, took a quick breath and swallowed twice as if he had eaten something too heavily peppered.

"My dear cousin! I don't know how you can possibly make such a request."

"Why not? His Majesty wants the Jesuit property used for advancing agriculture, among other things, and Doña Ana is a keen agriculturalist.

Her garden is next door. With the extra land, she will doubtless carry out many interesting experiments."

The Marques' mocking tone made the Bishop feel he was trafficking with Satan more than he usually did when having to engage in business with his cousin. It was all he could do to prevent himself from making the sign of the cross.

"It's impossible. The scandal would ruin me."

"Nonsense! There will be no scandal. Who would dare make one? But if you insist on giving way to these ridiculous fears, then the Extraordinary Council will be unable to consider your recent request."

Loans from Jesuit funds at low interest, or altogether free of interest, had already been made to several grandees, and the Bishop had applied for one so as to complete the new library which he was building. The ceiling was to be frescoed by Mengs.

"You are asking me to commit simony", the Bishop said, becoming more and more agitated. "If you are making the transfer of this property a condition of the loan, I'll do without the loan."

"You've grown very scrupulous, cousin. I don't remember your being so afraid of simony when your parents bought your mitre."

"That's untrue—outrageously untrue!" The Bishop's voice rose a half octave. "I was consecrated and installed without anyone having received a maravedi. There was nothing sinful in giving a few presents afterward to show the family's appreciation of certain kindnesses beforehand."

The Marques shrugged his shoulders.

"If I sell you a sack of flour, what difference does it make whether I hand over the sack first or you hand over the money?"

All this talk about simony, the Marques decided, must mean that the Bishop wanted a larger loan. He could not conceive that a man as worldly as his cousin might have scruples of conscience or that, living as he did, he would waste his time quibbling over an extra sin or two, being already up to his neck in past ones, unless he had some ulterior motive.

The Bishop, however, while not possessing much else in the way of virtue, still had faith. He was planning to repent before he died and saw no reason to add unnecessarily to the length of time he would have to spend in Purgatory. In this respect at least he was more intelligent than his cousin. He recognised that disobeying God was not a particularly good reason for disbelieving in him.

"I won't discuss it any more. The question is closed." He walked about excitedly, fingering his pectoral cross.

The Marques saw that if he wanted to get the Bishop and his conscience over this hurdle, he would have to make things easy for him.

"Come, cousin. I put the matter badly. We must deal with one thing at a time. There are two separate questions. First, the loan. I have authority here in my pocket to grant it to you."

"I won't take it! I won't take it! Not if you're attaching conditions to it."

"There are no conditions. The question of land at Sala doesn't come into it. We can think about that afterward."

"Understand that if I accept the loan, I am in no way binding myself to oblige you in the other matter."

"Of course not."

"Very well, then. I consent to take the loan."

They were silent for about a minute. The Marques picked up the Latin text of Horace's odes and turned the pages with bored curiosity. The Bishop paced about the room, apparently given over to thought.

"I agree to this lady having the loan of the land for the time being," he said at last, looking at his purple slippers, "but there can be no question of giving it to her."

With this the Marques was satisfied, knowing that with the passage of time the distinction between loan and gift would become meaningless, since no one would be brave enough to try and make Doña Ana give it up.

After kneeling to kiss the Bishop's amethyst a second time—with a show of deference that made a parody of the obeisance—the Marques departed. When he had gone, the Bishop's conscience began to give him the spiritual equivalent of indigestion. He knelt down on a prie-dieu, which had been given to him because he collected a particular kind of marquetry furniture, and looked up at the crucifix, which he had bought because it was a work of art.

"Lord have mercy on me, a sinner", he said, feeling it was unlikely, in his case, that such a prayer would be heard. How often he had read Dante's *Inferno* for the resonance of its cadences. But now he saw himself burning in hell with Boniface VIII. He resolved to write to the Marques and again refuse the loan. Immediately his heart felt lighter. Then another thought came to him. The library! Life without the library would lose all point and savour. And his spirits sank.

For a long time he remained kneeling on the prie-dieu.

The astonished chamberlain kept opening the door and then going away on tiptoe. The Marques, he thought, must indeed be a terrifying man if he could drive Monsignor to prayer, let alone prayer of such length.

At last, after a struggle lasting for three-quarters of an hour, the Bishop began to yield to the library. I made it quite plain, he said to himself, the loan had nothing to do with the business about the garden. And besides, it's only fitting I should leave some public monument behind me. It shows that the Church respects learning.

And with other arguments of this kind, he once more turned back from the narrow way onto the broad road he had been idling along since he entered manhood.

SEVENTY-EIGHT

On reaching his palace at Sala de Los Infantes—a medieval fortress with baroque wings—the Marques sent for his bailiff and ordered him to have the wall separating the garden of the Jesuit college from that of Doña Ana Mariano pulled down. The bailiff blanched.

"Well?" the Marques said impatiently.

"My lord, the people won't like it."

"And seeing how much they love me, it would be a pity to lose their affection for such a trifle?"

Not daring to say more, the bailiff went to have the order carried out, wondering where to hide if the people rose in revolt.

After sending word to his mistress that he would have supper and spend the night with her, the Marques made his way to the tower where Diego was imprisoned.

"Give me the key", he said to the servant on duty in the room at the bottom. He took the key and mounted the spiral staircase alone. At the top, an armed man stood guard outside the door of Diego's room. "Go down and stay there till I call you", the Marques said.

He waited until the sound of the man's footsteps echoing up the stone shaft had died away. Then he unlocked the door and went in.

Diego was sitting at a table, his head in his hands, reading a book. The Marques had not seen him for nearly two years; he looked somehow taller, heavier, burlier. Supposing that the door had been opened by one of his gaolers, Diego continued to read for several seconds. When he looked up and saw his father, he closed the book and stood up slowly. To the Marques' surprise, he did not flush or turn pale. In fact, he seemed unaccountably composed.

During his imprisonment, Diego had had little to do but think, and one of the conclusions he had come to was that as much blame for the evils of life attached to people of too yielding a temperament, such as himself, as to those of violent disposition like his father. If only the weak were less cowardly, the strong would have fewer opportunities for doing harm. And so he had decided that it was his duty to master his fears and, when necessary, stand up to his father calmly but courageously.

They stared at each other for several seconds, but this time it was the Marques who dropped his eyes first.

"I have persuaded the King to pardon you", he said coldly. "You don't deserve it, but I hope you are satisfied."

Diego, forgetting for a moment his decision to be calm as well as courageous, jumped to his feet and made a movement as if to throw his arms round his father's neck.

"However, you must sign this document first."

The Marques spread the document on the table. It was a deed of conveyance by which Diego made over to his father one of the estates settled on him by General de Pradanos. But, since it was written in Latin, a language Diego did not understand, he was unable to read it.

"What does it say?"

"It says you are grateful to His Majesty for his clemency and that you are sorry for having offended him."

Diego sat down eagerly and took up a pen. He dipped it in the ink and wrote a capital 'D'. Then he stopped. He looked puzzled and put the pen down.

"But I'm not sorry."

The Marques, who was standing behind him, clenched his fists.

Diego looked round.

"What finally happened to the Jesuits?" he asked.

"There's no point in going into that. His Majesty expelled them a year ago."

"Oh, my God! Then they must have caught Jean."

"You can worry about your friends later. All I want is your signature."

"I'm not going to sign."

"Very well. You needn't say you're sorry. We'll cross out that part. You can just say you're grateful."

But Diego had become suspicious. Nothing his father could say would persuade him to sign. Finally the Marques lost his temper. He walked up and down reviling his son, reviling the Jesuits, reviling priests and religion, reviling General and Doña Mercedes de Pradanos.

"Would anyone but a fool be taken in by that old humbug in epaulets and his whore of a wife with her jangling rosary beads? What d'you think he goes prowling the streets at night for? All Madrid knows that he's got so many bastards he can't even count them all . . ."

Suddenly the Marques felt himself caught from behind and lifted off the ground. He struggled, but Diego had gripped him around the chest so that he could not move his arms, and he realised that of the two of them, his son was the stronger.

"Let me go", he bellowed.

But Diego paid no attention. Breathing hard, he heaved the Marques across the room and set him down on a chair. Then, still from the back, he quickly moved his hands and locked them round his father's throat. The Marques could feel Diego's fingers gradually contracting and pressing against his Adam's apple. For the first time in his life he experienced what he had so often inflicted on others. He's going to kill me, he thought, sitting completely still. Why did I send the guard away? Why did I leave Manso in Madrid? Even if I shout, no one will hear me up here.

"Before I let you go," Diego said in a hoarse voice, "you're going to hear the truth for once. A long time ago, when I was still a boy, I made up my mind that one day I'd get even with you. One day I would kill you. And now I have the opportunity. I could strangle you. You would be dead before anyone could come to your rescue. Four years ago if I had had this chance, I would have taken it. Only the fact that I met a Jesuit who helped me to change my life has saved you. It's the Jesuits— the Jesuits whom you have persecuted, libelled, and ruined—whom you have to thank for not being dead already."

Diego took away his hands and stepped back. Immediately the Marques leapt up, turned, and rushed at him. The violence of the attack knocked Diego over, and the Marques, losing his balance, too, fell on top of him. For a quarter of an hour they fought, first on the floor, then around and around the room, knocking over the furniture, bumping into the walls, rolling on the bed, gasping, struggling, tearing at each other. This time it was Diego who kept thinking: "He's going to kill me."

At last Diego got the Marques in a corner and, ducking to avoid a blow from his fist, rammed his head into his stomach. The Marques grunted like a winded horse and slumped to the floor. Quickly Diego rolled him over and sat on his chest.

"Now," he said, panting, when the Marques opened his eyes, "if I release you, do you promise to go this time?" The Marques glared up at him but did not answer.

"You'd better", Diego said. "I don't expect Manso told you about the beating I gave him last time he treated me to his insolence, or that he's afraid to come near me now and leaves that to the other men."

He got up. After a second or two, the Marques did the same and stood holding his sides and breathing rapidly and noisily through his mouth. His lip was bleeding, his coat and breeches were torn, and his right stocking hung down round his ankle. Suddenly he snatched up his wig, which had fallen off and lay half under the bed, and backed toward the door.

"You cur!" he said, as he fumbled in his pocket for the key. "I'll keep you here till you rot."

He let himself out, locked the door behind him, and went down the spiral staircase two steps at a time. His raging thoughts found expression through his feet; with each step he was trampling on Diego's face.

At the guardroom door, he threw the key to a sentry and strode on down a vaulted gallery. An arch at the end brought him, with an abrupt transition, from the ancient to the modern part of the palace. In one of the great drawing rooms, he caught sight of himself in the mirror. Two eyes, like oysters without their shells, goggled at him from a face the colour of uncooked liver. He went to his dressing room. Having filled a basin with water, he plunged his face into it. Then he rubbed his face and neck with a towel and, without ringing for his valet, changed his clothes.

His heart began to beat less violently, but his thoughts hurried on. What could make up for the outrage done to him? He roamed about his room picturing ways of making Diego suffer. Starvation? Flogging? Suspending him from the ceiling by his wrists? He recalled a book he had seen called *The Torture Chamber*; a quasi-pornographic work with engravings, printed in Amsterdam. As his mind passed from picture to picture, he drank them in like a man dying of thirst.

But the mere accumulation of horrors could not, in the end, appease a pride of such magnitude. Nothing could make up for the insult and humiliation he had suffered. On the other hand, there was a limit to the pain he could inflict on his son by way of revenge. At some point Diego would fall senseless or die and in this way escape him. Besides, in modern Spain, one had to be careful. Searching for an outlet for his thwarted sadism, he picked up a Delft dish for catching the soapsuds when he was shaved and dashed it on the floor. Then he ground the fragments into the carpet with the heel of his shoe.

At dusk he had himself carried by sedan to Doña Ana Mariano's. The house was a copy, in miniature, of Lord Burlington's villa at Chiswick. Doña Ana, aged twenty-two and prettier than any of the Marques' previous mistresses, was waiting for him in her little drawing room, which glittered with enamelled and jewelled knickknacks, china, crystal, and silver gilt—the trophies of her success and the safeguards of her future.

Dressed in pale blue taffeta with pink bows, she lay spread out on a yellow satin sofa, like a meal prepared by an innkeeper for a specially demanding guest. Bursting breasts, barely held back by her bodice, bulged over its lace-edged top like little melons about to tumble out of a cornucopia; a creamy forearm rested along the sofa's back; and a diminutive foot, from which the buckled slipper had been allowed to fall, projected in a white silk stocking from among the flounces of her skirt and nestled among the cushions.

"Just imagine", she began gaily, as the Marques entered, "what Pilar has been telling me about the nuns of San Agustín." But, seeing her lover's expression, she stopped. My God, what had happened? He looked like Vulcan after finding Venus in bed with Apollo.

The Marques sat down in a chair six feet away from the sofa.

"What are you looking at?" he demanded roughly. "Say something. Do you think I keep you here to sit in silence?"

Doña Ana told the story about the nuns. Then quickly, to avoid a second reprimand, began another. She had a rapid, pointed way of telling stories which usually made the Marques smile. Through her gossip, he also learned things to the disadvantage of his dependents, employees, and tenants. But tonight every story met with a moody look that made her heart pound against her corsets.

They went into dinner. The Marques ate and drank as though he had been living for the previous six weeks on crusts and cold water. Every few minutes his hand reached for the decanter. Doña Ana, assuming she was still under orders to make conversation, continued, with increasing desperation, to chatter until the capon was served, when, deciding that her talk was not being listened to, she fell silent.

The Marques looked up.

"Who told you to stop talking? Go on. Amuse me."

Amuse him? Holy Angels, how was it possible to be amusing when her heart was pumping at 120 beats a minute! But she obeyed, all the same. "Did you know . . . ? Have you heard . . . ? They say that Don Basilio and his housekeeper . . ." And all the time she was thinking: "Holy Virgin, how much longer" and: "What can I say next?"

At last the meal was over.

"Go to bed and wait for me", the Marques said. "And don't go to sleep."

She went. The bedroom was all pearl-coloured silk and gilded wood-work—until a short time ago, her heart's desire. Tonight she wished herself once more in the back street of Burgos where she had been found by the Marques' procurer. Her maid undressed her.

"How my head aches, Pilar", she said. "If people knew what I have to put up with, they wouldn't envy me all this luxury." She felt sorry for herself. It was a new experience. She had often before seen the Marques in a temper. She was used to it. But this brooding silence, these long evil looks and abrupt commands were new and frightening. As she climbed into bed, her eyelashes were wet. She lay between the sheets, shivering and praying. Praying? Why not? God was merciful. Like the Bishop, she meant to make a good confession before the end.

At half past eleven, the Marques appeared in a long dressing gown, open down to the waist. He had undressed next door. Without his wig, he appeared ten years older, and his cropped rumpled grey hair gave him the look of a still fierce but aging wolf. Grey hair also covered his chest; the skin underneath was an unhealthy white. By contrast, his flushed face and the upper part of his neck looked the colour of old Roman bricks.

In his right hand he held a lighted gilt candelabra. Swaying as he crossed the room, he set it down by the bed and with a single puff blew out the six gently quivering flames.

During the night, the Marques, still raging in his thoughts against Diego, and, by extension, against the world indiscriminately, used his mistress so brutally that she frequently cried out with pain. She, on her side, while returning his caresses, which were like blows rather than endearments, was thinking: "I hate you! I loathe you! I wish you were dead!"

At last they lay still—the Marques satiated and asleep; Doña Ana wakeful from jangled nerves and the spinning of her resentful thoughts. It was then that a beam in the roof collapsed, and they were buried under twenty tons of plaster, wood, and rubble. When the bodies were recovered Doña Ana was dead. The Marques was still breathing but survived only a few minutes.

SEVENTY-NINE

By six in the morning, everyone in Sala de Los Infantes had heard the news. The effects were instantaneous. After ransacking the palace for anything small enough to be easily movable and salable, the Marques' servants ran away. The workmen, who had been pulling down the wall between the two gardens, hurried to the site and, after crossing themselves, began to build the wall up again. Canon Moratin of the church of San Andres set off for Lerma to find out from the Bishop what was to be done about burying the victims, who appeared to have died in a state of mortal sin.

The Bishop was in his garden with his architect. Between them they held a sheet of parchment—the plan for the new library. On hearing the Canon's story, the Bishop dropped his edge of the parchment and saved himself from falling only by clinging to the arm of a nearby statue of Ceres.

"Leave us", he said to the architect, in a voice that sounded as though he had a piece of felt in his throat. The Canon helped the Bishop toward a seat a few paces away. *What on earth is the matter with him?* he wondered. *Surely he doesn't expect me to think he's overcome with grief.*

When they had sat down, the Bishop made the Canon describe again the circumstances of the Marques' death. As he repeated his story, the Canon noticed that the Bishop's face was turning the colour of the lichened stone they were sitting on.

"What a warning to sinners, my lord", he concluded.

"Yes, indeed. A fearful lesson to us all."

"Of course", the Canon said impatiently. By sinners, he had meant sensational ones, not the commonplace kind that even he himself had to admit to being. "People are already taking it to heart. I saw men at Mass this morning who, as far as I know, haven't entered a church for years."

"Ah!" the Bishop said faintly.

"A terrible judgment indeed", the Canon went on. "One can only fear the worst."

The Bishop, who had been sitting slumped like a man in a coma, jerked into life. "That is because you don't believe in God's mercy", he said fiercely.

"But, my lord, think of the circumstances."

"How do you know? Deaths like these are a public judgment—a lesson to the living. We have no right to conclude from them what the private judgment of the individuals concerned may be. You, Canon, because you have always led an upright life, are content with God's justice. But I, who have great need of God's mercy, am prepared to hope that he will have given, even to the most criminal, a moment to repent." He stood up abruptly. "Let us go to the chapel and say the 'De Profundis'."

Later, when the Canon had gone, the Bishop sent for his architect.

"There will be no library", he said. "Draw up new plans. I want the palace converted into an orphanage. You will leave a small apartment of four rooms for me above the kitchens." He dismissed the architect, and, sitting down at his writing table, he dipped a quill in the inkwell and started a letter to the Extraordinary Council in Madrid, refusing the loan from the confiscated Jesuit property.

DIEGO, MEANWHILE, was still in his room in the tower, wondering why no one had brought him his breakfast. He listened at the keyhole. Silence. This, he thought, is my punishment for yesterday—no food.

At midday, hearing distant shouts, cries, and laughter, he climbed on a chair and, pushing his head through the bars of the window, peered downward. Crowds of people—clearly not his father's servants—were roaming about the courtyard at the foot of the tower. Others leaned from windows of the first and second floors of the more modern part of the building, while behind them still others were passing back and forth through the shadowy rooms.

He heard someone calling through the door.

"Don Diego?"

"Yes."

"Are you locked in?"

"Yes. Who are you?"

"Wait. I'll get a hatchet."

The footsteps moved away. After twenty minutes Diego heard them returning.

"Stand back."

Soon a jagged hole opened in the middle. A man looked through. "Wait," the man said again, "I'll make it bigger." He hacked at the wood till the hole was twice as large and then climbed through.

"Who are you?" Diego repeated, never having seen the man before.

"One of the General's men."

"General de Pradanos? But he's in prison."

"No, sir, he's not in prison. He and her illustrious ladyship, the Countess, have been banished to their estate at Fonsagrada. As soon as the General knew where they had taken you, he sent me here to help you escape. I've been living in the town for a year, looking for a way to get in touch with you. This is the first chance I've had. Be quick, sir. Everything's ready—money, horses, baggage."

"But what's happened?" Diego asked, still not fully realising he was free.

"Your father died last night, sir. The whole place is in a turmoil. That's how I got in. The servants seem to have vanished. I'm not surprised. They weren't all that popular; they must have known what would be in store for them if they hadn't run away. People from the town are wandering all over the place."

"My father has died?" Diego stared at the man as if he had said "the ocean has dried up" or "horses and cows are talking." Then, as the words sank in, he turned pale. "How?" he asked.

"Excuse me, sir, but I'd better tell you about that when we're on our way."

"You're right", he said, at last taking in all the implications of his situation. "We must go at once. Help me to get my things together."

"Don't waste time over them, sir. I've got everything you need. His illustrious lordship, the General, wants us to go to Italy. To the Grand Duchy of Panaro. He says we'll be safe there. Here's his letter."

The man helped Diego to clamber through the hole in the door. Downstairs, the rooms were filled with tradesmen, workmen, peasants, and their wives and children. They were prodding the upholstery, fingering the curtains, gaping at the pictures, investigating the cabinets and chests of drawers.

The General's letter, which Diego opened and read as they hurried along the marble gallery to the main entrance of the palace, said that he had asked the Grand Duke of Panaro to give Diego a post at his Court until it was possible for him to return to Spain.

EIGHTY

The only person in Madrid on whom the Marques' death made more than a passing impression was his wife.

Doña Ines de Torrelavega's first reactions were of unqualified relief and thankfulness. He had gone. He had gone. She need no longer live in continual dread and anxiety. Never again. But as the circumstances of his death sank in, considerations of a different kind began to preoccupy her. She had never been a particularly religious woman and, while her husband was alive, had stifled any momentary inclinations in that direction as a precautionary measure. The Marques would tolerate only the barest religious conformity unavoidable in an officially Catholic country. But, unlike her cousin by marriage, the Bishop of Lerma, she had nothing serious on her conscience to trouble her. So now that she could think and act as she pleased without danger, she liked to remember the nuns who had educated her. Most of her brief childhood and girlhood before she had been married off to the Marques at sixteen had been as loveless as her son Diego's boyhood and youth. Only in the convent had she experienced true affection, and in recalling her few happy years there, she began to reassimilate the nuns' ideas and outlook. According to their teaching, it was difficult to see how her husband could be anywhere but in hell. On the other hand, whenever a local criminal was executed, they had always had the children pray and do acts of penance for the salvation of his soul, even when he had shown no sign of repentance. From now on this thought became the mainspring of her life.

She did not undergo any striking conversion. She was a woman of very limited understanding and certainly not heroic. Yet there was a kind of heroism in the dogged way she devoted her newfound peace and security to succouring her greatest and most formidable enemy in his deepest need.

For most of the rest of the Marques' associates and acquaintances, his death was, for a few weeks, the occasion of satisfaction, jubilation, or ribaldry; then they forgot about him.

"A blessing of providence, I call it", said the Marquis Grimaldi, when his secretary told him the news. In Don Jeronimo's theology, providence tended to be an agency occupied exclusively with his interests. "He was always setting people at loggerheads. Now we shall have some peace."

Just at this moment a page opened the door and announced, "His Excellency the Vicomte de Fougères." The secretary withdrew, and Don Jeronimo went forward to greet Monsieur Charville.

In the past two years terrestrial blessings had poured down on Monsieur Charville like confetti over a bridegroom and bride. With the help and advice of the Parisian financier Duverney, he had multiplied his investments many times, so that he was now on the way to being a very rich man; his enemy the Governor of Languedoc was dead; the first volume of his great history of the Provinces of the Roman Empire had just appeared under his own name and was everywhere being praised; and he had been created Vicomte de Fougères after paying the card debts of the Duchesse de Gramont, the Duc de Choiseul's sister.

"Did you know that Torrelavega has just died?" Don Jeronimo asked.

"What a good thing it didn't happen a couple of years ago. One can't deny he was useful."

And they began to talk about the reception the night before at the Princess of San Martino's.

"To come to the point of my visit," said Monsieur Charville, or Monsieur de Fougères as we must now call him, when they had said all there was to say about the Princess' guests, food, and entertainment, "we want you to remove the Jesuits from Corsica."

"We", Jeronimo thought. He talks as if he were King Louis himself. "Why?" he said aloud.

"Because the conditions they are living in are causing criticism."

"You've been listening to their hangers-on. I know from our agents that they are really quite comfortable. If they were not, their superiors wouldn't be able to keep them together."

"Perhaps you will believe this, then", the newly-made Vicomte said, handing Don Jeronimo a cutting from a newssheet. "It appeared in a London journal and says some pretty sharp things, which is all the more striking when one recalls how few friends the Jesuits have in England."

Don Jeronimo put the cutting down on his desk without reading it.

"I can't really be bothered with the sneers of the English. They'll use any pretext to discredit us. They're not in the least sorry for our Jesuits. In the past they have butchered Jesuits by the score. In fact, the English were the first to start the hue and cry against them. It's all humbug."

"Nevertheless, it would be a pity if the Jesuits' misfortunes were to gain them sympathisers. Besides, since we purchased Corsica from the

Genoese in May, it now belongs to us, and it would be inconsistent if, having suppressed the Society in France, we allowed it to continue in some other part of His Majesty's dominions."

"Your Court is being most unhelpful. Almost unfriendly."

"Not at all. You don't like having them in Spain. Why should we want them on French territory?"

"Well, perhaps you can suggest what we are to do with them", Don Jeronimo said. "We've tried our best to get them to desert and escape to the mainland, but only a minority have responded. We can't tip them into the sea. Maybe you could ask the English to offer them a refuge, since they're so anxious about their comfort."

"We needn't do anything as drastic as that", the Vicomte said with a smile. "The logical place for them is still the Papal States. We can't land them there openly; it would lead to public conflict with Rome. But there's a way around the difficulty. We have been in touch with the Genoese. They are prepared to let you put them ashore at Sestri, provided they come unofficially and provided they don't stop there. Once on the mainland, they can make their way to the Papal States via Parma, and Modena—by the back door, as it were. We have grounds for believing that the Holy See will let them in, if they come like this, privately, and not as the result of a directly hostile act on the part of your Court. It will be all the more difficult for the Pope to object, seeing that he has recently given refuge to the Jesuits expelled from Naples, Parma, and Malta."

"We will consider it", Don Jeronimo said.

"Then please be as quick as you can. In spite of what your agents tell you, the situation is serious. We have had to send reinforcements to the island. Most of the buildings the Jesuits were living in have been requisitioned. Many of them are now sleeping in the open. There's less food than ever, and the older ones are falling sick and dying by the dozen."

After quitting Don Jeronimo, Monsieur de Fougères went to see Monsieur Laborde. There was no question of going on foot this time. He drove in his own carriage, with his own servants, who were wearing his personal livery.

Leaving the carriage in the street, he passed under the arch used by the wagons and went into the courtyard. It was beginning to fill with lumber again. The adornments bought to pacify Madame Laborde had to rub shoulders with crates and cartwheels; the basin of the fountain was dry; the evergreens were dying in their tubs for lack of water.

He recalled his first visit. Madrid had certainly been his lucky city. Without Laborde at the start, he could never have built up a fortune so fast. The chance that had stretched him senseless on Don Maurice's doorstep had worked in his favour, too. Not that he felt particularly elated at the public consequences of his activities. What was the use of having driven into exile hundreds of excellent schoolmasters? It could only mean that Spain would take longer than ever to come up to French or English standards of efficiency and civilisation.

Sometimes, he said to himself, I think that we who supposedly believe in reason are even more fanatical than our opponents who believe in the Trinity. The King of Spain behaves like an inquisitor, and theoretically enlightened people clap their hands and call him a friend of progress. Meanwhile the *parlement* of Paris, full of philosophically minded lawyers and free-thinking *gens de lettres*, has actually descended to burning the Jesuits' books. I suppose they would say that their end justifies their means. Which is what they accuse the Jesuits of preaching. I wonder if they do? Someone, I imagine, must have waded through all their impossible volumes of theology to find out. The fact is people only pretend to be shocked by the principle when it doesn't work to their advantage.

In this way, with what passes for wisdom among those who have decided to skate on the surface of life, he composed his thoughts and directed them into their customary channels. Seriously to regret any aspect of his activities in Spain was beyond the resources of what was now his nature.

Monsieur Laborde came out to greet his client and took him indoors. The house was full of boxes and trunks, some half full, some corded and sealed.

"What a good thing you called, Monsieur le Vicomte. I didn't know you were in Madrid. Your visit will save me writing a long letter."

"Are you leaving?"

"Yes, Monsieur le Vicomte. A nephew is taking over the business here. I'm going back to France to be with my wife and daughter. You perhaps remember, Monsieur, that Madeleine wanted to marry a Monsieur Mesnier, a Frenchman living in Madrid. But there's no foreseeing what women are going to do from one minute to the next. At the last minute she changed her mind. She decided to fall in love with a young man called Houdin who used to work here—an excellent fellow. He took the fancy of some rich Spaniards, who gave him enough money to start up in business on his own. He and Madeleine were married last year. Mesnier was annoyed about it, of course. But I said: 'She can choose whomever she pleases, provided the man can support her decently.' They've gone ahead with my wife to get things ready at home, while I'm teaching my nephew the ropes here. He's had plenty of experience handling other people's investments, Monsieur, and he understands your affairs perfectly."

Over the past year, many angry letters, full of reproaches and self-justification, had passed between Monsieur Laborde and his wife at Lyons. But in the end, the fact that Jean-Paul Houdin now had money of his own and that his business was prospering had gradually reconciled his father-in-law to what had happened. Monsieur Laborde still regretted the financial advantages that the marriage of his daughter to Mesnier would have brought him. But he knew that he was beaten. He was going back to Lyons because he could no longer bear life without a wife to look after the house and to keep him warm in bed at night.

"It has been a pleasure to see you again, Monsieur le Vicomte", he said, when he had presented his nephew and had satisfied Monsieur de Fougères that his money would still be in safe hands. "If you are ever in Lyons, I hope you will do us the honour of calling. The address is 12 rue des Martyres."

And at the thought that in future Monsieur de Fougères would be bullying his nephew instead of himself, he suddenly felt so carefree that he almost meant the invitation to be accepted.

EIGHTY-ONE

In late October, when the air smelled of bonfires and footpaths were coated with golden layers of sodden leaves, the Conte Malaforga, a young man in his twenties with the flushed and over-full face of a middle-aged *bon viveur*, was pacing the forecourt of his villa just outside the capital of the small but strategically desirable Grand Duchy of Panaro, which lay in the foothills of the Apennines between Modena and the Papal States.

A carriage drive led down from the villa to an entrance adequate for the triumph of a Caesar—arches of rusticated stone, urns, trophies, caryatids. The road to Parma, rutted and shining with puddles, was visible through the rusty gates. Beyond and below, the Po valley was still hidden by its covering of morning mist.

"They are late", Malaforga said, turning to his lawyer, who walked beside him.

"They are Spaniards", the lawyer said.

"Do you think we're asking too little?"

"If you ask any more, they'll lease some other place. They have already inspected the Villa Spinella and the Palazzo Testadandolo."

"But they sound as rich as English milords."

"The richer people are, the more they dislike being overcharged."

"Still, they expect me to forego the use of my villa for a whole year."

"Not much of a hardship, Excellency, since you live more in Venice than Panaro, and when here you seem to prefer Signora Tedeschi's house to your own. I must remind Your Excellency that you need money urgently. You can't afford to have these people go elsewhere."

"I wonder why they should want to spend a year in a godforsaken place like Panaro", Malaforga said, as though speaking to himself.

"Some people prefer peace to the excitement of the Venetian gaming tables."

Malaforga frowned. Undoubtedly, as his debts mounted, so did the impertinence of his lawyer.

"Look," he said, "here they are."

An old man, who guarded the property in the Conte Malaforga's absence, was pulling open the gates. A carriage drove through, climbed the drive, and stopped before the steps leading to the *piano nobile*. Jumping down from his box, the coachman opened the carriage door and helped the occupants, a man and two women, to get out.

As he walked forward to greet his tenants-to-be, Malaforga looked admiringly at the younger of the two women. "A beauty!" he thought. And a blonde beauty, too. Who would have expected that? She looks sad, though. I suppose she's been kept hidden in one of those dismal Spanish houses filled with duennas and dwarfs. And now they've brought her abroad to get her away from the lover she's never done anything more than wave a handkerchief to when he strummed his guitar in the street outside. The mother's a striking-looking woman, too. Not much of the proud Spaniard about the father, however. Crushed by the domineering wife, perhaps.

Malaforga presented himself, and the tour of the house began. The main reception rooms were sparsely furnished, disproportionately large, and frescoed with architectural fantasies that seemed to double their already overpowering size. Talking with the women, Malaforga led the way. Their presence had transformed him. The lawyer was astonished by his client's sudden fluency.

"This is the *salone*", Malaforga said. "The Signora will notice the ceiling. One of Pomponi's masterpieces. The view from these windows is admirable. The Signorina will find that temple at the top of the cypress walk a delightful retreat if she wants solitude or has an interesting book. Now this statue of Hercules in the alcove here has an appealing story attached to it. When my grandfather was absent, fighting for King Charles of Spain during his conquest of the Two Sicilies, my grandmother used every day to hang a fresh garland of flowers around that statue's neck. Its features reminded her of my grandfather's. My grandparents were distractedly in love with each other."

The girl, who up to this point had looked apathetic and listless, went over to the alcove and gazed at the statue attentively. "How touching. Did you hear that, Mother?"

"Yes, my dear. Very interesting. But . . ." The older woman turned to Malaforga, ". . . The rooms do seem", she hesitated, "a little empty."

"Yes? Yes, I suppose they might . . . at first. But I can't stand overfurnished rooms, you know. I must have space." He waved his arms. "It elevates the mind . . . inspires noble sentiments."

"What a beautiful idea!" the girl said. She looked at Malaforga approvingly.

Space! Noble sentiments! *Mio dio*, the lawyer thought, that's a masterly way of covering up the fact that most of your possessions have been carted off by your creditors. I've done this young man an injustice. If he handled money as cleverly as he handles women, he would be as rich as the Sultan of Turkey.

"I still feel these rooms are rather large for us", the older woman said. "We shall not be entertaining much."

The lawyer glided forward.

"The Signor Conte will be happy to make more reasonable terms."

Malaforga gave him a quick scowl, then turned back, with a smile as bland as custard, to the women.

"I understand. The Signora will perhaps prefer the intimacy of the *sala rosa* and the *salotto*." He threw open a door. "My mother's apartments. Perfect for the family circle. I can see that the Signora approves of them."

If the other rooms had been too big, these, by contrast, seemed rather small. But the rose-coloured damask on the walls gave a feeling of warmth, and the gilt chairs and tables, which were decorated with pieces of glass, twinkled prettily.

"What do you think, Maurice?"

437

"Just as you wish, my dear. If you like the place we will take it."

"Do say 'yes', Mother." The girl spoke pleadingly. "I'm sure we shall be happy here. As happy as we can be."

"Very well, my darling."

The husband turned to Malaforga.

"It is settled, then. We would like to move in as soon as possible."

EIGHTY-TWO

In the *sala da pranzo*, the afternoon sun, caught by the Venetian looking glasses on the walls, filled the upper part of the room with light, as the footman, in a shabby Malaforga livery, circled the table, removing the Meissen soup plates.

Doña Teresa de Vallecas waited until the footman had handed the next course and had left the room, then she turned to Diego de Torrelavega, who sat on her right, dressed in his uniform of extra-assistant equerry to the Grand Duke.

"I think", she said, "we ought to be careful how we talk, except among ourselves. One of the servants may know Spanish."

Under her high lace cap, her hair was whiter, while her face, instead of being lined and sharpened by care, had simply been mellowed by it and made more gentle, the outlines softened, the colours muted.

It was the de Vallecas' first day at the Villa Malaforga. At noon, while they had been unpacking, Diego had come cantering up the drive. He had just heard of their arrival while on duty at court. They had greeted him with the excitement natural to exiles finding a fellow exile unexpectedly and had made him stay to dinner. Beatriz, her parents noticed, had changed into one of her prettier dresses. It was a long time since she had made any effort to please.

"You're quite safe in Panaro, Doña Teresa", Diego said expansively. "The Grand Duke is on the side of the Holy See and the Jesuits, and the people all hate the King of Spain."

Don Maurice, whose head was bowed over his plate, looked up slowly.

"So we have heard, Don Diego", he said. "So we have heard. Yes. Undoubtedly you're right. But Doña Teresa is right too. We must be prudent; it is always possible that some of the servants may have been bribed by Spanish agents."

His tentative way of expressing himself made Diego feel uncomfortable. He would have preferred to hear the Don Maurice he had known in the past—vigorous, confident, authoritative—even though he had been half-afraid of him.

"Something rather disagreeable happened to us in Parma on our way here from Vienna", Doña Teresa said. "Our rooms at the inn there were searched while we were at the theatre. It has made us perhaps unnecessarily suspicious. And now you must go on telling us what became of your servant after you were arrested."

"Jean-Paul? He's in Lyons."

"But did he get to Rome?"

"Yes. But he had difficulty in getting to the Pope. You can imagine what it was like for a fellow like Jean-Paul, all by himself. The papal chamberlain, to whom the General had given us a letter, had just died. Jean was passed from one official to another. Then, one night, when he had been in Rome for about a week, he was attacked in the street. He escaped, but not without some nasty stab wounds, and he was a month recovering. By the time he managed to see the Holy Father, it was too late."

After dinner they moved to the *salotto*, where portraits of Malaforga's ancestors—a warrior in wig and cuirass, a girl peeping from behind a domino, a dissipated-looking Canon of the Lateran—hung on the panels of faded Genoa velvet.

They talked for a while to the sound of the hissing chestnut logs in the fireplace. Then Don Maurice went into the *sala rosa* next door to take a siesta; Doña Teresa moved a tapestry screen closer to her chair so as to shield her face from the heat and picked up some embroidery; and Beatriz led Diego to a table in the window to look at her portfolio of sketches.

"And Doña Isabel?" Diego said in a low voice, holding up to the light a watercolour of the Lake of Constance. "Why did you leave her behind?"

"She didn't want to come", Beatriz answered in a half-whisper. "She was afraid to. So Father said that while we were away she could live with Gaspar and Luisa."

"But she used to be so anxious to travel."

"You don't understand, Don Diego. We aren't ordinary travellers. We're in disgrace."

"Because of your brothers?"

"Not just that. Many people have Jesuit sons and brothers. But immediately after the expulsion, my father resigned all his positions. The King was terribly angry. But what else could Father do? Soon it was being said that he had taken part in the plot to have the King assassinated. People stopped coming to see us and asking us to their houses."

"They wouldn't have kept me from visiting you", Diego said indignantly.

"That's because you are brave, Don Diego. But in the last year I've learned that there are far fewer courageous men than I used to think. They may be brave about losing their lives, but not many are brave about endangering their social position or property. It was thought there would be arrests and executions as in Lisbon. It hasn't been as bad as that. But no one could be sure. It's high treason to defend the Jesuits or to criticise the King's action."

"Your father is an exile, then?"

"A voluntary one. He thought that from Italy we should be able to send help to Jaime in Corsica and get news of Alfonso. We can't see them, of course. If we did and were found out, Father could have all his property confiscated."

"In view of what you say, I'm surprised you were allowed to leave."

"Father let it be known that we had been invited to stay in Vienna with my mother's cousin, who is a *hofdame* to the Empress and very close to her. The King, it seems, is especially anxious not to annoy the Empress."

"I would have thought Doña Isabel would have felt safer out of the country with you and your parents?"

"It was Luisa's fault. She kept telling her that Father was out of his mind, that we should be reduced to poverty, that the only way to avoid total family disgrace was for her to stay behind in Madrid. You mustn't, please, blame Isabel. She's only a child still, really. You couldn't expect her not to be scared. Much older people were."

Diego stared at the carpet; he seemed to have fallen into a trance. For almost a minute he remained silent and motionless. Then, recollecting himself, he looked up, blushing.

On the other side of the room, Doña Teresa was dozing. Her head nodded rhythmically up and down; her embroidery had slid from her lap onto the floor.

"And your Father?" Diego whispered. "Has he been ill?"

"No, it's the shock. You remember how he revered the King? Up to the last minute he was assuring everybody that the Jesuits weren't in the slightest danger. He couldn't believe that His Majesty was their enemy. Ever since, he has seemed to have no more trust in himself." She hesitated, as if weighing up how much she had the right to say. "To make things worse," she went on, "he reproaches himself for having quarrelled with my cousin Rodrigo. He feels he ought to have been more understanding. After all, if the King could be misled about the Jesuits, it isn't surprising Rodrigo was. And on top of everything else, he's discovered that Monsieur Charville, whom we all thought so devout and whom he paid to act as Rodrigo's travelling companion, was a French spy and a well-known unbeliever. Poor, poor, Father! He has had one humiliation after another."

Her left hand and forearm, soft and dimpled, lay in her lap close to Diego's knee. On an impulse he bent forward, took her hand and kissed it. Then, appalled at himself, he waited, still in the same position, for her rebuke.

She drew her hand away, but all he heard were the murmured words, "Kind friend!" Then, in an ordinary tone again, "Look, you haven't admired my sketch of Prince Eugène's Belvedere."

EIGHTY-THREE

It was late in the afternoon by the time Diego left the Villa Malaforga to return to Panaro. Above and below on the hillsides, wavering lights pierced the luminous blue beginnings of darkness. He rode slowly, listening to the suck and pull of his horse's hooves in the mud and occasionally singing, gruffly and out of tune, a fragment of one of the arias that the tenor Corradini warbled so effortlessly at the opera house.

Suddenly, with the feeling that he had been doing something indecent, he broke off. What was he thinking of? What was he doing feeling happy? He had just heard that Doña Isabel, the woman he had once thought he would like to marry and whom he had been expecting to find with her parents and sister, was hundreds of miles away in Spain. Why wasn't he disappointed?

Then, abruptly, as if he had been awakened by an explosion, he saw the truth. He did not in the least care about Doña Isabel. He never had. He had persuaded himself that he liked her to give himself an excuse for continuing to see her sister. Doña Beatriz was the one he had been in love with all along, only he had been so much in awe of her that he had never dared admit it to himself.

Oh, my God! he thought. What am I going to do? She's probably still in love with her cousin. From the way her voice shook when she mentioned him, it's almost certain. But perhaps the cousin has married someone else. That might explain why she was upset. Or he could be dead. No. No. Not that. I'll think about it all later.

Shocked by his callousness and egotism, he dug his heels into the horse's sides and urged it to a trot. At the gate of the town he was forced to stop. The vaulted brick tunnel, built in late Roman times by one of the Exarchs of Ravenna, was blocked by a crowd of excited Panarese.

"What's the matter?" Diego asked, leaning down and shaking the shoulder of a *contadino* with a shovel over his shoulder. Half a dozen people turned their heads and answered simultaneously.

"The Jesuits."

"From Corsica."

"They walked all the way from Sestri."

"The Spaniards put them ashore . . . just like that. Without money, clothes, anything."

"The barbarians! The infidels!"

"Down with Spain! Death to King Carlo!"

Diego stood up in his stirrups. A lantern hanging by an iron chain from the centre of the arch faintly lit the scene below. In the middle of the crowd, a corporal of the grand-ducal guard was questioning a group of about fifteen bearded men dressed in a random collection of clothes, none of them clerical.

"Friends", suddenly shouted a six-foot man with rolled-up sleeves and a neck almost as thick as his head. "King Carlo's a long way off, but his representative lives here in Panaro. Let's go and show him what we think of him."

There were cries of "Down with the Spanish representative", and part of the crowd broke away, following the man at a run up the cobbled street to the centre of the town, where the Spanish representative Don Henrique Lerida had his residence.

Diego urged his horse farther under the arch. Peering through the twilight, he saw a face he thought he knew.

"Don Jaime!" he shouted. One of the men looked round. "Don Jaime, it's I", Diego called in Spanish. "Diego de Torrelavega. Your father and mother are here. I've just left them."

For a few moments Jaime de Vallecas stared at him uncomprehendingly.

"It's true", Diego shouted again. "I'll take you to them."

Jaime spoke hurriedly to one of his companions and began pushing his way through the mass of gesticulating bodies. "*La mia famiglia, la mia famiglia*", he kept repeating. At these words, once so powerful over Italian hearts, the Panarese not only made way for him but propelled him toward Diego with cries of "*Son fratelli. Va bene!*"

"Don Diego! What are you doing here? Where are they?" With his weather-beaten face and uncut black hair and beard, he looked not unlike an early Franciscan.

"They're living in a villa only a mile away", Diego said. "Where's Father Padilla?"

"He's with another party. We split up to make it easier to find places to sleep at night."

"Jump up behind me."

Jaime felt his legs gripped by half a dozen hands and was heaved onto the horse's back.

"*Grazie, grazie*", he called.

"Hold tight", Diego said, and shook the reins.

In a short time they were back at the Villa Malaforga. Diego threw his right leg over the horse's neck and slipped to the ground. "I'll go ahead and warn them", he said, and ran up the steps. Jaime dismounted and walked the horse up and down the forecourt. He was still wondering confusedly what his parents could be doing in Panaro when Diego came back.

"I've told them", Diego said. "They're waiting for you."

"But aren't you going to come in, too?"

"No, no. They've seen enough of me. I'll call tomorrow."

He vaulted into the saddle and, leaving Jaime in the darkness, cantered off down the drive. Before turning into the road he slowed his horse to a walk and looked back. A figure with open arms stood at the top of the steps silhouetted against the lighted doorway, and a voice cried "Jaime!" in a tone that made Diego's nerves tingle. If only there were someone in the world to call his name with that ecstatic joyfulness.

He rode on. Halfway between the Villa Malaforga and Panaro he stopped at an inn, and, after tying his horse to a nail on the wall, he went inside, ordered a glass of wine, and sat down at a table. He was filled with a longing for love, a wife, a home; for someone who belonged to him and to whom he belonged; for a place he could come back to with the feeling that he was rejoining a severed part of himself.

Why shouldn't I try to win her love? he thought. I have as much right to it as the cousin has. If I succeed, the fault is his for neglecting her.

No. It was useless. He was incapable of inspiring love. Her kindness to him was merely the expression of her general goodness of heart. He would go away and fight in the armies of the King of Prussia, dying at last, unmarried, on some central European battlefield.

But he knew he hadn't the strength of character for prolonged self-sacrifice.

What was he going to do, then?

After three-quarters of an hour he got up, paid, and left the inn without having decided anything. While unhitching his horse, he saw a glow in the sky above the centre of the town. My God, he thought, Don Henrique. They've set fire to his house.

Throwing himself into the saddle, he started off at a gallop—down the road, through the Modena gate, up the Via dei Falegnami, past the ghostly white marble Gothic front of the cathedral, along the Corso Cevalcore.

In the Piazza Gran Ducale, a crowd of several thousand were dancing and yelling around a twenty-foot high bonfire, with a dummy wearing a pasteboard crown and a placard around the neck saying *"Carlo, Re di Spagna"* perched on top.

DURING THE NEXT FEW DAYS, increasing numbers of destitute Jesuits passed through the Grand Duchy on their way to the Papal States. The Panarese mob, delighted at having repeated excuses for working off their feelings of hostility toward a power they saw as altogether too big and interfering, smashed Don Henrique's windows, scrawled insults on the walls of his house, and, whenever his carriage appeared in public, plastered it with mud.

After delivering a protest to the Grand Duke's chief minister, Don Henrique departed to the town of Bagno del Cavallo to "take a cure".

On the evening of Jaime's third day at the Villa Malaforga, a servant came into the *salotto* and told Don Maurice that he was wanted in the library.

The library was a gloomy, unused room on the far side of the hall. The books had all been sold, and in place of their close-packed leather spines, the walls presented ranks of gaping shelves.

Don Maurice opened the door and paused. In front of the empty fireplace stood a man in a greatcoat glistening with raindrops. His face was in shadow. The only light came from a single candle above and behind him on the mantelpiece.

"Yes?" Don Maurice said in Italian. "What can I do for you?"

"You have a son, a Jesuit, staying here."

"Who are you?"

"Don Henrique Lerida wishes to remind you that the Spanish subjects are forbidden to harbour Jesuits. You have until tomorrow to get rid of him." And before Don Maurice could reply, the man slipped from the room, buttoning up his greatcoat as he went.

"What is it?" Doña Teresa asked anxiously, when he returned to the *salotto*.

Don Maurice sat down, flushed and trembling. "It's no good", he said despairingly. "You will have to go, Jaime. It was a message from Lerida. They already know you're here."

"Never mind, Father", Jaime said, sitting down beside him and taking his hand. "I would have had to leave in another day or two, anyway. The others will be expecting me."

"I know, I know", Don Maurice said. "But the infamy of it all! God forgive me, but may they live to suffer for it."

EIGHTY-FOUR

Don Maurice's first audience with the Grand Duke did not take place until the middle of December.

Gian Achille VI Cevalcore was the only enlightened autocrat in Europe who, while cultivating his mind, had not attenuated his faith or, while professing to believe that the Pope was Vicar of Christ, did not allow his ministers to treat him like a defaulting debtor. He was also an example of the fact that, in certain circumstances, an inferior political system can work as well as, or better than, a superior one. Everything depends on the quality of the man or men in power.

In the Middle Ages Panaro had been a republic. But early in the sixteenth century, Gian Achille's family, the Cevalcores, the richest of its citizens, had, through a mixture of clever manoeuvres and propitious circumstances, become its ruling house. To begin with, their fellow rulers, while willing to borrow their money, had looked down on them for having made it in trade. But time, which makes almost everything respectable, had in the end made the Cevalcores indistinguishable from other reigning families. They dressed like them, thought like them, married into them, and eventually had come to look like them. For the past hundred years, they had been incapable of winning a battle and had so completely forgotten the art of business that they were always in debt to half a dozen different banking houses.

Just before the birth of Gian Achille, it had seemed likely that the Cevalcores would die out. The three previous Dukes had each been more eccentric and indolent than the one before. But in Gian Achille, the decaying family had unexpectedly put out a healthy shoot.

The Grand Duke received Don Maurice in a drawing room of his private apartments. He was tall, and his lean face, hooked nose, dark eyes, and big supple mouth called to mind the portraits of his shrewd mercantile forbears hanging in a group at the far end of the room rather than those of his later more exalted ancestors scattered about elsewhere.

The Grand Duchess and their six youngest children were present. After a quarter of an hour of conventional courtesies—"We hope", the Grand Duchess said, "that we shall see your wife and daughter with you at the gala on the twenty-ninth"—the Grand Duke took Don Maurice into the cabinet where he kept his collection of prints and drawings.

"We lay aside ceremony here, Don Maurice", he said, sitting down and indicating with a gesture that Don Maurice was to do the same. "We have heard all about you from young Torrelavega." As he spoke, he fondled the head of his favourite mastiff, which sat beside him with its muzzle resting on his right knee and its eyes adoringly watching his face. "But we have waited before summoning you so as not to arouse speculation, which, if reported in the wrong places, might cause inconvenience for both of us. You know our friend General de Pradanos, we hear." He looked quickly and searchingly at Don Maurice, who realised that he was being weighed in the balance.

"Yes, indeed, Your Highness, and I love him dearly. Your Highness, I expect, will have heard how he has recently been made to pay for his courage." The emotion with which Don Maurice spoke, the slight tremor in his voice by which he was himself surprised, must have tipped the scales in his favour. The initial reserve in the Grand Duke's manner evaporated.

"You yourself, Don Maurice, from what we have been told, have been no less brave," he said warmly, "and we wish you to know how much we admire the stand you have taken. Unfortunately, prudence compels us to keep our sentiments hidden from all except you. Defiant gestures are not for states like ours. If Panaro is to keep its independence and you and your family are to remain unmolested, we must not provoke His Spanish Majesty. But, insofar as we can, we shall give you our protection, and we hope that you will regard Panaro as a home. And now we would like to hear about the events leading up to your departure. It has been difficult to get reliable news. You can safely open your heart to us. Nothing you say will go beyond these walls."

Before his meeting with the Grand Duke, Don Maurice had been harassed by the thought that he had perhaps exposed his family to trouble and danger merely for the sake of a quixotic display of principle. The Grand Duke's friendliness and approval did much to restore his peace of mind and self-confidence.

THIS FIRST AUDIENCE was followed by many more—generally in the evening and usually in the print room, to which Don Maurice was brought by an equerry up a private staircase from a side entrance. Although they talked about many subjects, their conversations nearly always ended with the escalating conflict between the Catholic courts and the Holy See.

At first the Grand Duke's frankness embarrassed Don Maurice. He was not used to discussing the failings of princes so bluntly—especially not with someone who was himself a prince. Throughout his life, the intelligence that in a courtroom had enabled him to see in a flash who was telling the truth and who was lying, had always appeared to abandon him in the face of royalty. To use common sense about them had seemed like sacrilege. However, the Grand Duke viewed them from a different angle. He had several times had to thwart attempts by Vienna, Paris, and Madrid to filch his duchy from him.

"The Catholic kings do not see where they are going", he said, late one January night after they had been talking for more than an hour. "Absolutism, if that is what we are to call the concentration of authority largely in one man, appears to be at its apogee in Europe today. But its death knell is already sounding, and the kings themselves are helping to dig the grave."

He was silent for a while, watching the light of the flames flicker on the marble putti around the fireplace. Outside it was snowing. The mastiff, lying between them on the carpet, whimpered in its sleep, and its back legs kicked. "Bella, Bella! Wake up! You're dreaming", the Grand Duke said, touching the dog lightly in the ribs with the toe of his buckled shoe. The dog opened its eyes, closed them again, and turned on its other side.

"As a form of government," he went on, "absolutism seems to me

449

essentially a system for emergencies, for restoring order after periods of social turmoil or disintegration. It can last over extended periods only where there is a long-established way of life to which the majority of the people are attached, where there are few new ideas; and where there are no powerful social groups who feel that their interests are not sufficiently attended to. But today in Europe at least two of those conditions for survival are absent. There is a wealth of new ideas; and there are at least two social groups anxious to have more influence: the new literati who disseminate the ideas and the expanding mercantile class anxious to throw off the customary restraints that limit their capacity to make money. We have some of them here in Panaro. For the time being these two groups are content to let things go on as they are, provided they have the ear of the prince or his minister. Also, they are still uncertain of their own strength. But were they to discover it . . .''

On another occasion he said, ''The objection to absolutism is not that the ruler will necessarily be a tyrant. The system is as likely to throw up King Log as King Stork. The objection, in my opinion, is that it enervates the classes who ought to be sharing in government, either because of their natural capacities or their social position, turning them into sycophants, intriguers or good-for-nothings, or, for want of their having nothing better to do, forcing their energies into unprofitable activities—unprofitable, I mean, for the good of society as a whole.''

He drew Don Maurice toward a window. By this time it was spring, and beyond the parterre below, they could see an avenue of stone monsters leading up to a cavern formed by the open mouth of a gigantic frog.

''Built by our grandfather with the help of his first minister, and that sort of thing was his principal occupation during a reign of more than thirty years. But he probably did less harm than a ruler with ideas bent on reform at all costs. On the whole, he was popular. Rulers do not need ideas so much as wisdom, intelligence, and a sympathetic understanding of their people's real needs.''

The Grand Duke's two youngest children, aged five and three, were playing in the parterre with a go-cart, watched by a nurse. Catching sight of their father, they waved excitedly. The Grand Duke waved back.

During the course of the summer, he approached the subject from a different angle. "If, as I believe," he said, "our cousins in Paris, Madrid, Lisbon, and Vienna are moving blindly toward disaster, it is because they forget that absolutism in Europe is of recent origin and something foreign to its genius. Up to two hundred years ago authority was dispersed. The nobles, we can say, ruled the countryside, the merchants the towns, the monarchy presided over the whole, and the Church, from outside the temporal order, spoke in the name of God. These four sources of authority worked together in theory for the common good and, to some extent, achieved it by acting as a check on each other. It was not a perfect state of affairs, but it was capable of improvement. It was destroyed by the cult of classical antiquity, which corrupted the minds of princes by reintroducing the principle that the will of the prince is law, by giving them a taste for imperial splendours, and by teaching them to regard fame and glory as worthy goals of national policy. As I see it, it is this essentially pagan approach to government and the state that is responsible for the attitude of today's Catholic courts to the Church and the Holy See. Caesar, whether a single man or a group of men, has never wanted his subjects to hear a voice that contradicts his own. But in the past he accepted that such a voice had a right to exist. Today, by prohibiting the publication of papal teaching and injunctions without special permission, they are trying to silence that voice completely. Like England's Henry VIII, each wants to be Pope as well as Caesar. If they continue on their present course, they will soon have taken their countries into schism. They could learn a lesson from England. What happened to the English monarchy after it destroyed the old balance of social forces by crushing the feudal nobility and enslaving the Church? It was gradually crushed in its turn by a powerful new land-owning class of non-noble origin. Once a workable social balance has been destroyed, it is extremely difficult to restore. By emasculating the nobility and now trying to muzzle the Church, our Catholic kings are opening the door to the eventual rule of the literati and the new men of money."

"If you will forgive me, Your Highness, I cannot see the King of Spain ever openly breaking with the Pope. His Majesty, in his peculiar way, is so very devout."

"So was our great-uncle, after his second marriage." The Grand Duke pointed to a bust of Louis XIV in the role of Apollo. An aureol of silver-gilt rays projected from the marble curls of his wig like blunted dinner knives. "That did not prevent him, when he quarrelled with Innocent XI, from turning the French embassy in Rome into an armed camp or having the heretical Gallican articles taught to the French clergy."

"Is it perhaps because Your Highness is Caesar in Panaro", Don Maurice said with a smile, "that you are so hard on Caesar? Surely it is not always the temporal ruler who is at fault? Louis IX of France was a saint, yet he had his differences with the Pope of his day. Your Highness will surely admit that it is possible for churchmen to trespass beyond their domain."

"Indeed, yes. We had our differences with the last Archbishop of Panaro. He tried to force the university here to accept one of his nephews as rector. But between the papacy and the Catholic courts today, the trespassing is now all in the other direction. None of today's rulers is a saint."

"Saintly kings have always been rarities, Your Highness."

The Grand Duke's long, rather sensual-looking mouth was smiling, but his dark eyes looked melancholy.

"True. We mustn't set too high a standard. But we mustn't set it too low either. The kings and their flatterers say the Curia loves gold. But whose fault is that? The fault of the kings, surely? They provide the gold. If they stopped bribing the Pope's servants, there would be more hope of having none but honest priests in the Curia. The kings talk about reforming the Church, but if they really loved reform, they would appoint holy bishops. Nearly everywhere they have usurped the power of nomination, and look at the kind of men they choose."

IN FEBRUARY 1769 came the news that Pope Clement XIII had died. The conclave to choose his successor met on February 15. From Rome the Grand Duke's representative reported the manoeuvres of the French, Spanish, Portuguese, and Neapolitan courts to get a candidate to their liking elected.

Outside the conclave, the French and Spanish envoys, Aubeterre and Azpuru, were working with bribes and threats. They were letting it be known that should a cardinal be chosen of whom their master did not approve, they would refuse to recognise him as Pope and leave Rome. Inside, the Bourbon and Braganza cardinals were using methods of persuasion considered more suited to the dignity of their office and the sensitivities of their colleagues. The Spanish Cardinal Solis was said to be trying to extract a signed promise from every member of the sacred college willing to listen that they would suppress the Jesuits if or when elected.

In May, on the feast of San Bernardino, Don Maurice was unexpectedly summoned to the palace in the morning. As usual, he was taken to the print room. When the Grand Duke entered, he stopped on the threshold and said gravely, "*Habemus papam.*"

"Who, Highness?" Don Maurice asked anxiously, when he had made his bow and kissed the Grand Duke's hand.

"I will give you a hint. A member of a religious order."

"A Franciscan?"

The Grand Duke nodded.

"Ganganelli?"

"I fear so. He has taken the name Clement XIV."

"Then Your Highness was right. The Catholic kings, or their ministers, have won."

EIGHTY-FIVE

"There is something I want to talk to you about, my love", Doña Teresa said to Beatriz, as they sat together in the grotto at the bottom of the cascade.

Beyond the serrated entrance, a wall of green shut in the view— the deep shadelike green of ilex, cypress, and bay. The only sound was the drip and splash of the water that trickled down the avalanche of sham rocks in which the cascade ended and fell into the stagnant, weed-

453

choked basin at its foot. Inside the grotto, whose walls were lined with shells and artificial stalactites and whose floor was paved with different-coloured pebbles worked into a pattern of scallops and conches, the air was cool, the light muted and toneless.

It was a June morning in 1771. The de Vallecases had now been at the Villa Malaforga for nearly three years. During that time they had heard neither of Rodrigo nor of Alfonso. All they knew, by letters from Spain, was that Rodrigo had not reappeared in Madrid. As for Alfonso, they had begun to fear that he must be dead. Other Jesuits from Paraguay had long since reached the Papal States.

As soon as her mother spoke, Beatriz's face became expressionless. For the last six months she had become more and more withdrawn. Now it was as though the windows of a house had suddenly been shuttered and barred from inside.

"Since we've had no news of Rodrigo for so long . . ." Doña Teresa said. She hesitated and glanced at Beatriz. "What I wanted to say", she continued, "was that under the circumstances I don't think you are still bound by any promise you may have made him. So if you feel your heart drawn elsewhere, you ought to feel free to follow it."

Beatriz bent over her work. Doña Teresa allowed a minute or two to go by in silence.

"I wonder if you realise", she continued, "that Don Diego de Torrelavega is very much in love with you."

Beatriz, who was stitching a piece of embroidery, held up her needle to rethread it. For more than a minute she struggled to push the silk through the eye. Then she dropped her work and stood up quickly.

"It's not true", she said vehemently. "He wanted to marry Isabel."

"If he did, I don't think he wants to any longer."

"Oh, why do you say this, Mama? You must know it only makes me miserable."

She snatched her straw hat, which she had laid on the seat beside her, and left the grotto. A few minutes later she came running back and, with a pathetic expression, knelt crying beside her mother. "I don't know what to do. I love them both. If I encourage Don Diego, Rodrigo may come back when it is too late, and then I shall be miserable. And if

I wait for Rodrigo, Don Diego may give up hope, and I shall perhaps lose them both. Life is horrible . . . horrible. . . .”

ABOUT A MONTH LATER, mother and daughter were again sitting in the grotto, working at their embroidery and talking quietly about the peasant families they had got to know on their walks about the estate, when they were interrupted by the sound of hurried footsteps on the gravel and, glancing up, saw, framed in the grotto's entrance, an agitated servant bowing apologetically.

"What is it, Vittorio?"

"If I might speak a word with the signora in private."

Doña Teresa went outside.

"There is a foreigner here, signora." Vittorio said in an undertone. "He insists on talking to you. He says he has a message from Spain."

"From Spain? Holy Virgin, protect us!" Doña Teresa began hurrying down the steps toward the villa.

"Let me go first, signora", Vittorio said, running to catch up with her. "He looks like a vagabond. Who knows if he is telling the truth?"

He took her around to the side of the villa and through a door on the ground floor into a cavernous passage giving onto the kitchens, the laundry, the storerooms, and the cellars. Halfway along it, a man sat slumped on a wooden bench. In the shadowy light he resembled one of the beggars who, back in Madrid, used to cluster like hungry birds on the steps of San Placido. Hearing footsteps, he looked up, then slowly rose from the bench like a soldier injured in battle whose wounds have grown stiff. He was tall, emaciated, and very dirty.

Doña Teresa felt frightened. Terrors and expectations tumbled in disorder through her mind like sticks being swept over a waterfall. Vittorio was right. Who would have sent a message by a man like this? He looks like a convict—an escaped convict. Perhaps a prisoner from the galleys. What shall I do? But why does he look at me in that strange way? Perhaps he's mad. Now he's smiling. It isn't possible . . . it isn't possible . . .

She ran forward. "Oh, my darling! My Alfonso!" They clung to each

455

other. Vittorio tiptoed away and disappeared into the kitchens. After several minutes, still holding hands, they sat down together on the bench.

"Mother," Alfonso said in a flat, husky voice, "there's a further surprise for you."

"Rodrigo?" she said quickly, half-afraid.

"He's had a complete change of heart. And he's with me."

"It can't be true! It can't be true!" Now Doña Teresa was crying and laughing.

"I had to leave him six miles back along the road. He was too weak to walk any farther. We've been together for the last two and a half years. I'll tell you about it later."

Doña Teresa dropped Alfonso's hands and stood up. "Vittorio," she called, "tell them to bring the carriage. Hurry, please. Hurry."

"Can you send someone for a doctor, too?"

"Yes. Yes. And they can be getting a room ready while we are fetching him. Poor boy! Oh, my poor boy!"

LATER, in the twilight of the *salone*, which had been shuttered against the afternoon heat, beneath Pomponi's gods and goddesses tumbling in lustful frenzy across the ceiling, Alfonso and his parents sat talking in lowered voices. A few feet away, the door to the Pompeian room stood ajar, and through it they could see the end of the canopied bed in which Rodrigo, watched over by Beatriz and her maid, was lying unconscious.

"We had no idea he had gone to the Americas", Doña Teresa whispered. "And then?"

"On the way back we were shipwrecked off the coast of Portugal, near a place called Lourinha", Alfonso said. His hands, moving nervously on the arms of his chair as he talked, were wasted like those of a very old man. He had bathed and was wearing a black suit belonging to his father. "When the authorities there found that seven of us were Jesuits —seven, that is, with Rodrigo, who was dressed as a lay brother—they shipped us to Lisbon, and in Lisbon they imprisoned us in the fortress of St. Julian, where they left us until they let us out three months ago."

For about a minute Alfonso was silent. He sat staring at his lap and seemed to have forgotten about his parents.

"It wasn't so much the physical conditions," he said at last, in an even lower voice, "the lack of food, the damp, the dark, the vermin. It was the thought that we were there for good."

Don Maurice leaned forward to catch his words. Alfonso rubbed his hands together as if they were cold. "We were in an underground chamber, half the size of this room, chained to the walls. I was at the end of the inside wall, in a corner. If it hadn't been for Rodrigo, who was chained next to me, I would have gone out of my mind. How can I describe what he was like. He never murmured, never seemed to think of himself. His patience and courage were inexplicable. When I had fever, he stripped off most of his clothes to cover me and make a pillow for my head. He gave me the greater part of his rations and drinking water. And I took them, God forgive me. That's what prison can do for you."

"He wanted to make up for what had happened", Doña Teresa said gently.

"He's done more than that . . . a hundred times over. It's he that ought to have been the priest, not I."

"My dear one, you mustn't reproach yourself. You have all of you suffered appallingly."

"Yes, I suppose it's true. Yet it's nothing to what the Portuguese Jesuits are going through. All told, it seems, there are about sixty of them in the fortress. In our cell, we had ten chained in pits in the floor, which at high tide filled with a foot and a half of water. They've been like that for twelve years."

"How can they possibly still be alive?"

"I don't know. It's even more incredible if you've actually been in the place. We used to get a glimpse of them by the light of the lanterns when the gaolers brought us our food—just their faces, framed in the tops of the holes. Sometimes we heard them singing to keep up their spirits and reciting the psalms aloud. And we would try to talk to them in Latin. Their clothes rotted away long ago. They get a new shirt once a year. In winter the cold is deadly."

"Why were you and the other six set free, do you think?"

"I believe the Imperial Ambassador heard about us and protested. Father Huber and Father Mayer were Austrians. So they let all six of us out."

"All seven, you mean."

"No. You see . . . you see . . . Father Huber . . ."

Don Maurice slipped quickly down on his knees beside Alfonso's chair and put his arms round his shoulders. Alfonso bent his head and shielded his eyes. His starved body shook.

"I loved him so much", he said in a piteous voice. "For pure goodness, he was like nobody else I have ever met. And he died only the day before we were released."

EIGHTY-SIX

After a month, Alfonso, still looking prematurely aged and gaunt, left for the Papal States to join the Spanish Jesuits, who had formed a community for themselves at Faenza.

By this time the Spanish representative in Panaro had received instructions from Madrid not to trouble Don Maurice and his family any further.

When Alfonso had gone, life at the Villa Malaforga was caught into the rhythm of Rodrigo's illness. Doña Teresa and Beatriz, with the help of maids they had brought with them from Spain, took turns nursing him. Don Maurice did his share, too, and surprised the women by his gentleness and skill. His reconciliation with Rodrigo had brought out a tenderness in his character that, like subterranean waters suddenly released by a geological upheaval, had only now, through adversity, found a way to the surface.

Volpi, the Court physician called in to attend Rodrigo, diagnosed his weakness as "general debility". Nature, he said, was the best doctor, and time, sleep, and good food would eventually restore the patient to health. But time and sleep did not cure Rodrigo's continuous cough, did not heal the sores round his ankles and wrists made by the irons he had worn in prison, did not relieve the attacks of fever and delirium that recurred at intervals of ten days. And, in spite of food, he remained as frail and light as a young girl.

Losing faith in Volpi, Don Maurice sent for Bamberelli of Padua. The famous doctor arrived, listened with a scornful smile to Volpi's opinion, examined Rodrigo as cursorily as a connoisseur inspecting a doubtful antiquity, and announced the "correct diagnosis"—infection of the pulmonary tissue and morbid condition of the bile duct. His remedies were brutal: boiling hot plasters for back and chest, purgings, bleedings, plunging of the patient's fever-racked body into ice-cold water.

Rodrigo submitted to the treatment with only an occasional, involuntary moan. In the end it was the nurses, not the patient, who rebelled.

"I can't stand any more of this", Don Maurice said. "Bamberelli may have a great reputation, but his treatment goes against common sense. And I distrust the judgment of a man with so little human feeling. We must get someone else."

The Grand Duchess recommended Guastaverza, a doctor at Bologna, who treated diseases with herbs.

Guastaverza came and prescribed tisanes, broths, inhalations. Gratefully they banished Bamberelli's instruments of torture and set to work steeping leaves and simmering roots and berries.

Rodrigo began to improve. Soon he was strong enough to spend the day in a chair. As the winter went on, the hopes of his family rose. In March, with the first warm days, they had him carried into the garden. For hours he lay in the shadow of the gigantic columns of the portico, holding Beatriz's hand and gazing at the sunlight on the shrubs and paths.

In Easter week they were married. The wedding, conducted by the Grand Duke's confessor, Father Morosini, took place in the *salone*. Rodrigo made his responses sitting. Thirty-six hours later, the wound on his right ankle started to suppurate again. Gangrene developed; the infection spread quickly, and before they had adjusted themselves to the seriousness of the relapse, Rodrigo was dead.

The funeral followed within two days. In a hearse like a state coach, with silver angels weeping on the corners and horses caparisoned in black, his body was taken to the nearby village of Milminore and there, after a Requiem Mass in the church of San Filastro packed with peasant women saying their rosaries, was buried in a corner of the *camposanto* on the hillside.

THREE WEEKS LATER, the abbess of the Poor Clares of Panaro was talking to a visitor in the whitewashed parlour of her convent, an ancient rustic-looking building that stood above the gorge of the River Becchia just outside the Rimini gate. She sat sideways to the grille with her veil raised, her rough hands folded in her lap, and her bare feet tucked out of sight under her habit. Although she was seventy, her features had the gentle roundedness of stones worn smooth to the touch over the centuries by the sea.

The young woman on the other side of the grille was dressed all in black—black silk dress, black cloak, black hood, and from a black velvet ribbon around her throat hung a pendant set in a circle of brilliants containing a lock of black hair. The band of fair hair framing the white face beneath the hood gave the only touch of colour to the picture.

"But what, my child," she asked, "makes you think you have a vocation?"

The abbess' voice, in which all vibrations of disordered or exaggerated emotion had long ago been stilled, fell on the silence of the parlour with the calming effect of summer rain.

Beatriz was looking at the wedding ring gleaming on the third finger of her right hand. "So many things, Mother, that have happened in the last seven years seem to point to it."

"Yes, yes. I have read the Archbishop's letter of recommendation. You have suffered greatly, my poor child. But the loss of your husband so soon after marriage is not in itself a sign that you are called to the life of the cloister."

"There are other reasons, Mother."

"What, my child?"

"It's difficult to explain." Beatriz's voice quivered. She remembered the night on the road to Aranjuez when the carriage had overturned and the Queen's ladies had shrieked like half-strangled peacocks. Had not an inner voice seemed to tell her that if she trusted God, everything would come right? In a sense, of course, it had. Rodrigo had returned. They had been married. How terrible it would have been if he had died in prison and she had never known what had happened to him. How terrible if they had never been reconciled. But if God could do so much, why could he not have done that little bit more and have kept Rodrigo alive?

"Oh, Mother, I'm afraid", she said, and there was anguish in her voice. "Afraid of myself. I didn't know what I was like before. But now . . . There have been times in the last three weeks when I have almost hated God. Why did he bring my husband back only to let him die? But that's not all." A sob broke from her. After a pause, she went on in a lower voice. "The moment before my husband died, he suddenly said 'Jesus' and then 'Father', and such a wonderful expression came into his eyes that I knew he was seeing God. I ought to have been filled with joy. Instead, I thought, 'All he cares about now is God. God matters more to him than I do.' I felt jealous of God. Oh, Mother, if you don't take me, I shall lose my soul."

The abbess said, "My dear child, it's just as possible to lose your soul in a convent as in the world—it's done differently, that's all. You mustn't pay any attention to these feelings. They are the result of all the sorrow you have had. Do you think that if you really hated God you would be offering to give the rest of your life to him? And your husband, now that he is in heaven, loves you more, not less. Genuine love of God unites us; it does not divide." She turned away to cough. "And now, about your request", she went on. "It seems to me that at present you

461

are far too upset to make any important decisions. I suggest that you come back and talk to me at the end of six months."

"But will you take me then, Mother?"

"We will see, my child. We will see. If it is God's will."

EPILOGUE

Extracts from the Diary of
Father Alfonso de Vallecas

Faenza, Papal States: August 18, 1773

Today they gathered us together in the refectory to read us the papal brief, *Dominus ac Redemptor*, by which the Society of Jesus is dissolved forever throughout the entire world.

Although the Holy Father had been expected to do this from the time of his election, it has taken the Bourbon Courts and the King of Portugal four years to get him to sign and issue the brief—four years during which their ambassadors in Rome have ceaselessly bullied and insulted him.

It seems that the turning point came when the Empress, too, agreed to ask for the suppression of our Society. Before this, she had held back. They say she was won over when the Court of Versailles suggested the marriage between her daughter the Archduchess Marie Antoinette and the Dauphin.

By the terms of the brief, we are now secular priests, released from our vows of obedience and poverty, forbidden to live in community or to work together in any way.

May God's holy and adorable will be done in this as in all things.

Faenza, 5 Via Maiano: September 26th, 1773

Jaime and I are living here in a couple of rented rooms. For the last two months our Father General, Father Lorenzo Ricci, has been confined to the English College in Rome. There had been some kind of trial, but although he was cleared of the accusations brought against him by the agents of the Portuguese and Bourbon Courts, he was not released. Today we learned that he has been moved to the Castel Sant'Angelo. The present Holy Father has never been favourable to us. Nevertheless the pressure on him must have been tremendous.

Total spiritual darkness. In the afternoon Father Pignatelli called. I opened my heart to him. He said: "We are poor, we are reviled, therefore we are close to Christ. If misfortune makes us feel farther from Christ, then we are only half-Christian and our enemies have defeated us in every sense. But if we understand Christ properly, our enemies can't

win, since for us it is through defeat that we win our greatest victories."
There was nothing new in this, but he can say things you have heard
many times, and you feel you are understanding them for the first time.

Faenza: September 1774

Letter from Panaro. Beatriz and her husband, Diego, have a son. They
have called him Alfonso.

Faenza: March 1775

The lot of our priests and brothers is hard indeed. To have released
them from their vow of poverty was scarcely necessary. Most of them
live alone in little rooms in foreign towns, spied on by agents of the
Bourbon courts, threatened if they try to get in touch with their relations
at home, and forbidden in many cases from acting as priests. They are
without occupation or resources. Their pensions are paid irregularly and
often not at all. How can anyone judge with severity the few who give
in or fall into bad ways and fail to admire the many who accept injustice
without complaint? I can speak for them because, thanks to my father,
Jaime and I are not in want.

My father's generosity to the former members of the Society seems
endless. Father Pignatelli, who, by common agreement, has become our
spokesman and representative, tells him who are most in need. But there
are so many to help, and although everybody gave at first, after a while
enthusiasm cooled. You can't blame people. Other events come along to
distract them. To the world at large, the story is over.

Faenza: August 1775

Our Father General is said to have appealed to the new Pope, Pius VI,
to ask for his release.

Faenza: December 3, 1775

Death of our Father General, still in prison, on November 24. The Holy
Father ordered a solemn funeral. He is said to have been considering his

release. Why did he not free him as soon as he became Pope? Because, we can assume, it would have been interpreted as a sign that he was planning the immediate restoration of the Society, with who knows what countermeasures from the powers.

The Jesuit College, Polotsk, White Russia: February 1776

We reached this town last night by sleigh from Warsaw—Jaime, Father Padilla, and I along with four other priests of our former Society—one French, one Neapolitan, and two Portuguese. The journey from Italy took three weeks. Jesuits from many different countries have joined the community here. They gave us an overwhelming reception.

Now I must explain why a Jesuit college still exists here, three years after the Society's suppression.

By the recent treaty between Russia, Prussia, and Austria, the Empress Catherine acquired a number of Polish provinces, and with them a great many Polish Jesuits as subjects. As was to be expected of a correspondent of Voltaire, she did not initially have a very favourable opinion of us. However, in the course of a visit to Polotsk, she inspected our college here and was, it seems, impressed by what she saw. So much so, in fact, that she decided our schools were a good influence and would raise the standard of education in her Empire. Because of this, when the brief suppressing the Society arrived, she forbade it to be published in her dominions, and a brief that is not published does not canonically come into force. This is why we can continue to exist as a religious order inside the Russian empire without being in schism. Furthermore, the Catholic Bishop of Mohilev, in whose diocese we are, has forbidden us to disband for fear that our doing so would anger the Empress and endanger the rest of her Catholic subjects. Rome, under pressure from the Catholic Courts, has publicly been pressing the Empress to execute the brief but, we understand, is more than happy to tolerate the situation.

Polotsk: June, 1778

Yesterday, Jaime got into an argument about the Society with a Russian visitor. In defending it, Jaime made extravagant claims for us. Afterward,

Father Padilla said: "When a man has been unjustly convicted of certain crimes and executed for them, it is not necessary, in order to restore his good name, to prove that he was totally without faults. All that is necessary is to prove that he did not commit the crimes he is accused of. That is what we must do. Our members are not, and never have been, without failings. There have been Jesuits who were, in some measure, overbearing, narrow-minded, petty, tactless, mediocre, or weak. In admitting that, we are not playing into the hands of our enemies. If ordinary human failings that are common to everybody deserve the treatment we have received, then there is no class of men—whether lawyers, statesmen, writers, scientists, scholars or merchants—that ought not to be rooted out and suppressed."

St. Petersburg, The Oregin Palace: December 1780

I reached the capital two days ago. Last winter, Prince Oregin asked our rector at Polotsk for a priest to educate his sons and act as chaplain to his wife, who is a Catholic.

St. Petersburg: May 1782

The other day the Prince showed me a book by the German naturalist Baron Cornelius Voss, describing his travels in Paraguay. Here is what the Baron says about the Reductions:

> I examined everything that was to be seen and questioned the Indians carefully about their customs, system of government, and way of life under the Jesuits, and all that they told me, coupled with the evidence of the buildings, roads, and farm lands that still remain, compelled my admiration. But the traveller today sees only the decaying relics of what was once a flourishing civilisation. The buildings are ruinous and abandoned. The fruit trees are running wild. The fields and gardens are poorly kept. In many places the forest is swallowing what was once cultivated land, and the number of inhabitants diminishes year by year. One of the Reductions I visited was deserted. In another, the priest

468

had an Indian mistress and went about armed to protect himself from his flock!

The words wrung my heart. At the same time I couldn't help thinking, "At last we are vindicated." But what does that matter compared to the loss for the Indians, and how many people are going to read the book.

St. Petersburg: November 1788

A letter from Panaro. Now that King Charles III is dead, Beatriz and Diego, with their five sons and two daughters, are going back to Spain. Gaspar has persuaded the new King to pardon Diego.

Beatriz writes: "Do not be anxious about the graves of our parents and Rodrigo. The Micheles, who have been so kind to us here, have undertaken to see that they are properly cared for after we leave."

St. Petersburg: December 1794

Yesterday evening I was in the Princess Oregin's drawing room, playing chess with Andrei Vassilievitch while the Princess made a crayon sketch of us. The clock, I remember, had just chimed six when Andrei Vassilievitch looked up at his mother and said, "Listen! A sleigh in the courtyard. I wonder who it is?" "Aunt Tatiana, I expect", the Princess replied. Scarcely a minute later, or so it seemed, Prince Oregin's steward, Mikail Nicolaiev, came hurriedly into the room and spoke to the Princess in an undertone. She started up with a slight cry and followed him out. Five minutes went by, in which Andrei Vassilievitch and I pretended to be still absorbed in our game. Then the doors of the drawing room opened again, and an elderly woman entered. Her dress and hair were concealed by a black velvet cloak and hood lined with sable, on which a few frost crystals still sparkled. "The Empress, Father!" Andrei Vassilievitch whispered to me as we both got quickly to our feet. He hastened forward, knelt, and kissed the Imperial hand. I did the same. The Princess, looking troubled, was just behind her.

"This is Father de Vallecas, Your Majesty", she said. "You can talk to him here without fear of being disturbed." She made a sign to her son, curtsied, and then the two of them withdrew. The Empress and I were alone.

It is difficult to convey the feeling of awe one has at suddenly finding oneself in the presence of an absolute ruler like the Empress Catherine. Outwardly there was nothing impressive about her—a stout woman in her sixties with a white puffy face and breathless from climbing the stairs. But the knowledge that she has the power of life and death over millions of people—including myself—made me feel exceedingly small and defenceless, as though I had been exposed all at once without protection to all the elements at once. Fantastic thoughts ran through my head. What had I done, said, or written that she would take exception to?

Meanwhile, the Empress had moved toward the fireplace and had taken possession of the Princess' chair.

"Come and sit down here, Father", she said, pointing to the chair on which Andrei had been sitting. "We have often heard Princess Oregin sing your praises, and so we thought it would be pleasant to have a quiet talk with you. But we do not want there to be any misunderstanding. We like the conversation of intelligent men. That is all. We are not interested in learning about the teachings of the Church of Rome. We are a faithful daughter of the Holy Orthodox Church."

Having lost most of her teeth, she looked older when speaking. She pushed back her hood and opened her cloak. Underneath she was wearing a scarlet jacket, frogged and braided like an officer's uniform, and a green velvet skirt like a riding habit. Her fingers played continually with the buttons on the jacket. She began to talk about the work of our Society in Poland. After paying us some compliments, which I think she meant sincerely, she moved on to speak about the education of her subjects in the rest of her Empire. I took advantage of a pause to thank her for all that she has done for us.

"The Fathers of our Society pray daily for Your Majesty," I said, "and I am sure no more fervent prayers are offered for Your Majesty's welfare."

"Enough, Father! Enough!" she said. But she looked pleased, nevertheless. "We have simply profited by the stupidity of our fellow sovereigns." She played for a moment with her muff; then she looked at me with a curious expression, half-suspicious and half-hopeful. "We have been wondering, Father, what you think about the death of King Louis? We suppose you regard it as a divine punishment."

"Why, Your Majesty?"

"For having suppressed your Society."

"But, Your Majesty, that happened under King Louis XV. And besides, the King of Portugal was the first to exile the Jesuits."

"Then you see no connection between the two events?" She sounded, I thought, disappointed.

"A connection, yes, Your Majesty. But I would not like to maintain that in dying on the scaffold King Louis was necessarily expiating this one act of his grandfather's reign, or that this act was anything but a remote and tributary cause of his death. In no sense was he himself to blame."

"But if God does not punish your persecutors, is one to suppose that he will not reward your protectors?" She sounded affronted, like a child who has been denied a promised doll.

"God will certainly reward Your Majesty", I said. "And in the most abundant manner. But Your Majesty forgets that rewards and punishments are not all distributed in this world. One has to be careful, I think, not to take too simple a view of the way God acts in history."

"What about those French writers, then? You can't say that some of them have not been punished. Condorcet, dead in prison. And Charville, or de Fougères, as he started calling himself . . . did you know him?"

"Not personally."

"Guillotined. Had you heard?"

"Yes, Your Majesty."

The Empress was silent for about a minute. Her thoughts must have agitated her considerably, because her face suddenly became mottled with red blotches.

"What a pack of scribblers, the whole lot!" she said abruptly and angrily. "To think that I corresponded with them! So did the King of

471

Prussia. We must have been out of our minds. Look at what it has all led to. I regret nothing in my life so much as having let myself be flattered by that cynical intriguer Voltaire and the rest of his cabal of literary sycophants. Surely, Father, you can't say that they are not very largely to blame for this . . . this . . . this diabolic revolution in France?"

"It would be hard to maintain they were not responsible for the turn it has taken."

I began to understand the way the Empress' mind had been working and the reason for her visit. She wanted to discover whether God would allow a revolution to break out in Russia to punish her for having corresponded with the encyclopaedists, or whether, even though she had been guilty in that respect, he would reward her generosity to our Society by giving her his protection.

"It seems to me, Your Majesty," I continued, "that where the French philosophers did most harm was in substituting for Christianity a new and, in my opinion of course, an erroneous view of man and history—a new religion, in fact."

The Empress opened her eyes wide. She makes great use of them in talking, and they are very expressive. "You are playing with words, Father. Religion is the one thing the *philosophes* detest."

"The Christian religion, yes. But not, in a broader sense, religion as such. Are they not trespassing on the field of religion when they tell us that the destiny of man is to make a heaven on earth?"

"Then you do not believe in progress?"

"It depends what is meant by the word, Your Majesty. If to Your Majesty the word implies useful change, then certainly I believe in progress. But see what use the word has been put to by the present French government."

This time her eyebrows came together, making a double furrow above her nose.

"Hypocrites! Murderers!" She spoke with such energy that I almost jumped in my chair.

"And yet they always act, so they say, with the highest intentions. That, Your Majesty, is the curious thing. Never have so many fine

472

speeches been made about the greatness and goodness of man as while the guillotine has been cutting off men's heads. The revolutionaries believe they have the truth and, consequently, that everything they do is justified. Only another year or two of violence, only a few more laws, and the world will be transformed. Perfect freedom, perfect justice, perfect equality, lasting forever and ever! Such a goal seems worth almost any sacrifice."

"A false and wicked doctrine!"

"Unquestionably. But Your Majesty must surely see how compelling it is to men who no longer believe in the immortality of the soul or in an absolute moral order. Otherwise, what meaning would life and history have for them? They are atheists who, because they were brought up as Christians, cannot tolerate the idea that history is meaningless, though that is the conclusion that atheism necessarily implies. We Christians are more fortunate. For us, the salvation of the individual is what comes first, so that history finds its meaning, not in some remote future that no one now alive can possibly live long enough to enjoy, but in the present moment, at the death of each man and woman, no matter what is happening in the world as a whole, no matter whether civilisation is advancing or retreating."

The Empress looked at the jewelled watch fastened by a ribbon to the lapel of her jacket. Then she folded her hands in her lap, and there was something mocking in her expression as she said; "So the philosophers are right to say that Christians are more interested in getting to heaven than in trying to make the world a better place?"

"Only insofar as they are speaking of selfish Christians, those who can imagine that they can love God and yet neglect his command to love their neighbour. Let me put it this way. Which will benefit society and civilisation more, Your Majesty? Which will provide men with the stronger motive for acting well? A religion that requires us to make the best possible use of our talents and to help each other in our material needs, promising heaven to those who obey and, according to the degree of our disobedience, Purgatory or hell to those who do not; or a philosophy that has no unalterable standards, that can justify any

473

course of action provided it appears to lead to the hoped-for goal, and that offers no better reward for virtue than the promise that one day, if all goes well, our remote descendants are going to be less unfortunate than we are?"

"And why, Father, are you so sure there can never be a utopia? I have heard that you used to rule one in Paraguay."

"The Reductions, Your Majesty, were not a utopia, though it is unlikely the world will ever produce a society more closely resembling one."

"I did not expect to find you such a pessimist, Father. You surprise me. Why should not wise rulers be able to make their people happy?"

"That is always possible, Your Majesty, within the limits fixed by circumstances. But the revolutionaries—who, in this, are simply the most logical of the philosophers' disciples—are aiming at something higher."

"Higher!" She shook her head, and a little shower of powder fell from her hair onto the shoulders of her cloak. "Now you speak as if you approved of them."

How could I explain that although I do not approve, yet with a corner of my heart I understand? Should not we all long to make the world a paradise, even while recognising that we cannot? Is not this a form of hungering and thirsting after justice? But, alas, the desire for justice, when it is untempered by mercy and the other virtues, is a cruel thing, like zeal for the faith in Christians who lack prudence or charity.

"Perhaps I should have said, Your Majesty, that the revolutionaries are aiming at something more ambitious. And, as we know, an ambition that ignores reality is always disastrous. The revolutionaries want to create a social paradise. But paradise can exist only when men are united in their aspirations and are masters of their passions. In fact, men are neither, and so long as they are free here on earth, there will always be disagreement and sin. What, then, must the revolutionaries do to make men virtuous and of one mind? They must use force. But if force is used, what becomes of the paradise?"

The Empress smiled.

"The Princess was not mistaken when she praised you so highly, Father. You have a nimble mind."

Then she thanked me and held out her hand, which I kissed, and I realised the interview was over.

Later, after I had gone to bed, I lay awake a long while, thinking. Somewhere across the Neva a bell was tolling, and I could heard the jingle of sledges and the creak of their runners on the snow. But my mind was far away at San Miguel as it was on the day of my arrival. I could see the cattle grazing on the grasslands, the sun touching the towers of the church, the smoke from the hearths rising in plumes above the trees, the procession moving toward me through the fields. I could hear the Indians singing. I could feel the peace and harmony of it all. Then this scene was followed by the picture of desolation and ruin described by Baron Voss.

Oh, my dear friends—Anselmo, Tarcisio, Cayetano, Jacinto, Dídaco, Xavier, Methodius—if you knew how much talk there is in Europe about the rights of peoples, about constitutions, about liberty and brotherhood. Yet you, who were free, who were equals, who held your possessions in common, had your beautiful republic destroyed by the efforts of the very men who have written so many burning pages on justice and good government and against despotism and tyranny. They valued reason, but that did not save you. Do their followers still believe that human reason alone can lead us into a Promised Land?

Note by the Archivist at the Gesu, Rome, after the Restoration of the Society of Jesus in 1814:

This diary was brought from St. Petersburg by Father Jaime de Vallecas in 1816. Father Alfonso de Vallecas died of typhus in 1813, at the age of eighty-three, caught while ministering to the French prisoners who had been captured the year before during Napoleon's invasion of Russia.